Tulips from Mal

GABRIELLA MARGO

First published in 2022
ISBN 978-0-6454051-0-1 Paperback
ISBN 978-0-6454051-1-8 Hardback
ISBN 978-0-6454051-2-5 eBook
ISBN 978-0-6454051-3-2 Audio book

Book cover design and interior typesetting by Vanessa Mendozzi

Any references to historical events, real people, or real places are used fictitiously. Names, characters and places are products of the author's imagination.

All military aspects of this book are fully fictional. While every effort was made to ensure factual accuracy, all views, expressions and information are for entertainment purposes only, and do not represent the Australian Department of Defence or its components.

As the author, I acknowledge that this story was written on Bidjigal land and pay my respect to Elders past, present and emerging. I humbly give thanks to all Aboriginal and Torres Strait Islander peoples who have been telling stories for tens of thousands of years.

Tulips from Mal is dedicated to
all the pets currently living in shelters.
Despite often experiencing trauma,
you always change our lives for the better.

Here's to finding your forever home.

10% of profits from book sales goes towards the
Animal Welfare League NSW, who work tirelessly
to ensure quality of life for abandoned pets.

SUMMER

1

GEORGIE

I spotted him at the most inconvenient time.

I was rummaging through my kitchen drawers, looking for a Band-Aid and cursing the metal grater on the marble bench as hot pain seared down my hand. Wincing, I brought my finger to my mouth and sucked on it, annoyed at myself. For someone who once single-handedly catered an event for two hundred and fifty people, it was ironic that I couldn't be trusted not to slice off the top of my finger in my own kitchen.

I grabbed a large Band-Aid and struggled to pull the packaging off with one hand.

And that's when I saw him.

I froze, blood oozing down my finger, anger seeping into my veins instead.

Behind the sparse row of bushes that lined the boundary of our houses, I could see him through my window, standing on his front lawn.

"Are you kidding me?" I muttered, noticing the stream of foam that was coming off the roof of his car and snaking its way across the grass, pooling at my door.

Yet again.

The guy had moved into the house next door a week ago, tops, and this was already the third time he was washing his beloved car and consequently flooding the front of my house. Normally, I couldn't care less what my neighbours did – and I wasn't bothered by much that didn't involve me. But the first time he'd done it, I was coming home with a glass baking dish in my hand and didn't see the water. I'd slipped at my front door, dropped and smashed the dish on the concrete steps, and rolled an ankle.

The guy was synonymous with pain, apparently.

My stomach turned, remembering how Byron hadn't spoken to me for days after I broke his mother's favourite baking dish.

I bit down on my lip and managed to wrap the Band-Aid around my finger, then stormed out the front door, dodging the foamy puddle this time. I'd been inside with the air conditioning set to seventeen all day. The scorching summer sun and stifling heat knocked the wind out of me, taking my frustration up a few notches.

"Hey!" I yelled at him, getting closer. "Do you think you could stop flooding my garden and front porch? It's been a mud pit since the day you moved in!"

Tone it down, Georgie – the guy is just washing his car on his lawn.

But my rational brain was nowhere to be seen.

He glanced at me briefly as I stomped closer to his charcoal-grey Hilux, but his lips remained pressed together.

"Hey!" I shouted again, looking at the chunky tyres on the tall four-wheel drive.

He twisted the nozzle of the hose to stop the water, with something like amusement flashing across his face.

"Hello, do your ears *work*?" I huffed, ignoring the pain in my right hand. The heat was making my finger throb with agony.

"Morning," he said, casually lifting a hand to his forehead to shield his eyes from the sun, then pointing to his left ear. "Actually, I *do* have a bit of an issue with this one, but that comes in handy sometimes." He winked.

My eyes trailed south. He was wearing a pair of dark green shorts. And that was it.

Barefoot on the glistening grass, my new neighbour stood there looking at me as my gaze continued down to the V-shaped muscles on his lower abs for a split second. He didn't have an overly defined six-pack, but he was a solid guy. Toned, a bit scruffy – one of those outdoorsy types, not someone who spends hours working out in a gym.

I quickly averted my eyes from his tanned body and looked up again, trying to remember what I was going to say. A silver watch sat loosely on his left wrist, reflecting the sun into my eyes. I blinked.

He was trying hard to contain a smile, but the left side of his mouth was inching towards the sky. "I'm sorry. Is there a problem?" he asked.

"Yes, there's a problem! You keep flooding my garden. And my front steps. Seriously, how often do you need to wash your car?"

He finally broke into a smile, but didn't move. Kind of an unusual reaction to a strange woman practically screaming at him.

"Also," I continued my rant, "there's this thing called water restrictions. You heard of those?"

It was bad enough that Byron couldn't care less about trying to save water. *I'm one person,* he'd say to me. *What difference will it make if I leave the water running?*

I couldn't stop looking at my neighbour's muscly arms. I was sure he was flexing on purpose as he held the hose.

He cocked his head. "And here I was thinking that you

were coming to welcome me to the street with a nice basket of muffins or something."

I put my hands on my hips. "It's not the 1950s. And do I *look* like the kind of woman who bakes muffins?" I said, forgetting I had an apron on, and hoping he couldn't see the bowl of muffin batter through my kitchen window from where he stood. The scorching heat and the pain in my finger were unbearable. I was sure I'd sliced the top of my finger right off, and I knew that Byron wouldn't respond to anything less than a detached limb. That thought on top of the searing pain wasn't helping the situation with the new neighbour. It was making me feel like a few of my screws had come loose. I knew I was being unreasonable. But I was in agony – and this guy was more annoying than having to do a three-point turn in my rusty work ute, sans power steering.

"Okay, look, I'm sorry. I promise I won't wash my car again in this spot."

I lifted an eyebrow. "Starting right now?" I said, wondering how far I could push it.

"Sure." He shrugged again. "Starting right now."

Well, that was easier than I'd anticipated. My shoulders dropped a bit, and despite my annoyance, something about the neighbour made me feel at ease. He was so … calm? Easy going? And he obviously had a sense of humour.

Too bad he was so infuriating. I hesitated, then went to walk away. I'd barely taken two steps when the water started back up, a stream of it flying past me and starting up the small river flowing down towards my front steps again.

I turned around and glared at him, but as I opened my mouth to protest, a jet of water hit me square in the chest and face. He was hosing the car's roof, whistling, like the last two minutes hadn't even happened. His thick, dark hair sat swished to one side, like he'd just been to the barber. Even his beard was perfectly trimmed, adding to his overall manicured-but-somehow-scruffy appearance. I stood staring at him with my hands on my hips again.

What a smartass. It wasn't hard to see we were not going to be friends. I took a step towards him, then paused, thinking twice about my strategy. I looked at the green hose snaking a path down along our shared fence and into his backyard.

Game on.

I turned and went back inside, wiping water off my face angrily, not wanting to admit to myself that the cold water had actually felt refreshing. Hurrying down the hallway, I glanced to my left. Byron was sitting in our study with his headphones on, oblivious to my antics. I continued to the back door, opened it, and made my way to the garden, contemplating my next move. I grabbed onto a giant pot plant against the fence. The pot wasn't very tall, but it was thick and sturdy. I looked around, craning my head to the right.

Car Wash Guy was still out the front, hosing. I smiled smugly to myself, feeling childish, but annoyed enough to go ahead with the plan.

I put one foot on the pot plant and hoisted myself up onto the fence. Then, in one swift movement, I launched myself over it and landed with a thud on the other side, slightly less elegantly than I had imagined. One of my shoes had fallen off. I brushed the grass from my shorts and headed towards the tap that the hose was attached to. But as I reached for it, something sparkling in the backyard made me pause. It was stunning. The expensive-looking stone around it made it look like one of those Balinese resort pools, its surface rippling with a beautiful sapphire colour. Trust me to notice it. Of all the pools I was contracted to clean and maintain, this was up there as one of the most gorgeous ones, and I wanted to jump right in, apron and all.

The rest of the garden was perfectly manicured, grass freshly mowed and gorgeous lilies, tulips and vivid yellow roses lining the fence. A stone path led to a modern-looking deck behind the house with a jacuzzi on it. The people who lived here before this guy had put a *lot* of money into their backyard – it was like I'd tumbled straight into the Ritz-Carlton.

I looked down at myself. One shoe, a dirty apron, and saturated hair – I was a sight. Plus, my injured finger was now bleeding through the Band-Aid. It was going to need a proper bandage.

I turned back towards the tap. I'd been so engrossed by the pool that I had missed the giant dog who'd snuck up behind me, the soft grass absorbing its footsteps. It was sitting about two metres away from me, next to the tap, like it knew what I was going to do and needed to guard it.

My head spun, images of a dog latching onto my leg flooding my thoughts. "Jesus," I murmured, flailing backwards and gaping at the animal. It was huge – one of those big black and white Siberian dogs that had no business being in the Australian heat.

And I had no business being in its backyard.

Ice-blue eyes were boring holes straight into me. It was ready to attack.

2

DREW

I twisted the nozzle of the hose to turn it off and looked at the car, which was gleaming in the sun and dripping water onto the grass. It had been absolutely filthy. No matter how much I washed, wiped and polished it, I was still finding dust everywhere since driving across the Nullarbor last week.

It was sweltering outside today, and the cold water felt nice on my feet. Sometimes I wished I'd bought a lighter car – this dark paint showed every bit of dust, every bug I'd collected along the way. It'd had a few close calls with some pretty big roos, too – one I'd only just missed – but thankfully I'd made it across to Sydney without too many hiccups.

The Navy had offered to fly me. But I needed my car anyway, and besides, I loved a good road trip.

I'd seen my neighbour once or twice since moving in, but I'd never spoken to her. She often left for work right before I did, hopping into the driver's seat of her white ute before I could go and say hi. But after what I'd just witnessed, that was probably a good thing – she didn't seem like much of a morning person.

She was wild, yelling at me like that – although, she was completely right about the water restrictions. I had totally forgotten, and I was usually so mindful about not wasting water. But despite how much I was clearly pissing her off, I couldn't help noticing she was actually pretty cute.

And it was *very* cute that she thought she could sneak into my backyard without anyone noticing.

I just hoped she liked big dogs.

I glanced into the backyard again, down the straight stretch of grass along our shared fence. It was kind of a dead area – wasted space. But it wasn't wasted today. I could see her with Mal, in what looked like quite the standoff. There they were, eye to eye, neither of them moving. And she looked petrified.

I didn't even know her name yet, and she was already trespassing on my property.

I smiled, watching her. She was sort of cowering, and kept glancing at the fence, absolutely freaked out. Kind of served her right for jumping the fence to do … Well, whatever she was planning to do. She probably didn't quite deserve to fear for her life, though. I sighed and put the hose down, opened the gate, and walked down the grassy strip.

"Mal! Come here, boy," I whistled as I tapped my thigh. Mal came bounding over to me and sat down at my heel. I scratched him on the head and grinned at her. "So," I said, "I see you've met my dog."

She was backed up against the fence. "Get that *bloody* thing away from me."

Mal wouldn't hurt a fly. He was timid – I'd even seen him run away from tiny puppies before. And he was a terrible guard dog – exhibit A.

"I am *not* a dog person," she muttered.

"Yes, I can see that," I said. "What on earth are you doing, anyway?" I nodded at the fence she'd just climbed.

Her apron was loose around her neck, the plain white T-shirt underneath it soaked from when I'd hosed her. It was big and baggy, but now that it was wet, it clung to her chest, almost totally see-through.

I couldn't stop staring. But I forced myself to tear my eyes away from her before she thought I was a massive creep.

"Nothing," she said, her lips tight. "I ... I fell."

I raised an eyebrow at her, trying not to smile more than I already was. "Right. Well, now that you've fallen into my yard and scared my poor dog, are you going to tell me your name?"

She stared at me. Then, clutching her right hand to her chest, she took off towards the back door of my house. Was she for real? I followed her inside, just catching the screen door before it slammed shut. Mal continued standing outside, watching us curiously.

"Please, come into my house," I said under my breath. She ignored me and kept walking, making her way through the kitchen and living room, towards the front door. "Hey. Can you please stop?"

She turned around. "What?"

"Look. I'm sorry about the car washing, all right? I'll do it further away next time." I really didn't want to start off on the wrong foot with my new neighbour. She seemed legitimately angry.

Standing in my living room, she studied my face for a moment. She must've been a couple of years younger than me, at a guess. Her shiny, caramel-coloured hair was in a high ponytail that reached halfway down her back, the colour fading until it was a very light blonde at the bottom. I'd seen this kind of hair colour on other women. But it was different on her. Like she wasn't trying to look good on purpose, but somehow managed to do so anyway.

She stared at me with enormous hazel eyes, and her shoulders dropped. She sighed. "I'm Georgie."

Light freckles peppered the tops of her bronzed cheeks. She was definitely attractive, and had a kind of sultry look about her.

In fact, with those soft, full lips and bright eyes, she wasn't just attractive – she was downright stunning. Something fluttered in my chest. It was too bad she was so … unhinged.

"Nice to meet you, Georgie. I'm Drew." I extended my hand, but she just looked at it.

Well, okay then.

She didn't move. We stood in my living room, looking at each other. Now *I* was the one in a standoff with her.

She was a bit shorter than me, slim but fit-looking. And whatever she did for work, she must've spent a lot of time outside, judging by the deep golden glow of her skin.

My gaze fell to her hand, which she was still clutching. It was bleeding. In fact, blood was seeping through to the fingers of her other hand.

"Hey, did you hurt yourself climbing the fence?" I said, quickly ripping a handful of tissues out of the box on the coffee table and moving towards her.

Her eyebrows furrowed. "What, are you worried about your fancy white carpet?"

"I wasn't. But now that you mention it, I'll send you the steam-cleaning bill." I grinned, wrapping the tissues carefully around her finger. She didn't object, but she didn't thank me, either. "This looks pretty bad, Georgie. What did you do to it?"

She hardly skipped a beat. "Your dog got me. He just … He came over and went for my hand."

I glanced down at her as I held the tissues to her soft hands. Mal sat at the screen door gazing at us with wide blue eyes, his tongue hanging out in the heat. He looked like he was smiling at me. I smiled back at him. *She's a little different, huh, pal?*

I turned back to Georgie. "Yes. He's a *very* vicious guard dog."

She rolled her eyes, and took her hand away from mine while glaring at Mal. "What is that anyway – a Husky?"

Mal was black on top and white underneath, like a reverse Cadbury Top Deck. White legs and chest, black body. His face was white, too, except for a black arch that looped down between his eyes. The white parts highlighted those pale blue eyes that I loved so much. He had a lot of thick, silky hair, but thankfully didn't shed as much as I thought he would when I adopted him.

"Nah, he's an Alaskan Malamute cross," I said.

"And his name is Mal?" she snorted. "Mal like Malamute? Original."

"Mal is short for Malcolm, actually," I said. "He prefers Mal, though. Says Malcolm makes him sound like an old man."

She rolled her eyes again, not even cracking at my lame joke. "It's too hot to have dogs like that in Australia." She looked at me like she was trying to gauge my reaction, before squeezing the tissues around her hand and looking back down at it, sighing loudly. "I think I cut the top of my finger off. I was grating dark chocolate for my neighbour's muffins, and the grater slipped."

"Ah. See, I *knew* you were making me muffins!"

She scowled at me. "My neighbour across the road. I'm not making *you* anything."

"Ha. Right, well you just got dropped from my Christmas list." I said, trying to poke her back. She was in a terrible mood, but I couldn't stop grinning. She narrowed her hazel eyes at me, and as I looked into them, something passed between us for a brief moment. Her eyes softened, like this wasn't the real side of her, somehow – that this was some fired-up version of an otherwise very nice woman. And this feeling between us … Well, I wasn't exactly sure what it was. To me, it was like a sudden flutter in my chest had taken over – but in the space of a millisecond, she broke our gaze and made for the front door.

"Hey – wait. Do you … Do you want to, uh – stay for a drink?"

She paused, turned around and looked at me. "Stay for a drink?"

I smiled, putting my hands in my pockets nervously. "Yeah. I mean – it'd be nice to get to know you, um, a bit better."

She raised an eyebrow at me.

"You're – you're really beautiful." I cleared my throat. Did I really just say that?

"Drew. I'm *married*."

Standing frozen to the spot, I gaped at her. If I'd known that, I never would've said anything. Not a chance. But then ... I hadn't exactly asked. "I'm so sorry," I finally managed to say, scratching my head. "Um – I didn't mean – well, you aren't wearing a ring."

Right away, I could tell I had made a huge mistake.

"What?" she said slowly, taking a step towards me. "So that means I'm anyone's game, does it? Not everyone wears a ring, you know."

I blinked, opening my mouth but not forming any words. Anyone who knew me would vouch for the fact I would never ask out a married woman. Ever. Especially after everything I'd been through with John.

"I'm really sorry," I repeated. *What the hell, Drew?* What a pathetic excuse about the ring. I couldn't have said anything worse if I'd tried. I'm not even sure where I was trying to go with that one.

She shook her head and made for the front door.

I didn't try to stop her this time. But I did notice her finger was bleeding through the tissues now, too. "Hey, you should get that finger looked at," I called out as my screen door slammed shut behind her.

Without turning around, she held up a finger to me.

And it wasn't the injured one.

3

GEORGIE

I spent five hours in the accident and emergency department. Five.

That's how long I had to wait, clutching my bloodied finger, before someone gave me a couple of stitches and sent me home. I kind of thought the word "emergency" implied it would be fast, but I guess I was wrong. I understood that my injury wasn't exactly life-threatening, and I knew there were people coming in with suspected heart attacks, head injuries and other horrendous things – I wasn't that unreasonable. But I was still frustrated, and in a lot of pain.

If I was being completely honest, I was more annoyed about the fact that, despite being married to a surgeon, I couldn't get it sorted at home. Apparently, he couldn't put a couple of stitches in my finger because "he was busy". He had every type of medicine and every piece of equipment at home anyone could ever possibly need, but he was on some important call all afternoon sorting out an upcoming work trip. At least he'd dropped me off at the hospital while he talked on loudspeaker.

And somewhere amid my annoyance, there was also a tiny fleck of anxiety. What the hell was that next door – Drew asking me out? At least – I think that's what it was. He'd only asked me to stay for a drink. It's not like he made a move on me or anything. Was I overreacting? There was something about the way he was looking at me. It was like … total adoration. How was that possible? The guy didn't even know me.

But I hadn't done anything wrong – so why had I felt that small wave of nauseous guilt ever since? I definitely couldn't tell Byron about it. Nothing good would come of that.

Who does that, though? Who asks out a total stranger?

My time in emergency wasn't completely wasted. At least I'd had the chance to catch up on some work admin, reading and replying to emails on my phone while I waited. It was a little awkward trying to navigate my phone with my injury, though, but there were new clients, and I didn't like to keep them waiting. There was a luxurious, newly finished apartment complex not far away with an indoor and outdoor pool, as well as a couple of penthouse apartments each fitted with a jacuzzi. And I really, really wanted The Pool Chicks to get the contract.

Plus, it kept me distracted from the thought of telling Byron about the Drew incident. I also didn't want to annoy him with something so trivial. He was so busy these days. But I could understand Byron's motivation for working every minute of every day. He was so passionate about his job … Just like I was about mine. It was one of the things that had drawn me to him in the first place – the way his eyes lit up when he talked about operating; the way he loved helping people, giving people a second chance at life. The bonds he developed with some of his patients. He had this deep passion for his job at the hospital – everything he did there, he gave a hundred and ten percent to.

"How'd you go, babe?" Byron asked when I got home from the bus stop, sorting a folder of papers on the coffee table in front of the TV. He didn't look up as I walked into the house. I went straight to the kitchen and started cleaning up from my earlier baking adventures. Disgusted, I looked at the grater, wanting to throw it straight out the window.

There was a tiny flicker of annoyance in me that Byron hadn't even attempted to tidy the kitchen while I was at the hospital. Crumbs littered the benchtop, and the milk was still out. It was my mess, I knew that – but surely, he could've at least thrown the fridge items back in.

"Fine. Got a couple of stitches. Hurts like hell." I studied my wrapped finger. This was going to make work pretty tricky, given I spent half my time at the bottom of chlorinated pools. "What do you want for dinner?" I said, bending over and looking in the fridge. I was glad I'd done a decent shop in the morning when I'd got the ingredients for the muffins. "Do you want me to make that sour orange curry, the one with barramundi? Or I could slow-cook a lamb shoulder? With those potatoes you like?" There were also ingredients I could use to make a simple gnocchi – a vegetarian one. My mouth watered. Gnocchi was one of my personal favourites. And lately, I was enjoying vegetarian meals more and more. Nothing against meat – I just felt so good after a meal that was filled with all kinds of vegetables instead. Red cabbage had recently become a favourite. It had such a unique flavour, and I loved the crunchy texture. Shame I didn't use it more when I was a chef.

"We're going to Kev's tonight, remember?" He paused and looked up at me. "You didn't forget, did you?"

"No." *Crap.* "But I'm going to sit this one out. My hand is killing me."

He gave me a look. "You cut your finger cooking, babe. You're not dying."

Oh god, please don't make me sit through one of his speeches about how there is always someone worse off than me. Staying home seemed like a good plan, anyway – it was Saturday night and I just wanted to cook something and relax on the couch with a book. By myself, preferably.

And I really didn't want to see Kevin. Not after what happened at Byron's birthday. Even the thought of it was enough to make my skin crawl.

"He's making his amazing paella tonight, too," Byron continued.

In that case, I was most definitely *not* going. The guy couldn't cook to save his life. Kev, Byron's older brother, couldn't even pull off two-minute noodles if his life depended on it. I'd seen it with my own two eyes. Perhaps it was due to the fact that he'd lived at home until he was thirty-six ... Then again, when your parents own more vineyards than you can poke a stick at, and live in a multi-million-dollar home, it's not exactly a tough way to live. Kev and Byron had always been looked after – even as adults. But the difference between the two sons was that Byron actually worked hard now – even if he *had* had some pretty significant handouts – whereas Kev just used his parents' money to pay the rent in his Kirribilli penthouse and buy female company when he felt like it.

In general, I really didn't care what someone did for work or how they lived their life. But I had my reasons for hating Kev.

Once Byron gave up on convincing me to go, I took out the ingredients for the gnocchi and got to work, trying to avoid using my right hand too much. I also finished the muffins and took them across the road to Kate's.

An hour later, Byron was gone, and I was on the couch with my bowl of steaming gnocchi. I'd put some chilli in, seeing as Byron wouldn't be having any. God, I loved the stuff. The fact that my husband didn't eat any chilli whatsoever had almost been a dealbreaker for me.

Almost.

After two bowls of gnocchi, I was lying down on the couch, grateful that I'd gone for a lengthy run in the morning. I suddenly felt nostalgic, hearing Dad's voice as he'd joke: *never regretti eating spaghetti*. I sure as hell didn't regret the second bowl of gnocchi. I propped myself up on some cushions and opened my book, finding the dog-eared page.

I'd just got into the chapter when there was a knock at the door. *Kate must be here to talk about how good those chocolate muffins are*. I knew they were delicious – they never got a complaint – but I still relished every compliment. I jumped up and opened the door in anticipation. I loved Kate. She was so down to earth, and we'd become close in the last few years since Byron and I had moved in. She was throwing this year's street Christmas party, which she'd asked me to do some baking for. Those muffins were part of a "trial batch" I'd offered to make. Any excuse to bake.

But the person at my door wasn't Kate.

My eyes shot up to meet Drew's. He smiled down at me. "Hi."

"Um … Hi."

My gaze shifted down to the obnoxiously large bunch of flowers he was holding. I looked back up at him. He was wearing a white, collared shirt and dark jeans, and looked freshly showered. His cologne was woody and crisp. I took in the delicious scent of it.

I raised my eyebrows at his shirt. "So you *do* own clothes. Nice to see you know how to put them on."

The flowers were a bright mix of pinks, yellows, and oranges. Tulips – a flower I could never manage to grow in my garden. The thick bunch wasn't wrapped in anything, it was just bound together with some brown string. Drew handed it to me gently.

I took the bunch with my good hand.

"Well, I thought I should put clothes on before I came round," he said, smiling awkwardly.

Through his shirt, I could see the contour of his chest. I was glad it was covered.

Kind of.

I put the tulips up to my nose and breathed in. They smelled so alluring that I involuntarily closed my eyes, feeling like I was in a cheesy romance film.

I could feel his gaze on me. "How's your finger?" he said, eyeing my hand.

"Not bad." I held it up to him. "Couple of stitches."

"Wow. I had a feeling it was bad."

I shrugged. "It's fine."

"So … Um, anyway, I wanted to apologise for this morning," he said.

I looked at him and frowned, realising something. "Wait a sec. Aren't you even a little worried about being at the house of the guy whose wife you recently asked on a date?"

He paused. "It wasn't – I mean I didn't …" He stopped, then sighed and shook his head, like he was annoyed with himself.

When I didn't respond, he continued. "These are … from my garden." He smiled softly, eyes warm and friendly as he spoke. "Look, Georgie, on a serious note, I am really sorry for this morning. Obviously, if I'd known, I … Well, it wouldn't have happened. I'm not that kind of guy. I know they probably all say that, but I mean it. I'm sorry."

I nodded, before putting the tulips back into his hands. What was I going to do, put them in the kitchen and tell Byron, *Oh, these are from the ridiculously hot guy next door who maybe asked me out*? No way. And I'd already made the decision not to tell him. There was no need to have bad blood with the new neighbour. And also, *I* hadn't done anything wrong, so there was that. "I can't accept these from you. Sorry."

"I had a feeling you'd say that. They're not from me, though."

I furrowed my brows. Drew grinned, eyes sparkling. I couldn't look at him – that annoying expression was getting under my skin again. How could one person be so infuriating? I hardly knew the guy. I looked away from him and at the flowers again, still not inviting him in.

"They're from Mal," Drew continued. "Tulips are his favourite and he thought you might like them, too. He picked them himself. In fact, it was all his idea. He is sorry for scaring you and he wants you to know you're welcome in his backyard any time."

My face softening, I looked down, worried I would crack a smile if I glanced up at Drew again. I took the bunch back from his hand, ignoring the feeling that ran through me when my fingers brushed against his.

"Tell Mal I said thanks for the flowers. And next time, I'd love to watch how he ties that brown string with his paws." I sighed, pushing away the impending smile. "I guess Mal is forgiven, then."

"Only Mal?"

I hesitated. "For now, yes."

"How come?"

"Because. You can't be angry at a dog."

"Hmm." He scratched his chin with one eyebrow raised, thinking. His thick beard really suited him. "Interesting. I thought you weren't a dog person."

"I'm not. I'm not even an animal person." That wasn't a lie; I really didn't like them. But I had my reasons for that, too. "He is pretty cute though, I guess."

"Yes! See, you're going to like him, I promise."

"Look, Drew. I've got a lasagne in the oven. I have to go."

"Oh. Okay, yeah. Well, I'll see you around."

I forced myself to smile at him, then closed the door as he said something quietly about being a big fan of lasagne in case I had leftovers. After I'd put the flowers in a vase with some water, I flopped back on the couch with my book. But instead of looking at the words on the page, I found myself watching Drew from the corner of my eye, through the window, as he walked off in the opposite direction to his house.

He must be going out.

He looked fantastic in those dark jeans as he walked down the road and I wondered whether he was going on a date. He certainly was attractive. But he was one of those people who annoyed me by simply being around. His face was annoying; his *smile* was annoying. I couldn't stop thinking about just how annoying he was. And once I'd forced myself to turn away from the street, I had a very hard time getting back into my book.

4

DREW

"So," Jess said, "did you miss me?"

I sat across the table from her, stifling a yawn. She was in Sydney for work, and I hadn't seen her since I'd left Perth. It had only been a month since I'd sold most of my things, packed up the Hilux, thrown Mal in the back, and driven across the Nullarbor after being posted to Sydney with the Navy, but the way Jess was talking, it was like we hadn't seen each other in years.

And a bit like she'd forgotten that we were never officially together.

I'd loved the drive across the desert, with Mal sitting in the tray of my Hilux. And I swear he loved it there, too. He was an excellent travel buddy. I'd offered him the passenger seat, thinking he'd enjoy the air-conditioned cab a lot more, but it seemed that he preferred sitting in the back with his tongue hanging out in the wind. We passed lots of utes with dogs in the back – I think he just wanted to look tough like those desert dogs. We stopped for a couple of weeks in Adelaide, visiting some ex-Navy mates, and then continued on to our new home in Sydney. Buying the house had been a surreal feeling. I'd thought it would take months to find what I wanted, but that wasn't the case. And I was getting the chance to settle in a bit before I started work again – the holiday was officially over in a few more days.

"Did you miss *me*?" I directed the question back at her.

I felt bad lying. Truth was, I hadn't really thought about Jess at all. But now that she was here, it was good to see her again. A familiar face from Perth. Her eyes had a mischievous glint to them. She was not bad to look at. I could see why I'd been interested for a while there. I smiled back at her.

"I sure did," she said, raising her eyebrows up and down quickly. "So, are you going to wear your uniform for me tonight?"

I almost choked on my beer. Come to think of it, I wouldn't even have a clue where my uniforms were. I thought I saw one of my green flying suits somewhere the other day, but who knew where the rest were. I still had a couple of boxes to unpack that'd arrived in the truck a few days ago. I didn't have a lot, but the house was coming together nicely, and the backyard was perfect for Mal.

I thought about Georgie climbing my fence, and grinned.

"What?" Jess asked.

"Nothing," I said quickly. "So, how's work going?"

"It's good, they're promoting me to the …"

My mind drifted to meeting Georgie. I definitely did *not* start off on the right foot with her. Hopefully after some time, we would at least be on speaking terms. It'd be awkward to have a neighbour who hated me. And I felt terrible about the way things had played out. If I wanted us to be civil, or friends at some point, I would need to steer clear of her for a while – and hopefully get a fresh start.

As I looked back at Jess, watching as she talked and trying to replay what she'd just said, I couldn't help thinking that while she was quite pretty, she was nothing compared to Georgie.

Had Jess asked me a question? I took a swig of beer to stall. No, she was still talking. This dinner had been more boring than watching paint dry. What the hell had we even talked about in the past?

I finished my beer and took out my wallet. I wasn't feeling it. Not enough to keep it going, anyway – and not enough to string her along.

"What are you doing?" she said, eyeing the money I was taking out.

"Uh, actually, Jess, I've gotta be up really early tomorrow. I'm going to make some tracks."

"Are you kidding me?" Her expression changed in a split second. She looked at me with daggers in her eyes.

I nodded slowly.

"I fly to Sydney to see you, you make me come all the way out to the 'burbs, and now you're sending me home?"

"You said you were here for work," I reminded her.

She scoffed. "Whatever. You're an asshole."

Well, that escalated quickly.

"Look, I'll get your Uber home." I unlocked my phone and clicked on the app. "Where are you staying?"

"Not at yours, apparently."

We looked at each other silently for a moment. I was really winning with women this week. "I'm sorry, Jess. Let me get dinner and your Uber. Okay?"

"Screw that. I'm gonna go out. I'm sure I can find a guy elsewhere. A more decent one." She pursed her overfilled lips and puffed out her chest.

I'm sure you probably can, I thought. But I was done. And I didn't want to lead her on any more. It wasn't fair to her.

"Sorry again, it's—"

"Don't worry about it, Drew. Go home and fly your dumb planes."

I sighed. I flew helicopters. Like I hadn't told her sixteen times already. Like it even mattered now.

She grabbed her handbag and took off without another word.

I paid the bill and walked home.

It was dark – the streetlights were pretty spaced out. But I was enjoying the walk; the night hadn't cooled down at all. I loved these warm nights – they felt so tropical. Usually in Sydney, the summer evenings slowly got cool. It was rare that it was over thirty once it was dark. But tonight it was, and I wished I'd worn shorts instead of jeans. What was I thinking? Rookie error. I walked up the last hill towards home. At least Mal would be happy to see me – always a given. I walked past Georgie's house to my left, noticing her lights were still on. Pausing, I wondered what she was up to, but I couldn't really see anything without getting closer and feeling like a creep.

Her husband must be a pretty patient guy, to put up with that temper.

I looked at her work ute curiously, the one I'd seen her getting into in the mornings. It was really old, its silver tray full of equipment. There were a couple of steel boxes bolted down, some plastic pool hoses, and blue drums of chlorine. A sign on the side of the car read "The Pool Chicks" in giant letters, painted like drops of water.

She was certainly intriguing. And very, very attractive.

And despite that temper, I found myself hoping I would get to speak to her again soon.

5

GEORGIE

I crossed the street with a glass tray in my hand, having guilt-baked some lasagne after lying to Drew about putting one in the oven last night. I hardly knew the guy, but he seemed like the honest type, and not being truthful with him just didn't sit well with me. He did that thing where he looked into my eyes so intensely that there was no way I couldn't be honest. It almost felt like he could read my mind.

And I really hoped he couldn't.

As always, I'd baked extra. Making my way up Kate and Tony's driveway, I could hear voices coming from inside. Raising my hand to knock on the door, I realised it was Han and her father arguing. I hesitated, wondering if I should come back later. But Han noticed me through the window, waved, and came to open the door.

"Hey!" Her face was bright, like she wasn't in the middle of a fight. Tall for sixteen, with flawless skin and plump cheeks, Hanako took after her Japanese mother, who had also struck gold in the looks department. Unfortunately for the family, she had passed away when Hanako was eleven or twelve. Tony remarried a few years later and, luckily, Kate and Hanako got along well. Hanako could be quite moody, but then again – what teenager couldn't?

"Can we go driving this Sunday?" she asked, glancing at the aluminium foil on the tray, eyes widening. "Oh my god, *please* tell me this is your famous lasagne?"

I nodded, handing it to her. She needed to get her driving hours up, and I often took her out for lessons – neither Kate nor Tony had the patience (or the time) to go with her. I liked it, though, and Hanako and I got along well. Anyway, I'd always enjoyed a challenge. And a challenge it was, teaching a teenager to drive.

"Sure. Sunday works for me."

She took the tray, brought it to her nose and breathed in. "Delicious. Did you—"

"Hey, Georgie." Tony walked up behind Han. "Let's wait and see about the driving, yeah? Hanako might be grounded this weekend."

Han rolled her eyes. "Japa*nese* parents don't ground their kids," she retorted.

"Come on, Han. You're the most Aussie kid going around. You can't just claim your Japanese heritage whenever it's convenient for you." Tony looked up at me. "She can't even speak Japanese, you know. Her mother tried to teach her. But no."

This was not really a conversation I wanted to be a part of, but there I was. I followed Tony inside after an offer of iced coffee, and Hanako sat down at the table with me, arms folded. She looked at me with anticipation, like she wanted me to ask why she was being grounded.

"I got suspended from school," she burst out when I didn't say anything. There was almost a bit of pride in her voice.

"Oh shit. What for?" Dammit. Byron was right. I really *did* need to set up a swear jar at home.

"For swearing." A mischievous grin crossed Han's face as she said this to me. I loved Hanako. She was clever and sweet, and her frankness reminded me a lot of myself at that age. Although, I'd never got suspended … and I'd certainly never sworn as much back then.

I frowned at her as Tony brought the two coffees out. "Sounds like a pretty rough punishment for saying a bad word."

Her grin got wider. "I swore at the principal."

"*Oh.* Well, uh … that's not so good," I said as Tony spoke over me loudly to scold her.

She shrugged. "We had a career advisor talk to our year group. And the principal was there. He said that women weren't good at work that involved physical labour."

I nearly spat out my coffee. "Um … That's—"

"So, like, we got into this massive debate, and I called him out on it, but he wouldn't take it back or apologise. So I told him he was a sexist pig. Then I swore at him." She seemed pleased with herself. "A lot."

Tony was rubbing his temples. "Okay, Han. That's enough."

She flashed me a cheeky look. "It's pretty cool being suspended, though. Got me a little street cred." She said this in a deep voice, making some funny symbols with her hands. I couldn't help smiling. "I don't wanna go back anyway. I want to leave school."

Tony pointed a thumb at her and gave me a look. "The latest. *Have kids,* they said. *It'll be fun,* they said." He shook his head.

I finished my coffee, wanting to get myself out of this situation. It was only going to escalate with me here, I could tell.

"*Georgie* never finished school," Han said, as if on cue, folding her arms again.

Tony sighed. "Georgie trained hard to become a chef. For six years." He looked at me. "Six, right?"

I nodded.

But Han wasn't deterred. "I want to do physical work. Like the pool-cleaning stuff she does. I want to work at multi-million-dollar houses like she does."

"It's not always so glamorous, Han. Also, you're there to work. Not to have a pool party."

Tony shot me a thankful look.

"You love the pool job, though, don't you?"

She had me there. "Yeah." I loved the industry I was in. And I had the best colleagues going round. Roisin, my business partner, was wonderful. And we had a fantastic group of women working for us at The Pool Chicks.

"And you earn good money, right?"

"Yeah … Good-ish. It's not easy running a business, though."

She gave her father a *See, I told you so* look.

"All right, I have to run, but let me know about the driving, okay?" I stood up, put my glass into the dishwasher and headed out the door, looking across at Drew's house. Han walked me down the driveway, then went back inside.

I wondered if I should take Drew some lasagne. First, he'd unwittingly made me bake a lasagne, and now he was unwittingly making me take some over for him. But if I did that, it would mean seeing him again, which would lead to some sort of frustrating exchange. I was sure of it. Seeing him felt like an effort – and a little bit like playing with fire.

I hesitated, noticing his car wasn't there. I could drop some off at his door and not have to actually see him. But then, he might come over later to thank me. I stood outside his house and chewed on a thumbnail. When did I become such an overthinker?

Whatever. I'm never going to get through three trays of lasagne.

I grabbed one from my fridge, scribbled a quick note on a scrap of paper, and walked to my front door. I turned towards Drew's house, after making sure nobody could see me.

Just to be safe.

6

DREW

"Wow," I said to Mal. "That is the *best* lasagne I have ever had."

The top was crunchy. It was cheesy. It was meaty. And it had gone down damn well on a night when I couldn't be bothered to cook. I'd scraped every last bit out of the ceramic dish, even picking the melted cheese off the aluminium foil.

The dish was quite big; it probably could've fed a whole family. But tonight, it just fed me. I'd come home from doing some landscaping for my sister and found it in a bag on my front step. I was starving, too. There was a note on top that read: *Warm up in the oven – 10 mins. PS. Thank you for the flowers.* Of course, I'd been way too hungry to wait for the oven to heat up, so I'd microwaved it instead. As half the lasagne went round and round in the microwave, I wondered what would happen if Georgie came round right now. She'd probably yell at me again. I felt like a naughty kid, disregarding the note's instructions. But I figured what she didn't know couldn't hurt her. Or *me*. After I'd shovelled the lasagne in, I put the other half on the plate and repeated the microwaving process.

So she *did* know how to be nice. I read between the lines to assume she had forgiven me, too. I washed and rinsed the dish once I finished eating. I'd have to return it to Georgie sometime, and that meant I would meet her husband. Safe to say, I was more than a little curious.

I flopped down on the couch, exhausted. Mal jumped up next to me, settling into a neat round ball of fluff at my feet.

"You're lucky it's a long couch, pal," I said, scratching him between the ears. He looked at me, doing that thing dogs do where their eyebrows alternate going up and down, and I smiled. "What do you think of Georgie? She's cute, huh?" I motioned towards her house. "And far out, can she cook a lasagne." Mal's expression suggested he wasn't impressed that he didn't get any. "Dairy's not good for dogs. Come on – we've been through this." I looked at my front door, remembering how Georgie had stormed off and given me the finger. It was strange. She was so stubborn, and so tightly wound. So why couldn't I stop thinking about her?

Not to mention how much she despised me. And I couldn't really blame her.

But still. If she were single …

Drew, you can't think like that. You only want her because you can't have her.

I flicked through the TV stations and settled on an ocean documentary. About ten minutes into David Attenborough's soothing narration, my phone rang. When I saw the number, my heart sank. It was Tom, and he was calling from his Defence Force-issued mobile number.

"Sir."

"Drew. How are you?"

"Good thanks. What's happening?"

"Flooding in Queensland – squadron's leaving tomorrow for disaster relief. You'll be there for a week. Full details at the morning briefing. See you at zero seven hundred hours."

I hung up and looked at Mal, shrugging. "Sorry, bud. You'll have to put up with Elena for another week." Elena, my sister, used to look after him for me when I'd lived in Perth – she had lived there, too, only moving to Sydney a month or so before me. Luckily, Mal liked my sister, and didn't mind staying with her. Then again, Mal liked everyone. But he always came back from Elena's a little on the chubby side. She didn't care that dogs weren't supposed to eat dairy. And Mal capitalised on that.

I sighed. So much for my final three days of freedom.

I dialled Elena's number.

7

GEORGIE

I picked at my thumb and it started to bleed. I wished so badly I could stop picking my fingernails. It was the worst habit, but I'd done it for as long as I could remember. So often I wished I had a different bad habit to try and give up. It annoyed me to no end when people said, *Why don't you just stop picking them?* I didn't often talk about it, but when I explained it to people, I compared it to an attempt to quit smoking if you had ten cigarettes attached to you at all times.

I used to smoke, too. It was never an addiction – more a social habit. And I'd always loved it. But that was an easy one for me to stop – I just didn't buy any. I never missed them, either. I usually did the nail-biting when I was anxious, or bored. Or deep in thought. Actually, I did it all the time, and I couldn't stand it. It seemed there was nothing I could do about it, though. I'd tried that nail polish stuff that makes them taste bad. But that made everything I ate and touched taste bad, too. Cooking with it on my nails was awful. And it didn't stop me picking at them, either. I'd tried wearing a ring to fiddle with instead. But the problem was, I couldn't wear rings to work. The chlorinated water got trapped under them and then the skin would get red and irritated around it. That's why I never wore my wedding rings anymore, especially to work. I usually only wore them if I went out in the evening, and even then, it was rare.

I was standing in my kitchen, biting away at my thumb. I was both deep in thought *and* anxious.

I was going to have to tell Byron the truth. I couldn't not. Too much time had passed, and I wouldn't be able to keep up the charade for much longer. Byron would soon cotton on to the fact that something was up.

I looked across at Drew's window and wondered if he'd enjoyed my lasagne. It wasn't my best effort, but it was okay. In all honesty, I'd been waiting for him to come running over with the tray all squeaky clean, probably with more flowers to say thanks. But he hadn't come round.

It wasn't Drew I had to tell Byron about. I figured our meeting was innocent enough – Drew had been legitimately sorry, I could tell. And I didn't know him from a bar of soap, but it just seemed to me that he was a decent guy. Slightly annoying, sure – but there was nothing sly or malicious about him.

And if I told Byron about the conversation, the only thing that'd happen would be a confrontation between the two of them, because Byron would *not* take it well. And if he tried to throw a punch, I didn't like his chances against the solidly built Drew.

But I had no idea how he was going to react to the other thing I had to tell him. I stared out the window, wondering how to say it. A wave of nausea threatened my stomach as the doorbell rang.

"Babe, are you in the kitchen? Can you get that?" Byron's voice bellowed from the study. "I'm in the middle of something."

I really didn't like it when he called me *babe*. But I'd given up on asking him to stop. It was a lost cause.

I turned the oven off and opened the front door. Drew was standing there, a worried expression on his face.

"Hey," I said, excitement brushing the pit of my stomach. I tried not to let it show.

"Hey. Um … I know this is a bit left field …" He paused and looked at me. "I have a favour to ask. And I will really, *really* owe you one."

I frowned. He looked quite nervous as he stood on my doorstep, wide-eyed. I contemplated whether to invite him in or not. I decided on *not*.

"What is it?" I asked.

"I'm being deployed tomorrow. Last-minute disaster relief. Normally I'd ask my sister to look after Mal while I'm gone – but she's away with her partner. I'd take him to a kennel, but the truth is he hates it there. And I haven't had a chance to even find one in Sydney yet." He scratched his head, not breaking eye contact. "So … I was wondering if I could pay you to do it instead? I – I have to leave early tomorrow, so I'm pretty stuck. I mean, you could drop him at the kennel the day after if—"

"Drew." I took a breath. "I *told* you I'm not a dog person." The thought of being with that dog again made me shudder.

He narrowed his eyes at me. "Are you a person who can throw a handful of biscuits into a bowl?"

I rolled my eyes. Seriously? I couldn't believe he was asking me this. I didn't even know what he did for work, let alone want to offer to be his pet-sitter.

"Look, he's really low maintenance. Could you … If you could just feed him tomorrow night, I can sort something else out after that. And he'll be okay during the day."

"Well, good evening." Byron had come up behind me. My heart skipped a beat.

How is this going to go, Drew and Byron meeting? I swallowed.

Drew stuck his hand out and introduced himself, looking at me subtly and explaining the situation again to Byron.

"Of course, mate. We can help you out. No worries at all." Byron said warmly.

How did I know that my husband would agree to help, but it'd be me doing all the work?

"So, what do you do for a living?" Byron asked him, looking up. He was at least a head shorter than Drew. And about half the width.

"Helicopter pilot," Drew said. "Defence."

"Oh, you're in the Air Force? I used to have a buddy in the Air Force."

"No. Navy. Recently got posted to Sydney from Perth. Fleet Base East."

I pictured him in a helicopter. *Dear God, never, ever let me see that man in uniform.*

"Wow. Well, we can swap work stories when you're back."

I smiled at Byron. I loved the guy – but he certainly never missed an opportunity to mention his job. And what he thought being a surgeon had to do with being a helicopter pilot in the Navy, I could only guess.

"Okay." Drew didn't ask what Byron did for work. He didn't strike me as a small talk kind of guy. He looked back at me. "I'll leave you some instructions in the morning in the kitchen. Thank you so much, Georgie." I noticed he was directing it at me – not Byron. He hesitated, then broke our gaze. "Nice to meet you, Byron."

"Babe. Why don't you go over with Drew now and see what we have to do?" Byron pointed behind him with his thumb. "I've gotta finish this proposal. Hope the deployment is okay, mate. We'll look after the dog. Come over for a drink when you're back."

I forced another smile. This whole exchange was making me queasy. I breathed out slowly. Why the hell did he suggest I go over to Drew's?

"Uh, well, only if you have time?" Drew eyed me.

I shrugged. "Sure."

Byron headed back to the study, and Drew and I stood at the door, looking at each other. His gaze fell to my hand. I was hiding the finger that I'd been picking at. It was so embarrassing. And yet, Drew's gorgeous eyes were so warm as they flickered back up to mine. "So, uh, did you want to come over and I can show you the dinner routine and where Mal's leash is and stuff?"

Leash? Was I going to have to walk it, too?

Drew grinned suddenly. "Also, would you like to walk to mine, or just jump the fence?"

I gave him the most disgusted look I could muster. "Give me a sec." I walked over to the oven and took out the cupcakes, then chose a big one that had risen perfectly. I put it on a piece of paper towel and walked back to the door. Opening the oven made the kitchen smell like chocolate all over again.

"Mmm, that smells amazing. You really *do* bake a lot, huh? Muffins again?" he asked as I put one in his hand, then walked past him out the door.

I turned around. "Are you coming, or not?"

"Uh, yeah." He looked at his hand, puzzled. "What's this?"

"A cupcake."

"I know what it is. I mean, why are you giving it to me?"

"It's pumpkin and dark chocolate. It's supposed to have more dark chocolate grated on top. I haven't had a chance to do that yet. Also, I'm not super keen to use the grater again any time soon." I held up my finger as a reminder and made my way across the front lawn, waiting for him to follow me. "They're for an elderly client I see on Mondays."

"Quick question," he said, jogging to catch up to me. "What's the difference between a muffin and a cupcake?"

That was actually a pretty good question, seeing as the two

looked similar and were even baked in the same kind of tray. "Cupcakes generally have icing on them," I said. "They're sweet – usually lots of sugar and stuff. Muffins can sometimes be savoury."

He grinned at me in the dark. "Wrong. The difference is you've never given me a muffin."

I rolled my eyes, making my way along the bushes that separated our lawns. In the dark, it was easier to walk onto the street and then back down to Drew's front door again, rather than weave between the bushes. I'd seen the spiderwebs in there. When I got to the road, I stopped. "See that house there?" I pointed across the road and Drew nodded. "That's Kate and Tony's place. Kate is hosting the street Christmas party this year. She's asked me to do all the cooking and baking for it."

He was standing next to me on the road, looking at their house. "When is it?"

"The Christmas party? Twenty-third. Five, six weeks away."

"How does one get an invite to such an event?"

I paused, noticing he was looking at me again. "Um – you move into the street?"

"You're hilarious," he said, chuckling.

"All right. Let's do this." I made for his house, wanting it to be over quickly. I knew I would resent agreeing to look after his dog, that slobbery mess, and I knew Byron wouldn't lift a finger.

"So am I like your guinea pig then? With the cupcake?" Drew asked, opening the front door.

"Sure."

He held the door open for me, then led me out the back and sat on the steps of the deck. I hovered awkwardly near him until he motioned for me to sit next to him. There was one down light that shone onto the jacuzzi, but otherwise it was fairly dark out there. He sat on the top step, facing me, watching as I sat down next to him and crossed my legs. Mal had followed us outside and was sitting next to Drew, which I was grateful for.

"Mal's bowl lives there," he said, pointing towards the base of the jacuzzi and peeling the paper away from the cupcake before taking a bite. I looked at his hands as they held my little cupcake. They looked strong. "He normally eats at about six, but—" He paused. "Sweet baby Jesus." He studied the cupcake with wide eyes, then took another bite. "Georgie. This is *amazing*."

My face went hot.

"Seriously. This is the best cupcake I've ever eaten." He was talking with his mouth full, but trying to keep it shut at the same time to be polite, and looked ridiculous. It made me smile. "This is … *wow*. Oh my god. I don't know whether to shove it in my mouth, or savour it forever." He turned to me, swallowing. "Then again, if I shoved it all in and choked, I'd hate for you to have to give me mouth-to-mouth."

I just shook my head.

"Lasagne, *and* the most amazing dessert in the same night. You're setting a high bar here." He wiped his mouth and beard. "Wow."

"So it tastes okay?"

"Okay? Jesus Christ. I could eat a tray of them. They're incredible."

I could feel myself blushing again, grateful it was dark. "Thank you. I'll bring you some more later."

"Seriously. You should cook for a living."

I let out a small laugh. How ironic. But this was getting too comfortable. "Drew, can you show me the rest of the stuff so I can go home?"

"Uh, sure." He stood up, a slightly disappointed look in his eyes, but didn't say anything. Damn, that was a bit harsh. Mal had jumped up when Drew did, and was looking at me. He was a tall dog, towering over me when I was sitting down. I hugged my knees to my chest, hoping he wouldn't come over to me. He may not have been a good guard dog, but he sure as hell looked intimidating. I stood up slowly, not taking my eyes off him. I wondered if he was marking his territory, trying to say Drew was his.

"Why did you buy a winter dog in a summer country?" I said, eyeing the dog's thick coat.

Drew laughed, turning around to go inside as Mal trotted behind him. "I didn't buy him. My neighbour in Perth got him from a shelter. Apparently he'd been dumped as a puppy. So my neighbour took him home as a birthday present for his son. But eventually he got too big for their apartment, and the kid got sick of looking after him. I was leaving for work one morning and I saw them walking out with Mal. They never walked him, so I was glad to see him getting out. But when I said hello, they told me they were taking him back to the shelter. Mal looked at me with those huge blue eyes, and the next thing I know, I'm a frickin' dog owner."

I followed Drew into the kitchen. He stopped after his story, turning to me suddenly, one corner of his mouth rising towards the ceiling. *Yep, he definitely knows that that story makes him even hotter.*

"So you just adopted him?" I said as he opened a door that led to an internal laundry.

"Yeah. Seven years ago." He opened a cupboard. "Can you imagine him as a puppy, though? He was like a mini black-and-white teddy bear. So bloody cute. Apparently he's not a purebred though, because the purebreds don't have blue eyes." He shrugged, then pointed to a bulky white bag and opened the velcro bit at the top. "Those're his biscuits. He gets one large scoop each morning when we get back from our run. But it doesn't really matter what time. And usually at night I give him some chicken necks or beef. To keep it simple, though, just give him the biscuits morning and night. His leash is there, if you or your husband feel like going for a walk." He shrugged. "He'll be fine without it, though. He's happy lying around doing nothing. A bit like his owner," he added with a grin.

Mal was at the laundry door, sitting patiently.

"Are you gonna feed him now?" I asked.

"Nah. He's already eaten dinner. He wanted some lasagne, too, but I said no."

"You just rustled his food bag, but you're not giving him any?"

He waved his hand towards Mal. "He's a big boy. He'll be fine." He walked back into the kitchen, leaving me and Mal staring silently at each other in the laundry, while he said something about filling up the water bowls. I hesitated, then quietly stuck my hand into the white bag and grabbed a few of the biscuits. Mal's eyes darted to my hand. I opened it up and let him lick the biscuits from my palm. It was a bit slimy, and I scrunched up my face. His collar jingled as he basically inhaled the biscuits. I followed Drew into the kitchen innocently, wiping my hands, glad he hadn't seen what I'd just done. He definitely would have made a big deal out of it.

"That's basically it. Keep the back door open, screen door locked, and then he can come and go through the doggy door. So, any questions, or is it clear as mud?" He walked to the sink and turned on the tap. I watched the muscles on his back tensing and relaxing under his shirt as he washed and dried his hands.

"Um, no, it's all clear."

"Great. How's fifty dollars a day? If Elena gets back before I do, she can take over from—"

"Fifty a day? Are you joking?" I frowned.

"Oh, well, if that's not enough I can—"

"You're not paying me, Drew." Was he for real? All I had to

do was put biscuits in a bowl.

He leaned back against the kitchen island onto his palms, his triceps standing out. *Good lord.*

"Come on, Georgie. You don't even like Mal. You're saving me money anyway – if I had to put him in a kennel I would—"

"You're not paying me," I repeated, pausing to think. "Okay, how about this. I'm short-staffed Saturday after next. You can help me then, instead of paying me."

His eyebrows shot up. "You want me to come and work with you?"

I shrugged. "Why not? You're back by then, right? I really need someone to help. And who doesn't love free labour?"

He laughed a genuine, warm laugh. I couldn't stop looking at him – which made me wonder if this was a bad idea. I instinctively put my thumbnail to my mouth, then pulled it away when Drew looked at me doing it. I hated that disgusting habit so much. What would he think if he ever looked at my hands?

"Okay, sold!" He laughed again, breaking me out of my thoughts.

"I better go," I muttered. "Key?"

"Oh, yeah, almost forgot. Here." He took a key off his keyring and put it in my hand, then walked me to the front door. "Seriously, thank you so much. You're a lifesaver."

I walked out without saying anything, still annoyed at myself for the deal I'd just made.

I was halfway across the lawn when he called out to me. "Hey, Georgie?"

"Yeah?"

"Mal said to say thanks." He paused, and I swear I could feel the grin spreading across his face. "And he also said to tell you that we're both big fans of cupcakes. *And* muffins!"

I walked to my front door without saying anything.

But I couldn't keep the smile off my face.

8

DREW

I threw some clothes into a duffel bag and looked down at Mal, who was lying next to my bed. "All right, mate. Now, you know the rules. The house is fair game, but not the bed, okay?"

He cocked his head, giving me a blue-eyed stare.

"You're cute and all, but you're too big and hairy for it. We've already got one big hairy dude in there; we don't need any more. Right?"

Mal never got in the bed while I was around. But sometimes when I got home, there would be a warm dent in the blanket at the foot of the bed, and some white hairs scattered around.

He wasn't stupid.

But neither was I. Still, I wasn't going to close the bedroom door while I was gone.

I zipped up the bag and put it on the ground, then fell back onto the bed for a moment, scratching Mal's head as he stood next to me. "You get a whole week alone with Georgie, you lucky bastard. You better be good for her." I thought about the lasagne she'd left me. She was a seriously good cook. And that cupcake? Not like anything I'd ever tasted before. I realised I'd forgotten to return the lasagne dish.

Having her next door was going to be trouble. She was drop-dead gorgeous. It was all I could do not to stare when she was around. I couldn't look at or think about anything else when she was there. I turned over and looked at Mal, already anticipating coming back home, as my phone vibrated with a text from John.

Hi Drew. I hope the move from Perth went smoothly and you made it to Sydney all right. Now that you're on the east coast, maybe one day you could come visit. It'd be really great to see you. I'm sorry again. I just wish I could tell you that in person. I miss you, Elena, and Pete. Love, John.

I threw the phone back on the bed next to me. The old guy was relentless.

And I had no plans to visit him any time soon, despite being back in Sydney.

My mind wandered to Georgie slowly, and how she'd fed Mal those biscuits in secret when I wasn't watching. Warmth spread through me. It meant that she wasn't as much of a dog-hater as she made out to be. And that was good, given I was about to leave my dog with her for an entire week.

Well, her *or* her husband. Who knew which one would actually come over and look after Mal? Maybe Georgie would just ask him to do it all. But somehow, I didn't think so.

He was a lucky guy, being married to Georgie. It didn't add up, though. She was cranky all right, but she seemed like a good person. I honestly couldn't say the same about him. It wasn't anything I could put my finger on. He just didn't seem very … genuine, perhaps? And they seemed like a mismatch of a couple. Of course, it could be my jealousy – even if it was hard to admit. It kind of felt like more than that, though.

I was still thinking about the situation as I showered, brushed my teeth, and hopped into bed. I couldn't get her out of my mind.

"Well, goodnight, Mal. Don't worry, buddy. Tomorrow I'll be gone, and you can sneak onto the bed again. But not under the covers, okay? And no drooling on my pillow!" I switched off the light, listening to the cicadas outside.

At least I was about to have a week away from here.

And that was good, because I needed to reset my thoughts. They were headed in a bad direction.

9

GEORGIE

I emptied the skimmer baskets, put them back in place, and popped the plastic lids on them. Lou's pool was looking good. It just needed a vacuum and then I was done for the day. I wiped my arm across my forehead and gazed out over the azure Pacific water of Balmain; white boats dotting the smooth surface. I loved the view, and this was an easy pool to maintain, so it was often left as the last job of the day. Lou was usually home, and she was one of my favourite clients. She always made me tea, and would come and chat to me while I worked. It was a nice change from all the other jobs. I never felt like I had to hurry. And during summer, she always offered to let me have a dip before I put the chlorine in.

Today had been another thirty-something-degree day and I was cooked. I really wished I'd packed swimmers so I could take Lou up on her offer. Usually, that was a no-go at jobs. People who owned these multi-million-dollar homes and pools didn't appreciate you swimming in them. One of the pools I looked after, in Potts Point, recently had a four-million-dollar upgrade. Just for the *pool*.

Earlier, I'd had an iced tea with Lou, which was a touch sweet for my liking – especially coupled with my chocolate cupcakes

– but it went down so much better than a normal tea on this sweaty day. She'd enjoyed the cupcakes, which I'd kept cold in an esky with ice. Lou generally liked everything I baked for her. Today, she'd eaten six of the cupcakes in front of me, asking, "What's the point of being old if you can't be fat?" as she shoved the sixth one in.

I packed up my gear once I finished vacuuming the pool, yelled a farewell to Lou and headed to my ute to drive home.

Truth was, I'd been feeling tense and agitated all day – and it was good for me to have the distraction of work, and of Lou. Otherwise, I would only be thinking about the inevitable – what I had to tell Byron. It was time – and it wasn't going to be pleasant.

And then there was Mal. I had to feed him from tonight, and I wasn't really that keen.

When I got to my house, I parked out the front, but went straight to Drew's to feed Mal. As I turned the key in Drew's front door, I could hear the swinging of the doggy door out the back. I hesitated and stepped inside. Mal paused for a moment, then wagged his tail and bounded over towards me. His expression and the way he was panting kind of made it look like he was smiling. It *was* cute when dogs did that, I had to admit. I hesitated again, then leaned down and scratched him on the head cautiously.

"Drew wasn't lying – you really are a terrible guard dog."

He eyed me with a funny expression. I stood up and walked to the back deck, filling up his water before grabbing the food bowl beside the jacuzzi. I took it into the laundry, Mal trotting along behind me. I was about to fill the bowl with dog biscuits when I spotted his leash. I glanced at it for a moment, and Mal looked at me. As if sensing my contemplation, he sat down in front of me eagerly, waiting to see what I would do. His fluffy tail swished back and forth along the floor like a broom.

I sighed. "Well, I guess I could use a walk, too." Despite being in the sun and working hard all day, a peaceful sunset stroll did seem appealing.

"But don't tell Drew, okay?" I raised my eyebrows at him.

Jesus Christ. You're talking to a dog.

When I reached for the leash, two things happened simultaneously. One, Mal jumped up at me, making me realise he was almost as tall as me; and two, I lost my balance, fell back onto the laundry bench and knocked over the entire bag of biscuits.

The race was on. Me, trying to scoop up the biscuits with my hands while swearing, and Mal wolfing them down before I could get to them. I could just imagine the expression on Drew's face right now. He would be absolutely losing it laughing at me.

Mal beat me to the last few bits and gave me a triumphant look. I stood up, hands on my hips. "Well, I guess you just halved your dinner portion, then." I grabbed the leash, clipped it onto his collar and walked out the front door with him. As soon as we were out, I tightened the leash a bit. It wasn't that he was pulling on it, it was more that I was petrified of losing him. What if he ran off? Drew would never forgive me. I hardly knew the guy, but I could tell he loved his dog a lot. And he must've been *really* stuck to leave Mal with me.

As we turned the second corner, I relaxed a bit and let the lead slacken. We plodded along together in silence down the back streets. I passed a few other people walking their dogs, or running with them, and they all gave me a knowing look. It was like being in some special dog-owners club. Plus, I liked that it made me get out for an evening walk. Normally, I would've just flopped down on the couch with a book, or watched some sitcom I'd seen a thousand times, while Byron worked in his study. And, of course, I would've been answering work calls and returning emails, too. I tried to avoid doing that in the evenings. But I had just as much responsibility to ensure the smooth running of the business as Roisin did.

I realised Byron hadn't even messaged me to see where I was.

Mal stopped to pee on a tree. He wasn't so scary after all. His fur was so thick and shiny, and his eyes were mesmerising – what a beautiful breed. If Drew had adopted him as a puppy seven years ago, Mal must've been around eight years old, if that.

I looked at my watch and wondered what Drew was doing. I hoped he wasn't worried about me taking care of Mal, although I wouldn't blame him if he was. Then again, he hadn't seemed too worried when he was showing me the food and talking about going away. I pictured him leaning against the kitchen bench as he was talking to me. The way his muscles had moved under his shirt as he animatedly explained something. The way he looked with a bare torso when he was washing his car. Those warm eyes, and—

I jumped when a tiny dog barked at us and threw itself against the metal gate, making it rattle. Mal stopped, curious, his long tail swishing back and forth in a friendly way. The dog was lunging at us, baring its teeth and frothing at the mouth, patchy white fur standing on end. Mal was not bothered one bit, while the other dog looked like it wanted to eat him. It wasn't much bigger than one of Mal's paws.

"Come on, mate. Let's go." I pulled him away and we continued down the street, heading home, completing what must've been a five- or six-kilometre loop.

When we got back to the house, I poured some of the biscuits into Mal's bowl. I had intended to give him less dinner than he was supposed to get, given our mishap before, but I couldn't do it. I gave him the normal amount, writing off the earlier feed as a bonus. Besides, our walk had been almost an hour, and I figured that had to count for something. I fed Mal, and admired the pool, deck and jacuzzi again while he ate. When I went back inside, I couldn't help looking around the house a little. It was simple but modern, and had all the basics. I guess Drew had only recently moved in, and probably hadn't accumulated a lot of stuff. Or he just liked being a minimalist. Either way, it was nice – simple but elegant. There were a few pictures on a cabinet by the wall in the living room. I walked up to them. I figured it wasn't snooping if the photos were on display. It wasn't like I was planning to go into the bedrooms or anything.

There was a photo of Drew with an older couple, who I assumed were his parents. His expression was nothing less than ecstatic, standing behind them in a restaurant, his hands resting on their backs. He had the most amazing smile.

In another photo, he had a young girl sitting on his shoulders. He looked like he was living the dream, grinning wildly at the camera. And he had no shirt on. Good lord. I stared at it for a moment, before noticing something else – a photo of Drew with a very pretty young woman. She looked about his age, with blonde hair and hazelnut-brown eyes. They had their arms around each other.

A pang of jealousy flashed through me as I wondered if it was his girlfriend.

I sighed. *You have absolutely zero right to be jealous.*

Mal had come into the living room and was watching me carefully. I crouched down and gave him another pat as he licked his lips post-dinner. "See you, buddy. Thanks for the walk."

Well, I could handle a week of this. Living next door to Mal would be fine. Enjoyable, even.

It wasn't him that I was concerned about.

10

GEORGIE

I breathed out slowly as I took the crispy skin salmon out of the oven. My finger still hurt, but at least cooking didn't bother it as much as work did. I arranged the salmon carefully on top of the cauliflower puree and tempura zucchini flowers, my stomach rumbling from hunger. But I was also incredibly anxious. It was time to be honest.

I had to tell Byron tonight. He was going to be pissed – but I needed to do it. There was no point putting it off any longer – for his sake *and* mine.

He came out of the study ten minutes after I told him dinner was ready. That used to annoy me – as a chef, you wanted people to enjoy the meal as soon as it was served, not ten minutes later. But Byron did as Byron pleased, and I'd stopped putting up a fuss, learning to just go with the flow. I needed to work on my flexibility, anyway.

"Smells great, babe, thanks!" He gave me an appreciative smile and dug in without waiting for me. I dried my hands and sat opposite him at our dining table, annoyed that I had waited for him and not started right away.

He had a sip of his sauvignon blanc. "Mmm. Nice pairing."

"Is the salmon okay?"

"Yeah. It's phenomenal."

"So, how's the planning going?"

He swallowed. "Good. We're almost done with organising the trip," he said. "We've got the nurses and doctors all sorted, flights and accommodation booked."

"That's great, so what's left to do?" I made myself eat, despite the ill feeling in the base of my stomach. I wiped my forehead with my napkin, feeling silly for being so anxious about this. He was my husband. He would hear me out, and he would be understanding – towards *my* actions, anyway. *It'll be okay, Georgie. Just be honest.*

Byron continued talking about his trip to Tanzania. He was one of the surgeons on the Surgeons with Heart International team going to do cardiac surgery in the local hospitals. He'd done it before – it wasn't anything new – but this time he had a lot more to do with the organisation of the team and overseeing the general planning and itinerary, as well as liaising with the staff over there. He recently joined some board, and I could tell he loved talking about it a lot, so I listened intently. It was cute when he got so passionate about his trips, and they were a welcome change to the day-to-day operating he did.

The way he was looking at me with soft eyes as he talked about the trip made my heart break. *He's not going to be angry about this – he's going to be really, really sad. And disappointed.*

I wiped my mouth and finished my glass of wine. I was so nervous, I'd pretty much necked the entire thing. I swallowed. "Byron – I have to tell you something ..."

"Everything okay?" He frowned. "Please stop picking your nail, babe. It's so gross."

"Uh ... Sort of." I took a deep breath, trying to calm my heart rate. "Actually, no. It's about Kevin." I gave him a smile that said everything would be okay and put a hand on his. "He tried – well, he tried to hit on me."

I thought Byron was going to choke on his wine. He frowned, and then started laughing. "Very funny."

I put my fork down. "I'm not joking."

Studying me like I was a stranger, he said, "Are you kidding me, Georgie?" He shook his head and drank his wine, still staring at me.

"No. I'm not kidding. I just said that."

He said nothing.

"It was your birthday night, when he and Sean were here. After he came back inside from the garage," I said, starting to recount the events that were so clearly burned into my memory.

The other two had stayed outside, but Kevin came in to go to the bathroom. I hadn't heard him as I walked back to the bedroom with only a towel on. We were going to a fine-dining restaurant in the city for Byron's birthday dinner and I was getting ready. Kevin passed me in the hallway, and kind of blocked me so I couldn't get past. He'd glanced outside towards the garage before his gaze fell south, and even though I was covered by the towel, the way he ogled me made me feel like I was naked. He scanned me up and down and said, "Mmm, you're so ... hot ... And such a tease ..." before biting his bottom lip. It made me want to be sick. Kevin raised his eyebrows at me quickly, then moved in towards me, backing me up against my bedroom door, his sour breath on my face. I snapped out of my shock and pushed him away from me with one hand, the other gripping onto the towel tightly, and slammed him into the wall – hard.

I'd always known he was a massive creep. I just hadn't thought he was *that* big of a creep to crack onto his own brother's wife. What would've happened if that door had been open, or if he'd come into the bathroom? My skin still crawled with a thousand bugs even thinking about it.

I hadn't gone to the restaurant with them that night, claiming Kate needed urgent help with a family crisis. And I hadn't seen Byron again until he came stumbling home at two in the morning, with a new Rolex on his wrist. Telling him about Kevin then wasn't an option. Neither was the following day. And after that, I kept putting it off.

The two brothers were close – I knew this wasn't going to go down well. I just didn't think my own husband would laugh it off.

Byron looked at me as I finished recounting the events, then chuckled again. "Wow."

"What do you mean, *wow*?"

"You expect me to believe that *Kevin* hit on *you*? And – and – pushed you up against a wall?"

"Why are you saying '*you*' like that? And yes, I expect you to believe what I'm saying. I'm your wife."

He smirked and refilled his wine glass. "Okay, listen. It's not that I don't believe you. I just think maybe you, you know, misinterpreted something."

"I didn't *misinterpret* anything." I glared at him.

He sighed, putting his fork down. "Well, saying it was true, what do you expect me to do about it anyway? He's my brother."

I gaped at him. "Seriously?"

When he didn't respond, I grabbed my plate, stood up, and made for the kitchen. "You know what?" I threw the plate in the sink. "It doesn't matter."

He gave me a smile that didn't reach his eyes and kept eating. "By the way," he said between mouthfuls, "we got an invitation to Dr Lee's sixtieth next month. It's black tie."

I stood at the sink, staring at him in disbelief. I couldn't believe I'd been worried about him getting angry, or worse – really upset – by this news. But I should have known better. It was only a couple of weeks ago that I'd got this same feeling after confiding in him – a feeling of … I don't know … insignificance. My brother's wife had had a miscarriage – and Byron couldn't understand why I was so upset about it. In fact, he was so unfazed by it that I almost wished I hadn't shared something so private with him. And not long before that, when our neighbour Tony was in hospital for a few days, Byron didn't understand why I went to all the effort to cook for Han and Kate.

Feeling like that with your own husband just felt wrong.

But this? This directly affected me. *Us*, actually. It was significant. At least, it was to me. And I always thought that what mattered to me, mattered to him.

It clearly didn't, though. In fact, it really didn't seem to faze him at all. It was like his compassion was growing for his work, and his patients – and disappearing for me. Like he only had one small bucket of compassion to borrow from, and more and more of it went to his work, and less came to me. I stared into the kitchen, at nothing in particular, everything blurring into one, and let that thought sink in.

Byron drank his wine, reading something on his phone, laughing loudly. "Oh my god, babe, you have to come and see this," he chuckled.

I grabbed the spare key to Drew's house. "I'm going to walk Mal."

"Again? But it's almost dark out."

I didn't mention it was also raining. "I'm a big girl."

I walked towards the front door, but Byron was back to sniggering at something on his phone before I'd even got there.

11

DREW

I picked up the Hilux from the airport carpark and drove it straight to the mechanic, grateful they were open for servicing on Saturdays – it was overdue. Then, with my duffel bag on my shoulder, I jogged the three kilometres home, wondering why I hadn't just left the bag on the backseat for a few hours while the car was there. My tired brain wasn't working.

At least the bag wasn't very heavy, and it was only a short run home. Despite the scorching day, the exercise felt good – I was missing my morning runs with Mal. And I was dying to get home and see him.

Georgie hadn't given me her number, so I had no way of contacting her during the week I was away. I wasn't really worried about her with Mal, but with Elena away, I realised I had literally no way of contacting anyone back home. My house could've burnt down and I wouldn't have known. I made a mental note to get to know the other neighbours, too – starting with Kate and Tony across the road. Georgie seemed to really like them, and for some reason, I trusted her opinion.

I unlocked the door, grinning as I waited for Mal. But he didn't come.

"Mal?" I called, looking around. "Mal!" He usually came bounding to the front door as soon as he heard it open. I walked through the house and checked the backyard, too, but he was nowhere to be seen. Georgie or her husband must've been walking him, because there was no way he could get out anywhere with all the tall fences surrounding the backyard. It was one of the first things Elena and I had checked out when we came to inspect the property. I only had two requirements for my new home in Sydney – that it had a spacious, secure backyard for Mal, and a garage or storage space for my surfboards and spearfishing gear.

I hesitated, then went next door. My chest tightened at the thought of seeing Georgie – but it was her husband who opened the door.

"Hey, mate, how was the week?" He seemed surprisingly happy to see me. "This is my brother by the way, Kev." Kev stepped forward and shook my hand, a little harder than necessary, eyeing me suspiciously.

"Oh, yeah, good thanks. I was wondering if you had … if Mal was here? He isn't in the backyard."

Byron frowned at me. "That's the dog, right? Must be with Georgie. She left ages ago. I thought she went to Kate's." He shrugged. "She's been out with that dog every day this week. I guess people change, huh?" He let out a throaty laugh. There was definitely something off about him, but I still couldn't quite put my finger on what it was.

You're just jealous of him. I swatted the thought away. But I knew it was more than that.

"All right then, well, thanks for looking after Mal this week. I owe you."

"Don't mention it. Any time."

Something told me he hadn't so much as lifted a finger – that it was all Georgie, despite the fact she didn't even like Mal. I walked back to my place and stripped off my sweaty clothes. It was already over thirty-five degrees, and the jog hadn't helped my cause. I threw everything into the laundry basket on my way to the shower. It felt good being naked, the air drying the sweat on my body as I walked. I hopped in and was about to turn the tap on when I realised I hadn't brought any soap back in after my trip. I opened the glass door and got out. That was when I noticed them out the bathroom window.

Mal – and Georgie. They'd walked up along the side of the fence, rather than through the house, and were right outside where I was.

Luckily for me, the bathroom window was higher than my waist.

I waved at them wildly from inside, excited to see them both. But Georgie didn't see me. I went to shout something to her, but decided to just go outside and see them instead. I was looking around for a towel to cover up with when I heard her start talking to Mal on the back deck.

I glanced out the window again and craned my neck to see them. She was crouching down on the deck, wearing orange running shorts that complemented her tanned legs, and a baggy white T-shirt. She always seemed to be wearing those baggy T-shirts, much to my disappointment. She was scratching behind Mal's ears and looking at him in complete adoration. My heart fluttered. I'd never seen her smile like that before. She certainly never smiled at *me* like that. And she obviously didn't despise Mal quite as much as she made out to everyone.

"All right, I admit it," I heard her saying faintly through the window. "You're very cute. But can you do any tricks? Can you … roll over?"

I stifled a laugh. No, he couldn't. Apart from being able to make you feel guilty for not feeding him, he had no tricks.

She laughed, crouching at eye-level with Mal and holding his head between her hands. "You have the most amazing eyes, you know that?" she said, pausing momentarily and then lowering her voice. "Just like your owner." She stood up. "But we won't tell him that, will we?"

I almost choked. *What?*

I stood in my bathroom, fully naked, frozen to the spot with my heartbeat quickening by the minute. She would be so embarrassed if I went out there now and she realised I'd heard what she said. Since my car was at the mechanic and not out the front, I guess she'd assumed I wasn't home yet. Had I even told her when I was getting back? Maybe not. But it seemed like the best thing to do was hide and hope that she went home sooner rather than later. Something told me she wouldn't laugh it off – that she would be really annoyed at what I'd heard – and that would only give her more reason to avoid me. I sure as hell didn't want that.

So I'd just have to wait quietly until she went home. I glanced out the window again. Georgie was walking towards the pool. Her arms crossed over the front of her body and lifted her T-shirt off over her head. She dropped it on the ground behind her, then unclipped and took off a sports bra, revealing her toned back and a white bikini top underneath.

Good lord. I felt like a creep watching her. But I couldn't tear my eyes away.

She was moving fast. Her shorts were next, which also ended up on the ground after she'd kicked them off. A pair of white bikini bottoms matched the top. I tried hard not to stare.

Georgie is in my backyard in a string bikini.

She took her long hair out of its elastic band and shook her head, letting it swish down her back before diving into the pool. I looked around the bathroom, still naked. Luckily it was warm, because at this rate I might be here for a while.

I could sneak out now and pretend I just got home.

Unfortunately for me, all the towel racks in the bathroom were bare, rendering my plan useless. I'd have to go out to the laundry, past the big glass doors, to get a fresh towel – or make a run for the bedroom where all my clothes were. I groaned and opted to stay where I was until it was safe, still looking around my empty bathroom uselessly. When I glanced back up again, Georgie was hoisting herself out of the pool facing me, water running down her face, her neck, her breasts … I tore my gaze away quickly. She was so damn sexy. I closed my eyes, feeling terrible watching her without her knowing. But it was too late. The image was seared into my memory. The water running down her body. Her full breasts in that white bikini. Those long legs. I imagined sliding my hands around her waist and kissing her neck, her jaw, those soft lips …

Well, now I *really* couldn't go anywhere – which was unfortunate for me, as Georgie had started making her way towards the house. I watched in horror as she walked up the path, water running down her body, and reached for the screen door.

12

GEORGIE

I squeezed the water out of my hair before I walked into Drew's house. That pool was everything I'd thought it would be. I'd been eyeing it every day after I got home from walking Mal. And this morning, I'd thrown on my bikini under my running gear, deciding it was high time I gave it a go. I was pretty sure Drew wouldn't mind, especially as I was dog sitting for him. And besides, in the week he'd been gone, I'd also looked after the pool. I'd kept all the leaves out of it, vacuumed it and tested the PH, chlorine levels and alkalinity. It was the full Pool Chicks service, except Drew had got it for free. Even if it *was* mostly for selfish reasons – so I could swim in it. And it was such a beautiful pool, I couldn't let it sit there gathering dirt and leaves anyway. I'd even scrubbed the stone around the pool, and the back deck. And that was definitely *not* part of the Pool Chicks service. I enjoyed being at his house, and I enjoyed hanging out with Mal in the backyard.

Plus, exercise was helping the tension that seemed to have made a home in my chest and spread itself out through my body when I thought about the whole Kevin situation. Things Byron had done in the past – lack of compassion, putting his work before me, not really listening – they weren't great. But not believing me about Kevin? Unless something changed, this was pretty much a dealbreaker for me.

And I couldn't ignore the implications of that.

Since I told him, I had been walking around like a zombie – part of me disbelieving, part of me realising that it really wasn't that weird for Byron to act like this, and that maybe I should have expected it. That in itself made me clench my fists.

And it was the first time I'd actually thought about leaving him.

I understood that Kevin being his brother made things harder, but still, the situation spoke volumes, and was totally unforgivable that he thought I would make something like that up.

I'd forgotten to bring a towel over, and going home for one seemed a bit pointless, so I thought I'd use one of Drew's. If I was being honest, I didn't really feel like going home yet, anyway. Sitting on the back deck in the shade seemed like a better option. And a bit of Georgie-time sounded like just what I needed.

Inside the house, I opened the laundry cupboard, but I couldn't see any towels. Chlorinated pool water was dripping off me and leaving a trail on Drew's kitchen and laundry tiles. Nothing I couldn't fix up afterwards, though. As I closed the door, I heard a sound inside the house. Frowning, I stopped to listen, thinking it might have been the wind, even though I didn't recall leaving any windows open. I heard nothing else, so I made my way to the bathroom to look for a towel – surely I'd find one in there, given the laundry didn't have any, and I hadn't seen a linen cupboard anywhere. I hurried, not wanting to be inside the house too long; it felt like I was snooping.

I turned the doorknob to the bathroom, right as I heard the shower go on. My heart skipped a beat. What the hell? Drew was *home*? I hadn't seen his car – he must've got home in the five minutes I was in the pool.

Unfortunately, that fact didn't register in my brain quickly enough to stop me from opening the bathroom door.

I squealed and slammed the door shut again.

Drew. Naked in the shower. He was facing away from me, at least. I stood at the door with my heart racing. Did he hear me? *Please no.* I closed my eyes and tried to erase the visual of the back of his tanned, muscly body. Tried to forget the way the water was cascading down his hamstrings and calf muscles. Lord help me. I smiled at the fact that his butt was extremely white compared to the rest of him.

"Um ... Georgie?" he called out cautiously. "Is that you?"

I paused. I didn't really want him to know I was still standing there. But I guess he probably wanted to double-check it was me and not some burglar coming to steal all his possessions. Not that he owned very much. "Yeah. It's me."

"Do you ... Uh ... Could you bring me a towel? I forgot to grab one."

I glanced down, realising I was still soaking wet and now creating dark patches of water on the new carpet.

"It would be helpful if I knew where they *were*," I grumbled. The water in the shower stopped. Oh god. "Don't get out!" I yelled, out of breath.

Poor Drew. I was always so cranky with him. I don't think I'd ever even smiled at the guy. And now I was essentially trespassing in his house and swimming without permission. Then again, he hadn't turned around and seen me in my swimmers, so he didn't need to know that. "Um ... Just tell me where they are?"

"Laundry. Top right."

How did I miss them? As he said – they were there, folded and stacked on the right-hand side in perfect alignment. I grabbed two of the towels, wrapping one around myself as I walked back to the bathroom door cautiously. I didn't trust Drew when it came to being serious, and I had no reason to trust a naked Drew, either.

I was ready to cover my eyes if he emerged completely nude.

"I'll just – leave it here!" I yelled at him through the door, placing his towel on the floor. "Give it two minutes, then come out!"

"Okay, thanks. Hey, wait …" He paused.

I turned away from the door. "Yeah?"

"Was everything all right with Mal? Did you manage okay?"

"Yeah. Fine."

"Oh, good. Um … Do you— Are you free tonight?"

I frowned. It was Saturday, but I didn't have any plans. I glanced over at my house. I bet Kevin would be staying all night. Kevin and Byron – I couldn't think of two worse people to spend the evening with. But I could hardly hang out with Drew on a Saturday night and not feel guilty about it. "I'm not, sorry." I closed my eyes.

"No worries, well, another time. I want to cook you dinner to say thanks for looking after Mal." His voice came out all echoey from the shower. I tried not to imagine him standing there naked with the water dripping off him, waiting for me to leave so he could grab the towel.

"I better go, but thanks, dinner sounds good. Byron and I would love to come over." Better not give any false hope. On the other hand, what made me think that it would be more than just a "thank you" dinner? How conceited was that?

"Uh, okay, sure, sounds good."

"See ya." I let no emotion seep into my voice, to be safe.

"Okay, see you, and thanks again." *His* voice was full of disappointment.

I headed towards the back door, grabbed my clothes from the pool, and made my way home along the side exit. I couldn't walk through the house again in case he'd hopped out of the shower.

There was no way I could deal with a half-naked Drew right now.

13

DREW

"Hey, buddy!" Mal came bounding over at the sound of my voice, wagging his tail. "I missed you! Did you have fun with Georgie?" I shook my head at myself as I ruffled the fur on Mal's head and scratched him on the belly. That was a bloody close call – almost busted by Georgie. She didn't seem to know, at least, that I'd been there the whole time and had heard her comments to Mal.

She definitely had a bee in her bonnet, though, and she definitely did *not* like me very much. What exactly did she have against me? I didn't really understand. But it had been obvious since the day she came over and told me off for washing the car.

I walked outside to fill Mal's water bowl. The pool was cleaner than before I'd left. I bet she had come over and cleaned it – even the edges had been scrubbed, and I had definitely not done that myself. I scratched my head. Not only had she looked after Mal, she'd even cleaned the pool.

If I hid all the chemicals and water testing kits I bought, I could hire Georgie officially and have her over regularly to clean the pool for me. Of course, I'd have to pretend I didn't know what I was really doing.

Drew. That is a dangerous road.

Besides, knowing Georgie, she would probably send someone else from her company to do it, just to annoy me.

Sighing, I had to ask myself: what was happening here? She was *married.* Not in a relationship; *married.* Naturally. But she had constantly been on my mind since I'd met her. I definitely had a crush on her, even if she was a bit fiery and over the top. All I knew was that every time I saw her, my chest felt tight. And that was bad news. I couldn't be falling for a married woman. Talk about never going to happen – even if she showed any signs of interest, which she did *not*, I would never go there, especially after everything John had put our family through.

I stood by the kitchen island, contemplating the situation and staring into space. *You're gonna have to get over whatever this is.*

I put on a load of washing and wiped down the kitchen absent-mindedly, even though it hadn't been used in a week, and I thought about John, Georgie, and my move from Perth. I did miss Perth. Perth wasn't this complicated. Perth didn't make me think so much. But then, it made me happy being close to Elena again. And I loved my new house; as did Mal. For how nice the house was, it wasn't as expensive as I'd anticipated, either. The pool and jacuzzi were an added bonus – a crazily luxurious bonus. And the bedrooms were more than I needed, but at least it'd be great for when Pete and his girls visited. There'd been nowhere for them to stay back in my Perth house, and I was already anticipating them visiting me at my new place.

I tidied the garage, picked up my car, and had just sat down on the deck with a sunset beer when there was a knock at the door. Apart from Elena, nobody else would pop over randomly. And Elena was still away on her holiday.

My heart skipped a beat as I raced to open the door, hoping it was Georgie, and mentally telling myself off for the thought.

And to my utter delight, it was her. There she stood, in front of me, in a simple green summer dress that stopped just north of her knees. It was casual, but she looked absolutely gorgeous. I couldn't hide my joy.

"Hey," she said quietly, without moving, a serious expression on her face.

"Hey!"

She didn't reply, standing awkwardly at the door.

"You wanna come in?"

She studied my face, her gaze dropping after a moment. "Depends. Can you put a shirt on?"

I grinned. "Sure. I mean, it is my house and all, and I am home by myself, but if you insist, I can put a shirt on." I pointed a thumb behind me. "Alternatively, I also have an alpine jacket and pants, a ski mask and some sheepskin boots which I can totally cover up with if you prefer?"

She glared at me, tight-lipped, then glanced towards her house. "Um, is it still okay if— Are you still ..."

"You want to stay for dinner?" I asked gently, scared of frightening her away by being a dick and making any more jokes.

She shrugged. "Okay."

My heart was threatening to beat itself out of my chest. There was only one small problem. Sure, I'd invited her for dinner on a whim earlier, but I had absolutely no food in the house. I was planning to order some pizza for myself if I got hungry, as I hadn't got around to doing a grocery shop since I'd been back – out of pure laziness.

"Well, come on in," I offered.

She seemed a bit frazzled, or perhaps upset. I led her into the living room and motioned for her to sit on the couch while I got us both a glass of cold water.

"Hey – is everything okay?" I asked as she sat on the couch, sipping away at the water. I noticed she'd brought my house key back with her and had placed it on the coffee table.

"Yeah."

"Are you sure? 'Cos it doesn't seem—"

"I'm fine." She put her glass down on the table and started picking at a nail, looking down. She was definitely *not* fine.

I watched her as she sat with her legs tucked under her dress. Her hair was up in a messy bun, the blonde part sitting in a donut shape on top of her head. Her face was a bit red. She noticed me looking at her picking her nail and stopped, a blush rising up her neck.

"How was the week away?" she said, her voice tight.

"Yeah, not bad. Disaster relief in northern Queensland after the cyclone."

She nodded. "Was it hot?"

"Yes. Sweltering." I laughed. "Especially in the uniform."

She blinked. "Uh, speaking of heat, I hope you don't mind, but I had a swim in your pool."

"Of course not. You're welcome to do that, any time. You don't even have to jump the fence."

The corners of her mouth tugged upwards a little. *Excellent.*

"So, how was your week with Mal?"

She seemed to relax a touch at the mention of Mal and leaned back into the couch. "Yeah, not bad. I enjoyed walking him, actually. He's so good. There's this annoying dog that wants to attack him through its gate and Mal just stands there unfazed."

"Yeah, I know the one. Mal's a pretty good dog. Well behaved. He must have a good owner."

Rolling her eyes, she said, "Hey. Can I ask you something?"

"Of course, go ahead."

She looked down. "What was your first impression of me?"

I hesitated at the odd question.

"In three words. Go."

"You know the first time we met was that day you yelled at me, right?"

She shrugged. "Three words. Go."

Gorgeous. Confident. A little scary …

"Um, okay. Confident, honest …" I hesitated. "And fiery."

She smiled, not seeming too bothered by this. "Fair enough."

"So I get to ask you the same question, then, right?"

"Do you really want to know the answer to that?"

"Sure." *How bad could it be?*

"Annoying, childish, immature, frustrating," she said without skipping a beat.

"Hang on. That's four. Besides, frustrating and annoying are the same thing. And so are childish and immature. You owe me one more."

"Okay." She paused. "Predictable."

"Predictable?" Was that good or bad?

"Yep." She gave me a lopsided smile, and something told me she was trying to poke me on purpose. She didn't elaborate on her comment though, instead looking around the living room before settling her gaze back on me. I melted. Smile or no smile, she was a total knockout. And I couldn't do anything about it.

Cocky as it may be, usually once I had a woman at my place, on the couch, it was game on. But unfortunately that was not going to be the case with Georgie. And I was really attracted to her. It was irony slapping me in the face.

"Who are they?" She motioned to the framed photos.

"My parents, one of my nieces, Gracie, and the blonde woman next to me is my sister Elena. The one who lives up the road."

"Ah." She flashed me a funny look. "No girlfriend?"

I shook my head.

"So, quick question. Why did you ask me to stay for a drink? On that first day?"

I'd been hoping that would never come up again. I swallowed. "Listen, Georgie, I'm really sorry about that. Honestly, I shouldn't have done it. I wish I could take it back. I just – I thought – maybe … Well, I don't even know what, to be honest. Anyway – I'm sorry."

I remembered the moment clearly. It had felt like something was there between us. But I'd been wrong. So very, very wrong.

"So you wouldn't say I led you on, then. That I was flirting?"

I frowned. "What? No. Not at all. I—"

"So you're not attracted to me?"

Shit! "Um, no, I'm n—"

"Because if you are, I don't think we should be hanging out. At all."

"Georgie. I'm not attracted to you." My chest tightened. Wow. It physically hurt saying that, but I knew where she was going with the comment. And despite the fact I would never, ever act on anything, I didn't want to stop hanging out with her, either. I'd rather be friends than nothing. It would suck never seeing her again.

Mal came in through the back door and ran straight over to Georgie. She untucked her legs and placed her bare feet on the floor, then cuddled Mal. The light pink nail polish on her toes made her feet seem even more tanned. Mal dropped a tiny, chewed bone in front of her and wagged his tail, like he had given her the best gift ever.

"Traitor," I said to him under my breath.

"So, what are you making us for dinner?" she said, still patting Mal, but facing me.

"Oh, I, well, I was going to cook, but then I didn't get … I mean, I was actually just going to get some takeaway."

She scrunched up her face. "I'll go to the shop and buy something to cook. I don't do takeaway."

"You don't do takeaway?"

"I know that sounds … funny. But I … I like cooking."

"Yeah, fair enough, but I invited *you* over as a thank you for looking after Mal." I paused. "All right, how 'bout this. We can go to the shops and grab something quickly, then come back and I'll cook. Deal?"

She nodded. "Okay, sure."

Great. Now I had to think up something to cook. She stood up and grabbed her keys. "I'll drive."

"So, is there anything you don't eat?" I said as we made for the front door.

"Yeah. Takeaway food."

It was my turn to roll my eyes.

But I got another smile! And I wanted to hi-five someone. I hopped in the passenger seat of her white work ute. She didn't say anything the whole way to the shops.

"So what should I buy? What do you feel like?" I asked as she pulled up the handbrake.

She shrugged.

Man was she moody. As I got out of the ute and slammed its creaky door shut, I noticed a piece of folded paper on the ground, and for some reason picked it up. "Hey, check it out. It's someone's shopping list," I said after unfolding it. She didn't look like she could care less if she tried as she locked the car and started walking towards the supermarket. I jogged to catch up to her. "We should buy whatever is on this list and try to make a meal out of it."

She turned around and frowned. "You are so weird."

"But how cool is this? Some total random's shopping list." I raised my eyebrows, realising my discovery wasn't even remotely "cool". She didn't seem impressed, either. "It'd be a challenge. Like *The Amazing Race*, except for cooking! They should totally make a show like that," I said with more enthusiasm than a kid in a candy store. It wasn't the list – I think being with her was what was making me feel so elated.

"Like where people are made to cook something with a time limit?"

"Yeah! Maybe."

"Yeah. That's called *MasterChef*."

"Do you like taking the joy out of everything?"

She sighed, suppressing a smile. "What's the list say?"

I unfolded the paper again. "Prawns, bananas, Fanta, potatoes, nappies, cherry tomatoes, Band-Aids, milk, fish, garlic, laundry liquid." I grimaced. "Okay, maybe this was a bad idea."

Georgie stopped walking, turned to me, and clasped her hands suddenly, excitement beaming from her face.

"What?"

"Are you sure you don't need some nappies?"

"Oh, I get it, because I'm childish?" I gave her a look. "Well maybe *you* need the Band-Aids, because you might actually cut off your entire hand this time if I let you near a grater."

She laughed. She actually laughed. "And Band-Aids would help in that instance how? Come on. I know exactly what we can make with it."

"I'm not sure I want to make any dish with milk and Band-Aids in it," I said.

"Come on, Drew. This was your idea! Get creative."

"Okay, but I have no clue what to cook with any of this stuff. It was a terrible idea."

"Well, I used to be a chef. How about you sit on the couch with a beer and I'll cook?"

She used to be a chef? And now I'd offered to cook for her, from some totally random shopping list.

Nice one, idiot.

"Um … That's … I'm supposed to cook for you, remember?"

"You can cook for me another time. I can make something good from this. Come on. I'm excited for the challenge. *Drew's Cooking Segment* – first and only contestant, Georgie!"

I was pessimistic, but she was also giving me a chance to have dinner with her another time, too. And I was not saying no to that. Besides, her mood had done a complete one-eighty.

"Done."

We walked through the aisles, getting what we needed. At one point she grabbed a bag of nappies and pretended to put them in the trolley, looking at my face, laughing and putting them back again. I loved hearing her laugh. And I was enjoying walking through the supermarket with her. It was hard not letting my imagination run wild with it. We made our way towards the seafood section to grab the prawns and fish.

"Hey, Georgie!" the guy at the deli counter said, wiping his hands on his apron. "Are you picking up some more of those dog bones? I can give you a whole bag for a fiver – we've got loads today."

She went bright red and turned towards me. "Uh … No, thanks."

"Oh. My. God. Georgie, the dog hater, buying bones? For Mal?" I was grinning ear to ear. "Yeah, she'll take a bag, thanks."

She glared at me while the guy went out the back.

I slapped my hand to my forehead. "*Now* I know why Mal likes you so much!"

"He likes me because I'm nice to him. And I walked him. Not because I gave him *one* bone, *one* time while you were gone."

"Oh, really. *One*?"

"Yeah."

I couldn't stop grinning. "Don't try and lie to me, Georgie … uh, hey wait, what's your surname?"

She paused, like she was contemplating whether to tell me this piece of information. "It's … De Luca."

"Georgie de Luca? Is that Italian?"

She took the bag of bones from the guy, muttering a thank you and throwing them into the trolley.

"Mine's Thomson, in case you care," I teased. We grabbed the seafood, paid, and walked back to the car. I was still blissfully pleased about the fact she'd got busted with the bone thing. "But what about Georgie? That's not Italian, is it?"

She just about winced. It was almost like talking to me was painful. But I was enjoying getting these tiny snippets of information from her.

"It's – technically Giorgia. But no one ever calls me that."

"Giorgia …" I repeated. "It's nice. I like it."

Unlocking the car, my side first so I could get in, she smiled at me but didn't say anything.

"Thank you. So, tell me about The Pool Chicks," I said, glancing at the painted logo on her ute.

"What do you want to know?" We got in and she reversed out of the parking spot.

"Anything. How long have you worked there? Or do you own the business? And how does one go from cooking to maintaining pools?"

"My friend Roisin and I run the business. Well, she's the owner and boss, but I guess I'm more or less second in charge. The two of us run it together and make all the decisions. We have four other girls working with us. Mostly Irish, like her."

"That's cool, and how did you get into it? You said you used to be a chef?"

"Yeah."

I hadn't really had a chance to ask her much about it. I hadn't had a chance to ask her anything, really. Since we'd met, our time together had been lots of yelling, a drink offer turned down, me calling her beautiful randomly, a deployment, and an awkward naked shower encounter. This was really the first proper conversation we were having. I waited for her to continue, looking at her from the passenger seat.

"When I was sixteen I went to Italy and trained as a pastry chef."

"Wow, really?"

"Yep. And then as a regular chef. My parents are Italian. I was born there but we moved to Australia when I was four. They decided to go back to Italy when I was in Year Ten. My grandparents were getting older and they wanted to be closer to home. And I hated school, so I dropped out and went back to Italy with them. My Italian wasn't good enough to do well academically, so even if I wanted to go back to school I wouldn't have done well. So I did the chef stuff instead."

"Ah. So you grew up here. Hence the Aussie accent."

"Yeah. But I also lived in England. After my training in Italy, I moved over to London and worked in a restaurant. Italy wasn't my cup of tea. I mean, it's gorgeous. Lake Maggiore – it's amazing. The food is delicious. Stunning lake, wineries; it's the best. But at the time, I didn't want to live there long term."

"And you moved to London, instead."

She nodded.

"So then how did you come to live in Australia again?"

"I met Byron."

Damn. I wish I hadn't asked. "Where did you guys meet?" Better not let her think I felt awkward talking about him, though.

"I was catering a private event in Chelsea, after a medical conference. He'd flown over for it and ended up staying longer than planned. He moved to London shortly after that. But after a while he wanted to move back to Sydney, where he'd been living, and he wanted to get married. I didn't really mind where we did it. And I missed Sydney, even though I hadn't lived here in years. Plus, I was sick of the work I was doing. It made me resent cooking, and I really love cooking, so that wasn't good. I was always working on weekends, late nights – I never saw anyone. Being a chef was tough – very anti-social. And it was a high-stress environment. If you messed up, you messed up for the whole team. In the same way, if someone was lazy in the kitchen, it affected everyone. I was so over it. There was also a lot of bullying. And I mean, a *lot*."

"Wow. Sounds full on."

She nodded. "Once, when I was new, I messed up a risotto. I was marched out to the customer's table and made to tell them I had messed it up personally, and I had to apologise." She gave a half-smile at the memory.

"That's really harsh."

"Yeah. But I never messed up risotto again." She laughed, her eyes gleaming.

"And how'd you get into the pool job?"

"When I moved to Sydney, I had already decided to do something completely different. I didn't wanna spend my time in Australia working stupid hours. I met Roisin through a friend and she took me on board in her new business. It was good timing – she was looking for a business partner. She trained me up in all the pool stuff, and then a few other girls Roisin knew were interested in getting on board. The business didn't even have a name yet, so we came up with 'The Pool Chicks' together. Original, huh?" She laughed. "Funnily enough, my brother married an English woman, so they live in London. And now, my parents and nanna are there, too."

"It's a pretty cool story. You're all very well-travelled. And I love the story of The Pool Chicks. I like the fact it's all women. What would happen if a guy wanted to work for you?"

"Why, you interested?"

"Nah. I would just distract all the women." I winked, anticipating an eye roll – and it wasn't long before I got one.

"We wouldn't say no to hiring a guy. They'd just have to be happy with being called a Pool Chick, I guess." She laughed. "But you'll get to see for yourself next weekend, anyway. You know – be a stand-in Pool Chick."

"True! Maybe you can call me … The Pool Rooster?"

She looked at me like I'd told the worst joke in the world, which, to be fair, was probably accurate. I laughed. "Maybe not. So, it sounds like you're pretty happy here in Sydney, then."

"I love living in Sydney, but to be honest, I really don't like our area."

"Oh yeah? How come?"

"Too suburban. I miss the beach a lot."

"Why did you move here, then?"

She frowned. "I dunno. I grew up here. So – familiarity? Also, it's convenient for Byron to be close to his work. And once again, I didn't really care where we lived. Though now that we've been here a few years, I think I want to move back to the coast, where we used to live."

"You should." I hesitated. "Mal would miss you, though."

She smiled at that. "That's exactly what we'll be doing once the current lease is done."

My heart sank. I'd actually thought they owned their house. "Fair enough. So you enjoy the pool job, then?"

"Yeah. I absolutely love it. It's outdoors, it's physical, most of the time I don't deal with people, and I work with a great bunch of women."

"Worst part of the job?"

She drummed her fingers on the steering wheel, thinking. "Rich clients who are demanding. The ones that have six-million-dollar pools and expect us there at the drop of a hat. Doesn't always work like that. Oh, and also not being able to jump in when it's forty degrees outside."

"Yeah, that would suck. Hey, that reminds me, can I hire you to do my pool? I mean, if you're not too busy?"

She gave me a look as she parked the car out the front of her house. "Why? You don't need help with it. I've seen the pool. It's immaculate."

"I don't have the time," I said, thinking quickly. "And I get deployed a lot. It'd be nice to know someone is taking care of it regularly. The jacuzzi, too."

She shrugged. "All right. But you're not paying me."

"Why not? I want to hire you, officially. Not on mates' rates. It's not a favour."

"Because you're going to help me out at work on the Saturdays when I'm short, remember? Starting next Saturday."

"Geez, you drive a hard bargain. I thought that was a one-off thing. But, okay, deal." Once again, this was working in my favour. More time with her was never going to be a punishment, no matter how many pools I had to scrub.

We got out of the car and made our way into my house.

"I've already been cleaning your pool anyway," she admitted, "even though it didn't really need it."

"Oh, really?"

"I've also been putting this salt mineral stuff through it. It's similar to Epsom salts. You won't notice much difference, but when you get home from your run every morning, go swim in it – it's really good for your muscles."

"What if I don't *want* a special salty mineral thingy in my pool?" I teased. I was actually really touched she'd been doing such a kind thing for me.

"Then I'd think you were silly to give up something that's good for your muscles and skin, not to mention free. It's expensive stuff."

"How expensive?"

"About forty dollars a bag. A pool the size of yours needs about eight bags, added in slowly."

"Wow. That *is* expensive. You're not gonna get busted taking stock?"

"It's not like that."

"I'm just being a smartass."

"Oh, really? I've never noticed that about you." She grinned, then handed me the grocery bags she was carrying. "I've gotta grab some stuff from mine."

I put a few things in the fridge while she ducked over to her place. She returned with two glass containers.

"What's that?" I asked.

"Linguine, and chilli oil."

"You make your own linguine?" I asked, eyeing it.

"I'm an Italian chef. Are you really surprised?"

"Is Ms Georgie de Luca, Italian chef, making fun of me?" I paused. "I wouldn't put it … *pasta.*"

She looked at me, wide-eyed. "Yeaaah. That is the worst pun I've ever heard."

"Drew Thomson, out with the jokes. How *dairy!*"

She held up a hand. "Okay, stop, or I'm going home." But I could tell she was really fighting the urge to laugh.

"Well, in all honesty, now I know why your lasagne was the best lasagne I have literally *ever* tasted. Oh, and remind me to give back the dish."

"I'm glad you liked it. It wasn't my best effort."

"It was absolutely incredible."

She took the cherry tomatoes out and rinsed them under the tap. "Did you put the lasagne in the oven like the note instructed you to?"

I blinked. There was no way I could lie to her face. "Uh, well, no, I was starving, and—"

"See?"

"What?"

"Predictable. I knew you'd microwave it. I told you you were predictable."

I stood looking at her, mouth gaping. I had no retort.

She got to work in the kitchen while I opened two beers. "Can I help at all?" I asked, jumping up to sit on the kitchen bench and handing her a bottle.

"Yeah, you could get your ass off the bench."

I had a sip of beer but didn't move.

She gave me a dirty look and flung a tea towel at me.

"Okay, okay, I'll move," I said, holding a hand up in defence and grinning. This was turning into a great night. And she could boss me around as much as she bloody well wanted.

14

GEORGIE

I took the two bowls of prawn linguine to the living room and paused at the table. Wafts of tomato and garlic were making my mouth water.

Dinner with Drew. I was starting to feel guilty about how much I was enjoying this, and wondered what Byron was up to. He was probably playing some video game with Kevin. He hadn't texted me or anything, which was fine – I was still angry at him anyway. It made matters worse that not only had he brushed off what I'd told him about Kevin, but had also invited the guy round a couple of days later. No wonder I didn't want to be there.

And I could see myself becoming good friends with Drew. He was so easy to hang out with – such a sweetheart. So kind, and very, very funny – despite how hard I was trying not to laugh at him. He was one huge smartass.

He had gone to get something from the backyard, so I yelled out to him, "Hey, do you want to eat at the table, or …"

"Up to you," his voice came through the back door. "I reckon couch, though. Put on some crappy TV, have another beer."

"Look at that, you *do* have some good ideas!" I sat down on the couch and put the two bowls on the table.

"Turn around for a sec," he said.

"Huh? Where?"

"Like, towards the TV or something."

"Okay …" I turned away from the back door and kitchen, and could hear footsteps – both human and dog. Then silence. I waited. What the hell was he doing?

"Okay – you can look!"

I spun around to see Mal sitting in front of me, all alert and tail wagging. He gazed at me with those gorgeous baby blues. He was holding a single yellow tulip delicately between his teeth, and a little card was tied to it with a piece of brown string.

"What's this?" I asked Drew.

He shrugged. "Beats me. Ask him." He nodded at Mal, who was still staring at me and brushing the carpet madly with his bushy tail. What a bloody obedient dog. I took the tulip gingerly from his mouth and opened the folded cardboard note.

Thank you for taking care of me. I had a nice week-long break from Drew. And don't worry. I won't tell him that you fed me bones all day and swam in the pool. He doesn't mind and he says you have to let him cook you dinner next time. He's not the best cook, but you should give it a chance anyway. Love, Mal.

I turned to Drew. "That's … You didn't need to do that," I muttered through a smile.

"I didn't."

I couldn't help rolling my eyes. "Linguine's ready," I said, nodding at his coffee table. "I put some chilli oil on mine, but I went a bit easier on yours."

He gave me an unimpressed look as we sat on his couch. "*Please.* I love the stuff. What, you don't think I can handle chilli like you?" He grinned. "'Cos you're a chef?" he said the last part in a posh voice.

"Suit yourself," I said, passing the bottle of chilli oil.

He took it, and started draining it into his bowl, making eye contact with me to show how brave he was.

"Hey, whoa, ease up there, can you please try it before you drown it in chilli? You've gotta be able to taste it, too."

He chuckled, putting the bottle down. "I thought chefs loved chilli."

"We do," I said. "But we also like to be able to taste our food. If you're gonna have *that* much, you may as well just enter a chilli eating competi—"

"Damn, Georgie. Who are you?" he asked through a mouthful, looking down at his bowl and shaking his head. My body felt warm – I was so pleased when people loved my cooking. "This is … *wow.*"

"It's my mum's recipe. She used to make it for me on my birthday all the time. It reminds me of European summers, and spending them in Italy."

He took another bite and ate wordlessly, sinking into the couch. He sat facing me rather than the TV, which we hadn't even switched on.

"This is incredible. I'm seriously speechless."

"Well, that would be a nice change … So," I said, twisting some linguine onto my fork, "how long have you been in the Navy?"

"Hmm. Nearly twelve years?"

"How old *are* you, speaking of which?"

He swallowed his mouthful. "Guess."

"No thanks."

"Okay, it's cool, I'll go first," he said mischievously. "Are you … fifty-nine?"

I pretended to flick my linguine at him. "I'm twenty-nine, and seriously considering Botox now after that comment."

"Well, *don't* do that. I mean, uh, that didn't come out right. I meant, do what you want, it's your body, but I personally don't think you need it."

"What about you? Eighty-nine?"

He chuckled. "Close. Thirty-one."

I crossed my legs underneath me and leaned back on the couch, bringing my bowl up into my lap. Byron would have a heart attack watching me eat a tomato-based linguine on the couch. But Drew didn't look like he could care less. "So, what made you join the Navy?" I asked him.

"Actually, my dad was in the Navy. He was a Qualified Flying Instructor, too. Helicopters. I was always in awe, so I joined as soon as I could, to do the same thing. Mostly because I saw how much he loved it. I guess, well, the only annoying thing, as a kid, was having to move a lot. But I've always been drawn to flying and being a pilot. It's so interesting. Sitting up so high, looking down on the world, in an aircraft that's totally under your control – I dunno – it's an incredible feeling."

I contemplated his answer. "How long did it take to start flying? Like, the training part?"

"From the day I joined, to the day I became an operational pilot ... about five years."

"Wow."

"Yep. You have to commit to eleven years of service after they train you up. It costs them something like seven million dollars to fully train up a pilot."

I looked at him, studying his face. "So how come you're allowed a beard? I thought they had strict rules about shaving and stuff."

"You're allowed to have a beard in the Navy. But it has to be trimmed nicely; it can't just be all over the shop. And in the Air Force and Army, you can have a moustache."

"So weird that it's different. And your hair is a lot shorter now than the first time I saw you." I picked up my beer and had a drink.

"You mean the day you yelled at me for washing my car?" He grinned. "Yeah, the hair we have to keep fairly short. Under five centimetres. Also, you can get in trouble for being sunburnt. So, really, I should thank you for screaming your head off at me that day and making me go inside and get out of the sun." He winked.

I nearly spat out my beer. "What? You can get in trouble for being *sunburnt*?"

"Absolutely. Happened to me once. Pretty embarrassing being a grown man getting told off in front of everyone in the morning parade. I get it, though. I accidentally got lobstered. It's not a great look."

I burst out laughing. "And what happened?"

He waved his hand dismissively. "Nothing much. Got given a formal warning. Luckily didn't get my pay docked – that can happen too – and that's all I cared about."

I laughed loudly. "That's hilarious. So, what do you do – on a daily basis I mean?"

Drew put his bowl down. It had pretty much been wiped clean.

"By the way, there's more linguine in the kitchen."

He didn't need to be told twice, bolting to the kitchen like a kid and returning with his bowl filled to the top. I smiled to myself again.

"Well, obviously I get deployed pretty often on the Navy ships, and there's a bunch of us who fly the aircraft on them. Around Australia, it's mostly human aid and disaster relief, like what I did in Queensland, but I've been to the Persian Gulf area a couple of times, too. The overseas missions are about maintaining regional stability. Our squadrons do patrols, as well, for anti-terrorism and that sort of thing."

"So how long do you know before you go away? I mean, how much notice do they give you before a deployment?"

"It varies. Sometimes you know a month before; sometimes it's a call in the night saying be here at x o'clock."

"*X* o'clock?" I teased.

"Ha … ha. You know what I mean."

"Ooh. I've also always wanted to know what War Games were. Is it, like, military guys doing sport and stuff?"

He let out a roaring laugh. I was starting to really like the sound of it. "Not quite. It's basically us getting together with coalition partners, doing different kinds of military exercises. They usually go for three to six weeks. So no, it's not military personnel shooting hoops for fun."

I laughed. "And how fit do you have to stay?" My eyes drifted over to his arms. The muscles were defined even when he wasn't flexing them. *Stupid question.* He caught my gaze.

"It's pretty job specific. There's minimum requirements, of course – we train three or four times a week at least, but ours aren't as hectic as some of the special ops guys. Commandos and stuff. Those guys have to stay super fit."

"You seem pretty fit."

"I have a good running buddy. It helps," he said, motioning towards Mal.

"Is it hard? Getting deployed all the time?"

"Yeah. It can be tough. I miss Mal a lot. But, you know …" He paused for a moment. "It's easier for those who are single."

I nodded, feeling slightly awkward about the comment. Single or not, it would still be hard leaving family and friends behind. "Did you say you had a sister?"

"Yeah, Elena, she lives up the street. She … We both lived in Perth, and she moved here about a month before I did."

I nodded, looking across at the blonde in the photo. "She's

very attractive."

"Yeah. I've had to fend off many a drooling-bloke. Which is actually quite funny."

I put my bowl on the coffee table. Drew had had two heaped bowls before I even finished my first one. "Why's that?"

"Because she never had any interest in men. She's gay. And she's been with her partner, Therese, for a very long time."

"Ah! I see."

"We had their engagement in Perth just before we moved across, actually. I also have a brother – he lives in Singapore with his wife and two kids. Pete."

"I have a brother, too, in England. Sucks having him so far away."

"Yeah. I get that. Do you talk much?"

"Every two or three days."

"That's impressive. Pete's kids send me letters sometimes."

"I *love* receiving letters," I said. "They are so much better than emails, or texts. It's like you really know the person spent time putting it together, that they are thinking of you. That you're important. You know?"

"Yeah. I love getting them too. *Hate* writing them, though." He shuddered.

I laughed at that. "Fair enough. So, were you born in Perth?"

"Born here in Sydney, moved around a bit for Dad's work, but settled in Sydney more or less when we were teenagers. There was a stint of about five years when my uncle John took care of us. Dad was being constantly sent away for work, and training – Mum was looking after her sister who had leukaemia. She wasn't great at keeping in touch. So often the only contact we had was the occasional call from Dad. And John kinda became a stand-in dad, really. We were very close most of my life. Until … Well, he kind of messed things up. But anyway. That's neither here nor there. So Mum and Dad live up in Brissy now, Elena and I are here, Pete's in Singapore. John's in Sydney, but I … I don't see him."

He had a slightly deflated expression in his eyes, but before I could ask, I noticed Mal making his way to the table. He sat down next to Drew. Drew leaned down and cupped his ear to Mal, pretending to listen to him. "Mal said he enjoys having you here for dinner."

I raised an eyebrow. "Oh, really?"

"Yeah. Hold on." He bent down again. "He says the house smells great and you're a fantastic cook." He looked at me and grinned.

Our eyes locked, for just a moment too long. I tore my gaze away and stood up. "All right. I have to go. You still good for next Saturday?"

"Yep! Sure am. Free as a bird, and ready to be bossed around by your highness!"

"Great. See you at zero six hundred hours."

He chuckled. "Is that military talk?"

Shrugging, I took out my house keys. "Gotta make sure you're on time."

I walked away, Drew's affectionate laugh sending a flutter of warmth through me.

15

DREW

"Yeah. I'm out the front," Georgie said into the phone impatiently. "Yeah, Darlo penthouse. Can you send your guy down to let me in?" She drummed her fingers on the steering wheel of her ute as we waited outside the ritzy Darlinghurst apartment complex.

And some complex it was. I had to crane my neck to see the top of it from her ute's cab. The real kicker, Georgie had told me, was that the whole apartment block belonged to one family. And they didn't rent it out. They lived in it. On each and every floor.

I stole another glance at her as we waited to be let into the building's secure car park. She was wearing a light blue polo shirt with a Pool Chicks logo on it, and some white shorts. We were at our first job for the day, on the first Saturday I would be working with Georgie.

When the wide garage door finally opened and she drove in, stopping briefly to say hi to the foreman who'd let us in, my jaw dropped.

Holy shit.

The garage was filled with luxury cars: Porsches, Bentleys, a Ferrari and a Corvette. Millions and millions of dollars all under one roof. There was only one narrow car space left. I don't know if I could've fit a car in there, let alone Georgie's old work ute with its wide metal tray. But she handled it like a pro. Still, I basically had to close my eyes as she reverse-parked it in a spot between the vintage Corvette and a black Bentley without so much as glancing behind her. And she looked so cool doing it, reversing with one palm turning the steering wheel only, her other hand resting on the gear stick casually. I'm sure I had sweat running down my face just thinking about her hitting one of those luxury cars. But it was obvious she'd done this a thousand times before.

The pool and jacuzzi at the penthouse were breathtaking, occupying the entire rooftop and overlooking Sydney Harbour. The sun was already burning. Georgie crouched down and unlocked a gate under the wooden deck to grab something, then asked me to go back to the ute and bring up two twenty-litre drums of chlorine as well as some equipment. I got out of the lift and delivered everything to her as she was leaning down and trying to reach something at the bottom of the pool. Even though she'd told me to do two separate trips, I didn't. I'd like to think I could carry two drums of chlorine, a couple of hoses and a new pump at once, but carrying all those awkwardly shaped things was tougher than I'd thought it would be. She glanced up as I walked towards her, trying to walk instead of stumble. I could see she was struggling not to smile.

"Thanks."

"No worries."

She sat back and stretched out her legs, shielding her eyes from the sun. "I hope those aren't good shorts," she said, motioning towards my legs.

Elena had very recently bought me a pair of black shorts, and I loved them. Also, I thought they looked pretty good on – and

I'd be lying if I said I wasn't trying to impress Georgie a little. They were my favourite pair.

"No, not at all – they're really old. Why?"

"Because they're officially ruined."

I studied my now-chlorine-bleached shorts, cursing myself internally and realising why The Pool Chicks uniform consisted of white shorts only.

I waved it off. "That's all good." *You idiot, Drew.*

"Great. I didn't think you'd be silly enough to wear anything good around chlorine." She stood up, brushing herself off. "By the way, make sure your phone is *never* in your pocket. Trust me. Leave it in the car, or put it somewhere else. I guarantee, if it's in your pocket, it'll be at the bottom of a pool before the day is out." She motioned around the panoramic rooftop with her hand. "This whole deck is new." The Harbour Bridge was in front of her. What a spectacular view. I could absolutely see the incentive of living here – if you had a few million dollars to spare, that is. "We only refilled this pool last week. Took two days."

"Two days to fill a pool?"

"Yep. Leave the hose in, come back the next day."

"Is it expensive?"

"Not as much as you'd think. This one would probably add … around a hundred dollars to the water bill." She wiped her hands. "Right. Let's go. We've got a really cool job next."

"Yeah? What is it?"

We made our way down the lift and back to the ute.

"It's a very large mineral pool. For some very special swimmers."

"Who?"

"Police sniffer dogs."

"Seriously?"

She nodded as we pulled out of the garage, and I took a final glimpse at the luxury cars. But I was more interested in this sniffer dog swimming centre.

"Should've told me. I would have brought Mal."

She gave me a funny look. "I'm glad you didn't."

"Come on. You can't tell me you still don't like him."

"I don't *hate* him, no."

I rolled my eyes. "Can I ask you a question?"

"You just did."

She was lucky she was focusing on the road and didn't see the faux-dirty look I gave her.

"Okay, well here comes the second one. How come you changed your mind and came over last Saturday?"

"Huh?"

"Last Saturday. You said you couldn't come for dinner, but then you changed your mind and came over."

The expression on her face, and the subsequent silence, made me regret asking the question one hundred percent.

But eventually, she addressed it. "I ... I kinda had a disagreement with Byron."

She said nothing more, and I didn't press it. If she wanted to tell me, she would.

"Well, I'm glad you felt like you could come over. You're welcome at mine any time. Not just because of Mal."

Georgie let out one of her rare laughs. And then a deep sigh. "His brother made a move on me a few weeks ago."

It took me a second to realise I had stopped breathing. "His *brother*?"

She nodded, indicating and turning left. "I think he ... Well, I'm just glad I wasn't home alone. I don't – I mean I don't think he'd ..." She sighed again. "Anyway, Byron didn't believe me when I told him. So I was pretty pissed off."

It was like I had to switch my breathing from automatic to manual. Remind myself my body needed oxygen to function.

"That's …" I couldn't even come up with the right word. And I had to put effort into unclenching my jaw so I could try to speak. "Georgie, that's terrible." I shook my head. No wonder she had to get out of there. What a prick.

Breathe, Drew.

I tried to put myself in Byron's shoes. If I were married to Georgie, and she came to me with something like that … My knuckles were starting to turn white just thinking about how I would feel.

We drove in silence for a moment, and I tried to think of something else to say. How do you tell someone their husband is a piece of shit in a diplomatic way?

Is that even what she would want me to say?

"Wait," I said, thinking. "Is that why you asked me about my first impression of you? Whether you had, I dunno, led me on or something?"

She nodded, slowly.

"Georgie, trust me when I say that couldn't have been further from the truth. And I don't know you that well, but I'd be willing to take a stab at the fact that you didn't do *anything* to lead his brother on, either."

I remembered meeting the brother briefly. He looked like an absolute creep, and Byron didn't seem much better. And now, Georgie was even questioning herself, doubting herself. My anger at this admission stopped any words from coming out of my mouth. I tried to focus, hesitating, and wondering how to frame my response as her phone rang with a work call. Why didn't Byron believe her? His own wife?

"So," Georgie said, "are you ready to take care of the next pool all by yourself?"

I took a deep breath, pushing away my thoughts about Byron and focusing on Georgie's beautiful smile and sun-kissed cheeks, instead. "That sounds like you're … throwing me in the deep end."

"I hope that's your last joke for the day," Georgie said with a groan as she hopped out and grabbed some equipment from the ute.

"That was the first. And there are plenty more!"

We did four more jobs after the sniffer dog pool, which had been super cool to see. We'd stopped at a little hole-in-the-wall woodfire pizza restaurant for a takeaway lunch, where the owner – a plump woman with bright red lipstick – talked to Georgie like a long-lost daughter. Then we made our way to the last job, Georgie sheepishly admitting to me that she always made an exception to her "no takeaway" rule when it came to this little pizza joint, mostly because the woman reminded her of her Italian "Nonna".

"Well, you should work with me more often," Georgie said. "It's going a hell of a lot faster than when I'm on my own."

"So would you say my traineeship is going … *swimmingly*?" I grinned at her. I thought she was going to punch me. "All right. So, where's this last one, then?"

"It's near Wisemans Ferry. Furthest one out for the day. But at least home isn't too far from there. It's easier doing that drive in the afternoon rather than trying to get back home from the city."

"You guys definitely cover a huge area."

"Yeah. Well, with six employees, we can spread across a fair bit of Sydney. I pick up the leftovers on a Saturday, the ones that the girls didn't get to during the week, and any emergencies."

After we'd been driving in silence for a while, Georgie turned on the radio.

"So, what are you doing tomorrow?" I said.

"Sunday. Let's see. Probably … swimming in your pool, and

finishing a book I'm desperate to get through this weekend."
She chuckled. "I mean, if that's okay."

"Absolutely. What's the book?"

It did seem a bit odd that she didn't mention spending any time with Byron. After what had happened with the brother, that made sense. But even before that, they didn't seem to do a whole lot together, from what little I had seen and heard from her.

She was definitely independent. And spending time apart from one's husband was fine. Healthy, even. In normal circumstances. But these just didn't seem like normal circumstances to me. And if I were the one married to Georgie, I would be grateful for every moment spent with her.

"It's this book about the— Oh, bugger!" She slammed on the brakes on the quiet, winding road, and jumped out of the ute.

"What?" I said, not seeing anything around us. No cars, no animals. Or so I thought, until Georgie emerged carrying a giant turtle across the road, holding its muddy shell with two hands.

"Come on, buddy. That's no place to sunbake. You're going to get run over!" She carried the turtle across to the bush, turning it around so it faced away from the road.

Once again, I caught myself holding my breath as I watched her, a warm feeling spreading through my chest. *Animal hater, my ass.*

Georgie reached into the ute's cab and grabbed a hand wipe from behind her seat.

"They're adorable, but they stink!" she said through the open window, laughing as her phone rang. She hopped in, moved the ute off the road, then answered the call and jumped out of the vehicle again. When she was done speaking, she got back in, giving me a matter-of-fact smile.

"What is it?"

"You okay if we stop in at one more job after Wisemans?"

"Yeah, sure."

"Great. It's not far from home. That was Roisin. She couldn't get to her last job."

Georgie started laughing. And then the laughter came roaring out until her eyes were wet and her face was like a tomato. I loved her sound, her energy – and suddenly wanted to soak it all up like a sponge; save it for later.

"What is it?"

"Roisin's … ute …" She gasped between laughs. "It got vandalised."

I frowned. "Why's that so funny?"

"Someone scratched off one of the letters."

I thought about The Pool Chicks sticker on Georgie's ute. Roisin's must've been the same.

"Okay … ?"

"They peeled off the 'L'," she managed to get out between howls of laughter. Tears were coming down her face unstoppably now. "I'll just give you a minute to think about that one."

Uncontrollable laughter hit me a moment later, too, and we sat on the side of the road for a good five minutes, red-faced and gasping for breath. Eventually, Georgie wiped her face and started the ute, then pulled out onto the road. "Right. Two more jobs. They're fairly quick ones. Then home, and you're free to go!"

I looked over at her as the deep red afternoon sun bounced off her caramel hair and dark eyelashes.

I didn't want this day to end. Not even a little bit.

16

GEORGIE

I was bending down, vacuuming the deepest part of the pool. Normally, I would rather cut my arm off with a butter knife than work on a Sunday, but this was Drew's pool – and that was different. Plus, I'd been looking forward to it all week. As much as I didn't like to admit it, it was an excuse to see him.

He was pottering around with something in the backyard. Mal was lying in the grass watching me, tongue hanging out on what was another forty-degree day. I really hoped the weather would cool down soon, at least a little, before Kate's Christmas party. Baking and barbecuing would be a nightmare otherwise.

I enjoyed cleaning Drew's pool. It was a simple one, no weird corners, everything easy to reach and clean. Also, I could jump in if I felt like it. Not that I'd really wanted to get in a bikini in front of him. I hadn't quite reached that level of comfort yet.

I grabbed the net and knelt down again on the stone to reach some of the bigger leaves at the bottom of the pool that my vacuum couldn't get. I cast a quick glance over at Drew, who was tinkering near the jacuzzi now. Unfortunately, he was taking up a huge portion of my thoughts these days. I was definitely attracted to him. I couldn't see how anyone *wouldn't* be. Not with those looks. That *body*. But he was such a sweetheart, too. It was so easy hanging out with him.

And then there was Mal.

I was going to have to start being more careful. I was being too open with Drew. Too … *myself*. I needed to be a little less friendly or something, rein it in a bit. Maybe that made no sense, but I somehow felt like being happy around him was playing with fire. I needed to tone it down a touch, for my own good. It was just that being around him *was* so much fun. It was a slippery slope, and I had to make sure I could hold myself steady at the top.

It had been easy hanging out with Byron when we first met, too. His passion and enthusiasm had been second to none. And he'd been so into me. Everything moved pretty fast.

Maybe too fast.

But it had been fun, meeting him back then. Now, it was like he was a totally different person. A person with no interest in me or my wellbeing. And fun? I couldn't even remember the last time we laughed at something together.

I missed those times. Carefree, happy. I didn't feel like that any more.

Deep down, I knew this was more than just the romance and the fun fizzling out of our marriage, or something we simply needed to work on.

It was more than that.

And as a tiny lump of guilt rose up through my chest, I reminded myself: these feelings were around way before Drew was.

I wondered what would've happened if I'd met Drew before I met Byron. What if I'd met him years ago? What if I'd met him *first*? One thing was for sure, I certainly would have—

There was a huge splash in the pool next to me as I knelt on the edge, scooping out the leaves. It made my heart leap into my throat.

And it also made me lose my balance and tumble straight into the deep end of the pool, fully clothed. I didn't even have a chance to close my eyes or mouth. A flurry of black-and-white fur swirled in front of me among the bubbles. Bloody Mal. He'd jumped into the water and scared the living daylights out of me. I grabbed the side of the pool and hoisted myself out to see Mal paddling to the edge to do the same.

As I stood on the stone, dripping wet and coughing up chlorinated water, I pulled my shirt up to my ribs to wring it out. And there was Drew, frozen to the spot and staring at my stomach. He looked away quickly, as Mal bounded towards him with a sopping wet tennis ball in his mouth. Drew grabbed it, suddenly looking at me like someone who had pulled off a very funny prank.

"Did you just throw that to him?" I said. "Into the pool? On purpose?"

He held his hands up in the air and shrugged, peering at me innocently. "I cannot confirm nor deny such allegations."

But I was not impressed as I continued coughing up the pool water. "Shit, Drew," I said, patting my shorts. "My phone!"

I gaped at the bottom of the pool, spotting my phone under the rippling water, and dived back in to retrieve it.

I emerged eventually, fuming. "What the *hell*, Drew. It's dead! What were you thinking?" I shook the phone and tried to dry it on my shirt. The shirt was soaking wet – I knew what I was doing was completely pointless.

He jogged over to me while Mal lay on the grass, chewing on the ball. "Damn," he said, taking the phone and drying it on the bottom of his shorts. Of course, he wasn't wearing a T-shirt. "I'll get you a new one," he said, inspecting it. "Didn't exactly mean for *that* to happen."

"Oh what – but you did mean for me to fall in, fully clothed?"

I narrowed my eyes at him.

"Would you kill me if I said yes?" he said, grinning.

"You're out of your mind. What the hell's wrong with you?"

He held up his hands in defence. "Lots, clearly. I'm sorry. I only wanted to give you a little scare. It's hot, and Mal needed to cool off. Remember how you're always complaining about it being too hot for him here?"

I glared at him, snatching the phone back. "It's totally ruined."

For some reason that just made him laugh more. "Okay, well, as I said, I'll buy you a new one. Today. So really, you could look at this scenario in two ways. You could continue to be pissed off at me, or you could enjoy the fact that you've cooled down on a forty-degree day *and* scored a new phone, by doing absolutely nothing." His eyes sparkled as he continued: "I mean … nothing aside from falling into my pool fully clothed." He was beside himself laughing as he waved his arms wildly above his head, imitating me falling into the pool.

"Don't think for a second I'm going to let you buy me a brand-new phone."

"Why? It was my fault. Although," he said through fits of laughter, "you gotta admit, it *is* kind of funny you had your phone in your pocket when the entire time I was working with you, you kept telling me not to do that." He wiped his face. "Oh, man. It's too good."

I shook my head and put the phone in the pocket of my wet shorts, picked up the pool net, and handed it to Drew. "We're done here." I stormed off towards the side gate and swung it open, letting it slam behind me.

This was definitely me overreacting, I was fully aware of that – I wasn't even cross with him about the pool.

I knew full well my problem was a lot deeper than that.

17

GEORGIE

The ute's temperature gauge was climbing and had passed the halfway mark. I wondered if there was a problem with the thermostat again. Now, at three in the afternoon, in the absolute scorching peak of the day, it was not happy. I frowned, looking at the dash again. Luckily, I was done for the day, so I could always pull over if I needed to. It'd been a less-than-ideal day at work. With no phone, I couldn't ring any clients, and at two jobs I wasn't able to get access to the pool. A complete waste of my time, and now I had a list of additional clients I would have to visit again first thing tomorrow. I cursed Drew under my breath. I'd done all the right things. I'd put the phone in a container of rice. I'd put it out in the sun. I'd even got the hairdryer onto it on its coldest setting – but it was all useless. The phone was dead.

I glanced in the rear-view mirror as I drove along the main road, hoping I wouldn't break down right here. The guy in the soft-top sports car was still on my ass.

"Go around, dickhead," I muttered. He'd been tailgating me for quite a while – and when people did that, I had zero intention of going any faster. It was like they saw a tradie ute and auto-matically assumed it was slow. But I was doing the speed limit.

I glanced at the dash. In fact, I was even going a touch quicker. A bike rider merged in front of me, one of those home-delivery guys, with a green box sitting on the back. The box was so full that it made the entire bicycle seem really wobbly. I despised those food delivery companies – there was something so wrong about having these poor young teenagers riding their bikes or scooters to homes of those who couldn't be bothered cooking. How lazy were people getting? Was it that hard to buy a barbecue chicken, if you were really that unmotivated to cook? Especially late at night, when it was raining and cold – how did people have no conscience about sitting on their ass in front of the TV while someone pedalled their dinner to them? It frustrated me. Plus, it made me feel bad when they were on these busy, multi-lane roads. Drivers in general didn't look out for bikes in Sydney. I kept my distance, feeling like I could somehow protect the rider from behind at least.

The driver in the sports car behind me got so close I could no longer see his bonnet in my rear-view mirror. My right arm was resting on the windowsill and I lifted my hand up to give him the finger. He was a scrawny guy with slicked-back balding hair and a thick gold watch. Of course. There were three lanes, anyway – it's not like he couldn't get past me if he really wanted. Finally, he got the message, put his foot down, and went around. And when he passed me, he returned my gesture.

"Asshole," I hissed, glad I didn't have to look at his ratty face in my mirror any more. I wondered if Byron drove this obnoxiously in his sports car. And I was pretty sure I knew the answer to that, from what I'd heard.

In his anger, the driver swerved in front of me, presumably to cut me off, and didn't notice the bike. He merged straight into the rider, who didn't even have a second to register what was happening.

"Shit!" I slammed on my brakes, tyres screeching, as the rider came crashing down in front of me in slow motion. The ute stopped, and for a split second everything was frozen. I couldn't move.

And neither could the bike rider, now sprawled on the ground only inches in front of me.

As cars zoomed past in the other two lanes, I sprang into action. The sports car had taken off. I put my hazard lights on and ripped up the handbrake, patting my pockets frantically, then searching the centre console. I needed to ring an ambulance, now. Where the hell was my phone? I craned my neck to the back of the ute's cab before I remembered. It was at home. Dead.

Cursing, I jumped out and ran to the guy. A thin stream of blood was running along the road and under my vehicle. I pushed away the lump in my throat and ran across to the footpath, flagging down two people walking past.

"Hey. I need a phone!" I yelled, breathless. One fumbled around and grabbed his mobile, and I dialled 000 with shaky hands. It didn't go unnoticed that no one else had stopped; no one else had offered to help. Cars kept streaming past, and some even honked at me for blocking my lane. I bolted back to the rider. At least the ute was there; he wasn't just lying in the middle of the road. But still. The situation was less than ideal, especially given that it was peak-hour traffic on a multi-lane road.

"Police, fire, ambulance?"

"Ambulance!" I yelled down the line.

The operator put me through, and I glanced back at the rider. He looked like he was trying to move.

"No, no, no!" I forced myself to get closer. I was going to have to rein it in – freaking out was not going to do anyone any favours. Especially if the rider could hear me.

"What is your location?"

I realised the person on the phone was talking to me. I moved the box of food and forced myself to check the rider.

"Um, Anzac Parade," I said, looking up. "Cleveland Street corner. Right before it. Headed north ..."

"How many people involved in the accident?"

"Just one."

"The ambulance has been dispatched, but I am going to stay on the line with you until they arrive, okay?" I didn't respond. "Talk to the person, reassure them, if you can ..." her calm voice said as adrenalin pumped through my veins.

I peered down at the rider, forcing myself to take a deep breath. The blood was coming from his ear, and I knew that was not a good sign. He looked young – maybe seventeen, eighteen.

White hot anger blazed through my chest.

"Hey," I said to him as calmly as I could, crouching down now and trying not to stare at his ear. The pedestrian whose phone I had and his friend had walked out beside my car and were trying to stop the cars driving past in the lane directly next to me. I was grateful. "What's your name?"

He groaned, but didn't speak.

Okay, that's a good sign, he can obviously hear me. He's conscious.

"Help's coming – hang in there."

The operator was telling me to keep talking to him. She reminded me not to move his head, and asked a few other questions about the rider's condition. I reported back to her, while continuing to talk to the guy. He was giving me no response and I could feel my pulse in every part of my body, pumping away, threatening to explode the calmness I was trying to channel.

The ambulance arrived within a couple of minutes, sirens blaring. It made me appreciate living in a big city. Some paramedics jumped out, and someone started putting orange traffic cones on the road to close off two of the lanes. I couldn't tell if it was a tow-truck driver or a medical person. I had no idea what on earth was going on; I was only concentrating on the rider. Soon, the police turned up too, so I stood up and gave them some space, looking at the rider on the ground and feeling a sudden prick of tears behind my eyes as I leaned back on the bonnet of my ute, hands still shaky.

A police officer took my statement, but halfway through it, I had to sit down on the footpath. My legs were jelly – they just wouldn't hold me up any more. The rider had been taken by the ambulance and there was nothing more I could do. The reality of what had happened finally sunk in. I did my best to give a description of the driver, annoyed I hadn't taken note of the sports car's number plates – not that I would have had time anyway. All my effort had been focused on not running over the rider. I gave the phone back to its owner and thanked him.

One of the cops motioned for me to move my car.

"I'm sorry, I – I can't even stand right now," I said, looking up at him from the footpath.

"Okay, no worries, relax there for a minute," he said, and asked for a number to contact me on later.

When I'd finished giving him my mobile number, I sighed and said, "But you can't ring me on that. Well, 'til tomorrow or something. I don't have … I need to buy a new phone later." Another officer moved my ute up onto the walkway so it wasn't obstructing traffic. I thanked him, then sat in the passenger seat, and buried my face in my hands, bawling my eyes out.

Once I calmed down, I drove home slowly and parked the ute out front, glad to be home more than anything.

A dish was sitting on the front step. As I got closer, I realised it was the one I'd given the lasagne to Drew in. It was covered in aluminium foil. I picked it up, wondering if he'd baked me something in return, but the dish was cold. I peeled back the foil, revealing a small box wrapped in paper with a familiar brown string around it. Still standing at the front door, I pulled at the brown string and opened the box.

Holy shit. Drew bought me a new phone ...

I don't know why I was surprised; he did say he was going to do exactly that. And despite my objections, he'd done it anyway. I wondered if he hid it inside the dish so only I would see it. Not exactly a fool-proof plan, but still. I opened the white box and took out the folded note that was inside it, eyeing the brand new, plastic-wrapped iPhone.

I'm sorry about your phone. This one is water-resistant – it can survive for up to thirty minutes in four metres of water, but it's probably still best not to have it on you when you're planning to fall into a pool fully clothed.

P.S. Here is the first number to add to your contact list.

It was followed by his name and a mobile number.

A massive lump sat in my throat, and a sob escaped my lips. What an awful day. What a crappy outcome.

And then here was Drew buying me a new phone and writing a sweet, thoughtful note.

Hot tears ran down my cheek as I stood out the front of my house. Would Byron be home? Would he want to listen? And more to the point, would he even care about what had happened to me?

I didn't have to contemplate that question for too long. And I didn't open my front door.

Instead, I went and knocked on Drew's. And when he opened it, I threw myself in his arms.

18

DREW

She said nothing when I opened the door, and it took me a moment to realise she was, or at least had been, crying. A split second later, she was inside with her arms thrown around my waist, almost making me lose my balance, her face buried in my chest. She was in her blue-and-white work clothes, her shoulders moving up and down as she sobbed into me. She smelled like something sweet and floral, with a slight hint of chlorine.

Instinctively, I wrapped my arms around her and pulled her close. Her skin was so smooth, so warm. What the hell had happened? What had that prick Byron done now? The sight of Georgie crying was unsettling. She always seemed so tough and unaffected by things. Seeing her like this was a dagger through my heart. It was like whatever she was feeling, I somehow felt, too.

I gently put my chin against the top of her head. "Are you okay?" I said after a few moments.

She nodded but didn't say anything, and I wasn't going to push it.

"Thank you for the phone," she said eventually, sniffing. "You didn't need to do that."

I smiled when she looked up at me. "You're welcome. I wanted to – the whole thing was my fault."

She shook her head, wiping her glassy eyes. Her tear-stained cheeks were red, too. But she was so beautiful, and all I wanted was to keep holding her.

"If you want to talk, I have two very good ears." I took an arm off her briefly and pointed to my ears as evidence. "Well, that's a lie. I have one *very* good ear, and one very average one."

She laughed at that, feeling warm and snug against me, her arms still around my waist. And I couldn't help but feel that she was right where she was meant to be. I didn't even care that my chest and stomach were wet from her tears.

"Do you want to come in?" I said eventually. We were still standing in the doorway, the afternoon sun beating down on us and making me sweat. And I was sure we weren't far off her having a go at me for being shirtless yet again.

But we stood still like that for what felt like a long time.

And yet not nearly long enough.

"Wait. You like Incubus?" She frowned, gazing behind me at the framed poster in the hall.

"Yeah, you haven't seen that before? They're my favourite band."

She looked at me, then wiped her forearm across her nose.

I laughed. "I can get you a tissue, you know, so you don't have to use your arm?"

She narrowed her eyes, but not in an unkind way. "Why are you such a smartass all the time?"

I shrugged. "Life's more fun that way."

She took her arms off my waist and made a move for the living room. She sat down on the couch, kicked off her work boots and pulled her legs up underneath her in her signature position. I closed the front door, and went to sit next to her sideways on the couch so I could face her. Her hair fell softly down around her face, with a few kinks in it, like it'd been tied up all day and only recently freed.

She let her head drop, gazing at her hands in her lap. "I saw a really bad accident. On my way home. A bike rider got hit, right in front of me. And no one else stopped."

"God, no wonder you're shaken. You poor thing. Hold on, I'll grab you a water." I stood and walked to the kitchen as she kept talking.

"I had to borrow a phone to call 000. He was bleeding from his ear."

I winced. Of all days, it had to happen when she didn't have a phone. And that was because of *me*.

"And you know the worst part? I won't ever even know if he lived."

I thought about that as I passed her a glass of water. "Maybe you could ring the hospital? Or the cops, and tell them who you are?"

"They would never give out that sort of information," she said, frowning.

"Yeah. You're probably right. But you can always try."

She looked down at the ground and said nothing else.

"Can I get you anything else, Georgie? Tea? Coffee?"

"Nah. Thanks. Alcohol would be great, though." She gave me a hint of a smile.

I grabbed us two beers from the kitchen. She had a drink, then put the bottle down on the coffee table. "Okay. I need to think about something else for a bit. So tell me about the poster. What's your favourite Incubus song? And album?"

"I got it as a thirtieth birthday gift, actually. Signed by the band. Um … favourite album – probably '*S.C.I.E.N.C.E*'." I thought for a moment. "Favourite song – 'Vitamin'. And 'Wish You Were Here'. Oh, and 'Pardon Me'."

"That's three," she said, looking at me with a lopsided smile. "Do you know how to count? I'd think that would be an important skill for the Navy."

"Who's being a smartass now?" I said. Mal came in through the doggy door and ran straight to Georgie. Of course. She took his face in her hands and scratched his ears.

"Hi, cutie," she said.

"Hi, Georgie," I replied without skipping a beat. Her expression said it all – *Shut up, Drew.* Mal jumped up on the couch and sat next to her. That dog had no spatial awareness. He couldn't possibly get any closer to Georgie if he tried. He rested his head on her thigh, and I shot him a disapproving look.

"Your dog loves me."

"You don't say. Hey," I said, glancing at her hands, tucked under her folded arms again. "How come you hide your hands so much?" It was like she was always making sure I couldn't see them.

She shrugged, and hesitated. "I bite my nails. It's gross. I've done it since I was a kid. I'm repulsed by it, but I can't do anything about it. Byron says it's disgusting."

I looked down. "Can I see?"

She shook her head.

"Can Mal see?"

She paused, then sighed and slowly unwrapped her hands, holding them out to me.

I took them in mine. Her nails were unpainted, but they weren't gross at all. They weren't even that short. The skin around the nails was a little red, but that was it.

"They get so dry from the chlorine. I can never stop picking at them. It *is* disgusting," she said as she went to pull her hands away.

I held onto them and looked at her, squeezing her hands gently. "I can tell it bothers you. But honestly, if you hadn't told me, I never would have known," I said. It was the truth. She didn't try to pull her hands away again. "And they're not disgusting.

They're fine. And you're beautiful."

I paused, knowing I had probably been a bit forward. But it was the truth.

We sat on the couch, her hands in mine, and she looked into my eyes. I melted. Staring at her forever would not be difficult. And as I looked deep into her eyes, and studied her expression, I just knew. She liked me, too. I wasn't imagining this.

And I hadn't imagined that initial attraction, either. It was there on that first day, and it was certainly here today. There was something between us.

She must've felt it, too. Because she suddenly pulled her hands away, grabbed her shoes, and walked out the front door without a word.

I stared at her unfinished beer on the table, then at Mal, who returned my gaze curiously with his big eyes. He glanced towards the door.

"Yeah, buddy. She's got me good, too."

19

GEORGIE

I put the kingfish and watermelon carpaccio on a serving dish, with chilli and dill oil drizzled on top. It was Monday night, and I had a rare day off work tomorrow. A delicious meal and some quiet reading time were on the cards – Byron was still at work, giving me yet another night at home alone. I had got used to these nights alone – but that didn't mean I liked them. Tonight was a different story, though. I couldn't wait for some peace and quiet, especially after everything that had happened today. The accident, the new phone. It had been an emotional day.

And I felt horrible for how I'd left Drew's. There was no doubt in my mind – I had to leave when I did. But now I was feeling pretty bad about it; I'd have to apologise to him later.

I looked at my new phone, still in its box, and hesitated. I took it out and connected it to the charger to set it up. Eyeing the note that had come with the box, I sighed, and added the mobile number to my contact list. *Okay, Drew. You win.*

Then I composed a new text to him.

Hey. Thank you for the new phone – you really didn't need to. But I appreciate it. You have my number now. And thanks for listening this afternoon. Hope you have a great week.

Succinct, polite.

A few minutes later, the phone vibrated on the kitchen bench. *Who's this?*

I grinned. Smartass.

Your worst nightmare.

He replied immediately. *Ah, ok great. Then that's how I'll save your number in my phone :) By the way, did you end up ringing the hospital?*

I chewed on a nail. *No, not yet. By the way – sorry about before. That's ok. Me too.*

I drummed my fingers on the bench, wondering what to write next. *Nothing, Georgie. Stop the chat and put the phone away.*

But Drew had already sent me another text: *P.S. Mal would like to know if you're free for dinner this week.*

I could hear the low rumble of Byron's Maserati pulling into the garage.

Sorry. I can't.

I turned the phone on silent and placed it upside down as Byron came in with a look on his face that said it had been a tough day, and he was ready to tell me all about it.

"Hey, babe," he said, putting his keys on the kitchen table and taking my hands in his.

I immediately felt guilty. And while nothing had happened with Drew, I couldn't deny the fact I'd kind of wanted it to. But wanting and doing were two different things. And I would never, ever do that to Byron. It was a crush, and it'd go away.

"You all right?" He peered at my eyes. They felt very swollen. And I was sure they were still red. My face did not hide crying very well.

"Yeah, I … I was the first on the scene of a road accident today."

He frowned. "You okay? What happened?"

"Guy on a bike got hit and I nearly ran him over. Had to slam on the brakes, then call the ambulance and wait with him. It was horrible."

"So you knew the rider?"

"Huh? What do you mean?"

"You didn't know him?" He shrugged, then shoved some kingfish into his mouth. "I mean, well, why did it upset you so much then?"

I stared at him.

He picked up the entire serving dish and turned away from me, shoving more fish in his mouth and talking while chewing. I hadn't even had any of it yet. "Well, I had *the* roughest day at work today," he said. "We're having this audit done on the hospital, and it was one admin thing after the other. I mean, it's such a joke, all this red-tape bullshit, really."

The more he talked, the more I tuned out, standing numbly at the bench, looking out at the dining room.

"So, what else is for dinner?"

I shook my head. He'd never been particularly sympathetic. I wasn't sure why I'd expected, or hoped, this time to be different. "Uh … Squid with grilled eggplant and pistachio baklava, if I can be bothered. Bit of an odd mix, but …" I shrugged.

"Sounds great. Hey, so, quick question."

"Mmm?"

"I was trying to call you all afternoon. Where have you been?"

"I … My phone isn't working."

"Why?"

I grabbed a tea towel and wiped a bit of oil off the bench. "It fell in a pool. And I only just set up my new one." I held up the phone to him.

He frowned and looked at me like he was trying to work something out. "How? You never have your phone with you near the pool."

I swallowed. "It was … actually Drew's pool. I was cleaning it for him and Mal jumped in, and I, uh, ended up falling in." I let out a mousy laugh.

Byron sighed impatiently. "Okay. I'll only ask this once. Is there something going on with you two?" He pointed a thumb towards Drew's house.

My heart literally skipped a beat. "I'm sorry. What did you just ask me?"

"I mean, you spend a lot of time with him."

I blinked, incredulous. "That's … What exactly are you accusing me of?"

"I'm not *accusing* you. I'm simply *asking* you."

I stared at him. "Nothing is going on, and I don't spend a lot of time with him."

"Kev said he saw him getting out of your car the other day."

"On Saturday? He was helping me. At *work*." When Byron said nothing, I continued: "And Kev *would* say that, wouldn't he, given the circumstances. But hey, you don't believe me about that, so whatever." I felt like an argumentative teen, unable to keep the sarcasm out of my voice. *What the hell.* "Drew has hardly even been here anyway."

"I'm sorry babe, it's just, you know, you get told something, and—"

"And we know how you like to believe your brother over your wife in any case," I muttered.

"But you *have* hung out with that dog a lot lately."

"Mal? So what?"

He smirked. "Come on. You don't even like dogs, Georgie. In fact, last time I checked, you hated them."

I threw the tea towel down and marched out of the kitchen. "Yeah, well, apparently people change."

2 0

GEORGIE

I grabbed my key out of the pocket of my running shorts and let myself into the house, panting.

"Hey, babe, how'd you go?" Byron was sitting in the kitchen, working on his laptop.

I took in a deep breath, trying to slow down the heaving of my chest. "Good. Thanks." I took the headphones off from around my neck, grabbed a gym towel and wiped the sweat off my face. My short response wasn't anything out of the ordinary, given the last few days. Byron and I had pretty much avoided each other when we could. But today, something in his tone had changed. He'd started calling me "babe" again. And he was actually attempting to make conversation, appearing interested in me again.

How ironic.

"Where'd you run to?"

I walked around the kitchen island and grabbed the glass bottle of water from the fridge. "Round the usual bush trails." I took my hat off, ruffled my hair and tied it up in a fresh bun. I was drenched in sweat after having run almost twelve kilometres. On the way home, I'd glanced at Drew's house before I got to my door. He had music playing.

I didn't go in.

"Babe. Can we talk for a minute?"

"Can I stretch and shower first?" I said, after taking a long swig of water straight from the bottle. Byron eyed me doing it, unimpressed, but didn't say anything.

"Uh, sure."

While I was in the shower, he made me a cup of tea. We sat on the couch together.

"I don't know what it is about tea," he said, laughing nervously, "but even in the heat I'm still happy to drink it."

I smiled. "So, what's up?"

"Uh – well, I think I owe you an apology."

I couldn't believe the words actually came out of his mouth. Byron was good at many things. Admitting he was wrong was not usually one of them.

"The other day. When I asked you about … Drew." He took my hands in his. "I know you'd never do anything like that, Georgie. You're not like that. I guess, well, it's hard not to be jealous when you're friends with a guy who looks like *that*." He laughed a sad laugh.

My shoulders slumped. "It's okay. I'm sorry, too, if I made you feel like that." It made my heart squeeze tightly, seeing that expression on his face. I guess I hadn't realised he was actually worried. I hadn't been a very good person.

I sighed, swirling the teabag around the mug. I would probably have to stop seeing Drew altogether – including as a friend. And as a dog-sitter. No more giggly dinners, no more help at work. It was unfair on Byron.

"Sometimes," he continued, "I feel like … I can operate on all these hearts, and fix people. Make them better again. But your heart? It feels like it's slipping further and further away from me, and there's nothing I can do to fix it."

My heart felt like it had a massive chunk of lead attached to it. But part of me didn't really get it. If he was so worried, he could try spending time with me. Listening to me. Being kind to me. I didn't even know he felt like there was a problem. He'd never mentioned anything.

All I said was, "I'm sorry you feel that way." But his sad expression awakened a sudden guilt deep inside me.

He took a breath, motioning next door. "I just, I think there's something a bit off about him, you know?"

"Like what?"

He shrugged. "I wouldn't trust him as far as I could throw him."

I almost laughed. How rich, given what had happened with Kevin. He clearly couldn't see the forest for the trees when it came to his own brother, but felt the need to warn me about Drew.

Level-headed, kind, sweet Drew. Drew who wouldn't hurt a fly.

I did not miss the irony, yet again. But I was too exhausted to get into it all.

"All right. Well, I disagree, but that's beside the point," I said.

"Just be careful. I mean, well, I don't think he's as honest and genuine as you believe he is."

I shrugged off the comment. He was clearly being territorial. And continuing this conversation was doing neither of us any favours.

"So ... do you love me?" The corners of his mouth lifted slowly.

"Of course."

"Good." He leaned across and gave me a kiss. "What do you say we have a nice dinner tonight? I'll take you out someplace fancy, yeah?"

"Sure. Although you know I'm just as happy staying in and cooking."

"I know. But I want to do something nice for you. And you know my cooking is awful." He laughed.

"Okay, sure. Thank you."

"You sure you're all right then, babe?"

"Yeah."

"Okay, good. Because I love you *so* much."

"I love you too, Byron."

"It's been so full on at Surgeons with Heart," he continued, "I've been … I haven't been myself. And I haven't had nearly enough time for you. But we're almost done with everything – and when I'm back from Tanzania, I'm all yours again. Promise. Okay?" He leaned over and kissed my cheek. I closed my eyes, breathing in the musky smell of his aftershave. It was nice. Familiar.

21

DREW

I sat at the wooden table in Kate and Tony's backyard with a fresh beer in my hand. It was another hot evening – I was still sweating at eight p.m. I put the cold bottle to my forehead for a moment before having a long drink of it.

It'd been a busy day of barbecuing, setting up furniture, playing games with the kids, cleaning up – none of which had been made easier by the stifling heat. I suggested having the Christmas party at mine next year, so everyone could swim. It'd been a pretty well-received invitation, especially by Kate, who seemed to regret having it here in the first place.

Georgie looked exhausted from all the cooking. She'd basically cooked for the entire neighbourhood, and was now sitting slumped in her chair sipping on a beer. Her freshly baked focaccia had put a totally different spin on the barbecue, as had the prawn milk buns with sundried tomato, caper aioli, and spicy iceberg. I'd written that one down in my phone and had been thinking of excuses to invite her over so she could teach me how to make them. I was pretty sure she was tired of me asking about each and every ingredient, and how everything was made. But it had been mouth-wateringly good. I couldn't believe she'd been able to pull it all off like that. There was a baked dish with eggplant and parmigiana that I'd forgotten the name of already and devoured like I hadn't eaten for a week. And her mini tiramisus had been demolished by everyone in seconds.

To my disappointment, she was being quite stand-offish again. The only help she'd accepted from me was carrying all the food across the road to the party when it was ready. It was like she'd reverted back to the old Georgie – the one who wouldn't even have a joke with me. She hadn't even spoken to me, or messaged me back, since our text conversation on the day she'd seen the accident. So I was pleasantly surprised when she sat at the table next to me.

All the other guests had now left, starting with the over-tired and cranky children who'd been taken home by their disgruntled parents. But what was a Christmas party with no family dramas? It had been a really fun day, and I'd enjoyed getting to know some of the other neighbours.

Byron, his brother, Kevin, and one of their mates, Sean, were sitting at the table opposite me. Kate and Tony were slowly gathering bottles and tidying up, accepting no help from their guests – no matter how hard we tried.

I stole a glance at Georgie, sitting to my left. She was wearing a short, white beach dress, and her hair was up in a messy bun, like she had zero interest in its appearance.

And she looked adorable. I had a hard time keeping my eyes off her, as usual.

I'd spent most of the night talking to Tony, whose nephew, it turned out, was in the Navy, too. Tony was great – a kind, jolly, come-round-for-a-beer-anytime kind of guy. He was short and a bit chubby, and, with his greying beard, all that was missing was a big red Santa suit. I could see why Georgie got along so well with him, and with his wife, Kate. They were honest, genuine and down-to-earth people.

As for Byron and his brother: I'd been polite, but otherwise had no interest in talking to them. They had a weird vibe about them – the things they said and did, the way they talked, seemed a little attention-seeking or something. I looked at Georgie, then at Byron. It was beyond me what she even saw in him. Admittedly, I was probably just jealous. But still, the guy could treat her better. I mean, he could believe his wife when she told him his brother had hit on her, for a start. Instead, she had to tolerate being face to face with him at this event. I peeled my eyes away from her and tried to tune back into the conversation across the table.

"So, tell us about this January trip then?" Sean said to Byron.

"Well, we're off to Tanzania this time," Byron said, placing his wine back on the table. "There'll be a team of twenty-nine of us – doctors and nurses. It's an educational trip, this one, which means we basically work side by side with the teams there – so for example, surgeons train surgeons, nurses train nurses, physios train physios."

"That's epic. And how long are you away this time? Same as Papua New Guinea?"

"Nah, a bit longer – we'll be gone a touch over two weeks."

Two weeks of Georgie being home alone without him. I mentally told myself off. Those kinds of thoughts were not helpful.

Georgie turned to me suddenly and smiled for the first time that whole day, clearly not paying attention to the conversation around us. "Hey, I didn't tell you," she said, speaking so quietly that only I could hear her.

"What's that?"

"That guy rang me – the one who came off his bike."

"Yeah? The one you helped?"

She nodded, eyes sparkling. "The cops left him my number.

Well, actually, it was his mum who rang me. But he was there. And he's okay. He had a bad concussion and had to be in an induced coma for a while, but he came good, and when they rang, they were really, really grateful."

I grinned, stoked for her. "That's *so* good, Georgie. I'm really happy to hear that. Good on you."

Our eyes locked for a second, and neither of us said anything. She looked so relaxed and comfortable, the deep colours of the sunset illuminating her golden skin. It made me wish I was on a tropical holiday with her.

Not sitting at a table opposite her husband.

My thoughts were interrupted by Sean's scratchy voice. He nodded at Georgie. "And what about you? You just stayin' at home, makin' sure all the pools in Sydney are scrubbed and cleaned to perfection while hubby's off in Africa savin' lives?"

What?

Kevin smirked, while Georgie ignored the comment and took another sip of her beer.

"So, we'll be operating for about eight days with the Surgeons with Heart International team," Byron continued, clearly not concerned with defending Georgie, "and the patients are usually split about half-half – kids and adults. The most difficult thing is, we have to be selective with who we operate on – those hospitals are not exactly equipped to deal with patients in intensive care, on life support, so we can't always operate on everyone if we think they'll need that level of support."

"Whoa, that's full on," Sean said. He turned to Georgie again. "How did you land this guy?" he asked, pointing a thumb at Byron and shaking his head.

I couldn't help myself. "What kind of question is that?" I said, trying not to glare at him.

He held up his hands in defence. "I'm just sayin', it's pretty funny that this guy is off operatin' on people in Africa, and his wife cleans pools for a livin'."

I glanced at Georgie, my hand tightening around my beer, and noted her expressionless face. As if being spoken to like this was nothing new. But there was a look in her eyes that was almost like defeat. Like she wasn't surprised, but didn't have the energy to deal with it.

"Why is that funny, exactly?" I said.

Sean ignored me, staring at Byron like he was royalty. "By the way, mate, heard you got a new car." He raised his eyebrows up and down quickly as I sat baffled, still processing his comments.

"Sure did. Maserati GT."

"New?"

Byron nodded. "Brand spanker."

Sean let out a low whistle under his breath. "Must've set you back a pretty penny."

"A bit over three hundred k, with on-roads."

"Whoa. No wonder you don't let her drive it, am I right?" He pointed a thumb towards Georgie again, turning to Kevin and laughing. "Makes sense you chose a Maserati. Italian wife, Italian car!" He chuckled. "I guess the question is, which one is a better ride?" That got them laughing again.

Anger rose to my chest. "Hey," I nodded at Byron, "aren't you going to say something?"

He chuckled. "Have you met my wife?"

Yeah. And I have no idea why she's with you.

"She doesn't need anyone to fight her battles," he continued.

"Maybe not, but if someone spoke to my partner like that, I'd have something to say about it."

I didn't look at Georgie, but my chest tightened in anger for what she was enduring. Not only was her husband a complete asshole, the other two were even worse. I hesitated only for a split second before I slid my left hand onto her knee under the table, without looking at her. She flinched ever so slightly, but didn't move or acknowledge it.

"What's your problem, mate?" Kevin asked me. Scrawny with a potbelly; squinty eyes and a bent nose, he was not an appealing guy. And he had the personality to match, apparently. Georgie had certainly not won the in-law lottery, that's for sure.

I softly squeezed Georgie's knee under the table and rubbed my thumb along her skin. Unfortunately, I hadn't noticed Tony's daughter, Hanako, right behind me, listening to the conversation.

And she was staring at my hand on Georgie's knee.

Damn.

Luckily, she quickly looked away without saying anything. I took my hand off Georgie's knee slowly.

Sean spoke before I could answer. "I'm not tryin' to put her down, man. Only sayin' she's lucky to be married to this guy, who is a surgeon, does charity work, drives a Maserati, and is a genuine, good guy."

I beg to differ. "You're being disrespectful, mate. And that's putting it lightly."

He stared at me. "I'm not tryin' to be rude or nothin', but everyone knows women just don't drive as well. It's a fact. But it's like – you're not allowed to say shit like that any more. You know. Everyone gets all antsy and politically correct and stuff. It's outrageous. You can't say shit these days."

I could practically feel my blood boiling. "Well, if it's so hard, you *could* try not opening your mouth at all," I said.

Georgie stood up suddenly, her chair scraping the ground behind her, and walked off towards home without a word. Hanako shook her head and followed her. I was suddenly very aware that I was alone at the table with three guys whom I'd clearly pissed off. This was not how I'd wanted my first neighbourhood party to go. But I wasn't going to let them talk about Georgie like that to keep the peace. Her husband was already doing that. Putting my feelings for her aside, these guys needed to be told they were out of line, anyway. What ridiculous, backward, sexist things to say.

Sean looked at me and snorted. "You don't even know me, whoever the hell you are."

"I live across the road. And you already know that. What you don't seem to know is that it's the twenty-first century, and you're being an obnoxious, sexist prick."

I glanced at Byron. He was despicable. I remembered Georgie reverse parking that big, bulky manual ute into that tiny space between those luxury cars without flinching. She was undoubtedly a much better driver than most people I knew. Why wouldn't Byron let her drive his car? Did he really value a vehicle that much?

Kevin stood up and glared at me. "Okay. You and me, mate. Outside."

I couldn't help but chuckle at the absurdity. "Okay. First of all, we *are* outside." I motioned around the backyard. "And second, we are at a family barbecue. I'm not going to fight you."

"Come on … Are you scared?"

I looked at Kevin. There were twigs in the backyard wider than his arms.

"Relax, mate. Take a seat," I said, chuckling again.

"I *am* relaxed," Kevin seethed. "But you need to pull your head in before I do it for you."

Good lord. The three of them were staring at me from the opposite end of the table. I guess we weren't going to be neighbourly friends, but I'd rather stick a hot needle in my eye anyway. They watched as I stood up, their stares almost willing me to say something else. I felt a bit macho thinking I wasn't threatened physically by any of them, but they didn't look like they could fight their way out of a paper bag if they tried. And I was keen to keep Kate and Tony on side. The last thing I wanted was to cause drama at their Christmas party. And I'd said just about enough to make things awkward.

I grabbed my empty beer bottle and pushed my chair in, turning to Byron pointedly. "She deserves better than this," I said, motioning around the table.

As I went to walk away, I heard Kevin snigger and say, "I *told* you he had a thing for her …"

I was sure he'd said it loudly on purpose. I walked across the lawn towards the street, but couldn't see Georgie. It was time to call it a night anyway. I jumped when Hanako's voice came out of nowhere. It had got dark; I hadn't seen that she was sitting on the steps leading to the footpath.

"He's a dickhead," she said, lifting a drink to her mouth. I eyed the beer, remembering she was sixteen, but didn't say anything. Not really my place.

"Who?" I said, knowing exactly who she was talking about.

"Byron," she said, disgusted. "Everyone loves him. But he's *such* a dick."

My thoughts exactly. But how the hell did I respond to that? "I don't know him very well," I said after a moment's silence.

She eyed me for a second, then smiled mischievously. "But you're getting to know Georgie quite well, I see."

"I— it's not like that."

"Like what?"

From her expression, I could tell she was loving this interrogation.

"I've gotta go. Enjoy the rest of your night and thanks for having us. Your lamingtons were very nice." I went to walk down the stairs.

"I will enjoy it, once those three halfwits leave," she said.

I smiled to myself. Hanako was a cool kid.

"Hey, Drew?"

I turned around at the bottom of the steps. There was just enough light left to see her wink at me.

"Don't worry. I won't say anything." She spun on her heels and walked up the lawn, back towards the house.

I crossed the street, shaking my head at the earlier conversation. Did Georgie's husband always let his mates talk to her like that? And his *brother*? Why didn't he say anything? Stick up for her? It was obviously a common occurrence judging by his reaction. Or lack of one, rather. And Georgie had been silent throughout it all. That was so unlike the yelling woman I'd met a couple of months ago.

I took out my phone to call her just as I noticed my front door was unlocked. When I opened the screen door and walked in, I found Georgie in my living room, pacing up and down.

"What the hell was that, Drew?" she said when she saw me walk in.

"So I guess you know where my spare key's hidden, then." I chuckled.

"I don't need you to fight my fights for me." Her eyes darted over at mine, then away. "Jesus. You could've been in a punch up."

"I'm sorry. I thought … Well, they were totally out of line."

"Yeah, well, you didn't need to say anything. It's my issue."

I sighed. "You're right."

She bit her thumbnail, her hand shaking slightly. My heart sank as I realised I'd upset her. And now she was angry with me again. But she'd also been worried about me getting hurt, which was slightly confusing.

I walked over to her and took her hands in mine without thinking, a gentle smile on my face.

"Please … don't." She took a deep breath in, but didn't move.

Mal was sitting by her feet, as usual, putting on an innocent face. But I knew full well he was only here to get the gossip.

"Georgie," I said. "I'm really sorry. Maybe it was out of line. I just … Byron didn't say anything, and it made me really angry, what they said. You deserve so much more than that."

She was looking at me, unmoving, her big hazel eyes searching my face. Her hands were still in mine, our faces only inches apart. As her expression softened, and as I gazed into her eyes, I was hit with a realisation: *I'm falling in love with her.*

She took her hands from mine, letting her arms drop to her side.

"Well," she said, "I should have been honest and told you this a while ago."

"What is it?" I managed.

"We can't see each other any more."

Then she gave me a tight-lipped smile and made for the front door, leaving Mal and me alone in the living room, staring out into the darkness.

22

DREW

"So let me get this straight," Mike said, pushing a wedge of lime into his Corona and making it fizz. "You're in love with the woman who lives next door. And she's married. *And* you tried to ask her out. And now she's not talking to you?"

I nodded, rubbing my temples. "Well, sort of. We had a *moment*. Actually, we've had a few of those. I thought maybe something could happen there. You know, not while she's with him. But ..." I sighed, inspecting my beer bottle and thinking about Georgie storming out of my house. "It's just not." The warm afternoon sun beamed down on us. I missed these west coast sunsets, watching them straight over the ocean. Nothing like it.

And I had missed my best mate.

"God. Talk about dramatic." Mike took a swig. "And her husband – is a dick?"

I nodded. "Naturally."

"Hold on. Didn't you say she was looking after Mal while you're in Perth this weekend?"

"Well, yeah, but that was already organised."

Mike shook his head. "Sorry to say, bud – sounds like a no-go."

I snorted, picking at the label of my beer. "You're not wrong."

"How was Christmas and New Year's?"

"Pretty uneventful. Mum and Dad flew down for three days over Chrissy. Had it at Elena's place."

"Speaking of hot," he said with a grin, "you gonna see Jess while you're here?"

"Jess?"

Mike raised an eyebrow. "You know – tall, slim, brown hair, great boobs, everyone wants a crack, you're the only one who has?"

I couldn't help but laugh at that one. "Nah. Didn't exactly leave things on a good note last time."

"What happened?"

"She was in Sydney and I didn't see her. I mean, I saw her, but nothing happened."

He almost choked on his beer. "The hell is wrong with ya, man? You may not be keen for a relationship, but you can still have a bit of fun. It's been, what – six, seven years since Eve?"

Eve had been my long-term girlfriend pretty much through high school and a few years after that. But when she'd wanted to get married, I realised quickly it wasn't what I wanted for us. She was such a kind-hearted person, though. And I'd made a promise to myself not to get involved with anyone unless I knew I was interested in something serious. Breaking up with Eve had been really tough. We were very young, but had a lengthy history. Seeing her upset was horrible.

It was why I'd always kept Jess at arm's length. And I'd never been dishonest with her about where we stood.

But even Eve hadn't made me feel the way that Georgie did. I couldn't even really make sense of what that meant. Like now that she was in my life, I couldn't imagine her not being in it.

That's why it hurt so damn much when she said we couldn't see each other any more.

I drank my beer, contemplating my answer, as my phone

vibrated in the pocket of my shorts. I took it out, my heart doing a backflip as I saw Georgie's name on my screen.

Hey. How's your Friday night going?

So this was not speaking? Talk about mixed signals. I went to put my phone back in my pocket, then hesitated. If I didn't reply, I'd just be thinking about replying until I eventually did. For God's sake, when did I become so indecisive?

I started typing. *Hey! It's good thanks. Having a couple of sunset beers with a mate. You? Mal behaving?*

Of course he is. As always!

I waited. Well, that conversation didn't last long. I was about to put the phone away again when it vibrated with an image from her. It was a photo of Mal, his head resting on her legs. She was lying on my couch, legs all tanned and gorgeous under Mal. How I wanted to be there. I was jealous of my own dog.

He's a pretty good tv buddy. Doesn't talk too much during the show.

I chuckled.

Well as long as you're not watching cat videos, he tends to be ok.

I glanced up at Mike. "Sorry mate. Give me one sec."

I can't tell you what we're watching. But you're right. Mal was a firm NO on the cat videos.

Haha. Why can't you tell me?

Mal swore me to secrecy. I think he is scared you're going to judge him …

Try me.

She could've been watching TV at her place. But the fact she was at mine with Mal, lying on the couch, was sweet. And also utterly confusing. What was she playing at?

She replied almost immediately. *We're watching The Bachelor. Last year's. He missed the last few episodes, apparently.*

No way. He made me watch that show, too! Coincidence? Haha! So who are you out with?

She sounded like she was in a good mood. Maybe I just had to be on the opposite side of the country for that to happen. The irony wasn't lost on me.

My best mate – Mike.

Well, have a great time!

I waited for a moment, then locked my phone. Mike was staring at me.

"Sorry, just sorting some stuff at home."

He waved the apology away and started talking about work as my phone vibrated again. I really wanted to check the message. I knew it'd be from her.

Mike was saying something about a work trip, and his boss. "I wasn't sure if she was agreeing for the sake of it, or saying it to get me off her back, but in the end …"

My phone kept buzzing and felt like it was on fire. I wanted it out of my pocket, and fast.

"Hey, man. You with me?"

I looked up at Mike. "Sorry, mate."

"Distracted?"

"A little. Sorry."

"All good. You want another?" He nodded towards my beer. "My shout for the next couple."

"Sure. Thanks."

He got up from the stool and went to the bar. I was grateful for an opportunity to check my messages. And then I would really have to start paying Mike some attention. I was being terrible company.

I had four messages from her.

Hey, I'm really sorry about the other night. I think I overreacted.

Well, no. I KNOW I overreacted. I know you were just trying to stand up for me. Thank you. And I feel awful for just leaving. I don't really care what those guys say about me these days, but I should have taken you with me – you could've been in a fight, and I left. I feel so bad. Terrible friend.

Anyway – it was nice having a beer with you at the party apart from that.

PS. When are you back in Sydney?

I scratched my chin. *No need to apologise – but thank you. I appreciate it. For what it's worth, I'm sorry too. I'm back Sunday night. About 7.*

Ok. I won't feed Mal dinner then – I think he'd rather wait for you to get home!

Come on. You and I both know he prefers you now :-)

OMG. Did you just write a smiley face the old school way? You know – there's this thing called an emoji keyboard.

There is? :-) :-) :-) What does emoji keyboard even mean? :0)

It means you are old. And yet still somehow very, very immature.

I laughed out loud, so much so that a couple to my left looked up at me from their dinner.

Truer words were never spoken.

My right knee was bouncing under the table. I knew I was playing with fire. But it was already lit, and I had the fuel.

So, I typed, *if you're free Sunday night, you're welcome to hang around at mine – we could watch The Bachelor finale? And in the breaks, you can teach me all about emojis. :D :D :D*

OMG. Stop it!! Sunday night sounds good. Text me when you're home. I'll bring the food. You bring the beer.

Mike sat down and pushed a pint of cold beer across the table to me. "Geez, mate, you look like you've just won the lottery."

I couldn't wipe the ecstatic grin off my face. "I have."

2 3

GEORGIE

I sat in silence as I drove the ute up the highway towards home. I didn't feel like listening to any music – I was still angry as hell from the trip to the airport. Byron was off to Tanzania, but instead of having a happy last day together, it had been a pretty horrendous goodbye.

I looked at the empty passenger seat next to me and felt guilty immediately. I was glad he was gone for a couple of weeks and I had the house to myself. I had one more night of hanging out with Mal, a dinner with Drew tomorrow, and then two weeks of blissful quiet in the house. I could cook whatever I wanted, watch whatever I wanted, and best of all – I wouldn't have to worry about Kevin being in my home.

On the way to the airport, all Byron had wanted to talk about was why I didn't get along with Kevin, and why I didn't make more of an effort with him. Since he'd apologised for accusing me of being with Drew, things were more or less okay – well, they were civil. We didn't address anything big. We just – coexisted, in a weird way.

We didn't even sleep together.

So when he'd brought it all up again in the car, on the way to the airport, to say I was furious would be a gross understatement.

Not only that, he'd spent a good chunk of time complaining about my ute smelling like chemicals when he got in, and shaking his head at the equipment on the floor. Admittedly, I probably should've tidied it up a little. Of course, he'd stopped himself pretty quickly and shut up when he realised what the alternative was – letting me drive the Maserati. If I weren't so angry, I would have laughed at how pathetic that was.

After a quick detour to the butcher, I parked the ute, grabbed a bag of raw bones, and went straight to Drew's place. I unlocked the door and put my keys on the kitchen bench, surprised Mal wasn't already inside and sitting at my feet, resisting the urge to jump on me because he was too bloody well-trained.

"Mal!" I yelled towards the back door, waiting in silence.

Frowning, I unlocked the screen door and stepped outside, letting my eyes adjust to the dark. I looked around, but couldn't see him.

"Hey. Where are you?" I tried to whistle, but after years and years of Dad trying to teach me as a kid, it still wasn't a skill I'd mastered. It sounded pathetic. I was attempting to whistle again, when I heard heavy breathing below me. Mal was lying on the ground behind the jacuzzi.

"Mal?" I let the door slam shut behind me and hurried over to him. How had he not heard me come in? He was lying flat on the deck, legs sprawled and breathing jagged. Adrenalin raced through my veins.

"Hey. Mal." I nudged him, hoping he'd get up. Bile rose in my throat. His eyes moved to look at me, but his head and body remained still, only his stomach rising and falling with his quick breaths.

"What the *hell*," I gasped, softly patting him on the head with a shaky hand. "It's okay, buddy. Come on. You'll be okay."

I fumbled to get my phone out of my handbag but dropped it. It clattered loudly onto the deck. As I snatched it back up, I took a sharp breath and opened Google Maps. Mal's eyes were locked on me as I typed "emergency vet" shakily into the search bar. There was a twenty-four-hour animal hospital five kilometres away.

"Hang in there, bud, you'll be okay …"

Mal's breath was shallow, and he was not going to stand up for me no matter how hard I tried. I scooped him up in my arms and tried to stand. He was incredibly heavy – about forty kilos, at a guess. My legs trembled under his weight, but I managed to stand, stumbling through the house and out the front door, kicking it shut behind me and hauling Mal onto the ute's tray.

"I'm so sorry, Mal." There was no way he would've fit on the passenger seat lying down, and I had nowhere else to put him. I wiped my eyes as I ran to the driver's door, got in, and drove towards the clinic as fast as I could, bearing in mind Mal was in the tray.

"Hey Siri!" I yelled at my phone on the seat next to me. "Call Drew on speaker!" I tried to take a deep breath in as the phone rang, looking in the rear-view mirror and pulling out onto the main road. "Come on. Pick up, pick *up*."

I looked in the mirror again, but I couldn't make out Mal in the tray. He must've been lying completely flat. *Please be okay.*

I was responsible for him. I was meant to be making sure he was okay. He was in my care. And whatever had happened, whatever had made him sick, was not good. I was no medical expert, but I wasn't naïve enough to think everything would be fine, either.

"No. No, no, no!" I hit the steering wheel, another tear rolling down my face. Not helpful. *Get it together, Georgie.*

I pulled into the parking lot, then realised I was going to

struggle to lift Mal out over the side of the tray. Luckily it was the weekend, and apart from a few bits of equipment on the floor, I didn't have a whole tray full of chlorine drums, hoses, and nets. With only a couple of things in there, there was enough space for Mal, and enough for me to climb up. I turned off the ignition and hurried out, unlatched the back of the tray, and jumped up. I scooped Mal up in my arms again, trying to compose myself as I crawled along towards the edge on my knees, all my strength going into lifting the limp dog. He gave me nothing, his head hanging off my arm.

I left the tray undone and pushed open the glass door of the clinic with my back, something wet running down my leg.

The young girl at reception dressed in green took one look at us and jumped up from the desk, leading me down the hall. She opened the first room and motioned at the table. I placed Mal onto it. Catching my breath, I glanced down at my leg and noticed a line of blood. God, he was bleeding, too? It took me a second to realise it was my own – I must have scraped it along the bottom of the ute's tray. I'd felt it at the time, but it hadn't really registered. Now the deep cut was throbbing.

"Are you okay?" the girl asked. "Do you want—"

"Just … The dog. What's … Why is he like this?" I was still trying to catch my breath, hardly able to form sentences.

"Yeah, let me get the vet. Hold on. She'll be—"

A slightly older woman came in, but her words didn't register as she spoke.

Please let him be okay. Please. This is going to destroy Drew. And me.

The vet snapped me out of my thoughts. After relaying what little information I knew, she asked me to wait outside while they did some tests. I didn't want to leave Mal, but I didn't want this to drag on, either.

Collapsing into a red plastic chair in the waiting room, I took out my phone and hit Drew's number again. Again, it rang out. I tried once more with the same result.

"Hey, your leg's bleeding ..." said a guy sitting opposite me with a cat carrier.

"Yeah ... I ... It's okay." I looked down, noting the blood was dripping down into my sock. He handed me some paper towel and I tried to soak up the blood as best I could, but just ended up smudging it around. A minute later, the guy came back with some tissues. His kindness made me start sobbing.

Please let Mal be okay.

I blew my nose and paced the room, unable to sit, conscious of the fact my leg was still bleeding. The girl behind the desk brought over a large adhesive patch, about the size of my palm, and some antiseptic spray.

"It's a waterproof dressing. It's got some padding on it – should help stop the bleeding," she said. "But you'll wanna wash and disinfect it."

I thanked her, then applied the spray and dressing to the wound. Washing it would have to wait.

After an excruciating amount of time, the vet nurse called me in just as I was about to dial Drew's number again.

"Is he okay? What's ... What is it?"

Her expression was sombre. "Malcolm has acute kidney failure."

I stared at her. "How?"

"He's on IV fluids and we're trying to flush it all out. Sometimes, it can be a snake or insect bite – sometimes, it's simply age. That doesn't help us anyway. The treatment does. But ..." She paused. "I have to be honest. Usually, by this stage, we don't have a good outcome."

A huge sob left my mouth, a giant claw ripping my heart

through my chest. "He's … He's not mine. I have to— When will you know?"

"We'll have to wait and see how he responds to the IV and the medication we've given him. In the meantime, I suggest getting in touch with the owners – they might have a difficult decision to face. I'm sorry I can't tell you more right now. We just have to wait it out."

My throat was closing up. I wanted to go back in time. I wish I hadn't taken Byron to the bloody airport and had gone to see Mal instead. Why had I left him alone all afternoon? What if I'd got there sooner and taken him to the vet earlier?

This was all my fault.

I got up and stumbled to the toilet, covering my mouth.

24

DREW

banged on Georgie's door, confused as hell. I'd had six missed calls from her on Saturday night that I hadn't seen until it was really late, and when I'd rung back, she hadn't answered. She also hadn't answered my call first thing on Sunday. There was one text, saying she would speak to me when I got back, and nothing else.

It was unlike her. The text was blunt, and a total contrast to the ones she'd been sending on Friday night. Seriously, what was up with this woman? I'd never met anyone as hot and cold as her.

I couldn't shake the feeling that she'd decided to cancel our Sunday night plans. And an even worse thought crossed my mind that I needed to push away as soon as I could – what if she had decided to stick with what she'd said to me after the party, that we shouldn't see each other any more?

But why all the missed calls on Saturday night? Had Byron seen her phone and got suspicious of our texts? I thought he had flown out to Tanzania already. Something wasn't right. And it had been one hell of a nerve-wracking flight back to Sydney. I banged on her door again, and when I got no response, I called her mobile.

"Hello?" Her voice was quiet.

"Are you home?"

"I'm at yours," she whispered.

"Uh, okay, I'll be there in two." I hung up the phone and jogged to my front door, which was unlocked. "Georgie?" I walked into the living room, but she wasn't there. I couldn't see her in the kitchen, either. "Hey. Where are ya?" My heart was pounding. Something was wrong; I could feel it. What was she going to tell me?

The place was completely dark. I flicked on the living room light, but still couldn't see her. The entire house was quiet and still.

Not even Mal came to greet me.

I walked around the kitchen to the other end of the hallway and opened my bedroom door. Georgie was lying on top of my bed, hugging her knees, in the dark. I could just make her out from the lights in the living room.

"Georgie. Are you okay? What's going on?" I dropped my duffel bag and moved closer to the bed, letting my eyes adjust to the dark. "Do you mind if … Can I switch the light on?" I said.

She let out a sob, but didn't say anything. I turned on the bedside lamp, thinking it would be a bit less intense than the main light. I sat on the bed and looked at her. "Are you okay? What – happened to your leg?"

Her face was tear-stained and blotchy. She continued to clutch her arms around her knees, her eyes puffy and red.

"Hey, what's wrong?" I put my hand on her arm.

She let out another sob. "Mal."

My breath caught in my throat as she glanced up at me with wet eyes.

And I knew.

25

GEORGIE

I couldn't stop picturing Mal's eyes. Those big, cobalt blue, innocent eyes as they'd looked up at me from the table, a large chunk of his paw shaved and bandaged where the drip had been.

Right after the vet had asked me to say goodbye.

She'd asked if I wanted to stay during "the procedure". There was no way in hell I was leaving Mal alone in his final moments. So I'd made the decision to stay with him until they put the needle in – the needle which would ensure I'd never see those blue eyes again.

And now I had to look into Drew's eyes and tell him that *he'd* never see them again, either.

When he hadn't answered his phone, I'd called his sister. I didn't have her number – I didn't have anyone's number that he might have known. But despite the state I was in, I managed to come up with the idea to find Elena on social media, and called her on there. It was lucky I'd seen the photo of her at Drew's, because her name was not uncommon. And thankfully she had answered.

I'd never forget her words: *"Do it, Georgie – he'd never want Mal to suffer. He would do the same thing."*

Mal had been labelled as "not for resuscitation" – the kidney failure was so advanced, they said that if he went into an arrest or had a seizure he would not be resuscitated anyway.

The vet's words still rang in my ears: *"It's just too traumatic for a dog of his size and age, at this stage of kidney failure."*

He's not even that old! I'd wanted to shout. *Do something else!* But they couldn't.

And before I knew it, it was dawn, and he was gone.

All I could think of was Drew.

My short nails dug into my palms as the tears streamed down my face.

Drew was sitting down on the bed. His jaw tightened, but he didn't say anything. He looked at the ground, then put his face in his hands and took a sharp breath in.

I didn't even need to say the words. He knew.

At least Elena hadn't told him, like I'd requested. The least I could do was be the one to tell him, in person. I thought about the collar and tag that sat on the kitchen bench. His ripped old dog bed that would still smell like him. The bag of bones on the kitchen floor he would never eat.

"He … I …" I started, but I couldn't get the words out.

"Don't," Drew said, with his face still in his hands.

The lump in my throat wouldn't have allowed me to say anything, anyway.

He took another breath, then turned the lamp off. I couldn't see anything for a moment, until I noticed his silhouette stand up in front of me and walk out the bedroom door.

I buried my face in his pillow and sobbed into it as I heard the front door close and lock.

He was gone.

Where would he go? Should I go after him? I doubted my ability to even stand. But a moment later, he came back into his room and closed the door. I was wrong – he hadn't left, he'd just locked his front door. He lay down on the bed facing me. I couldn't see his face, but that was probably for the best. Wordlessly, Drew wrapped his arms around me. I straightened my legs out and let him pull me closer. His warm embrace and the sweet, woody smell of his cologne was too much. He rested his chin on my head as I put my face into his chest. It felt like I was physically succumbing to him – finally. I had no energy left to fight the need to be with him – the need to touch him, to let him hold me. And I didn't want to fight it, either.

I sobbed into his chest all night long, haunted by Mal's intelligent eyes, one slightly lighter than the other. There are certain images you know you'll never get out of your head. A bad road accident; an animal's dying eyes.

Some sounds are like that, too. Drew didn't say a word all night.

But I knew I would never, ever forget the sound of his tears hitting the pillow.

26

GEORGIE

I ran a finger along my leg, gently feeling the cut. Today was the first time I was able to leave the bandage off the new pink scar. Part of me hoped it would stay there forever – my last memory of Mal. Unfortunately, I was only healing well physically.

My phone buzzed with a text from Roisin.

So, you got your drinking hat on?

I smiled. *I'll have a few. Won't be a massive one though.*

Oh come on. We both know that's not true. Byron's away anyway – make the most of it before you're back in jail.

I laughed, looking out the window of the taxi and taking a deep breath in. I always felt a bit nauseous when texting in a car. But I never learned. *I can't*, I replied. *It's been a big week. I'm exhausted.*

All the more reason. See you in 30. I'll have a tequila shot waiting.

And you'll be drinking it yourself.

It *had* been a huge week. Almost one week since Drew got back from Perth – and since Mal had been put to sleep. I closed my eyes, not letting the sting behind them get me this time. They'd got me every single day since last Saturday, and the tightness in my chest was still there. One wrong move, one flashback, and I'd be done for.

This night out had been organised for a month, to celebrate Kara's engagement and as a bit of a celebration for another successful year in business. All six of the Pool Chicks employees were coming – a rarity – and Jana was coming, too. She was the most recent addition to the team, taking the number to seven. Kara's fiancée was invited, of course, but ended up getting sick and couldn't come. So it was seven women, all colleagues who hadn't had been together in a very long time, going to a dinner with bottomless drinks. What could go wrong?

In all fairness, I needed to let off some steam. I'd spent the week giving Drew space. He sent me messages every day, but why would he possibly want to see me after what happened with Mal?

His dog was gone – because of me. He was heartbroken over it – because of me. And he would never see Mal again. Because of me, his life had been turned upside down. And still there he was, sending *me* messages asking to see how *I* was doing. He'd come over once, but I had Kate over, so he didn't stay very long. And I hadn't really asked him to. He was smiling, but I didn't miss the grief in his eyes. He wasn't okay. But he was putting on a front because he knew I felt guilty about Mal.

My grief for Mal overtook the guilt I felt for staying the night at Drew's house, in his bed, with him holding me all night. Not once had he let go, except to pull the sheets over us.

And not once had I wanted him to.

At the time, there'd been no guilt – only a debilitating sadness that had sapped me of energy, thoughts, and emotions. I'd even taken the Monday off work because I couldn't stop crying. But my eyes had remained red-ringed and puffy for the whole week, and on the numerous occasions my clients had asked about it,

I'd blamed it on a reaction to chlorine.

I gazed out the window again as my taxi crossed the Harbour Bridge. The sun reflected off the water's rippled surface, sparkly and blue. It was a beautiful late summer's afternoon, and it was going to be a good evening – I could feel it. I'd been stinging for this girls' night forever. I wished I could stop thinking about Mal and Drew, even just momentarily. I knew I'd never forget the last look in that dog's eyes. And I couldn't deal with how much pain and hurt I had caused Drew.

I took a deep breath as the taxi pulled up in the CBD, thanked the driver and got out, smoothing my dress down and catching my reflection in the window. The mint-coloured satin dress I wore was gorgeous – even I had to admit that. Its off-the-shoulder design showed off my now-very-tanned shoulders and arms, and it was a little shorter than I would have liked, but paired with the heels I was wearing it was quite elegant. I made my way to the restaurant, heels clicking.

2 7

DREW

Elena topped up her glass of red, finishing off the bottle, and grinned at me suddenly.

"What is it?" I asked, smiling back. It was such a relief seeing her, having her over at mine, despite what had been a horrendous week for both of us. But seeing my sister always cheered me up. She'd loved Mal as much as I did, and she'd been just as devastated as I had. I was glad to have her around – I'd tried as hard as I could to act like I was okay in front of Georgie, because I knew how responsible she felt for the whole thing. That in itself was ridiculous – but no matter how much I reassured her, nothing I did or said could change it. And she didn't really want to see me, which meant that I had been suffering over the loss of Mal by myself.

It'd been a long, tough week at work. I couldn't concentrate, and most nights I came home and had more beers than I should have, just to help me sleep. I knew it wasn't ideal, but the pain of losing Mal made me care about little else, including how much I drank.

His old bed was still on the deck outside. And his collar sat on the kitchen bench. I couldn't bring myself to do anything with them. Every now and then I'd get a faint whiff of his scent around the house, and I had to push the lump in my throat away.

So it was a relief to be spending this Friday evening with my sister.

"Nothing," Elena replied, "it's nice to see you smiling."

"Well, there *is* a beer in my hand, isn't there?"

She laughed. "The easiest way to your heart. Hey, I've gotta ask you something."

"Go ahead."

She hesitated. "Have you spoken to John?"

"I think you probably know the answer to that."

"Don't you think it's time to put it behind us?"

I shrugged. "I'll forgive him when Pete forgives him." Our brother was just as stubborn as me when it came to John. Pete also hadn't spoken to him in years.

Elena sighed. "Pete's been talking to him for over six months."

Well, I guess I was wrong.

I didn't know what to say.

"He's been a bit worried about telling you."

I shrugged. Normally, the comment would've annoyed me. But the truth was, after losing Mal this week, I didn't have the energy for any of that. Besides, I'd have a hard time being angry at my brother.

"I mean, the guy's apologised enough times. Don't you think you could just forgive him?" Elena said carefully.

I let out a slow breath. It had been years since John, our uncle, had had an affair and run off with a much younger woman. John was Mum's oldest sister's husband, and she'd been devastated. She hadn't seen it coming. Poor Gillian was a mess. And we'd been there to pick up the pieces. I'd even taken leave and flown back from Perth for a few weeks, the situation was so bad. It would've been easy enough to cut the guy from our lives – it was Gillian, after all, who was family, not John. But he had always been there for us when we were growing up. He'd often felt more like a dad than our own father, who – despite loving us – had not been around very much because of work. And even though we weren't even related to John by blood, he would do anything for us kids. There were so many good memories of him taking us rock climbing, snorkelling, fishing. He never once forgot a birthday.

And then he'd gone and done *that*. It still made me furious.

But it had been playing on my mind a little lately, something dawning on me. John was married, but had fallen in love with someone else. That was his crime.

The irony wasn't lost on me.

And compared to all the other stuff he'd done for us over the years … It was all so confusing. I scratched my head. If I was being honest, my situation with Georgie wasn't that different. Except for one thing. *She* was the married one, and *she* hadn't done anything wrong. It was just me who had fallen hard. Still, it was kind of difficult to ignore the parallels to our situation. Maybe I needed to stop being so hard on John – especially given that, after everything, he still made such a huge effort to reach out to me.

I looked up at Elena. "Did you come round here tonight with this agenda?" I asked her, half-seriously.

"I also brought Italian food …"

I laughed. "That's true. Listen. I'm not saying that I will – whoa, what on earth is …" I watched as she took out two massive containers of pasta and some garlic bread from the takeaway bags and put them on top of the three pizzas. "Jesus. You organise a party here or something?" I eyed her.

Her grin got wider, but she said nothing. I stood up and walked to the kitchen to grab two plates as there was a knock on the door.

"You should get that," she said. "And get an extra plate."

What the hell is going on? I walked to the front door and opened it suspiciously.

There stood my brother, Pete, with a suitcase next to him and a grin that matched Elena's.

"What the— What are you *doing* here?" I managed.

"I fly in from Singapore to see my bro and that's all I get?" he chuckled.

My jaw dropped as I stood staring at him in the doorway.

"Well, are you going to invite me in or not?"

I almost knocked him over with my hug.

2 8

GEORGIE

I gulped my water, eyes shut, trying to wash away the taste of the second tequila I'd downed since dinner. Despite wanting a quiet night, it certainly hadn't taken long for the girls to twist my arm. Shaking my head, I put the glass down. These shots were going to be trouble, and tomorrow was going to hurt. Luckily, it was a Friday night, and we'd organised it so that none of us were working tomorrow.

I looked around at the mahogany chairs and overhanging lights in the dimly lit restaurant. It was beautifully done, and the food had been delicious. I felt warm, comfortable and relaxed in my chair, and I couldn't stop smiling as the girls caught up on gossip, gushed about their lives, and complimented one another. I was sure the tequila played a big part, but there was nowhere else I would've rather been. It was also the first time in a week I felt anything other than utter devastation. I breathed in deeply as the smell of steamed dumplings floated over to our table, the girls' voices competing with the sizzling sounds coming from the kitchen. Roisin sat to my right and Jana, to my left, was admiring the giant rock on Kara's left hand.

"Holy moly, hun, that's amazing. Congrats!"

Kara beamed, breathing out a too-full sigh, but putting two more dumplings on her plate anyway. "Thank you!" She looked like a model in her hot-pink, skin-tight dress that outlined her gorgeous hour-glass figure. Her curls were pulled back into a sleek up-do.

I took the bowl from Kara and helped myself to some more dumplings, despite being way too full, too. They were a signature dish at Har Gow, a fancy Asian fusion restaurant – I couldn't *not* try them. I sat back in the chair after I demolished them, trying to catch a breath in my dress that had no give.

I looked around at the group, feeling so lucky to work with these women. Smart, hard-working, supportive women.

"How'd I get so lucky?" I turned to Roisin, my head spinning a little.

"What with, honey?"

"Working for you. Working with this lot." I swung my arm in a circular motion around the table, gesturing at the girls.

Roisin laughed and clinked my glass of water. "I'd say let's drink to that, but I'm thinking maybe we should slow down a tad."

"Huh?" I yelled. Despite the fact she was next to me, I couldn't hear a bloody thing.

"Nothing," she yelled even louder than me. "I love you. And by the way—"

"No, I love *you*," I interjected.

"You work *with* me, not *for* me," she finished. "Partners, remember?"

"Eh. Potatoes, tomatoes," I said, slightly knocking my front teeth on my glass of water. She was right – I definitely needed to slow down. Tequila had never been my friend.

A waiter in black came over with a tray of cocktail glasses, filled with an orange-coloured drink, and salt and chilli around the rim. "Sunburnt margaritas, ladies?"

"Good lord," I said, grabbing one. "Who the hell ordered these?"

Jana turned her long, elegant neck towards me, a frown on her face. "Uh, pretty sure *you* did," she said in her thick accent.

"Damn. They taste *gooooood*!" I said, licking the cocktail's salty edge and trying hard to focus on Kara and Fiona's conversation.

"Oi," Roisin said, laughing. "Slow down. You wanna make it to dancing later."

"Dancing shmancing," I slurred.

"So you guys are going to Greece and Malta in June?" Kara asked Fiona.

"Yeah! Booked yesterday."

"That is the best girls' trip ever. Can I, like, jump in your suitcase?"

Fiona sipped her margarita, laughing. "Probably not, but you are *way* more than welcome to come along. Seriously."

"Thanks, babe. But I have a wedding to save for now. I doubt Shauna would be too happy if I decided to jump on a flight to Greece with ya! I'll just have to live vicariously through your Insta photos. Of which I'm expecting a lot!" Kara winked at her.

"Hey, speaking of trips," Roisin said to me, "how's Byron's trip going? When's he due back again?"

I put my drink down on its coaster, its contents nearly gone. "Um. Eight days."

"Where is he?" Jana asked.

"Oh, he's on this amazing trip in Tanzania," Kara explained. "He goes with Surgeons with Heart International every year and they do all these heart surgeries on people who …"

I tuned out, ready for the usual responses of *Oh my god, Georgie, you must be so proud of him!* And *Wow, what a kind thing to do!* As the girls continued filling Jana in about Byron, I found my thoughts wandering to Drew. What was he up to?

Did he miss Mal as much as I did?

How can you even wonder that? He's absolutely heartbroken. I tried hard not to think back to that night. And I tried not to think back to the following morning, when Drew had been reluctant to let me go after holding me close to him all night. The intoxicating smell of cologne on his neck. The way he'd studied my face in the orange morning sun while he held me. The sadness in his eyes. The way the feeling had crushed my chest so hard I couldn't breathe. The way the heat from his face had radiated onto mine, a strong arm around my waist. The way I'd had to keep my eyes closed while he'd swept my hair from my face, because if I'd looked into his eyes while we were that close, I would no longer be able to deny what I was feeling.

But I'd have to get over the way he'd felt so warm and safe, and the way I'd felt in response – like I was home. I would definitely need to get over those feelings, and quickly. I drained the rest of my cocktail at the thought and ordered a round of Fireball shots. Jana had finished her drink and looked ecstatic about my order, but the others didn't seem so impressed.

"*Dunworry*," I slurred. "My shout."

"Yeah." Roisin said, chuckling. "That's ... not what we're worried about."

"Have they finished all the surgeries yet?" Kara was asking me.

"Oh, um, I haven't actually heard from him."

Byron never made contact while he was away, saying it was only a short trip and it was too hard to coordinate calls with the time difference. It actually didn't bother me – I always enjoyed the quiet time alone, and this two-week break was no different. I pulled out my phone, opened the Facebook app, and clicked on Byron's profile. Nothing had been updated since the day they'd arrived in Dar es Salaam, when he had posted their fundraising page again, reminding people to donate. "Nah, nothing online yet." Another round of drinks arrived, and I typed "Surgeons with Heart International" into the search bar. "Oh. They *have* posted something. Hang on."

"Cheers, ladies!" Roisin said, holding up her Fireball shot. I felt sick looking at it, but I *had* been the one to order them. Better suck it up. "Congrats to Kara on the engagement, and thank you all for making last year another successful one for The Pool Chicks," Roisin continued, "and also, welcome, Jana, welcome to the first Pool Chicks do. Please don't judge us for our binge drinking, we don't do it often – but when we do, we do it well!"

We clinked our shot glasses and downed the golden, spicy liquid. I shivered, and made a note not to order any more. The Fireball was so much smoother than that smoky tequila, though. It warmed my mouth and stomach immediately. I looked back down at my phone, and clicked on the Facebook photos that had been added two hours ago.

My finger froze on the third image, breath catching in my windpipe. There was a doctor making a presentation, whose smooth skin and brown eyes seemed familiar. I'd met him before. He was mid-speech, some people in the background watching on with interest.

And off to the side and behind him sat Byron, smiling warmly at a beautiful woman next to him. His hand rested on her thigh, slightly under the hem of her dress. I blinked and studied it again.

What the hell?

I stared at the photo as the girls chattered around me.

I stood up, almost knocking my chair over, and darted towards the bathrooms. As I ducked into a cubicle, slamming the door harder than I meant to, I leaned against the tiny copper tiles lining the walls. I looked at the photo again and zoomed in.

That smile. Half sleazy, fully confident. I remembered that smile like it was yesterday – it was the same expression he'd had the day we met. The way he'd watched me while I worked at the event – like nothing else in the world mattered to him. My gaze dropped to the woman's thigh again, where his hand rested casually – like it belonged there. The woman sat facing him, reciprocating his flirty demeanour.

Rage seared through my chest. I wanted to slam the phone against the copper tiles and throw it into the toilet. The only thing stopping me was the memory of the day it'd been delivered to my door, along with a note. A gift from Drew. I paused, stumbling over to the sink outside instead, and put the phone on the marble bench next to a tap that just seemed too fancy to use. I stared at it, trying to let my drunk brain work it out.

I straightened my arms out on the marble, enjoying the cold stone on my hot skin, then let my head and arms hang down towards the ground.

"Are you okay?" Two women near the door were looking at me, puzzled. I stood up, getting dizzy at the sudden movement, swaying on my heels and realising I was not feeling so stable. "Yeah … Fine. Thanks."

"Are you sure? Who you here with?"

I swiped my phone off the bench, flung the door open and said something unintelligible to them. Back at our table, the girls were talking loudly over the music. Everything was a blur. I grabbed my handbag from the chair without a word and stumbled towards the exit, out into the hot summer night, seeing a taxi not far away. I made my way towards it, steadying myself on the brick wall, cursing both the cobblestone street and my stilettos. I opened the door and slurred a greeting at the driver, noticing two missed calls from Roisin as I got in the backseat.

I wound the window down, taking in a gulp of fresh air as the driver looked at me cautiously in the rear-view mirror. *Yeah, I'd be worried if I were you, too, buddy.*

I definitely should've had a few more waters.

Or maybe fewer tequilas.

I wrote Roisin a text, squinting one eye. ***Hhey. Im out. Seen me your bank details so I can oay. Thnks for a good night.***

She replied immediately. ***Are you OK babe?? What happened?***

I didn't have the energy to reply. Nor did I think I could do so without throwing up. I stared out the window, eyelids starting to droop, as the warm wind hit my face.

Screw you, Byron. You piece of shit.

I thought about the photo. Did it really confirm anything? It was suggestive, but it wasn't definitive. I couldn't believe my drunk brain could think of such words. But soon after, it drifted to someone else entirely. I sighed. It had been doing so for weeks.

I gave the driver my home address, knowing full well that's not where I was going.

29

DREW

Pete handed me a beer and sat down, clinking his bottle against mine. "So good to be back," he said.

I grinned. "So bloody good to have you back."

He went to pick up the empty pizza boxes, but I jumped up before he could. I took them to the kitchen, flattening and folding them so they'd fit in the bin, then sat back down at the dining table. "Tell us more about Singapore – do you reckon you'll be there a while?"

"Drew, it's the best. A bit tough sometimes, with the humidity, but it's a small price. Amazing city. You gotta come visit."

I did feel guilty, not having been over to see him in the last two years since he'd moved there. I glanced at the collar on the end of the kitchen bench, sticking out under some mail. "Yeah, well, I guess I'll have a bit more time now." I had a gulp of beer, hoping it would push away the lump in my throat.

I miss you so much, buddy ...

Elena gave me a knowing glance, stood up, and squeezed my shoulder. "Right," she said. "You guys ready for dessert?"

Pete rubbed his stomach. "Ah, why not?"

"So, how are the girls?" I said.

"Yeah, they're great. They said to say hi. Oh, actually, they sent you two something. Remind me to grab it from my suitcase."

"Hey, Pete. Grab it from your suitcase."

"You are such a smartass," he said, taking a swig of beer. "I guess some things never change!"

I laughed at the comment, thinking about how Georgie always called me that, just as someone banged on the front door. I jumped up. "Yeah, hold on!" The loud banging continued until I got there. Whoever was at the door was adamant on getting in fast. "Yeah, yeah, hold your horses."

I unlocked the door, the stifling evening air coming in straight away.

Georgie stood in front of me with a faint sheen of sweat on her forehead, cheeks shiny, and an urgency in her expression. The way the green dress skimmed her body, showing her shoulder and collarbone, I couldn't tear my eyes away from her.

"Wow ..." I murmured. The pit of my stomach tingled as I stood staring at her.

There was a look in her eyes I'd never seen before. She stepped inside, steadying herself on the wall and moving towards me.

"You look so beautiful, Georgie. Have you been—"

Before I could finish my question, she flung her handbag to the ground and threw her arms around my neck. And in one swift movement, she jumped up, wrapped her legs around me, and pressed her lips against mine.

"Whoa," I breathed, stumbling as I tried to maintain my balance, and having to grab her so she didn't fall. Her perfume was floral and strong; her lips tasted like cinnamon and whisky.

She pulled back and studied me, her wide eyes a little hazy. And then she looked down at my lips, smiled and kissed me again, her mouth soft and smooth. Her skin was warm against mine as she held onto me tight, like she never, ever wanted to let go.

The beers I'd had definitely made me tipsy, but I was sober enough to recognise that she was next-level drunk. Out of the corner of my eye, I could see Elena staring at me from the living room, mouth agape, and Pete doing the same from his chair, a beer halfway to his lips.

Georgie had no idea we weren't alone. "D'you know how long I wanted to do that?" she said, holding onto my shoulders and burrowing her face into my neck. Her dress, which was already very short, had ridden right up her legs. There was definitely no extra room for wrapping your legs around someone. The fabric was tight around her thighs, almost revealing her underwear as she gripped onto me.

Good lord. I headed towards my bedroom. I hoped she couldn't tell how turned on I was, because this could not happen. Regardless of how badly I wanted it to.

I closed the door and lowered her down on my bed. She crossed one elegant leg over the other, one arm steadying herself on the bed. Her other hand reached for me and pulled me down to sit on the bed with her. She was so drunk, she had to tilt her head back to look at me. It was taking all my energy and then some not to kiss along that smooth neck of hers, down her collarbone …

"You," she said, pressing an index finger into my chest.

"Me what?"

She tried to kiss me again, but I moved away, took her hands softly in mine and stood up.

I can't let this happen.

"Where're you goin'?" she slurred, her eyes closing as she sat swaying on my bed.

"I'm going to get you some water, okay?" Even hammered, with eyes half shut, she was still a bombshell. "Wait there a sec."

I hurried to the kitchen and filled a tall glass with icy water, and also grabbed a bucket. Just in case. Elena and Pete were still staring at me from the living room in silence.

"Uh, I'll be out in a sec," I told them.

By the time I got back to the room, Georgie was lying face down on my bed, on top of the sheets, shoes still on. I put the bucket next to the bed.

"Drew?"

"Yeah?"

"Can I stay here tonight?" she said, her voice muffled by my pillow.

"Sure, um, of—"

"Drew … You are so hot. Someone should make a calendar of you. All twelve months."

I stifled a laugh. "Hey, have some water before you fall asleep." I tapped on the glass.

"Asleep?" she muttered. "I'm not asleep. *You're* asleep."

This time I really did laugh.

"What?" she said, sitting up slowly.

"Nothing. You're just funny."

Her eyes sprung open for a moment and she looked at me, moving her head slightly back and glancing around the room like she was trying to work out where she was. "I think my sixtieth drink was spiked," she said with a straight face, before erupting in giggles.

I laughed and handed her the glass carefully. It took her a second, but she eventually had a solid gulp of water. Then she put the drink down and looked at me without smiling.

"We need to talk, Drew."

"Sure. Why don't we talk in the morning?"

"Because I want to talk now."

"All right, well, I'm listening."

She flopped back down and let her head drop onto my pillow. Her eyes closed and her breathing steadily became heavier. I looked at her, with her hand under her head, lying on her side. The most beautiful woman who ever existed. I slipped off her shoes carefully, making her stir, and put them on the ground next to her.

"Why are you always so nice?" she mumbled. "All the time. So bloody nice."

"Well, I think—"

"Drew, I think I'm a bit drunk."

I pressed my lips together. "Nah. You're fine."

She cleared her throat. "Hey, Drew?"

"Mmm?"

"You're the best guy. The *best* one."

I closed my eyes and took a drawn-out, slow breath.

"I'm sorry if I was mean."

"When?"

"Always," she murmured into the pillow.

I put a hand on hers. "It's okay."

"Why did I meet you? And why didn't we meet, like, five years ago?"

I shrugged into the darkness. "I wonder that myself sometimes," I said quietly.

"When you … that day I climbed your fence?"

"Yeah?"

"And you … said I was beautiful? I … think about it all the time."

I smiled.

"And I miss that dog so much. I'm so sorry. I wish— I can't—"

I squeezed her hand. "Hey. You need to stop."

"It was my fault."

"Georgie, it wasn't. Please don't think that."

She was silent for a moment, then put a hand on her head. "Can your room stop?"

"Are you spinning?"

"No, your room is."

I laughed.

"Also. You should know."

I waited, but she didn't say anything else. I ran my fingers through her soft hair, loosening it and taking out some weird clip things that looked like they would hurt to sleep in. She was breathing steadily, now clearly asleep. I switched off the bedside light, turning the air conditioning on low for her. As I walked to the door, she said something quietly, and stirred in the bed.

I waited, but she just muttered something unintelligible into the pillow, then went quiet.

I was still smiling when I closed the door and walked out to the living room. Pete and Elena stared at me wide-eyed when I sat down at the table and took a huge swig of my beer.

"So that's my neighbour," I said, pointing towards my room with my thumb.

30

GEORGIE

I licked my dry lips and tried to open my eyes. It took them quite some time to cooperate, and once they did, I had to squeeze them shut again. My head was in a vice and someone was tightening it slowly. There was an unusual smell – something earthy … or woody? Cologne? I took a deep breath in, trying to work it out, and trying to fill my lungs with more oxygen. I opened one eye again slowly, the sunlight coming through the window immediately making me squint. My stomach ached like it had been punched repeatedly. What on earth? I ran my hands down over my torso, feeling satin material. A sheet was draped over my waist, too.

I slept in my dress.

I groaned as a wave of nausea hit me, followed by a coughing fit that made me sit up in bed. I looked around, trying to piece everything together. It didn't take long – the red bucket on the ground next to me made it all come flooding back. Dumplings. Kara's engagement. A taxi. *Way* too many drinks.

I tried to recall the end of the night with the girls. Did we go dancing? I definitely remembered coming home in a taxi. I didn't remember saying bye to the girls, though. Why didn't I take my dress off? I tried hard to recall the last thing I *did* remember. Nothing was really coming to me after the dinner. I rubbed my temples, annoyed with myself. This was going to be a rough day. I hadn't had a night like that since I was about twenty.

I looked around again – and that's when it hit me: *this isn't my room.*

Panic flooded my chest. I held my breath as I turned my head slowly to the right. The bed was empty, thankfully, but I knew exactly where I was. More precisely, I knew *whose* bed I was in.

I tried to locate my phone, taking comfort in the fact that I was wearing clothes. Things could have been worse. I found the phone on top of the sheets next to me and tapped on it, the screensaver of Byron and me at our wedding jolting my memory back to the bathroom at the restaurant, and to *that* Facebook post. To the photo that had made me bolt in the first place. Despite feeling sick just thinking about it, I clicked on the Facebook page again with a shaky hand. A sucker for punishment, I guess. And, in my drunken state, had I really seen what I thought I saw?

Would my own husband *really* do that to me?

The post was still there. Head spinning, I started swiping through the photos. But there was no photo of Byron and the mystery woman – it was gone. No picture of my husband, with his hand on another woman's leg. There was no evidence. I was drunk, but I knew I hadn't imagined it completely. There was no way. I clicked on Byron's profile, which still had no new updates.

I had six missed calls from the girls and two texts from Roisin asking if I got home okay. She must have been freaking out. I quickly typed a reply telling her I was fine.

And there was also a text from Drew:

Morning! Hope the head's not too sore. Come out to the deck when you're up!

I felt sick to my core. Feelings of regret and anxiety sat at the base of my stomach. Who knew what the hell I'd done or said last night? And in front of Drew – of all people. I sat up in the bed and swung my legs gingerly over the edge, wincing at my pounding headache. I stood up slowly, with the agility of a hundred-year-old woman, and made my way to the bathroom, where I was met with the sight of smudged mascara, frizzy hair, and a general greyish tinge to my face. Drew's bathroom was like the rest of his house – clean and minimalistic. I spotted a bottle of mouthwash which I immediately put to good use, and tried to wipe off the excess eye make-up with some toilet paper. Leaning on the sink, I took a few deep breaths, glancing at the shower and remembering seeing Drew in there naked. The memory sent an odd spark of electricity down my torso. I took another deep breath and headed for the back deck. I wanted – no, *needed* – answers, but I wasn't sure if I was going to like them.

Drew was sitting at the round glass table outside with a mug in front of him, typing on his phone. He glanced over when he heard the screen door opening. The smile on his face couldn't have been wider if he tried. He looked at me with such warmth that I almost had to turn away. I couldn't meet his eyes.

"*Heeeeeey*! She's up!" He put his phone face down on the table and stood up, pointing to his mug. "Want a coffee?"

I pulled a face that made him hold his stomach in laughter, my attention drawn to his shirtless torso immediately. Goddammit, Drew. Why did he always have to have half his body on display? The way those muscles moved as he laughed, skin golden and glowing in the morning sun. I stared, imagining what it would be like to go over there, sit on his lap, put my arms around his neck and kiss him slowly.

Stop it.

"I won't ask if you want any breakfast then, but can I get you some water?"

I folded my arms, suddenly feeling very exposed in my tiny dress. I was barefoot, and my feet throbbed from wearing heels. I put one foot over the other as I hugged myself, leaning against the wall. "Um, no, I can get it, thanks." It came out as a croak rather than a normal human's voice. I cleared my throat.

"Don't be silly. Here." He motioned at a chair. "Have a seat. I'll grab it." He went into the kitchen before I could argue, and returned with a tall glass of icy water. I sat down in the chair and gulped the water down, the cold liquid soothing my throat.

"Um … I'm sorry for— Well, for sleeping here. Did I … Did I wake you?" What I really wanted to know was, *Were you in bed with me?*

"No, not at all. I had my brother and sister over for dinner, actually."

"Oh. Right." I scratched my head. I had no memory of meeting them. Or of even coming around, to be honest. "Did I call you last night? How … When did I come over?"

Giving me a reassuring look, he said, "I had a few missed calls from you, but I didn't see them 'til after you'd come over. I guess you were ringing on your way here. I think you got here maybe about nine pm?"

I buried my face in my hands, mostly because the early morning sunlight was way too bright for my situation. "And did you … Did we …" I couldn't finish the sentence.

"I slept on the couch."

"Oh no. I'm so sorry."

"Don't mention it," he said. "Honestly. It was great. I put on Netflix and was asleep in five. It's quite a comfy couch, actually. I can see why Mal insisted on sleeping on it so much."

We smiled at each other for a moment. I was still confused,

and no memories were coming back to me. "What did we do when I arrived? Did I meet your family?" Not remembering anything was the absolute worst.

"Nah. You seemed pretty tired, so I just put you into bed."

"Oh. Okay. So I didn't even say why I came over?"

He shook his head. "You didn't say much, to be honest."

I relaxed a bit. Okay, well that was good news. "Hold on. Doesn't your brother live in Singapore?"

"Yeah. He was here for work, but kept it a surprise. He had a function on Thursday night, so unfortunately he was only free last night. And he went up to Brissy today to see our mum and dad for the weekend before he flies back to Singapore Sunday night."

I pulled my legs up to my chest, the icy water working wonders, and brought a hand up to my forehead to shield it from the sun. Drew was watching me intently.

"What?" I asked.

"Nothing," he said. "It's just nice having you here."

"I came over wasted, interrupted your dinner with your brother, whom you hardly see, kicked you out of your own bed and made you sleep on the couch, and now you're saying it's nice to have me here? I think we need to get you a dictionary and show you the definition of *nice*," I said, still shading my eyes.

He laughed, taking another sip of coffee. "Maybe. So, what are you up to today? You're not working, I hope?"

"God, no. I have this Saturday and next off, thankfully." I looked down at my dress and sticky feet. "Lots on the agenda today. Showering, then going right back to bed where this hangover belongs. Uh, to *my* bed, I mean."

"That's a terrible idea. Hangovers need fresh air, salty water and greasy food." He studied my face with a mischievous glint in his eyes. "And you look like you've got a good one."

"Gee, thanks."

"You're welcome." He grinned. "So, I'm going snorkelling today. Maybe take out the surfboard." He paused. "Wanna come?"

I snorted. "Absolutely not. That would involve movement. And effort." I shuddered just thinking about it. "*And* sitting in a car. Furthest I'll be going today is the bathroom, from my bedroom. Thanks, though."

Getting in a bikini in front of Drew? No thanks. Having to watch him in a pair of shorts at the beach all day? No.

"Come on, Georgie. It'll be good for ya. Better than sitting around moping all day."

"I'm not moping," I said defensively.

"Water's nice. Mid to late January is when it's at its warmest. And the visibility is really good at the moment."

"I've never snorkelled, and I don't plan to learn today."

His eyes flew wide open. "You've never snorkelled? And you lived on the coast?"

I didn't reply.

"Okay. Georgie de Luca. You are coming with me – no arguments! An Italian chick can't be living in Australia with no one having taken her snorkelling!" He stood up, a massive smile spread across his face, and reached his hand out to help me up.

I gingerly took it, his warm hand soft around mine. I never wanted to let it go. He must have sensed it, holding onto it for a second longer than necessary.

"Come on," he said, motioning to the door. "Grab your white bikini, I'll sort out the rest."

"Wait. How do you know my bikini's white?"

Drew paused. "I know *everything*." He chuckled. "Meet you at the Hilux in five."

I rolled my eyes at him, unimpressed. But my heart did a traitorous leap of joy.

31

GEORGIE

My sunglasses were doing nothing against the brutal morning sun that was beating in through Drew's windscreen. I cautiously glanced to my right, to Drew tapping away at the steering wheel as we drove towards the beach. The soft blonde hairs on his arms were illuminated by the morning rays. My eyes travelled north towards his defined chest, pushing against his white T-shirt. It was all I could do to stop my mind going to all kinds of bad places. I had to tear my eyes away from him and turn back towards the road. I took in a deep breath, slowly closing my eyes, as I had been doing this whole morning. I felt awful physically – but at least my ears and soul were being treated to an Incubus song, which was loud enough to drown out the sound of traffic, but soft enough that I could tell this driver knew exactly how hungover his passenger was. I closed my eyes, the sun warming my face as Brandon Boyd's silky voice transported me to another world. I took a deep breath in and let it out slowly. When I opened my eyes, Drew was looking at me fondly.

"What?"

"Nothing." He turned back to the road. "So you like Incubus, too?"

I nodded.

"Brandon is a pretty big hit with the ladies. Great voice, too."

"The man is a god."

Drew laughed. "Ah. I see. So *now* I know your type!" He slowed the car down and put the indicator on. "And you never told me *your* favourite Incubus song the other day, by the way."

"Oh. Um, I don't know …"

"Drunk brain not working?"

I smiled. "No. Let me get back to y— Hey, where are you going?"

"Trust me." He pulled the Hilux into a driveway, going past the giant golden arches into the McDonald's drive-thru.

"Oh my god. If you think I'm putting that crap into my body—"

He held up a hand, cutting me off. "Relax. I know you don't eat junk food."

"There's absolutely no way I'm eating McDonald's. Not even on this hangover." And it really was a nightmare hangover. I hadn't felt this sick in years.

Drew wound his window down, the warm air ruffling his hair. He combed a hand through it, the movement lifting his T-shirt up slightly.

Dammit. I couldn't stop staring. And I was going to be at the beach with him all day. I let out a sigh, turning away and trying to distract myself as he pulled up at the window and a skinny teenager came to take his order.

"Hey, how's it going?" Drew asked.

"Good thanks, how about you?"

"Yeah, great, thanks! Busy morning?"

"Was earlier, not so much now. What can I get you?"

"I'll grab two frozen Cokes, please – large."

So damn polite. To a young McDonald's employee he doesn't know from a bar of soap. Whenever I was at a café or restaurant with Byron, he wouldn't even so much as look at the person serving us.

"Sure, anything else?"

"That's it. Thanks heaps."

I'd always loved how only Aussies said "heaps". And I adored it even more after hearing Drew say it. Occasionally I would get odd looks in London if I ever used it, so after a while I stopped.

As we turned back onto the main road, I took a cautionary sip of the icy drink in my hand. Water dripped down it and onto my lap from the condensation.

"Here," Drew said, reaching behind me and giving me a whiff of his woody cologne. He grabbed an old T-shirt and put it across my lap.

"What, you worried about your car seats?" I joked. He gave me a lopsided smile.

He was right, though. The frozen Coke was the missing piece from my fragile, hungover body. The icy slush cooled my mouth and stomach, and when I slurped harder to get it into me faster, Drew laughed.

"Mmm …" I pointed at a tall apartment complex to my left which sat behind the highway barrier, my mouth full of frozen Coke. I swallowed, enjoying the numbness on the insides of my cheeks. "I have a job there on Monday. Brand new apartments. Quite a few pools inside, and I got us the contract. Mostly excited to see the penthouses."

"Nice one. I imagine they're worth a mint."

"Yeah. But who the hell would want to live in such a nice penthouse, out in the 'burbs?"

He laughed. "True. But it'll be a nice spot to work, huh? Good views."

I nodded, taking out my phone. I was already excited for a sleep-in on Monday morning, knowing the first job was so close to home. I opened my photo gallery to check the rest of Monday's schedule, of which I'd taken a screenshot on Friday afternoon.

My eyes did a double take at the first photo on my camera roll. *Byron in Tanzania. With the mystery woman.*

I must've taken a screenshot of it in my drunken state. There it was, in my own hands – the proof. His hand, on her thigh. Byron was turned in his chair, full attention on her, his other hand resting on the low back of her chair. She was doing the same, mirroring his posture and suggestive body language, pushing out her chest. It did *not* look innocent. No wonder he'd had the photo removed. He would've flipped out when he saw it online. And now, most likely, he would think he'd got away with it.

I wondered how many people had seen the post. Part of me wanted to go home and call Byron immediately. Except I knew he'd be hard to track down over there. But a big part of me wanted to see him face to face for this conversation. I stared at the photo for a moment longer, unable to snap out of it, and cursing under my breath.

"What's wrong?"

I clicked out of the image and locked the screen. Then I changed my mind and switched the phone off altogether, throwing it into Drew's glovebox. Out of sight. "Nothing," I said as "Pardon Me" started playing. "This," I said to Drew, "this is my favourite Incubus song." I leaned my head back against the headrest, my eyes closed.

"Now you're just copying me. This is *my* favourite."

"You said three songs. Don't be so greedy."

He laughed, and I relaxed into the seat, listening to the lyrics to take my mind off the photo. Jealous wouldn't exactly describe how I felt looking at it. Angry – yes. Disappointed – somewhat. But honestly, it didn't surprise me that much. To my knowledge, he'd never cheated on me in the past. Then again, I'd never felt like he fully trusted *me*. Not even in the beginning. And not once had I ever given him reason not to trust me.

Until I met Drew, that is. And even though nothing physical had happened, I knew it was deeper than that. That night I slept at his place after Mal died – it wasn't sexual. But it was the most intimate I'd felt with anyone, ever. I stole another glance at him. He had one hand on the steering wheel, the other resting on the gear stick.

I wanted them all over me.

I closed my eyes again, this time allowing myself to think those thoughts about Drew. Allowing myself to go to those thoughts I'd tried to keep buried all this time. Thoughts I knew I wasn't supposed to have. But they were there, and it was time to let them surface. Especially after that photo of Byron. As they say, a picture tells a thousand words.

Besides, it wouldn't mean anything would happen between Drew and me. But I was at least going to allow myself the luxury of imagining it.

The trouble was, I wasn't only attracted to Drew physically. He was so sweet, and loyal, and calm, and reliable. He was hilarious. And it was like he had this abundance of patience reserved just for me. No matter how prickly I was, or unpredictable, he was still so kind.

Was he simply a good guy, or did he actually like me? Often, I thought he did – and then at other times I thought he was just that type of guy. Always kind to everyone – like with the teenager at McDonald's.

I remembered the way he'd stood up for me at the Christmas party. Byron would never have done that. The way Drew responded to me on the day I'd seen the accident – compared to how Byron had responded.

I swallowed, pushing away the mixed feelings. The cold drink sat on my thigh, the water creating a dark patch on the T-shirt under it.

"Hey, are you all right?"

"Yeah." I paused. "Thanks. I'm just hungover."

He gave me a sweet smile. "Well, a swim will do you good. Salt water heals all, I reckon."

"Getting out of this car will do me good," I said, fanning myself. There was not a cloud in the sky and the sun was beating right down on us.

"Ah, come on, my driving's not that bad, is it?"

That smile. It was the cutest, most endearing smile I'd ever seen. And when it was directed at me, I felt something I'd never felt before. With anybody.

"It's not the driving I'm worried about. I just don't want to redecorate your interior."

He laughed hard at that. I took a deep breath and sat up in the seat. I actually *was* starting to feel slightly better. A frozen Coke – who would have thought.

"Ooh. Good tune," he said. "Living on a Prayer!" He started imitating Jon Bon Jovi … very badly. And with the wrong lyrics.

The frozen drink ended up lodged somewhere behind my nose, I snorted so hard at the deliberately awful, out-of-tune singing. If you could even call it that. "Yeah. Pretty sure those aren't the words, Drew."

He shrugged, singing animatedly and throwing his head back to project his voice, turning the song up a little more. By the time it finished, my cheeks hurt from laughing so much.

To my relief, Drew managed to get a parking spot quite close to the water. "Here we are. Gordons Bay. Fishies, here we come!"

He jumped out and opened up the back, pulling out two sets of snorkelling gear, a green shopping bag with beach towels and sunscreen, and a silver zip-up bag.

"I didn't bring the board – we can surf another time," he said. "This is a great spot for snorkelling."

"No way I could've attempted that in this state anyway," I

said, offering to carry some of the stuff. "Hey, what's that?" I pointed at the silver bag.

"A beach tent."

I burst out laughing.

"What?"

"A beach tent? Oh my god. You *are* eighty-nine!" I'm not sure why I found it so funny. Maybe I was still a touch drunk. But somehow, the image of big Drew in a little pop-up beach tent was very amusing.

He shrugged. "You'll thank me later."

We made our way down the steps to the tiny bay, which was thankfully less crowded on a Saturday morning than I had anticipated. Walking past the small wooden boats, we set our stuff down at one end of the beach. It dawned on me, as Drew was spreading out his beach towel, that I would soon have to be in a bikini in front of him. The thought made me shudder. Hangover-wise, I was feeling better by the minute, the cool sand between my toes providing instant stress relief somehow. God, I missed living by the beach. I took it all in. Clear blue water, the sound of curling waves crashing against the rocks, sunbathers dotting the golden sand.

I spread a towel out, too, grateful Drew had packed a spare, because I had, of course, forgotten to bring mine. He pulled his shirt off over his head, seemingly in slow motion, as I watched the muscles in his arms and stomach rippling under his skin as he moved.

Lord help me.

A group of teenage girls sitting a few metres away paused their conversation and stared in our direction.

It was certainly going to be a long day if I had to look at that for hours and not touch.

"Hey," he said, leaning over to grab something out of the beach bag, "mind chucking some of this on my back?" He handed me a bottle of 30+ sunscreen. "Would hate to get a patchy tan." He raised his eyebrows up and down quickly, grinning as he pivoted on the spot so I could reach his back, while rubbing some cream onto his face and chest.

I took a deep breath. *Good lord.* I squeezed some sunscreen onto my hand and touched his back carefully, like it was going to burn me. I rubbed it in slowly, careful not to miss any spots. My hand moved over his muscular back, fingers drifting slightly under the waistband at the back of his shorts. His body stiffened a little.

You're married, I reminded myself as I rubbed cream onto his neck, then finished by running my hands from his shoulders down his arms. I loved the feeling of his strong shoulders, the sunscreen lubricating our skin as my hands glided over his tanned body. The smell of the sunscreen and the salt in the air made me take a long breath in.

When I finished, I turned away, pulled my beach dress off over my head, and squeezed some sunscreen into my hands. I fiddled with the lid, trying not to get any sunscreen on it.

"Here," Drew said, grabbing the bottle and putting a hand on my shoulder to gently spin me around so he could do my back. Feeling his breath on my skin, I had to close my eyes momentarily as it prickled the tiny hairs on my neck. But being hungover with my eyes closed and trying to balance wasn't working for me, and I started to topple. Drew grabbed me, standing me up straight, chuckling. I swallowed as his hand moved over my back, the other one not letting go of my shoulder. His hand dipped under the knot at the back of my bikini, making sure not to miss any skin. He was taking his time applying the cream, making long, slow, deliberate movements. I wondered if it was on purpose. I couldn't help but close my eyes again, hangover or no hangover. Both of his hands slipped under the knot of my bikini. I wondered whether anyone was watching us, and if they could tell exactly what was going through my mind …

I really hoped not.

His hands moved away from each other, under the string, towards my sides, and I gasped as they brushed against the sides of my breasts.

I was sure he did *that* on purpose.

Before I knew it, he was done. I turned around to see him grabbing the snorkelling gear and making his way to the water awkwardly, and kind of in a hurry.

"Hey, aren't we supposed to wait until the sunscreen soaks in?"

He grinned at me, waist-deep in water already as he started putting his mask on.

"Waiting is overrated. You better come join me."

I stood on the beach, staring at Drew in the ocean as he winked at me from under his mask.

32

GEORGIE

The water didn't feel cold until I stuck my head below the surface. It took my breath away for a few seconds, but it was so refreshing that it seemed to physically dissolve my hangover. It was a strange sensation, having my face and body submerged in water, but still being able to breathe because of the mask and snorkel.

I had no idea so much colour existed beneath the surface. It made me feel pretty silly, to be honest, that I'd lived on the Australian coast and never snorkelled. I'd swum a lot, and spent a lot of time at the beach, but never seen what was truly underneath. And after seeing the marine life, I was in love.

Drew had laughed hard as I tried to hurry towards the water in my flippers, flinging sand everywhere. He was trying to catch his breath as he told me to walk backwards with them instead, or take them off until I reached the water. When I'd finally made it in, he wiped away tears of laughter from under his mask as he told me I looked like a newborn deer walking for the first time. I loved his laugh. It was warm and sweet, and the more I heard it, the more I fell in love with it. Being in the ocean, and with Drew, was the happiest I'd felt in months.

A bright yellow fish with black-and-white stripes swam past, getting close with a little bit of curiosity, then darting away when our eyes met. I smiled as much as I could with the snorkel in my mouth. The orange, pink, and yellow colours of the spongy coral shone from the ocean floor. I was swimming around to check out if there were any sea creatures hiding underneath the coral when I felt a tap on my shoulder. I turned to see Drew treading water, his head out above the surface.

I followed suit, bringing my head out of the water and taking the mask off for some fresh air. I spun around so I was facing him. He grinned at me, a faint red line across his forehead from the mask. "So?"

"It's frickin' *amazing*!" I said. "I'm so happy!" I knew the smile on my face was goofy and huge. And I didn't care. I was elated. I loved the ocean so much – it gave me this indescribable sense of peace; of freedom and joy. And my hangover was more or less gone, putting the cherry on top of what was already an incredible day. "I saw this … this weird squid thing – it came right up to me and everything!"

Drew's own smile went from ear to ear, the light green flecks in his eyes sparkling with the water's reflection. "There're a couple of sharks out a bit further. Wanna come see?"

"What?" My smile dropped. I must've had a panicked look on my face.

"Small reef sharks," he added quickly. "Not the sharks you're probably picturing!" He chuckled, then spat in the mask in his hand, spreading the saliva around the glass.

"What the hell are you doing?" I said, more curious than disgusted.

"It helps stop the fogging of the glass." He motioned to the mask on top of my head. "You should do it, too. Yours is really foggy." He put his mask in the water and washed it out. I hadn't even realised mine was foggy, but he was right. I took it off, eyeing Drew, and spat in it. "There you go," he said with a chuckle. "Now you're a real snorkeller!"

I laughed, rinsed it off in the salt water and put the mask back on so it was sitting on my forehead.

"Hold on a sec. You're all tangled." Treading water with his flippers, Drew adjusted something on the mask's strap at the back of my head, while I watched the low waves crashing into the rocks on my right. What a sound. The waves were gently pushing him into me. I could feel the hairs on his legs against mine in the water, his stomach against my back. My entire body was on fire in the cold water. And I might've imagined it, but it seemed like he lingered there a little. He brushed a small piece of seaweed off me as I moved to face him in the water, his fingers on my shoulder sending shivers down to my torso.

My body was buzzing with electricity. Had Byron ever turned me on like this? No. I'd never felt quite like this around anybody before.

We floated there for a moment, facing each other, our flippers occasionally making contact. He looked at me intently for a second, then smiled. It was so intense – I could clearly read his expression. He wanted me, too. I tried to snap out of the moment – before anything happened – but I couldn't tear my eyes away from him. The cool water lapped against my skin, Drew's body touching mine every few seconds as the playful waves pushed him towards me. His bearded smile, his dark hair which had started to curl in the salt water … I imagined what it would be like to kiss him right here, right now in the ocean. To taste the salt on his skin. His gaze drifted to my lips.

I wasn't strong enough to resist it if he tried. Not even close.

He turned away quickly, pulling the mask over his eyes.

"All right then," I said. "Show me these sharks. But if one bites me, you're not getting dinner tonight."

"I was going to get dinner tonight?" he said with his trademark lopsided grin.

Whoops. Guess I'd made an assumption. I put the snorkel in my mouth quickly and got back down in the water before he could ask more questions.

We swam side by side for a few metres, and as the water got deeper, the visibility got worse. I looked around me but couldn't see much. It was a bit scary, like we were out in the open ocean, totally alone. And it was silent except for the crackling sound of the water in my ears – another thing I'd never really experienced before. Eerie, and incredible at the same time. Drew tapped me on the shoulder underwater and pointed to his left. I couldn't see anything, but he made a waving motion with his hand for me to follow him.

Then he grabbed my hand and pulled me towards something. He stopped swimming and let his body float on the surface of the water. I did the same, copying him. Staying on the surface, gazing down, was so effortless, but such a wonderful feeling. We floated together, still holding hands. My heart thumped. He pointed down and squeezed my hand. I squeezed it back.

There was a shark about half a metre in length, with protruding eyes and black-and-grey patchy skin. My first shark! It swam along the ocean floor, quickly darting left to right, just as I caught sight of another one not far away. Drew turned to me and gave me a thumbs-up with the hand that wasn't holding mine, like he was checking I was okay. I nodded. And then all of a sudden, he let my hand go and dived down towards the sharks, keeping a fair distance away from them, but almost touching the sand at the bottom.

I watched in awe from the surface as he swam alongside the beautiful creatures, streaks of the sun's rays shining into the water and onto Drew's body. He moved through the water so effortlessly. I watched him until he finally came back towards the surface and we both came up for air, taking off our masks.

"Amazing, huh?"

"I saw sharks! Can't wait to ring my family and freak them out."

He chuckled. "Well, I might start heading back in soon. We can have another snorkel before we head home. I'm getting hungry."

My stomach grumbled at the thought of food. "Me too, actually."

As we swam back to the shore together, I felt a bit disappointed it was over – but a bit relieved, too. Being with Drew in such close proximity, with such a minimal amount of clothing on, was less than ideal. I was starting to lose all my willpower. The sun, sand, and salt were not helping the cause. I'd felt on top of the world being in the ocean – and with Drew – with little care about the consequences.

Drew set up the tent as I took the mask off my head, wincing as the soft plastic ripped into my hair. It had all become a giant tangled mess despite Drew's best efforts. The beach tent was like a standard two-person tent, except one side was completely open, facing the beach. We crawled in, the beach towels spread out next to each other in the shade.

"That sun is brutal," I said.

"So, don't you have something to say to me then?"

"Yeah. I just did. The sun is brutal."

"And?"

I sighed dramatically. "Okay, fine. You win. The tent was a good idea." I said the last bit in a disgruntled voice, but I couldn't help smiling at the same time.

He laughed loudly. "God, you're cute."

I blushed, suddenly very aware that I was in a bikini. I hadn't missed any of Drew's looks, either. He lay down on his side, resting on his elbow and propping himself up so he was facing me. I lay on my back, staring upwards, not wanting to face him. We were way too close inside the tent as it was.

"Hey," he said softly.

I swallowed. "Yeah?"

"Thanks for coming today. It's been fun."

"Yeah, it has. Thanks for bringing me. Those sharks were so cool. But my favourite was that squid! Oh my god. And so much coral. Those pink sponge ones were amazing!"

He chuckled. "Glad you liked it."

My eyes trailed down along his shorts to his left shin. "What's that scar from?" I said, pointing to a jagged white line running down just under his knee. Considering how little clothing Drew liked to wear, surprisingly I'd never noticed it.

"An accident when I was … ten?"

"I hope it's a good story …"

"Not so much. I fell down the stairs at home. Compound fracture and big tear down my leg."

I winced. "Oh, yuck!"

"Mmm."

"What were you doing?"

"Running away."

"From?"

"A kid's worst nightmare."

I frowned. "Maths homework? A gruesome horror movie?"

"Worse. Parents having sex."

I froze, then burst out laughing. "Oh my god. That is a great story. There're some things you can never un-see."

"You're not wrong."

I rolled onto my side to face him, mirroring the way he was propped up on his elbow. "One time, back in Italy, we were going through my nonna's stuff after she passed away. And we found," I paused for effect, "a *huge* stash of her old *Playboy* and

Penthouse magazines."

"No way. Are you sure they were hers?"

"A hundred percent. One was even signed and made out to her and her husband."

He started laughing. "Wow."

"Yeah. They were so old school, the pornos, from the seventies and eighties – there were all these hilarious photos, like naked chicks feeding dolphins and stuff. One of the magazines even came with those cardboard 3D glasses."

"Oh my god. That is gold! I hope you kept them, or at least took some photos!"

"We sure did."

It took us a while to compose ourselves. Eventually Drew looked at me. "There's something I need to tell you."

My stomach flipped. *No. Don't say it.*

His expression softened, and he gave me a cheeky look. "Speaking of porn, your left boob is out."

I froze for a split second, too mortified to move. My hand shot up to my chest and felt skin. And nipple. I shrieked, horrified that his statement was, in fact, true.

"No!" I quickly pulled the white material back to where it should've been, burying my face in my hands. "Oh my god. I'm *so* embarrassed."

Drew laughed. "Hey. Don't worry about it. I'm sure nobody on the beach was complaining."

"What do you— How long was it like that?" I asked, peering through my fingers a little. My face was red hot.

"Hmm … Not that long. Since just before the sharks."

"*What?*" I yelped.

Drew held up his hands in defence. "Hey, I showed you the Port Jackson sharks – and you showed me the white pointer in return." He grinned as I threw my beach dress at him, the closest thing I could find. "Ah, Georgie throwing her clothes at me. What a day this has been!"

By this point, I had tears streaming down my face in laughter. "You're such a jerk! You let me lie here and have those conversations with you that whole time!"

He shrugged, laughing. "Well, I knew you'd be embarrassed."

"So you just let me lie here? Oh, god. Thanks for nothing!"

We were in hysterics.

"Well, I might go and get some water from up the road," he said eventually. "Do you want some? I'm parched. And some food."

"Yes, please. Want me to come?"

"Nah. Chill here. Enjoy the peace and quiet. And," he said, raising his eyebrows quickly up and down, "the amazingly awesome tent."

When he took off, I searched my bag for my phone, remembering I'd left it turned off and in Drew's glovebox. That actually filled me with relief. There was no need to check it right now anyway. I lay back, making a pillow for my head out of my dress, and reached my arms out behind me.

Drew's phone started ringing on the towel next to mine, making me jump. I was surprised he'd left it there. Byron never, ever went anywhere without his phone. He would never leave it lying around alone with me. I thought about that for a moment before glancing at Drew's phone again. His mum was calling him, a photo of her face flashing on the screen. Her eyes were kind and warm, and green like Drew's. I hesitated, then let it ring out. What would I say anyway? It's not like she'd have any idea who I was.

When Drew came back, he startled me from a deep sleep. "Oh, sorry," he said as I sat up and rubbed my eyes.

"That's okay, I ... How long were you gone?"

"Maybe twenty minutes?" He had two brown bags in his

hands. He sat down cross-legged on the towel, facing me, and took out two mangoes and a punnet of strawberries that looked freshly washed. "Lunch?" He used a pocketknife on one of the mangoes on top of the brown bag, cutting off two sides and then slicing diagonal lines into it. He pushed the skin, fanning out the diamond shapes and offering it to me. My mouth was watering at the sight of the juicy yellow fruit.

"Do you always have a pocketknife with you?" I said.

"Yes, I keep one in the Hilux for all mango-related emergencies."

I devoured the sweet, cold piece of fruit and looked at him with admiration, before he cut up the other mango and opened the box of strawberries. We sat and ate them together in silence.

"What made you get fruit for lunch?" I said. "I kind of pegged you as a fish-and-chips kind of guy."

"Perhaps. But I'm with Georgie I-Don't-Eat-Take-Away-Food de Luca, so I went to the little fruit shop instead."

"Seriously?"

"It's no big deal," he said with a shrug. "I love fruit. Not to mention, it does wonders for a hangover."

I paused with a strawberry in my hand, staring at him.

"What?"

"Nothing. You're just … really thoughtful." My stomach grumbled. I actually felt like some of the greasy food he'd mentioned earlier, but I didn't want to say anything to him, when he'd already gone out of his way for me. I thought for a moment, then said, "Do you think I'm a snob?"

He snorted with laughter. "No. Why would I think that?"

"I dunno. I'm picky with my food."

"Not eating junk food isn't snobby. It's healthy. There's a big difference."

"Hmm. But I'm so annoying."

"Care to elaborate?"

"I dunno, I just … This entire time, since I met you, I mean, I feel like I haven't been myself. Like I've been … I dunno. Blunt. And annoying."

He considered this. "I don't know about blunt – and definitely not annoying. Honest, maybe. You say it like it is. Those aren't negative traits, Georgie. I think you know what you want, and you go for it. I … I like that about you."

I sighed. "I feel like you've been so nice this whole time. And I'm just a cranky bitch."

"Well, what's making you feel so cranky?"

Probably the fact that I have feelings for you and can't do anything about it.

"I'm not sure," I said.

"Okay. Well, you might work it out sooner or later. But I think you're being pretty hard on yourself."

"Drew?"

"Yeah?" he mumbled through the strawberry he'd popped in his mouth, making us both giggle.

"Don't laugh. But I think I want some fish and chips, too. Is there a place nearby where I can go get us some? I think I need the salty—"

Before I could finish, he reached behind him and brought out the second paper bag, pulling out a white tray with a pile of chips on it. It was covered in yellow salt. "Chips with extra chicken salt. I couldn't resist. I couldn't buy the fish, though, after looking at them in the water all day. I felt too guilty," he said with an embarrassed laugh.

Good lord. This guy.

I laughed as well, taking a handful of chips and shoving them in my mouth. "But don't you spearfish?"

"Well, yeah … I know. It's hypocritical. But I've always

thought spearing was better than regular fishing."

I stuffed more chips in my mouth. I couldn't get enough. "How so?"

"Well, I guess," he said as he copied me and put a handful of salty chips in his mouth, "it's different to fishing in that you can see what you're catching. You can get exactly what you want. No chance of catching any baby fish. And, if you know what you're doing, it makes it faster. They're not dangling on a line for ages, scared, out of water. It's speared, killed, and done and dusted."

I considered the statement. "Makes sense."

"I mean, you still get the idiots who don't know what they're doing, or do the wrong thing on purpose." He shook his head. "I dunno. Sometimes I think I'd rather just be a vegetarian."

"I've thought about it, too. But I think my family of Italian chefs would kill me."

"Worth it."

We wolfed all the hot chips down, still laughing. He watched me as I licked all my fingers and pressed my index finger onto the tray to catch the tiny crunchy bits of chips and chicken salt at the bottom.

"Why don't you just lick the whole tray?" he said, pretending to be disgusted.

So I picked up the tray and licked it theatrically, making him collapse onto the towel in laughter. When I'd packed up the rubbish, I lay down next to him on my towel. He looked at me for a moment before his expression turned serious.

"There *was* actually something else I wanted to tell you."

I froze. "Yeah?"

"When I lost … When Mal died, I was devastated." His gaze dropped to the ground and my chest tightened at the memory. Tightened with guilt. He looked back up at me. "But the thing that got me through it all was knowing that you were with him.

Right 'til the end. You were with him in his final moments and he knew he was loved." His chin quivered ever so slightly. "I'm so thankful that he wasn't alone. I'm so grateful for what you did. It makes me feel so relieved for him."

I couldn't handle it any more. A tear rolled down my cheek as he continued looking down at his towel. I moved in and put my arm around his waist, instantly feeling like this was where I was meant to be. Here, now ... Together. Touching, comforting Drew; feeling his soft skin against mine.

"Thank you," he whispered, then cleared his throat.

"I'm so sorry he's gone, Drew."

"Me too."

He brushed a strand of my hair behind my ear, sighing. "I wish things were different."

And I knew he wasn't just talking about Mal any more.

3 3

D R E W

I stole another glance at her in the passenger seat next to me, hair sitting on her bare shoulders, all wild and wavy from the ocean. Natural – as though she were free. It was almost eight p.m., and the sky only had a few hints of pink and red left on the horizon. It had been a breathtaking sunset, and it made me wish we were on the west coast, watching the sun go down over the ocean.

Just spending the day with Georgie, I was the luckiest man alive.

And if she were single, nothing could have kept me from telling her how I felt.

She'd seemed completely comfortable around me today. She'd hugged me; she'd smiled. She'd comforted me about Mal. She'd seemed ... *herself*, finally. I wondered if it meant she was happy being just friends. If she wasn't – if she had any feelings for me, then today would have been the perfect day to say something. The whole day had felt so ... intimate. But she hadn't said anything. And come to think of it, all she had really said last night when she was drunk was that she thought I was good-looking. And nice.

But she'd never said she liked me.

I sighed, driving along the highway towards home, feeling puzzled, and remembering the way she hadn't even batted an eyelid when the entire Sydney Roosters footy team had come wading into the ocean in their tight Speedos, all oily and tanned and ripped, enough to make any guy self-conscious. She hadn't given them so much as a glance, keeping her eyes fixed on me in the tent the whole time instead.

Talk about confusing times.

She reached for the glovebox, then seemed to think twice, and leaned back into her seat. Her feet were up on my dash, her legs golden from today's sun. The towel she'd wrapped around herself before we got in the car, after insisting on one final swim, had loosened, and was now only covering the seat.

And that meant she was just in her bikini sitting next to me. It was all I could do to keep my eyes on the road. Not to mention, the day wasn't over yet – she was cooking me dinner. The thought of spending more time with her made my heart swell. But a sinking feeling shared the space, too. *Nothing can ever happen here.* Why, why, why did she have to be married? If I wanted to keep seeing her, then I would have to accept the friendship.

"So," I looked over at her, "are you still up for cooking? What should we make?"

"You mean, what should *I* make?"

"Trust me when I say that you cooking will be the best outcome for us both."

"Right," she said with a laugh. "Well, following our no-fish theme, I was thinking of doing a gnocchi with basil pesto and pecorino, and a vanilla pannacotta with mulberries and a pistachio crumb."

I gaped at her. "Are you a fictional character in my wildest food dreams?"

"I have one rule though." She paused, and I nodded for her to continue. "No stealing any of the food 'til it's ready."

"No such promises can be made." I returned her smile as a phone call lit up the inside of my car, the word "Mum" flashing across the display.

"Oh," Georgie said, "I forgot to tell you she rang before when you went to get food."

My finger hovered on the green answer button. "Yeah, I saw that – do you mind if I get it?"

"No, no, not at all," she said hurriedly, waving towards the screen.

I pressed the button. "Hi, Mum."

"Darling," her warm voice came through the loudspeaker, "how are you?"

"Yeah, I'm good thanks. You? Oh – I'm just driving home … with a friend. You're on speaker."

"Gotcha. So it's lucky this old shagger didn't say anything embarrassing then, huh?"

Georgie struggled to stifle a laugh.

"Well, I won't keep you then," Mum continued. "I wanted to double check when you were leaving again?"

"That's all good. Monday morning."

"As in, the day after tomorrow?"

"Yep."

"Right." There was a pause, and my heart dropped. It couldn't be easy for a mum to deal with this kind of information. "Okay, darling, well I hope—"

"Let's do a video call tomorrow night, okay?" I interrupted her.

"Sounds good," she said in a soft voice. "Love you, Drew."

"Love you too, Mum. I'll speak to you soon."

As I hung up, Georgie turned to me curiously. "Where are you going on Monday?"

I'd avoided this. Not because I didn't want her to know – it was just something I hadn't even wanted to think about too much myself. I always knew it would happen eventually, but simply knowing it didn't make it any more real.

I cleared my throat. "I'm being deployed on Monday."

"Oh?" She turned her body so she was fully facing me now, legs curled under her on the seat. "How long for?"

"Uh, six months, at least."

"Six *months*?"

I took a deep breath in, knowing exactly what her next question would be.

"Where to?"

I hesitated. "It's … It's actually classified."

She was silent for a moment. "I'm guessing it isn't a tropical holiday destination."

I nodded, looking at her and smiling matter-of-factly. "It's in the Middle East."

Her expression changed instantly, like someone had flicked a switch. "What the hell, Drew?" She sat up suddenly, bolt upright. "Why didn't you tell me?"

The question took me by surprise. I took a right turn onto our street, realising I probably should've gone straight to the shops to buy the ingredients for our dinner, instead. But it seemed I had bigger things to worry about now. "Uh, I didn't … Well …" I scratched my head, then sighed. "I only found out a couple of weeks ago. And also, I don't have Mal to think about any more."

"You're going to a war zone for half a year, and you didn't even tell me? What the hell?"

"Hold on. Why are you so worked up about this?"

She put a hand to her forehead. "Are you kidding me?"

"No. What's the problem?"

She let out a sigh, staring out of the passenger window instead of facing me. Talk about a strong reaction to my news. I was confused. Confusion seemed to be the common feeling whenever I was with her, and it was getting a bit old.

"All right, Georgie. How about you just tell me what you're really thinking?" I looked at her. "Just be honest with me." *Say it. Say you have feelings for me.*

I was shocked at her reaction, but it was probably high time we started actually being honest with each other anyway. If there was nothing there from her side, my going away shouldn't be such an issue. Her words and her actions were so very different.

She continued staring out the window into the darkness, then put a thumb to her lip and started chewing the nail. I pulled the car up at the front of my house and switched off the engine. The air between us felt different now. Tense and unfamiliar, again – like it had been at the start. My heart sank.

We sat in silence as the interior light went out, neither of us addressing the elephant in the room. I let my eyes get used to the dark. There was only a faint glow coming in from a couple of streetlights.

"Look, I … I'm sorry, Georgie. It's been—"

"Don't," she whispered, not turning towards me.

"I'm really sorry. I guess I should've mentioned it." I wasn't really sure if that was true. If she didn't have feelings for me, why was this such a big thing? I was still confused, but reality was beginning to sink in. Whatever this was, whatever was happening between Georgie and me, she *was* bothered by the deployment. And not just a little. It killed me seeing her upset. And I had no idea what else to say.

Without really thinking, I put my hand on top of hers and squeezed it, her skin warm in mine, my heart beating in my throat. Maybe it was too much, but I wanted her to know I was here. And I was sorry. I wished so badly I could read her thoughts.

She gazed at me with misty eyes.

"Georgie …"

She looked down at my hand, then slowly turned hers around and threaded her fingers through mine. My hand twitched, bolts of electricity running up my arm and into my body as she faced me. Her eyes were wide and soft, studying mine. And for a split second, I could see into her soul.

I knew what was coming next. And I didn't know if I could handle it.

Our eyes stayed locked for a few seconds, neither of us acting. The silence around me was piercing.

She leaned closer to me slowly, studying me. And she held my gaze as she gently started stroking my face.

She's going to kiss me.

Goosebumps spread across my chest, my heart thundering, as she moved closer. Her lips brushed against mine, breath soft on my face. The smell of the sunscreen on her skin made me breathe in deeply and close my eyes. And then, I tasted the ocean salt on her lips as she finally pushed them into mine, kissing me softly. Her hands moved around to the back of my neck as she started kissing me harder.

The floor spun under me. *Georgie is kissing me.* The soft moans she was letting out between kisses, and the feel of her tongue on mine, were working me up fast. I was in heaven.

"Georgie," I muttered against her lips, but she ignored me, immersed in what she was doing. "Is this … Is this a good idea?" I whispered.

She looked at me like I was absurd before closing her eyes and kissing me again, one hand against my chest. Warmth spread through my body. I was floating, somehow numb but also feeling everything.

"Move your seat back," she instructed, making my body tense with anticipation, her breath hot on my neck. I fumbled with the lever to push the seat back as far as it'd go, doing what I was told. She watched me intently, hands still on me, but neither of us moved. Not allowing my brain to think too hard, I grabbed her around the waist and lifted her up onto me so she was sitting sideways on my lap. For a split second, everything froze. Georgie – on my lap – in just a bikini. I couldn't breathe; I couldn't think. She lowered her face to me and kissed me again, biting my lower lip gently and pushing down into me. "Oh, god, Drew," she whispered.

I was well and truly hard.

"Georgie," I repeated. I was two people right now. One who never, ever wanted this to stop. And one who thought this was a *very* bad idea. I glanced at her house, then away quickly. "What are we doing?"

She pulled back with one hand under my shirt, pressed against my chest. "Well, Drew, we're doing this thing called kissing, and," she said, making a point of looking down at my lap, "you seem to be enjoying it *very* much."

I slid a finger under her bikini top and pulled her back to me. "Smartass. I *am* enjoying it. Very much so. I'm just … I'm not sure it's a wise decision?"

What the hell are you doing, Drew? I couldn't believe those words had left my own mouth.

Luckily for me, she was not easily discouraged. "This is a very wise decision." She ran a hand along my thigh and looked up and down my body, sending shockwaves pulsing to my torso. "Remember at the beach today," she said, kissing my neck, "when you said I know what I want, and I go for it?"

"Mmm?"

"Well, I know what I want, and I'm going for it."

My heart was pounding so hard it was going to spring out of my chest.

"Drew, I've wanted this for weeks. No. I've wanted *you* for weeks. Months, even. Do you know how much I think about you?" She shook her head as though she didn't believe it herself.

I couldn't believe it. But no words came. I wrapped my arms around her waist, studying her neck, her arms, her hands that were moving all over my body, and kissed her.

"Here's what I want," she said, grabbing the back of my neck and threading her fingers through my hair, sending a shiver through me. Her expression was serious as she leaned down and sucked on my bottom lip. "I want to have sex with you, *all night long.*"

I thought I was going to pass out. *How is this happening?*

She trailed a hand down my chest, tracing my pecs. Yep, I was definitely going to pass out. I didn't think it was possible to get any more turned on, but clearly I was wrong. And almost instantly, the second person in me disappeared – the voice of reason, the logic.

It's happening.

She was so beautiful. And she sure as hell was determined. The little moans she was making were driving me wilder by the second. She kissed my neck, her heat sending electric pulses through me. Pulling back to look at me for a second with big eyes, she paused. "Is this … Are you okay with this? You haven't said anything in a while," she said with a sweet laugh.

Am I okay with this? With kissing the most beautiful woman I've ever seen, the woman I've been fantasising about for months, the woman I would do anything for?

I cleared my throat. "I'm the luckiest guy in the world. You are so beautiful."

And I am so in love with you.

"I'm the lucky one," she said, one eyebrow arched. Then she kissed me again, her breasts pushing into my chest. I slid a hand up her leg, along her smooth skin, and then over the soft fabric of her bikini top. She leaned back, her wavy beach hair cascading down her front, before I gathered it at the back of her neck and moved it off her breasts, savouring the view. Her nipples were hard, and she gasped as I took her breasts in my hands.

"Take off my top," she whispered.

I didn't need to be told twice. Running my hands down along her spine, like when I'd put the sunscreen on her, I found where the string was tied and pulled it free, sending sand flying everywhere.

She giggled. "Your car's gonna be full of sand. Sorry!"

I yanked the top off her completely. "I couldn't give a shit about the car."

"Wow," she said, "I think that's the first time I've ever heard you swear!" She ran a hand up my thigh again, like she couldn't get enough of me. I still couldn't wrap my head around the fact this was happening. And it was happening fast. Georgie – half naked and kissing me – in the darkness of my car. My heartbeat quickened as her hand drifted higher and higher up my thigh. She leaned forward and trailed her fingers underneath the waistband of my boardshorts.

"No briefs under those boardies," she mused.

"Nope."

"Excellent."

She grabbed the bottom of my T-shirt and lifted it up. I awkwardly helped her pull it off over my head. These movements were all a little tricky in the car. But I wasn't going to complain.

"Drew?" she said, leaning back and looking at me with her hands on my waist.

"Yeah?"

"I will never, ever," she shook her head, "tell you to put a T-shirt on, ever again. Because you are *so* damn hot without one."

I chuckled. "So I can wash my car shirtless then, without being told off?"

"You can walk around naked for the rest of your entire life and I wouldn't tell you off."

Something inside me melted a bit more every time she smiled at me like that. All the muscles in her face seemed to relax. Happiness and warmth had taken over her expression. But her body was tense, wanting more.

"What if I get arrested for walking around the streets naked?" I said as she swept a sweaty strand of my hair behind my ear. The car was heating up fast without the air conditioning on, the afternoon heat lingering in the dark, our hot bodies steaming up the windows.

She shrugged. "I'd come visit you in jail."

I laughed, pulling her closer and wincing as my elbow made contact with the car door.

"Well … This is a little awkward," she said, trying to catch her breath. It made my heart skip a beat. It hadn't felt awkward to me at all. It had felt totally right, and I'd thought that's how she'd felt, too, until she said those words. She noticed my puzzled expression. "Oh, I mean here in the car." Relief washed over me. "It's great, don't get me wrong, but it's a bit …" She motioned towards the handbrake under her leg. "How do you feel about going inside to yours?"

How do I feel about going inside to have sex with Georgie?

"Going inside with you sounds like all my Christmases coming at once," I said. Good – I didn't have any condoms with me anyway.

She put both her hands on my bare chest. Her kisses continued – sweet, warm, and fast. "Good. Because I want you *so* bad." She pulled back, watching me like a lioness with its prey.

And I did not mind being Georgie's prey.

The image of being naked in bed with her was almost too much. My hand flailed to open the car door as I kissed her back wildly, the cool air hitting us once I finally managed, goosebumps forming on my skin from the contact.

She climbed out and covered her chest with one arm, searching for my hand in the dark with the other. When she found it, she pulled me towards my front door and I followed her like a lost puppy, not even bothering to lock the car. I fumbled to find the main door key as Georgie stood behind me, wrapping her arms around my waist and touching my stomach and chest. A shiver ran down my spine as she kissed my back.

Come on, stupid door. My hand was shaking as I momentarily forgot which key went into the deadlock. *Goddammit.*

Georgie's hand snaked its way down my stomach from behind and dipped down into the front of my shorts, the sound catching in my throat as her warm fingers wrapped around me. The whole door-opening process, which was proving to be difficult for me anyway, was slowed down as her hand started moving. I groaned, closing my eyes.

When the key finally turned, we stumbled inside. She tore open the velcro at the front of my board shorts and pushed them to the ground. I picked her up, her legs wrapping around my waist, the front of her pressing against me. Exactly like last night, except this time, she was completely sober, and almost totally naked. Only her bikini bottoms were on her now. I walked us to my bedroom through the dark hallway, feeling around for the door with my free hand. I flicked on the hallway light, making us both squint a little, then headed into the bedroom.

"I can't believe we're doing this," she whispered in my ear. She pulled back to look at me. I was about to ask if she was okay, when she added, "*Finally.*"

I ripped back the sheets and gently threw her onto my bed,

the light from the hallway streaming into the otherwise dark bedroom, casting a faint tinge of light on us. Georgie – on my bed in only a pair of white bikini bottoms. The image would be forever stamped into my memory. She reached for me and pulled me down on top of her, running her hands over my shoulders and chest, then down along the muscles near my hips. Kissing my bottom lip, she groaned as I pressed further into her.

"Condom?" she asked.

I nodded, pausing. "Georgie, are you sure you w—"

"Drew. If you don't have sex with me right *now,* I will arrest you myself." She grabbed my hand that was on her breast and slid it down along her stomach and into her bikini bottoms. I closed my eyes again involuntarily. Her voice like honey, she whispered in my ear, "Now take these off me."

My breath caught inside my throat as I opened the bedside drawer, took out a condom with a shaky hand, and ripped open the wrapper. When I was ready and hovering over her, she ran her hands up my arms, then slid out from under me, moving me onto my back on the bed before crawling on top of me on her hands and knees. I pulled down her bikini bottoms, the final item of clothing left between us. She slowly lowered herself onto me, the heat from her stomach and breasts radiating onto my chest.

And it was here. All the times I'd thought of her over the last few months. All the times I'd wished I could spend just one more moment with her. The moments, the thoughts, the desire: it was all here, as Georgie moved on top of me with a determined rhythm. She closed her eyes as my hands moved over her back, her thighs, her arms, taking in her gorgeous body. I was pulled into another universe, where it was just us two alone, floating in darkness. Time didn't exist; I couldn't get enough of her. Slowly, I was dragged back to earth by her deep moans. Gripping her tight, I looked at her as she put a sweaty hand on my chest to prop herself up before she couldn't hold herself up any longer. She came down onto me, covered my mouth with hers, biting down on my bottom lip as she moaned into me for the final time. And I couldn't hold on any more, erupting into spasms that mirrored hers.

I was euphoric, shaking under her, meaningless thoughts taking over my mind. I closed my eyes, feeling her skin and breath against me. We gripped each other into a stillness that I'd never imagined possible. She lay on me, our chests heaving, hot and sweaty. My hands sat on her hips and I kissed her, coming to my senses slowly, tasting the salt on her skin again.

I loved the way she lay on me. I loved the way her caramel hair fell down in unruly waves around her face and sat softly on my shoulders. I loved the way we lay there together, still as one, her head turned to the side on my chest. Her hand twitched as it rested on my chest, and when my hand joined hers, she let our fingers slip through each other's and squeezed mine softly. We lay wordlessly for a few minutes, and every single muscle in my body felt heavy and relaxed. It was like a huge hit of Valium – my pulse was slow, like my heart couldn't be bothered to pump blood around my body any longer.

And yet, my heart was so full.

Georgie lifted her head with a lot of effort. Putting her chin onto the top of my chest, her eyes met mine and she smiled. "Holy. Shit."

I squeezed her hand. "Are you … okay?" Even saying those three words sapped me of any energy left.

She nodded, closing her eyes briefly before looking up at me again. "Glorious, actually." She lifted her head when my chest started moving from my laughter. A tiny part of me was worried she would freak out afterwards, that once the physical need was out of her system, the emotional stuff might get to her. But instead, she rolled over to my side and put an arm around me, her head resting on my shoulder. I got up carefully and went to the bathroom, and when I returned, I slipped back into the same position with her wrapped around me, pulling a sheet over the top of us.

I'd never felt this sated before in my entire life.

I didn't want to sleep. I didn't want this night to end, ever. Having her there, holding her, was so much better than I could have ever imagined. I rolled onto my side so I was facing her and put one arm around her bare waist.

A strange expression crossed her face. I didn't think she was going to sleep anytime soon, either.

"Do you think I'm a bad person?" she said, forehead lines slightly visible.

"No," I said without hesitating. I paused, wanting to add something, but not sure what. I kissed her on the forehead instead.

She lifted up her hand that was holding mine, examining our hands linked together. "You know this isn't … It's not just …" She paused, considering her words. "I really like you, Drew."

"I know. Me too." I kissed her on the lips.

"This is so messed up," she said, unlinking her hand from mine and drawing circles on my skin with one finger.

"Yeah." It was true. I had no idea what her plan was. And part of me was too scared to ask; too scared to hear the answer.

"Can we … Can we pretend it's just you and me, and no one else, tonight? No thinking or talking."

I nodded in agreement and we lay there, for what felt like eternity, in silence. Eventually, she lifted the sheet and moved her hand down my chest, allowing her fingers to roam all around my body. She propped herself up so she was lying on her front with her chin in one hand. Her eyes were devious as her hand continued moving south down along my stomach. She winked when it met its target. "So. I guess it's your turn."

"What for?" I said, putting a finger under her chin and tilting it towards me so I could kiss her again.

"Being on top." She grinned, gazing down at me.

"Gladly."

"Good. Because I did all the work the first time."

We dissolved in laughter.

"I could look at you naked," she whispered as she kissed me, "all. Day. Long."

I couldn't get over this new version of Georgie. The way the corners of her mouth creased when she smiled, the faint dimples in her soft skin, the blush of her cheeks and her defined cheekbones. So raw, so honest. And this kind of honesty I could get on board with. I groaned as I returned her kiss, so happy I didn't know what to do with myself. Then I climbed on top of her, kissing her neck and chin before moving down to her breasts and letting my tongue roll over her nipples. Her moans sounded better than any music I'd ever heard as I slowly kissed my way down her stomach.

34

GEORGIE

I woke up euphoric, with an Incubus song on repeat in my head, the sweet melody competing with the low hum of Drew's air conditioning. I opened my eyes slowly. It was still dark, not even five at a guess. I was warm in the sheets, the air conditioning cooling my neck and shoulders – the contrast strangely comforting.

I had sex with Drew.

Happiness swelled in my chest. Our naked limbs were a tangled mess, my arm around Drew, a leg between his somewhere. His naked butt was pressed against my stomach. Waking up next to Drew felt so right.

My face was pressed awkwardly between his shoulder blades. I pulled back a little, worried about drooling on him. Although I tried my best not to move too much, he stirred, then stiffened.

"Damn," he murmured.

"What?" I said, my voice still croaky. "What's wrong?"

He turned around under the sheet and under my arm, so he faced me with his sleepy eyes. "How did I end up as Little Spoon?"

I studied his face, then burst out laughing. "There's nothing wrong with being Little Spoon!"

"There's plenty wrong with *me* being Little Spoon. And having my butt in your face."

I laughed again, slightly concerned about my morning breath. "It wasn't *in* my face. And it's a nice butt. I like it." I paused. "How funny is the word 'butt'?"

He chuckled, then moved closer to me and kissed my forehead. "Are you always this funny in the morning?"

"Are you always this sexy in the morning?" I said, lifting the sheets for another peek. Drew's body. I knew it was good. I'd seen him shirtless enough times. But that wasn't the same as being in bed with him, fully naked, and getting to look and touch as often as I wanted.

It was heaven. I hadn't felt this happy, or this satisfied, in months. Nothing else mattered – I couldn't care less about anything outside of this room.

That is, if I didn't think beyond today, beyond this moment. If I did, I was sure my mind would go to dark places I didn't yet want to explore. I wanted to savour this morning with Drew. Before I had to return to reality.

And before he went into a war zone.

I squeezed my eyes shut, forcing those thoughts out of my head. I didn't need to try to focus on something else for too long – soon, he was kissing my neck with his drawn-out, slow kisses.

"Are you tired?" he said, an arm curling around my waist. I could feel him against me under the covers, already hard, sending shocks of hot electricity skyrocketing up my torso.

"Not *that* tired," I said, running my hands along his back.

I tried to maintain some sense of sanity as he moved his naked body against mine. *I had sex with Drew last night. Twice.* And he showed no signs of wanting to slow down.

I closed my eyes. *I could do this forever.*

*

I sat next to Drew, legs draped across his lap, my neck against the cool edge as the water fizzled around me. I'd always loved jacuzzis – the bubbly water, the coloured lights; the fact that when you were in one, it was usually with mates, relaxing with a drink. Or on a holiday.

But this was something else. The sun still wasn't up, and Drew and I were sitting in his hot jacuzzi in the dark, the jets and the occasional birds the only sounds we could hear, waiting for sunrise.

We were exhausted. At least, I was. Emotionally and physically. Sitting in the dark, tingling from the hot water that was leaving tiny bubbles all over my skin, I couldn't think of a time I'd felt more relaxed.

Drew had this special way of making me feel calm, no matter what. I felt like everything would be okay when I was in his presence. He sat in silence next to me with his head leaning back, eyes closed, the same way I was. His hand sat on top of my thigh, a thumb slowly rubbing against my skin. I was floating somewhere between being turned on again and falling asleep from being so relaxed. He was the best kind of meditation. And I'd loved his idea of watching the sunrise from the jacuzzi after neither of us was able to get back to sleep.

"You hungry?" his voice floated across to me quietly, breaking my meditative state. I couldn't bring myself to open my eyes.

"For your lovin'? Always."

He laughed so loudly that my eyes sprung open, snapping me awake. I turned my head and smiled at his silhouette, eyes slowly adjusting to his face.

"More specifically," he said, "I mean food. Would you like some breakfast?"

"I'm definitely hungry. But *way* too lazy to do anything about it."

It wasn't surprising we were hungry; we hadn't eaten since the fruit and hot chips at the beach. Nothing for dinner. He squeezed my leg. "Stay here. I'll be back."

I opened my eyes slightly and watched Drew hop out, a cloud of steam surrounding him, water running down thick, muscled thighs. I admired the shape of his chest and arms in the dark as he dried himself with a towel, before disappearing into the house. And as soon as he was out of my sight, someone else appeared in his place.

Byron.

I'd done a pretty good job of blocking him out in the last thirty hours. Of which at least sixteen were spent in Drew's bed. Once alone. And once … not.

I reminded myself of the photo of Byron and the woman. He'd probably been doing the same thing. *Stop trying to justify it. He might be sleeping with someone else. But you* definitely *are.*

I closed my eyes, remembering the way Drew had touched me, the spasms of pleasure throughout my entire body. The way he whispered in my ear, telling me exactly what he wanted … The way he kept asking if I was okay. How gentle he was.

I have to end it.

Drew walked out with a towel around his waist, carrying a plate. Light was starting to drift across the backyard ever so slightly.

I have to end it with Byron because I'm falling in love with someone else. Truth was – I'd known this for a while. I just hadn't been ready to admit it. But it was time.

Throwing his towel on a deck chair, Drew stepped back into the jacuzzi, goosebumps lining his chest. The plate in his hand had strawberries on it, cut in half, some blueberries, and wedges of pineapple.

I grinned. "With all this fruit you've fed me in the last twenty-four hours, I'm gonna start calling you Fruit Man."

Drew laughed. "So, does Fruit Man have any special powers? He sounds like a really cool superhero."

I sat up, taking a handful of strawberries and shoving them in my mouth. "Fank you," I managed, chewing and swallowing them. "Hmm, let's see. Fruit Man fights evil with the power of Vitamin C … Also, he is a gun in the sack and can get any woman he wants into bed."

"Wow. I wish I had discovered Fruit Man when I was sixteen."

"True story," I continued. "Fruit Man is a sex god." I took some more strawberries. They were going down a treat.

Drew took half a strawberry off the plate and popped it in my mouth. "Sorry. That was really lame." He grinned. "It was Fruit Man's cheesy rom-com move."

"The best kind." I grabbed another piece of strawberry and turned towards him, sliding the fruit along his bottom lip, like it was lipstick, before popping it in his mouth.

"Okay, wow," he said, licking his lips post-strawberry. "And I thought mine was a cheesy move."

Watching him lick his lips sent a warm buzz rushing through me. I took the plate away and placed it on a chair behind me, then sat in Drew's lap and kissed him, tasting the strawberry on his soft lips. *Naked in a jacuzzi, sitting on Drew's lap.*

He slid a hand up my leg teasingly. With the jets on in the spa, no movement could be seen under the surface from the bubbles. It was so hot, not knowing when and where his hands would be. He slid further down into the jacuzzi and hoisted me up, turning me so my legs straddled him.

"Are you going for number four here?" I said.

"Naturally."

*

"Georgie."

"Mmm?" It was bright when I opened my eyes.

"Sorry to wake you. I have to head out."

"Oh. Okay?" I yawned. I had no idea what time it was, but the sun was blasting through the blinds and onto my face. It couldn't have been that long since Drew took me by the hand, pulled me out of the jacuzzi and carried me inside, laughing, giving me a pathetic excuse of a towel down, and throwing me onto his bed. But clearly, I had fallen into a deep sleep right after we finished. I turned to face Drew, whose head was propped up in one hand, elbow leaning on the pillow. His expression softened when my eyes met his.

"Just so we're clear, you're kicking me out?"

He laughed. "You can stay as long as you like. There's more fruit and muesli if you'd like some breakfast. Tea and coffee. I have to do a few things today before I leave tomorrow – and I have a meeting at one."

The world came crashing to a halt.

Tomorrow. Deployment. Six months.

I swallowed away the bitter taste. The dream was over. "What … What's the meeting?"

"It's … a cultural briefing. I have to go. But … can I see you later tonight?" He kissed my forehead softly, lingering there for a while. "I'm going to video call my parents at five, but after that I'm free. I'd really love to see you."

I nodded, not thinking of the implications of this being his final night here. I had so many questions. Where in the Middle East? What for? How safe would he be there, really? But no words would come.

"I have so much I want to tell you," he said. "Come round for dinner at six? I'll cook."

I couldn't answer, tears threatening my eyes. I pulled him

close and buried my face in his chest, instead.

Stroking my hair, he said, "Are you okay?"

I nodded. Seeing the worry wash across his face only made my tears come faster.

"Hey. What's the matter?"

I sniffed. "I just …"

What, Georgie? "I don't want you to go"? "I'm going to miss you"? "I don't know what I'll do if you never come back"? There was literally nothing I could do about the fact he was leaving for six months. I took a breath. "I don't know what I'm going to do while …" I couldn't finish the sentence. Drew pulled me into him and wrapped his arms around me.

"Are you … Will you be flying helicopters over there?" I asked carefully.

"No. I'll be on ground as an operations watchkeeper."

"What's that? What do they do?"

"Mostly talk to intelligence guys and liaise with different groups … Direct convoys, that kind of thing. Generally oversee operations. It's not really my field, but they needed someone urgently."

I nodded, sniffling. "I'm sorry."

"It's okay," he said, still stroking my hair. "It's a horrible time. But let's chat tonight – and I promise we'll work this all out." He looked at me. "Together. Okay?"

I nodded. Minutes of silence passed before he peeled himself away from me, got dressed and left. I pulled the sheets over me and started picking at my nails.

I thought about telling Byron it was over. What would he do when he heard the words? Would he be angry? Would he even care? Now that Drew was gone and I was alone with my thoughts, a tsunami of guilt washed over me. I didn't want to hurt Byron. I didn't want us to have to go through a divorce.

Divorce. The word pounded in my temples. But the thought of not going through with it was so much worse. Not being with Drew again. I couldn't breathe. Gasping, I sat up in his bed, taking long, deliberate breaths.

I knew what I had to do. And I had to do it today.

I had to tell Byron it was over.

3 5

GEORGIE

I stood in the shower, letting the hot water sting my body, feeling a bit hypocritical that I'd once yelled at Drew for washing his car in the middle of water restrictions, when here I was, essentially wasting water, too. My brain was in overdrive, and the shower was somehow my emotional sanctuary. I was delaying the inevitable – calling Byron. Initially, I was going to wait for him to get home and talk in person. But now, all I wanted to do was get it over with.

Before the guilt really sunk its claws into me.

Plus, he had some explaining to do of his own. Despite the fact that I had a pretty good reason to believe he was cheating on me, none of this felt right. I was a liar – a deceptive wife. I didn't want to feel like that any more, nor did I want Byron to come home thinking everything was fine. Honesty would be the best policy, and the sooner, the better.

I closed my eyes and sighed. If I ended it today, it would make tonight with Drew so much better. I couldn't believe this was happening. *Drew and me. Finally.*

I rinsed the rest of the conditioner out of my hair and closed my eyes again, letting the hot water run down my face. What the hell do I do? What do I even say?

"Sorry, Byron, it's over."

"I want a divorce."

"This isn't working any more."

None of those sounded real. They were just lines out of a movie. How could I ever say it to his face? Or over the phone? All of this was so … *surreal.*

But saying it was inevitable. And even though there was guilt there – I'd known, deep down, that things hadn't been working with Byron. The ending would have been the same. I would have drawn the same conclusion, no matter what road I took to get there – it just happened that the road led me to Drew, and made me come to this conclusion faster, perhaps. But Drew did not take me from Byron. Drew did not change my feelings for Byron. That had happened a long time ago. And it was a hundred percent my decision.

Still, it was not a conversation I was looking forward to. But once it was done and dusted – once I'd told him – well, then I could get on with doing what I actually wanted to do. It wasn't an ideal situation – not even close.

But didn't I deserve happiness? Didn't Byron?

And didn't Drew?

I was excited for tonight. It made me smile just thinking about it. Dinner cooked by Drew. Lying on the couch with his arms wrapped around me. An episode of some crappy TV show. Maybe hopping in the jacuzzi again.

That could be my forever.

My doorbell went off, buzzing non-stop. I realised I'd heard it earlier, but it hadn't registered. I turned off the tap, grabbed a towel and dried my hair off quickly, followed by my legs and arms, before wrapping the towel around myself and making my way to the door as the bell rang again. Whoever it was really wanted to see me. A wave of anticipation flowed through me, hoping it would be Drew's face I'd see. Weird that he didn't just ring me when I didn't answer the door. That's when I realised my phone was still in Drew's glovebox.

I thought about the first time he came to my door, and how I wanted nothing to do with him. And how different things were now.

Hopefully, this wasn't Byron coming home early to surprise me – but then, it'd make me rip the Band-Aid off a hell of a lot faster.

The doorbell rang again as I padded down the hallway barefoot, my heart beating.

"Hold *on*, I'm coming," I yelled out, walking faster. "Bloody hell. Settle down." I realised there was no way Drew would act like this.

I got to the door and turned the round handle. And I was right – it wasn't Drew.

Instead, I was met with Kevin's face. "What the hell are you doing here?"

"Georgie. Where have you been? I've been calling you since—"

"I don't have my phone." I stood up straight, trying to appear confident despite the fact that, yet again, Kevin was standing there staring at me in a towel. I tightened it around me and glanced down at my screen door, thankful it was locked. "What do you want?"

"Georgie ..."

It was only then that I realised his face was drained of all colour.

"What?" My heartbeat was a stampede through my ribcage.

He swiped away at a tear that'd rolled down his cheek.

"*What*, Kev?"

He took a sharp breath. "Byron was in an accident." He shifted his weight to the other foot.

"What?"

He swallowed. "He ... The van that was transporting his staff to the hospital – it was hit by a truck."

I stared at him as he paused and started sobbing, shoulders heaving as he gasped for air. And I knew exactly what he was about to say.

My entire body lost its feeling. Complete numbness. I was lightheaded and needed to steady myself on the wall, black and white spots blurring my vision. And my heart pumped heavy blood through thin veins.

"He … He didn't make it, Georgie. Byron died."

3 6

D R E W

I stared down at my feet, my duffel bag sitting on the ground next to them. Who knew what I'd even put in there. I hardly remembered packing last night – the whole evening had been a blur.

"Oi. Are you even listening to me?"

I looked up at Elena, who had both hands on her steering wheel. "Sorry."

"Make me get up at the butt-crack of dawn to drive you to the airport, you can at least listen to my whinging!" she said with a laugh.

I cleared my throat. "I'm sorry. Could you … start again?"

"Drew. I'm joking." She glanced at me. "What's wrong? Are you worried about the trip?"

I still hadn't told anyone where I was going.

Well, except for Georgie, sort of. But I was sure Elena could probably work it out for herself.

I pictured the bunch of flowers sitting in the middle of my dining table. The dinner plates on either side of the flowers, the food slowly going cold. The dessert waiting in the fridge.

My unanswered knocks on Georgie's door.

And her empty front yard, no ute to be seen.

"No. Not really." I paused. "Can you please go round to mine in a few days and chuck out the flowers on the table? Also, there's heaps of food in my fridge. Grab it today so it doesn't get wasted." I glanced down at my hands. "Someone may as well enjoy it."

She paused. "Okay, Drew. Honestly. What's wrong?"

I shook my head. "Nah. It's nothing."

"Come on, Drew. I might be blonde and hot, but I'm not dumb. Now spill." She laughed at her own joke.

"Georgie." I sighed. "She was meant to come over last night. But she never showed."

"Georgie? Your neighbour?"

I nodded.

"The one who came round wasted the other night and threw herself at you?"

I nodded again. "Yeah."

"The *married* one?"

"Okay, don't do that. You don't know her."

Elena looked puzzled. "Did something happen between you two?" She took my silence as confirmation. "Drew. Are you kidding me? Of all people? *You?* After all the shit you put John through for doing exactly that?"

"Yeah, okay, I know, all right?"

Her expression made me cringe. "So, what? How long have you been seeing her?"

"I was never *seeing* her."

"Then what?"

"I was … I really liked her. It was only one time. But she was meant to come over yesterday. To see me before I left." I had to stop talking – my voice was getting dangerously shaky.

"So she said she was going to come over, but never did?"

"Yeah."

"Did you try calling?"

"Gee, Elena, that never occurred to me. Why didn't I think to *call* her?" Of course I had called her, multiple times – and knocked on her door, too. It was probably overkill but I also sent her a bunch of texts. And it wasn't until early this morning that I realised she had left her phone in my glovebox. It was lucky I'd even found it before I went away, as I was searching for my sunglasses. I'd placed the phone in her letterbox before I got into Elena's car and left for the airport.

My sister rolled her eyes. "What about her husband?"

"He's overseas."

"Doing what?"

I swallowed. "Operating in Africa. Heart surgery."

"What, like, volunteering?"

I nodded.

"Jesus Christ, Drew." She looked in her blind spot and changed lanes. A moment later, she turned to me. "She's never gonna leave him. You know that, right? They never do."

Yeah. I'd had exactly the same thought.

"Thanks for the honesty," I said, unable to stop the sarcasm in my voice.

"When is he coming back?"

"Um – in a couple of days, I think."

"He's coming home in a couple of days?"

"Yeah."

"And you're going to be …"

I closed my eyes, deflated. "In the Middle East for the next six months."

37

GEORGIE

A blur.

It was all just a blur. Life, death. *Byron.*

Fragments, movements, questions. Too many things happening.

Home calls. Tears. Blue uniforms. Family. Non-stop video calls from England and Italy.

Flowers. A smashed vase.

Vomiting.

Emotions.

No emotions.

I was drowning without being in water.

I couldn't speak, think.

There was no sleep. My eyes were wired. *I* was wired.

Hours reduced to minutes reduced to seconds.

Wishing I didn't exist.

Wishing he still did.

Just a blur.

3 8

DREW

Searing pain shot down my shins as I pounded the pavement around the expansive airport base. It was early morning, and the mercury hadn't even hit zero degrees yet. Snow-capped mountains dotted my view as tears from the icy air glided down my numb cheeks, ears throbbing from the cold. I glanced at my watch through the thick white clouds of my own breath. Sixteen kilometres. Round and round – and with each lap, I was more and more determined. My mind was running in circles, too.

Where was she?

Why hadn't she come over on my final night in Australia, like she'd promised?

When she was in bed with me, she was a different person. So sweet, so honest. *So genuine.*

Or at least, that's what I'd thought. *What the hell had gone wrong?*

But maybe that wasn't the real Georgie. Maybe the real Georgie was the one who'd been there all along. The one who'd yelled at me on that first day. The one who never showed any emotion or returned my flirting. Not the Georgie I really wanted; not the one I'd seen after our beach day.

Maybe that wasn't really her.

I could still feel her soft lips on mine, the shape of her body as she lay against me.

I ran faster, past the large section of the airport where the military unit was based. I had never seen so much barbed wire in my entire life. It was grey and cold, not a soul around except for security personnel. And me, gasping for air.

I pushed through the pain.

The trouble was, now that I'd had her, I couldn't imagine life without her. And that was a problem. Because a life without Georgie was all I currently had.

I wheezed my way to the end of the lap, glancing at the seemingly never-ending row of military helicopters on the other side of the airport. I walked the last hundred metres or so back to my room on the second level of the Australian headquarters, panting and rubbing warmth back into my hands. I stood in the doorway, hands on my knees, bending over to try and get more oxygen into me.

The guy I was sharing a room with, another operations watchkeeper, was there, gaping at me wide-eyed as I collapsed onto my bed in the tiny shoebox room, still trying to catch my breath. We were separated by a dresser in the middle, containing all our uniforms and belongings.

"Dude. You are bloody keen doing that. How long'd you run today?" he said from across the other side of the room.

I'd also gone running yesterday – and the day before.

"Seventeen."

"You're out of your mind."

"Thanks."

"That's not a compliment. It's *cold*, dude." He made a shivering sound. "Too damn cold for me, anyhow. What was it like in Sydney before you left?"

I sighed. "Perfect beach weather."

"Sounds like every day in Perth."

"You're from Perth?"

"Yeah. Best place on the planet."

I didn't respond.

"I mean, I'm from Perth originally," he continued, "but I've been away with the wife for years. Living abroad for work."

The last thing I wanted was small talk. I'd managed to avoid it for days, and I was at risk of him thinking I was a complete freak. I forced my question out. "Navy?"

"Nah. It's classified. Her job, not mine."

I said nothing.

"What's your story, then? You single?" he said, sounding excited to actually be having a conversation with me after days of silence.

I ran my hands through my hair and squeezed my eyes shut. "Yeah."

He chuckled. "Let me tell you, that makes this whole thing that much bloody easier!"

I got up and walked out without a word.

39

GEORGIE

There were two hundred and sixteen attendees at Byron's funeral.

Four poems were read.

One song was sung.

Sixty-eight bunches of flowers were delivered.

Three hundred and twenty-two texts and counting sent to me from people Byron had met through work. Patients. Patients' families. Surgeons. Anaesthetists. Nurses. Administrative staff. I didn't even know how half those people had got my number. My phone had been going off non-stop. I'd eventually turned it off and hid it in a cabinet. I'd misplaced it for a while, and then found it on top of some mail someone had obviously brought in for me. But I almost wished I hadn't found it again.

It was too much. Too loud. Too bright. Too many people.

Everything was just numbers to me.

Just numbers from zero to ten. Some big, some small.

It was all my brain could focus on. Nothing else made sense. *Life* didn't make sense.

It'd taken a week to arrange for his body to be brought home to Australia, working together with the funeral directors in

Tanzania. I was told the process had been quicker than normal due to the fact that an autopsy wasn't required.

Like that was a positive, and I should be grateful.

People checked up on me constantly. They sent condolences. Friends asked if I needed anything, randomly turning up at my door.

And yet I'd never felt so lonely in my life.

I'd started packing up Byron's things, but it was too soon. I'd get halfway through a drawer, or a shelf, and lose it.

I hadn't slept properly in weeks. I was dizzy, weak, and exhausted.

I had no idea what day it was.

And I was all-consumed by my own guilt – the guilt of what I had been doing at the time of Byron's accident. I'd worked it out, despite my brain willing me not to. It was just more numbers. At 5:29pm, I was in the taxi going out for the Pool Chicks dinner.

And at exactly the same time, at 9:29am in Dar es Salaam, a truck slammed into Byron's van, heading for the hospital.

They were all just numbers. My brain wouldn't comprehend anything else. After that, it would shut down. A blur. Numbers, numbness, and blur.

"Hey sweetheart. Can I get you anything?" Dad said, squinting into the darkness of my bedroom. The light from the hallway reflected off the top of his bald patch, a ring of thick black hair still circling it proudly.

He took my inability to respond as a "no".

"Okay. I'm off to bed. Yell out if you need anything, all right?"

I didn't respond.

*

My husband is dead.

I sat bolt upright in a sheen of sweat, unsure if it was a dream or a thought. My head spun, and I let it fall to the wall behind me with a soft thud. Closing my eyes didn't help. I lay back down, bringing my knees to my chest.

"Dad?" I managed.

I heard hurried footsteps before my door opened.

"What do you need, sweetheart?"

I shook my head as he turned on my bedside lamp, sitting on the edge of the bed.

"Can I get you some water?"

I forced a smile. "Thanks. I'm okay."

"What about some food?" he said gently.

I was so tired of being tired. He was drained, too, I could tell. I forced my eyes open and looked at him. "Thank you for flying to Sydney," I said weakly. I knew I was a burden.

"Of course." He put his hand on mine. "That was never a question. Your mother really wanted to be here, too, but, well with—"

"I know. Nan. It's all good." Nan wasn't well back in England. Mum and Max had stayed home to take care of her. She didn't speak English, and normally relied on help, even when she was well. And Max's wife was about a month away from giving birth. But it still hurt all the same that my own mum and brother couldn't make it to my husband's funeral.

"You sure you're okay?"

"Yeah, Dad. Thanks."

After a while, he closed the door and I could hear his footsteps as he went upstairs to bed. Our standard routine: Dad cooking a meal for me that he knew I wouldn't eat. Checking on me. Gently telling me I was losing too much weight. Going upstairs to bed while I lay on mine for another night of staring at the ceiling.

Groaning, I forced myself to stand, and headed towards the kitchen. I poured myself a glass of water, my hips and elbows aching. The pain was agony. It reached the depths of my bones, sticking its sharp blades into me.

I gulped the water down, my eyes traitorously glancing next door. All the windows in Drew's house were dark, the blinds drawn. I stood leaning on the kitchen sink, staring out at his bedroom window, and listening to the quiet buzz of my fridge.

Consumed by the darkness between our houses.

And I finally let my thoughts swirl around yet another truth: Drew was gone, too.

I let my head drop back, closing my eyes.

Please, please, please let him return alive.

An involuntary sob left my mouth. I opened my eyes a moment later and straightened out my back, then pulled the blinds down in my kitchen so I could no longer see his house.

The sea of flowers that'd kept coming after the funeral were now mostly dead, cards and gifts strewn around my living room and kitchen. And in that moment, it all became clear.

Regardless of whether Drew came home safe or not, I could never, ever see him again.

40

GEORGIE

"Hey, these ones are still alive, but I'm not sure about those roses over there." Dad crouched with a handful of weeds in his gloved hands, glancing at me from under his wide-brimmed hat. My garden was dead. Well, it was *almost* dead. He was trying to help me salvage it – and help it needed. I hadn't been outside in weeks, and the lack of watering on top of the February sun did not bode well for my plants. But I was actually enjoying being outside for the first time; enjoying the sun warming my back and the feeling of the fresh air on my skin.

Dad was a miracle worker to get me outside in the first place. Other than my immediate family, I hadn't spoken to anyone. In fact, I had hardly left my bedroom. In a way, I'd reverted to being a child again, with Dad looking after me, cooking for me, greeting visitors at the door (and subsequently sending them away), and collecting gifts and well-wishes. Once, I had seen Hanako and Kate, when they'd come around yet again to see if they could help.

They couldn't. No one could. Regardless, it was still nice to see those two, despite the fact that they didn't know what to say when they were here. Nobody really did.

And weeks later, everything – my limbs, my joints, my skin – ached and felt heavy.

I was weak from the grief.

I was weak from the guilt.

And I was weak from having nobody to talk to about the latter. Because the truth was, I was having an affair when my husband died. But nobody knew about it. I could hardly admit it to myself – and I hated myself for what I'd done. I hated myself for it more than I've ever hated anything.

Dad had given up on making me go to grief counselling. He'd realised after a while that I benefited most from just having him here, helping me around the house.

There were reminders everywhere that Byron was never coming back. I was haunted by the countless images that had been burned into my memory. The look on his mum's face at the funeral. Kevin choking on his words as he delivered the news to me. People sobbing as I read Byron's eulogy.

Watching a surgeon trying to navigate his wheelchair with one arm, the other arm in a sling.

The one who survived.

Everything was overshadowed by Byron's death. I'd never get the answers about the unknown woman in Tanzania, and I didn't care.

Nothing – no event, no emotion – was bigger than the fact that Byron was gone.

I walked over towards the roses Dad was pointing to. They filled the large pots lining the perimeter of my fence – including the side I'd climbed on to jump into Drew's backyard. I stared at the fence, running a finger along it and catching a glimpse of his pool through the gaps. His grass was getting long, and bird poo lay splattered and dried along the edges of the pool.

No Mal.

I stiffened, took a deep breath, and forced myself to look back down at the row of dead roses. "Hey, I think there're a couple here that survived!" I yelled over at Dad.

He glanced across the garden. "Okay. Well, first things first. Let's deal with this weed situation, then give everything a good water. We could go and grab some mulch down at the nursery?" he suggested gently. I knew he was trying to get me out of the house.

I pulled my gloves back on, brown and crunchy with age. I could hardly even move my fingers in them. Probably time for a new pair, I thought, as I bent down to rip out another handful of weeds. I could get some while we were at the nursery, if I decided to go.

I shuddered at the thought of being around people, though. Being outside was a big enough step. And going to the back garden for some air seemed a lot more appealing than the front yard, where people could be walking past.

I wiped the sweat off my top lip with my sleeve, squinting at Dad. "I'm about ready for lunch," I said, ignoring the joy on his face as I finally suggested a meal. "Want a sandwich?"

"That would be wonderful. Would you like me to make them?"

"Nah, that's okay. You enjoy the sun – I'll bring something out," I said, turning to walk inside.

I was pulling my gloves off when I passed the study, something making me stop at the closed door. It was the room where Byron had spent most of his time, typing away on his laptop. I opened the door slowly, holding my breath. Of course, nothing had changed in the room – Byron would've been the last person to go in there. It had been his sanctuary, like the garden was mine – he knew I never came in here. His laptop sat on the desk, plugged into the charger, the green light blinking, showing the laptop was asleep but not switched off. I straightened my back, hesitated, then stepped into the room, putting my gloves down next to the laptop, a few bits of dry soil falling off them.

It was just a laptop. A piece of equipment. A vessel for communication. And yet, I could feel my pulse in my throat as I opened it up and wondered what Byron's password would be, chewing on a nail. It didn't take long – my husband, predictably, had used the same one for everything. Not a good way to keep your wife out of your business, but he knew I would never, ever have looked through his personal things.

Until now.

The screen came to life. I felt dizzy. His laptop was synced with his phone messages, and there were eight hundred and fifty-four new message notifications. I swallowed, clicking on the app and scrolling absentmindedly, not really sure what I was looking for. I didn't know most of these names. I took a sharp breath and moved my finger on the mouse until I got to the last opened message. The date and time stamp told me it was the day Byron flew out. Immediately, nausea hit me when I saw who he'd been messaging. Saw the last person he had written to, from this study. With a shaky finger, I clicked on their message thread.

Kevin: *All in order?*
Byron: *Yeah, all ready to go. Exciting times. Leaving shortly.*
Kevin: *Let us know when you land.*
Byron: *Will do. This number won't be working over there, as usual*
Kevin: *Don't worry. I'll keep an eye on her while ur gone.*
Byron: *Nah. No need. But thx.*
Kevin: *You really trust her? With him next door?*
Byron: *Not exactly, but … I'm not worried any more.*

My mouth felt dry. And even though I hadn't eaten in days, I wanted to throw up.

Kevin: *What do you mean?*
Byron: *Well, he's away. And when he gets back, he won't want anything to do with her.*
Kevin: *??*
Byron: *Let's just say I took care of it. There will be no dog when he returns, and it'll be her fault.*

The walls in the room went dark, closing in around me. My head was made of lead. My legs gave way and I tried to grasp the chair as I tumbled to the ground, breathing in but not being able to breathe out, lungs filling but not emptying. Everything spun. I lay on the floor, blinking, clutching at the ground, clutching at my chest.

It was him.

Byron poisoned Mal.

My whole body was shaking. Convulsing. Unable to comprehend.

What the fuck?

I hardly recognised the animalistic howl that came out of me. Grabbing the edge of the desk, I pulled myself up, then read the message exchange again, and again. And once more.

And then my shock turned into rage. White, hot, pure rage. I picked up the laptop and hurled it against the wall, shattering the screen and denting a corner. Screaming, I pounded the wall with my fists, then picked up the laptop and hurled it against the wall again, this time much harder.

Hold it together, Georgie.

I took a deep breath, my fists still in balls, marched into my bedroom and opened the top drawer of Byron's bedside table. I rummaged through it, holding back tears and pressing my lips together. I knew exactly what I was looking for, even if I hadn't quite worked out why.

But they weren't there.

Where else could they be?

I threw the whole drawer onto the ground, swearing, then stormed back to the living room and started yanking drawers from under the TV, leaving items strewn around the house. I eventually found some sets of keys, but not the ones I wanted.

"You fucking piece of shit," I muttered, trying the kitchen drawers. "Where the hell are they hidden?" Not in the kitchen, either. *Don't tell me he took them with him to Africa.*

There was a small, wooden table near the front door with a single drawer, where I was supposed to keep the house and car keys but always forgot. I had mine; Byron had his. It had never been an issue.

But today, that drawer was locked. He'd actually *locked* it?

"You son of a bitch," I growled, searching for something heavy. I went around the kitchen island to get my large mortar and pestle, thinking of all the times I'd struggled to lift it from the bottom shelf, all the times I'd sworn at how heavy it was – but now its weight was finally about to pay off.

I grabbed it with both hands and stormed back towards the front door, lifted it up, and dropped it onto the wooden table. The old table didn't stand a chance, shattering into tiny, sharp bits of wood. There was a metal clinking sound as the keys hit the ground. To my surprise, the mortar didn't go through the floorboards altogether. I crouched down, finally spotting what I'd been looking for.

The Maserati keys.

"Dad?" I screamed out the back, but he was already coming in, presumably to find out what I'd done to make it sound like a train had crashed through the front door.

"Sweetheart, what … what's wrong?" He took in the scene as I stepped around the splintered wood, catching my breath.

Not only had Byron never allowed me to drive the Maserati – but he'd actually locked the keys up while he was away. *Unbelievable.* I shook my head, seething. "*Ass*hole," I muttered under my breath. But I didn't really give a shit about the car.

That fucking asshole poisoned Mal.

"I'm going out," I said to Dad, trying my best to sound casual.

He frowned at me as I made for the back door. "Are you … Can I do anything? What happened?"

"What happened?" I let out a hollow, cold laugh. "What happened is that I – is that he—" I couldn't get it out, choking on my words. All my energy was going into keeping the tears at bay – I couldn't even physically say the words. Shaking my head, I grabbed my wallet and walked out the back door into the garage, slamming the glass sliding door behind me, almost disappointed it didn't shatter.

The Maserati had a thin film of dust on it, its black exterior unforgiving. I swept a finger across the side panel and wiped it on my shorts as the rage burned through my chest.

What a stunning vehicle.

Shame, really.

I eyed the sleek sports car, my gaze dropping to Byron's personalised gold number plates. THE-DOC.

Pretentious prick. Apparently, driving a three-hundred-thousand-dollar car wasn't enough to say, *I have loads of cash.* I shook my head.

And then I put my right boot through the car's back bumper.

"You …"

Kick.

"Fucking …"

Kick.

"Piece …"

Kick.

"Of …"

Kick.

"Shit!"

I hit the button to open the garage's roller door. Out of breath, a huge sob escaped my lips. I swung the driver's door open and got in, put the key in the ignition and listened to the engine roar to life. I revved it a few times, putting my foot to the floor. It was loud, that's for sure, but the sound of the engine was hugely satisfying.

So powerful.

I put it in gear and accelerated, narrowly missing the edge of the garage wall due to how the car had been parked.

He couldn't even park his own damn car in a straight line.

I turned onto the road and put my foot down, driving towards the next suburb. When I stopped to put fuel in, two guys approached me, one of them letting out a slow but loud whistle.

"Hey. *Nice* car."

I ignored him, walking off to pay.

"How does she go?"

I stopped, then turned around to look at him. "That's exactly what I'm about to find out."

41

DREW

She leans over me, kisses my neck, laughs. She's in her white bikini, touching my chest, saying something about the sharks. The sun is reflecting on her skin through the material of the beach tent. I lean in to return her kiss, but we are smashed by a huge wave. It drags her out to the ocean, she reaches for my hand, I'm yelling her name, but I can't reach her. She's gone.

I woke suddenly in a cold sweat, trying to let my eyes adjust to the darkness. My lungs were desperate for air; heart pounding. I unclenched both my fists, one at a time, and squinted at my watch. Three a.m. I'd seen three a.m. a lot lately. Four and five, too – and not just when I was on night shift.

I lay on the bed wide-eyed for a while, wondering if I'd said anything in my sleep.

Three and a half weeks since I had arrived here – and the puzzle still wasn't getting any clearer. It was ironic, in a way – these were not the sorts of nightmares I'd imagined having while I was deployed. I let my mind drift to Georgie. Had I said something wrong? Was she upset when I left? I'd tried to replay our final morning together so many times, but I had nothing.

Did Byron come home early?

Was she back together with him?

Of course she's back together with him. They're married.

I'd been trying to force myself to think ahead, rather than back. What was going to get me through all this? When I had first arrived, I'd made myself visualise it – the long-awaited break. After the first four months of being here, I'd be allowed a break. I'd be allowed to take a holiday. A two-week holiday, and I could fly somewhere. I could fly *anywhere.*

Originally, I'd visualised flying back to Sydney. I'd visualised turning up at her door, seeing her face again. Kissing her one more time.

But those visuals slowly started morphing into *what if*s.

What if, rather than flying to Australia, Georgie came to meet me somewhere, instead?

What if we met halfway, just me and her?

What if I could convince her to come *somewhere* with me, that wasn't here, and wasn't in Australia?

I visualised that. A lot.

What if we could go to Italy together?

Or anywhere in Europe – France, Spain, Greece. I didn't care where. The thought of seeing her face again was what'd kept me going through the seven-day working weeks.

No breaks, no weekends. Just twelve-hour shifts – every single day.

I groaned, rolling over. She hadn't answered her phone on any of the occasions I'd tried to ring. In fact, her phone would go straight to voicemail. Is that what happened when someone blocked you? I had no idea. My twice-a-week call allowance had all been spent on her, bar one occasion when I'd rung Elena to tell her I was safe and to ask her to pass the message on to the rest of the family. The calls home were never very long – there wasn't a lot I could say about where I was and what I was doing, nothing I could really disclose. It was all classified, not to mention heavily monitored.

I'd started writing Georgie letters, thinking she might've changed her phone number. Because if that was the case, how would she even know I had called? She didn't have my email. There was no way she could contact *me*. I had to keep trying. So if she did have a new number, maybe she'd get my letters instead. But I was yet to receive a response. Surely the letters had arrived by now, even if it *had* taken me a couple of weeks to actually send them. Was she getting them? If she was, she wasn't responding to my Defence email like I'd asked. Somehow, I'd managed to keep the letters fairly upbeat. If it was a toss-up between Byron and me, the last thing I wanted was to send her a bunch of sad letters. That wouldn't do me any favours.

I let out a huge sigh and willed my eyes shut again.

If she *was* trying to decide between Byron and me, was that something I even wanted to be a part of?

I really thought there was something between us – something real. And even if I was wrong, there was a tiny niggling feeling in the base of my chest that wouldn't disappear. I couldn't understand why she didn't just send me an email. Or answer my calls. *"Hey Drew, stop calling me, I'm staying with Byron."* It didn't seem like her to ignore me altogether. She had more decency than that. Even if she felt nothing for me. I just knew it.

So what the hell is going on?

Of course, I knew there was a small chance I was wrong. And then perhaps I didn't want her in my life at all.

42

GEORGIE

I pulled up at the entry booth of the motorsport racetrack and a man came to the window. He eyed my car.

"Hey," I said. "What's the entry fee?"

He blinked, then roared with laughter, stopping when he saw the look on my face. "Oh, you're serious."

"Why wouldn't I be serious?" I said.

He frowned, still eyeing the car. "You don't just come here and pay a fee. What do you think this is?"

"I'm only after an hour. Tops."

He stared at me, then started laughing again. "That's not how this works. You don't just 'show up'" – he made inverted commas with his fingers – "and 'drive'." He did it again. "You know you have to pre-book the track days, and—"

"Yeah, okay, I got that." I interrupted.

He glanced at the Maserati again. "You ever been here before? On track?"

I shook my head, which was met by a roar of laughter again. My blood was starting to boil. "Look. Can I come in, or not?"

"No. There's not even a tiny chance of that happening." He paused, animatedly trying to stop his laughter. "You'll have to come another time. You know, actually be organised and sign up like everyone else? By the way," he said with a sneer, "you do realise that once you enter that track, your insurance is completely void? You can kiss that sweet-ass car goodbye the moment you crash it. You won't get paid a single cent from any insurance company with half a brain cell, I'll tell ya that much for free!"

I smiled at him. "My insurance is not your concern." *Asshole.*

"Hey, Al," came a female voice from behind him as I tapped the steering wheel, considering my next move. "Isn't it time for your lunch break?"

Al said something to the person behind him, then turned back to me. "Go home," he said, walking away without giving me another look.

A woman emerged from behind the booth, walked around the Maserati and came up to my window.

"Hey," she said. She couldn't have been more than twenty. "I love your car. That *sound*! Haven't seen anything that nice here since … well, ever, I don't think!" She giggled nervously. "What year is it?" She studied the Maserati in admiration.

"Last year's."

"Wow. New."

"Yep."

She stood staring at me curiously, probably wondering how a frail-looking woman in torn gardening clothes with dirt on her face drove a Maserati.

"Do you work here, too?" I said.

"Yeah." She looked over the top of the car and into the booth, then back down at me. "Well, if you really want to go in, I can take you to the registration office and see if Dane will let you do a late registration? I mean – if you want? You'll have to sit through the briefing with him, but it's not impossible."

"Thank you."

"No problem. Us women need to look after each other. Stick together."

I nodded in agreement. "So – you wanna get in?"

"Really?"

I shrugged. "Sure."

She climbed carefully into the passenger seat, looking around wide-eyed. "So, is this, I mean, is this your car?"

"It is now."

"Oh." She gingerly ran her fingers across the metallic Gran Turismo Sport badge on her side of the dash, then along the thick stitching on the leather seat.

I drove down the road slowly, obeying the 20-sign, the Maserati's engine grumbling underneath us. The road took us under a tunnel, the grandstand opposite us, pit lane and garages ahead. To our left was a line of ambulance and fire vehicles, ready for action. I could hear the distant rumbling sound of engines on the track already. A wave of adrenalin pulsed through me. I needed to be on that track, with my foot to the floor. I was keeping my anger towards Byron in check, but only just. I felt like a volcano about to erupt.

"Park here and I'll show you where to go."

"Thanks so much. I'm Georgie, by the way." I parked and took the key out of the ignition.

"Camille."

I nodded, sliding the Maserati keys into my back pocket. "Have you worked here long, Camille?"

"Um, not really. Six months?"

"How did you get into it? Not many women around here."

"Yeah, nah, there aren't. I just really love cars. But I'm only here part-time. I'm doing an apprenticeship and then hopefully once that's finished I can save up to buy my own track car. I've driven an old Corolla here on a couple of days. It's great. Love driving here. And the Corolla's a cool track car – it has over three hundred thousand kilometres on it; it's ancient. It's my boyfriend's."

"Not a surgeon then, I'm guessing."

"Um – He's actually a mechanic."

"And what do you drive?" I said as she led me to the registration office. "On the road, I mean."

She laughed. "Did you see that rusty orange bicycle locked up at the entrance?"

"No."

"Well, that's my reliable mode of transport."

"What's your apprenticeship?"

"Mechanic, too."

"Impressive."

"Thanks." She opened the door. "Hey, Dane? This is Georgie. There was an issue with her online entry form she did last month. Must've been that weird glitch we had in the system. Can she do the briefing now and join?"

"What glitch?"

She raised an eyebrow. "Don't you remember? We had all kinds of—"

"Of course I remember the glitch, Camille." He stood up straight, folding his arms defensively.

I pressed my lips together to stop myself smiling as Dane looked me up and down and glanced at his watch, sighing. "Fine. But you're late. There're only three more sessions left, and I only have space in the intermediate group."

I thanked him and filled out the paperwork, turning around and mouthing a massive *thank you* to Camille before she left.

Half an hour later, the engine was roaring to life under me, its sweet rumbling sound filling the cabin as I took the black

GT round the track. I'd never been excited by sports cars, or cars in general. But the sound and feeling were incredible – just me alone with all of its mighty four hundred and fifty-four horsepower. I remembered that fact from all the times I'd had to listen to Byron bragging about the car, and gritted my teeth just thinking about him again, putting my foot flat to the floor.

By the time I pulled into the pit lane for my second session, I'd got a good feel for the car, how it handled in corners, what speed I could take them at. By the third, I was overtaking cars, foot to the floor. I'd never thought I'd feel comfortable going that fast, but the speedometer hit two-sixty along the main straight and it only made me want to go even faster.

The sessions were over quickly. I exited through the pit lane and made my way up to Camille's booth.

She stuck her head out of the window as she heard me approaching, excitement written all over her face. "How was it?"

"Yeah, fantastic." I didn't feel any better about Byron – after what I'd found out about Mal, I despised him with every inch of my being; and the rage that had lodged itself in my chest was there for good. "Hey …" I tried to gauge if she was alone, but couldn't quite see into the booth. "Can I chat to you for a sec? Out here?"

"Yeah, sure, uh, hang on." A moment later, she was heading towards me and the GT. I pulled off to the side and parked next to her bike to free up the road.

"It sounded amazing on the track!" she said excitedly, looking at me with hands on her hips as I got out of the car and took the keys from the ignition. "I could hear it from here. Great car!"

"I'm glad you like it." I smiled at her. "Also, thanks for your help. That was really kind."

"Yeah, well, Alan's a dick. And so is Dane. There are some nice guys here – but those two are not among them. It's hard to tell if it's a sexist thing, or if they're just a pair of old douchebag shit-for-brains."

Instead of anger, it was laughter that erupted from me. And it felt good. I couldn't even remember the last time I'd laughed. Camille was funny; I liked her.

"So, I have a favour to ask," I said.

"I'm not sure I can pull that off again – you might want to actually register next time!" she said, still laughing.

"No, no, it's not that." I nodded to my left. "I was wondering if I could have your bike."

Her eyebrows furrowed. "Um, it's a *huge* piece of crap, but yeah, I guess – if you really want?"

"Good." I took Byron's garage remote off the keyring that also held both Maserati keys. "Because I need to get home. And your new car won't fit a bike in the back anyway." I held out the Maserati keys to her.

She stepped back, gaping at me with round eyes as though she were a cartoon character. "Huh?"

I reached for her hand and put the keys into it, hopped on the bike, and clipped the strap of her dented helmet under my chin. "Well, I hope these tyres will last the twenty ks to my house."

"Is this a joke?" She looked around us suspiciously as I rode the bike slowly in a circle, wobbling a bit, testing it out.

"She's a little less comfortable on the ass than the GT," I noted.

"Georgie. I can't accept this. This is … Are you for real?" She continued gaping at me.

"You can get my details from the office. To sort out the rego change."

"But … why?"

"Well, generally that's what happens when you get a new vehicle – you have to change the name over on the registration."

"No, I mean I know that, I mean why would you give it … to *me*?"

"Because I never want to look at it again. And you deserve it a lot more than the person whose it was, anyway." I took a breath and put my foot down on the gravel to steady myself. "Also, you helped me in a big way today. And I like you."

"But all I did was help you get on the track?"

"I guess that's what they call being at the right place, at the right time." I put my feet back on the pedals. "Enjoy!"

"But this thing must be worth, what – two, three hundred grand?"

I shrugged. "It needs a new bumper. And please, for the love of God, get rid of those *useless* number plates." I looked at her one last time, winked, then rode off as she stood there staring at her new ride home.

*

Dad was sitting on the deck, reading a newspaper. I struggled up the steep path to the backyard on the bike, gasping for oxygen. The thing didn't even have gears. Or, to be more exact, none that worked.

The chain had fallen off twice on the ride home and my hands were covered in grease.

"Hey," Dad said, looking up at me and frowning. "Where's the car?"

I got off the bike and lay it on the ground gently, like it would matter if I dropped it. I put my hands on my hips, breathing hard. "I gave it away."

"Oh," he said, sensing he shouldn't ask for more details. And a second later, he smiled warmly at me. "Okay. Well, I like your new bike."

"It's got character."

"The best things always do."

I took off the helmet and wiped my sweaty forehead. "Dad?"

"Yeah, sweetheart?"

I took another long breath. "I'm ready to move back to England."

His eyes softened. "Let's do it."

WINTER

4 3

D R E W

I stared out of the transfer car's window as we left Sydney airport, the sun warm on my face. I'd never been a fan of winter, and Sydney was welcoming me back with a cool seven degrees – just a slight contrast with the forty-degree summer I'd left behind at the end of my deployment. The seasons were extreme in the desert. But I didn't care about the cold. There was no feeling that could possibly rival this one – *safety*. I was back home now, finally, and the knowledge of being able to get around without a bulletproof vest on and a weapon slung across me was liberating. I'd disembarked from the plane feeling like a new person; the sensation of being able to relax, to be free of worry, was still unfathomable.

I couldn't wait to get in the ocean – I didn't care how cold it was. And I couldn't wait to see my family and friends.

I chewed my thumbnail as the car pulled up outside my place. Damn Georgie, her habit had rubbed off on me. I thanked the driver and hopped out, threw my duffel bag at my front door, and headed straight for her house.

I rang her doorbell, and knocked as well, for good measure. Her ute wasn't out the front, I noted. My heart pounded.

Six months. Six months I'd waited for this.

For six long months, I had added so many things to my list for when I returned to Australia: a swim in the ocean, a visit to see Elena, a trip to my folks' in Queensland. Fish and chips. A surf. Some four-wheel-driving. A pale ale with mates.

After six months of no response from Georgie, I'd written her off. Why should I keep trying to get someone's attention who clearly wanted nothing to do with me? Why should I keep wasting my time and energy thinking about her? Those were the questions that kept repeating in my head. And by the end of my deployment, I'd decided I didn't even want to see her. A bit of self-preservation, I guess. Some days I decided that's what it was – and on others, I was convinced I was over her.

Of course, as soon as I landed in Sydney, everything changed.

I had to see her. For six gruelling months, I'd waited for this. I had to know the truth.

Footsteps were coming towards me and I hoped they weren't Byron's. Heart pounding, I glanced down, wondering how much I looked like someone who had been cramped on multiple planes for twenty-plus hours.

The door swung open.

"Hi," a guy I didn't recognise said. A baby cried in the background.

"Um, hi – is Georgie here?"

He looked at me oddly. "Er – No?"

"Oh. Okay, do you … Do you live here?"

"Yeah. Moved in about, um, four months ago?"

A young woman came up behind him, cradling the baby, who was now wailing. "Hi."

"Hi. Sorry, I, I'm Drew. I live next door, actually. I was just looking for someone. But I guess she moved out."

"Yeah, I guess so, sorry. But nice to meet you anyway. I'm Raj, and that's Elise and Tommy. Actually, we were wondering who lived next door – we hadn't seen anyone around."

"Nice to meet you. Yeah, I've been away. So you didn't meet the couple who lived here before you?"

He shook his head.

"Do you know if Tony and Kate still live across the road?" I pointed in the direction behind me.

"Tony, is that the one with the old green station wagon? Japanese daughter?"

"Yeah."

"Yeah, I'm pretty sure."

I thanked him quickly, said goodbye to them, and ducked across the road to Tony's.

Hanako opened the door after I rang the doorbell. "Oh my god, Drew, hi! You're *back*?" She seemed so excited, but then her face dropped.

Tony came to the door behind her. "Mate, good to have you back!" he said, and reached out to shake my hand. It was good to be home, to see some friendly faces. But something wasn't right. Where the hell was Georgie?

"You wanna come in for a beer?"

"Oh, thanks, but no, I haven't even been inside my place yet. I was just wondering if – did Georgie and Byron move?"

Tony glanced at his daughter, who kept her gaze on me. It was hard to read her expression. But her father's wasn't.

What the hell was going on?

"Georgie, uh … She moved back to the UK."

My legs turned to jelly. "What?"

"Yeah, she, well, she moved, what …" he looked at Hanako, "in March I think?"

Hanako nodded.

"She" moved. He hadn't said "they". He said "she".

"Do you know why they moved? Her and Byron?" It was

obvious I was digging, and I didn't care.

"Han, why don't you go inside for a moment?"

She didn't move. Tony sighed. "Drew, Byron died. Georgie went back to the UK by herself. Well, actually, her father was here. He helped her move out and stuff."

I gaped at him. "What?"

"Yeah, he … was in an accident."

My pulse was in my ears. "Jesus. When?"

"While they were in Tanzania."

I steadied myself on the brick wall, a wave of nausea hitting me. I closed my eyes and tried to stay upright.

She'd worried about me not returning. But it was her husband who never came home.

No wonder Georgie had moved back to the UK. She must've been distraught. I swallowed, trying to keep myself composed.

"Can I get you a drink? Han, go grab a water. Please."

"No, I'm good thanks. I … I better go."

I hardly remembered saying bye to them, or walking back to my house. Han had been trying to say something to me about letters as I was walking away. Or something about the mail.

Byron's dead?

And Georgie is in England?

What the hell?

I pulled a hand down my face.

Georgie is gone.

Absentmindedly, I unlocked my door. I collapsed onto my couch and didn't move until the next day.

Her husband is dead.

I couldn't believe it. The fact kept repeating itself over and over, like a song without melody stuck in my head.

But so did something else.

Her husband died … and she still *didn't contact you.*

44

DREW

I lay sprawled on the bed of my new apartment, still fully clothed. I definitely needed to do a grocery shop. It was getting dark, but I didn't have the energy to get up and turn on the lights. Instead, I lay on top of my bedspread, listening to the cicadas outside and the distant sound of passing cars and people, a cool breeze coming in from the open window as the sun set over the water.

I'd been back in Australia just under two weeks and was still appreciating all the small things. And all the clichéd things, too. Vegemite. The beach. Family. West coast sunsets. Kosciuszko Pale Ales. I could do with one of those now, if I could be bothered to get up.

My phone buzzed on the floor next to me, but I couldn't be bothered with that, either. My mind was still a numb mess after hearing the news about Byron. The feelings I had were undesignated – I couldn't even put a label on them if I tried. I only knew one thing for certain – Georgie was gone. And there was no way I could live next door to her old house.

Before I'd left Sydney, I had made the decision to visit John. Appearing at his doorstep uninvited felt odd, especially after such a lengthy period of not seeing him and not returning his calls. Seeing all the new wrinkles in his face, that sad look in his eyes, made me feel broken.

How could you ignore him all this time?

He'd invited me in when he eventually got over his shock, staring at me wide-eyed like he couldn't believe I was there, and we sat on the couch in his dark living room drinking green tea.

"I'm sorry I was MIA for so long," I said, getting straight to the point. "It was a dick move."

"No. You didn't do anything wrong, Drew. This is all on me."

"Well, you might've made a mistake, but I was the one who acted like an immature teenager, and I'm sorry. It was just, well, it was really hard to take." I shook away the memory.

A sadness glazed over his face. "You of all people were never immature, Drew. You were upset. Disappointed, probably. But never immature. Do you remember the time Elena snuck out with her friends, and they got caught for underage drinking? You tried to sneak her back in through the garage, because you didn't want her to get in trouble? You were what, twelve?" He chuckled. "Or the time Pete got knocked out at footy and you rushed home from school with a bunch of DVDs and microwave popcorn for the weekend?"

I nodded, remembering those times clear as day.

"You might have been the baby of the family, Drew, but you were always the sensible one taking care of the rest of us."

He would have so many of these stories, considering how much of his life he'd given to us kids. My eyes pricked with tears and I had to turn away from him.

"It was so great, you know. Until I … Well, until I decided to …" His throat seemed to close up and he couldn't get his words out.

"John, you did nothing wrong by us. I just, I didn't understand. It felt like you abandoned us, but I know that's not true. I didn't get it like Elena and Pete did. I'm sorry."

He sighed and put his tea down. "The important thing is you're here now." He smiled at me. "But let's not waste any more time."

I nodded in agreement and we talked for a while longer about the Navy, about Elena and Pete, Mum and Dad – and eventually I felt courageous enough to ask him about Anita. They were still together, he admitted. A few months ago I'd have felt anger, but in a way all I felt sitting with him was relief at the fact that he wasn't growing old alone.

I just wished the same could be said for Aunty Gillian.

"I'm leaving Sydney," I admitted eventually. "Moving back to Perth."

"Oh?"

"But I'm sure I'll be back fairly often. Elena's here, and I'll make more of an effort to see you too, okay?"

His eyes softened. "I'd love that." He shifted on the couch as I gathered my phone and keys and made for the front door. "Hey, Drew?"

"Yeah?" I said, turning around.

"Why now?"

I knew what he was asking. He wanted to know why I'd decided to forgive him, after all this time. I stood at his front door and shrugged, thinking carefully about my words. "I realised that you can't help who you fall in love with." Then I gave him a half-smile and walked out.

*

I thought about that day now, my last day in Sydney, as I lay on the bed of my Perth apartment.

At least I'd got to see one person I wanted to see in Sydney.

I sighed and stared at the ceiling a little while longer. Eventually, pangs of hunger got me out of bed. Most likely another toast-for-dinner kinda night.

I couldn't contend with the whole cooking thing.

I sat up on the side of the bed, yawned, and picked up my phone. It took me a second to get used to its glare in the dark. The text that'd come through was from Jess.

Hey – Kayla said she saw you running this morning. Are you back in Perth????

Yes, being back in Australia was heaven. But there was no way I was staying in Sydney. Halfway through my flight to Perth, I'd gazed down on Australia from above, down on the Nullarbor, and remembered Mal in the back of my ute, tongue hanging out as we drove through the desert. I hadn't known what to do with Mal's ashes while I was back in Sydney. But not long after I had arrived back in Perth, it became clear. I took them to his favourite dog beach, where I had taken him swimming a lot after I adopted him, and I scattered the ashes in the waves, from where he swam, and from where he retrieved exactly zero of the sticks I'd thrown him. He just wasn't into fetching. Then I ran home, a huge lump sitting in my throat and tears running down my cheeks, mixing with my sweat and pooling in my sunglasses. Mal would always have a huge piece of my heart. He was the best dog in the world, and his collar would always serve as a reminder of the love and friendship he'd given me. No matter how much time passed, though, it would never feel like the right time to say goodbye.

But it was definitely time to say goodbye to Georgie.

I lay back down on my bed, my thoughts turning to Jess. Did I really want to keep avoiding her? Was she really as bad as I had made her out to be?

There was one thing that was certain. Jess actually *wanted* to see me. *She* never ignored my calls or texts.

I'd sent Georgie so many letters. She had once told me how

much she loved receiving hand-written mail. But she'd never even had the decency to acknowledge them, let alone take the time to send something back.

I shook my head.

Stuff that.

Six months. Six long months spent wondering.

Six months too long. I was done.

And, for a moment, I was grateful that it was Jess who was in Perth, and not Georgie.

I picked up my phone and hesitated only for a split second.

Yep. Back in Perth. You free tonight?

45

GEORGIE

My quads burned as I finished the eight-mile run and turned left onto Apple Grove. The crisp cold of the morning stung deep in my lungs, a feeling I actually liked – there was nothing quite like the icy English air. I stopped outside Mum and Dad's house, bent at the hips, catching my breath. Grabbing the key from under the pot plant and opening the green door, I took a final breath of the cool air, mentally converting the miles into kilometres as I stepped inside. Old habits die hard.

Glancing at the clock as I put the kettle on, I could hear Dad pottering around upstairs – not uncommon for six a.m. I knew Mum wouldn't be awake for quite some time. Even in the months I'd been living with them, she was starting to sleep later and later. I figured it was a good thing – she seemed so much more relaxed, finally switching off properly and enjoying retirement.

"Hey, sweetheart, how was your run?" Dad said from halfway down the stairs. He was used to my morning ritual – it had been the same every day since I'd moved to England.

Well, except for one day about five months ago, when I'd been completely rattled. I couldn't eat, couldn't think. I couldn't talk.

It was the day Drew was due back in Australia.

But I couldn't think too deeply about that. I didn't let myself.

"Yeah, it was good, thanks. No rain."

"You making tea?"

"Yeah, would you like one?"

"Thanks."

"Earl grey, splash of milk, teabag in?"

He smiled. "You know it."

I made the teas, took them to the white couch opposite the TV and draped a woollen blanket over my bare legs which were curled under me. Winter in England – I loved it. And these days, I hardly left the house anyway, so lying in front of the fire with a tea and a blanket, watching mindless TV, was perfect. But I knew that in the coming spring, I would start to feel more and more guilty if I continued to stay home doing nothing.

Dad joined me on the couch. "That dinner you made yesterday was phenomenal. I think the food coma it put me in made me sleep better," he said.

"Well, either that or the wine."

"True." He grinned. "Hey, what was that thing you put on the salmon again?"

"The buckwheat? Or the sweet potato? Those were roasted sweet potato crisps. Or did you mean the dressing?"

"Stop. You're making me hungry!"

I chuckled. "I'll make you some breakfast."

"So how are you feeling?"

"… Good?"

He fiddled with a cushion. "Do you ever consider moving home?"

"To Australia?"

He nodded, looking like he might be regretting bringing this up. It reminded me of Drew, always so polite, and whenever he asked me something that might've been a little too deep, a little too personal, he immediately got the same look on his face, like perhaps he shouldn't have said anything. But I loved that about him. He was such a gentleman – yet when he thought I might be upset or angry, he just said whatever he thought, and it was always the right thing. Simply thinking about him was like having a fifty-kilo weight dropped on my chest.

"Nah. I love being here. This is my home now. Besides, what would you and Mum do without my cooking?" I laughed.

"It's been a luxury, that's for sure. But I don't want you thinking we're relying on you. We're not that old, you know. We don't quite need care just yet. I don't know. I guess, with Nan gone now – I mean, I guess I'm wondering what your plan is."

It wasn't like Dad to ever pressure me into anything, or tell me what to do. This statement was the furthest he'd ever ventured into asking about my life choices. He was right, though – since I moved here, I'd spent my days cooking for Nan, always making enough for Mum and Dad, and when I wasn't with her, I was over at Max's house visiting my nephew. It had kept me busy. But with Nan gone, I was now spending the days at Mum and Dad's, not doing much besides cooking. And running.

She'd died in December. And with everything else that'd happened, it had been a pretty damn sombre Christmas for everyone. Besides Dad's jokes, that is. Nan and Nonna had despised each other, and Dad joked that now they were finally reunited, they would probably get kicked out of heaven for arguing too much. I knew deep down he missed them dearly. We all did.

I replied carefully. "I don't know. I guess I haven't really made any decisions."

"And you don't need to. I just wonder if you're really happy here."

"Wow, Dad, you're asking all the big questions today!"

"It's just, I mean, you must miss Australia?"

I miss the beach. I miss working with Roisin and the girls. I miss teaching Hanako to drive.

And I miss Drew so damn much.

I shook my head. "Nope. It's nice being home."

"Okay. Well, if you ever decide you want to go back, you know we'll support you."

I thought about the large sum sitting in my bank account I'd received from Byron's life insurance. Financially, the move would be easy. Emotionally, I wasn't prepared to do it. One international move a year was more than enough.

"Thanks, Dad. But I'm good." I wrapped my fingers around the warm mug and smiled. "I'd miss you guys and Max and Eddie heaps."

He chuckled. "You sound so Australian, you know. *Heaps.*" He laughed at the use of the word, mimicking me.

I grinned. "Haven't I always?"

"Well, yeah. Pretty much since Kindergarten!"

I did think about his question, though. In the last twelve months, I had lost my husband, moved to England, turned thirty, lost my nan, gained a new nephew.

And met the love of my life.

It was too much. I was living life day-to-day; I really had no plan. I didn't *want* a plan. I hadn't even thought about work. I hadn't thought about anything, really. The grief counselling that I'd finally agreed to attending helped, to some extent. But I had stopped because I didn't like the flashbacks it gave me of my marriage to Byron. And sure, there was grief. Grief for his young life. Grief for his family. Grief for the others who'd died in the crash.

But there were also memories that weren't particularly good. Kevin, and everything that'd happened there. Memories of Byron. Memories that made me realise something that I had never realised before.

I hadn't been happy.

And the thought of that only compounded my guilt, which was already too much.

There was the memory of our wedding day, for example – when we'd entered the room for the first time as husband and wife. But instead of announcing us as "Mr and Mrs", Byron had insisted on being introduced as "Dr and Mrs". Even on our wedding day, his title had been more important to him than the fact he was marrying me.

I hadn't put up a fight, though – I never did. And that made me feel weak.

My family thought I was healing, that I'd stopped the sessions because I was at peace. But I felt the opposite. I was a snowball turning into an avalanche.

Most of my guilt was over Mal, though. It was my fault. If I hadn't got so close to Drew, Byron never would have done what he did. I still couldn't even comprehend what he'd done. Affairs, deception, condescension – none of that compared to poisoning a dog. I didn't even know him anymore. And I couldn't believe I had *married* someone who could even think about doing such a heinous thing.

Since being back in England, I felt so – hollow; and so tired. One day I'd decided I was sick of my hair. Everything in life felt like such an effort, and having long, thick hair was a pain in the ass I didn't need. I'd gone to a local hairdresser, where they gave me a clipboard with a sheet of personal details to fill out. I froze when I saw the section on marital status. Single, married, separated, divorced, *widowed.* I'd stood staring at the word silently, heat rising in my chest. The fact that I had never, ever in my entire life understood why the hell those details were relevant to something like getting a haircut, or signing up for a new email address, or booking a concert ticket, did not help.

The poor hairdresser had copped an earful before I ripped the sheet into shreds and left.

Of course, a few days later I had gone back, requested to see that same hairdresser, and gave her a huge apology and a very big tip after she cut my hair. My guilt was through the roof.

I thought about Drew often. A part of me wanted to track him down – but I knew I'd left things too late. It was a vicious cycle. I missed him so much, but thinking about him only exacerbated the guilt. It'd been just over a year since our day at the beach. And now, we weren't even in the same hemisphere. I'd never even bothered to find out if he was okay in the Middle East.

I'd let him down.

And now he probably hated me. If I saw him right now, I wouldn't be able to look him in the eye. So there was no point dwelling on that. It was over, whatever it was, and he'd probably moved on. No way a guy like that would stay single for long. I wished so badly I'd had the chance to tell him how I really felt. The chance to explain what I'd meant when I said he was predictable. When I said he was childish, and annoying, I'd only been mucking around – but when I said "predictable", I meant it – even though I hadn't explained it to him properly. And what I'd meant was that, no matter what, he was always dependable. Reliable. It had just come out a bit funny. Good days or bad, he was always someone you could count on. I knew that right from the start. If our personalities were drawn as a line, mine would be all jagged and wavy, and his would be straight. No matter how moody or irrational I was being, he would always be there. How I wished I had taken the time to explain that to him back then. But now, I had to focus on pushing him out of my mind, and all the guilt associated with that time of my life.

I'd made the most of being in England. I'd visited my nephew, Eddie, a lot – even babysitting him a couple of times while Max and his partner went out for an early dinner, or to a film. He was sweet. But when we were alone, I was depressed, always feeling like holding a baby would never be something I'd get to experience.

I was lonely – but I had no desire to fix it.

Roisin rang me every Sunday night for a video chat. I really missed seeing her and working with her. The Pool Chicks business was going well, she said – they'd employed two new staff. I wasn't even needed there, by the sound of it.

My phone pinged with a text as Dad got up and collected our mugs. "Better go and put these in the dishwasher before your mother gets up and I get in trouble," he said, giving me a wink.

"Thanks, Dad." I looked down to check my phone. It was Roisin.

I'm off to bed, chat to you Sunday. 9pm your time?

Sounds good. I paused, chewing my bottom lip, thinking about what Dad had asked me.

I sent her another text. *Hypothetical question. If I came back to Australia, would you re-employ me? I mean not now, but maybe in a few years?*

I'd give you a job tomorrow if you came back.

ARE YOU COMING BACK? OMG PLS TELL ME YOUR COMING BACK?

*You're, she corrected.

I chuckled. *Haha. I said HYPOTHETICALLY!*

OK. Well are you HYPOTHETICALLY thinking about coming back?

I paused. *Maybe. In the future.*

Tomorrow IS the future …

I laughed again. *Good night.*

Putting my phone down, I stared at the firepit, still chewing on my bottom lip.

SUMMER

4 6

GEORGIE

———————

"So, where have you travelled from?"

"Brighton-Le-Sands," I said, following the lanky girl up the path of the animal shelter.

"Oh, nice, you live on the beach?"

"Yeah. Just off The Grand Parade, on the corner. You know the area?"

"Sort of." She opened the door to let me into the office, introducing me to the receptionist. "This is Georgie, she'd like to make a donation."

"Oh hi, Georgie. Thank you! Are you wanting to donate in cash?"

"Er, no …" I looked from one girl to the other. "I'm donating a hundred grand, so … I didn't exactly take that out in cash." I laughed, but my laughter was only met by two blank stares.

It was my first week back in Australia. I'd found an apartment on the beach, and had finally made a decision on what to do with Byron's money. It would be split in a few ways – and this was the first stop.

The decision to move back to Sydney had been a pretty easy one, in the end. For almost a year, all I'd done was sit around at my parents' place in England. I had looked after my nan; but my parents had looked after me. I'd got to meet my new nephew and spend time with my brother. But eventually, as much as I'd loved being there, I started to miss Australia. A lot. It'd become my real home. And despite my family being so far away, it was where I needed to be. It's where I *wanted* to be – Sydney was home. But there was no way I was returning to the suburbs; I went right back to where I always should have been, instead: the beach.

I'd made a pact to go back to England every year. Roisin had generously offered to give me as many holidays as I wanted (or, at least, she had used that promise to coax me back to Australia).

My new apartment was right on the water, and there was a long beachside footpath where I went running every morning before it got busy. I was back for the tail-end of the Australian summer, and I was in the ocean every day. I loved Brighton because the water was flat (I guess my European roots still set me apart from the "real Aussies" in that I despised the forceful, neck-breaking waves). My street was lined with cafés, restaurants, and little ice cream shops. It was busy, but the beach was stretched out enough that it never really felt too crowded.

I'd spent my first week back in Sydney swimming, running, eating at cafés alone (something I'd have *never* done before) and wandering the streets around me, getting to know the area. I sat on my ocean-facing balcony reading, staring out at the water and soaking up the rays. It didn't take long to be reminded of how harsh the Australian sun was, especially straight after an English winter. My skin was *not* prepared for that. A one-litre tub of thick 50+ sunscreen lived on my balcony permanently.

And for the first time, I almost felt happy. Well – not happy, exactly, but – content, perhaps. I was alone, and I didn't hate it.

Two days ago, I'd returned to work. Roisin didn't know what to do with herself. She didn't know whether to hug me, kiss me, or ask me a thousand questions. She gave me the keys to one of the Pool Chicks utes right away, wrapped in a little red bow.

"The bow is new; the ute is as old as the Egyptian pyramids. Sorry!" she'd said.

I smiled. "I don't care about that." I actually liked those beat-up old utes.

She wouldn't stop grinning and insisted we go out for dinner and a few drinks after work. The next morning, somewhat sore-headed and tired, I went for a light jog and jumped in the ocean. And on the walk home, I froze when I saw him.

A black-and-white dog with shiny fur and blue eyes. For a split second, I could've sworn it was Mal. But as reality sank in, I jogged home, filled with a deep sadness – only now, I had a good idea about what to do with Byron's money. I had already decided to donate a significant chunk to hospital charities and organisations like Surgeons with Heart International. And today was the day I gave it all away, starting with the shelter.

Besides, organising donations kept me busy – and stopped me from thinking about Drew every waking moment.

The receptionist at the shelter was the first to speak. "Um … That's … a sizable donation from an individual." She blinked. "Wow, thank you."

I wired the money across, gave the receptionist some details, and then the other girl walked me back out to the ute. I looked around at the rows of cages as she spouted information at me about the organisation, apparently feeling like she needed to treat me like royalty. I was nodding along and walking behind her, right as a loud bark just about made me jump out of my skin. I spun around to find myself face to face with an excited, panting dog. He whimpered and barked at me again, tail wagging wildly.

I loved how some dogs' mouths made them seem like they were really smiling. Mal had had it. And this dog had it, too. His smile was so wide, his eyes were almost squeezed shut. He barked again, then let his tongue hang out of his mouth as he panted and whined, standing on his long hind legs against the wire gate of his enclosure.

"Hey, buddy." I glanced over at the girl. "Is it okay to pat him?"

"Sure, I can let you in if you like?"

"No, that's okay," I said, poking my fingers through the holes in the gate. I couldn't pat him, though; he was too quick. Every time I stuck my fingers in to touch his velvet fur, he would lick them instead of letting me pat him. My hand was covered in his slobber. "What's his name?"

"Pepito Rodriguez III," she said, laughing when I gave her an odd look. "He seems to like you. You sure you don't wanna go in?"

She was unlocking the gate before I could decline. When I got in, he went wild – jumping on me, nearly knocking me over, nipping at my hands playfully.

"Wow. Energetic. What breed is he?"

"We don't know. The vet thinks he's a kelpie cross. Maybe greyhound and staffy, too. A bit of German shepherd." She shrugged. "He's never told us himself," she said with a nervous laugh.

I patted his head, his fur a little dusty and in need of a wash. "You have got the world's biggest ears," I said. He sat down and watched me eagerly, his huge ears pointing to the sky. His fur was a brown-black colour, with white all down his chest and on his paws like four white socks. His snout was white, too, and a thin white strip connected his nose to the top of his head. "What's with the long name?"

"Oh, we call him Pepper for short. His fur is kind of like pepper, the brown and black all mixed together. That's how he got his name. But Pepito Rodriguez III came from the way he sits, bolt upright with his chest out, looking so regal like he belongs in a royal family or something."

To Pepper's joy, I continued to scratch him behind his ears.

"He is very cute."

When I stepped out and closed the gate behind me, Pepper's eyes were glued to me.

"You're not looking to adopt, are you?"

"Oh, god, no. I only just bought a small apartment. No. I'm not a dog person anyway. He'd hate living with me."

She raised an eyebrow, probably wondering why on earth I'd donated a hundred grand to an animal shelter. "He doesn't *seem* to hate you ..." she said. "And he's a very friendly dog. Well, he gets pretty anxious around other dogs. But he's great with people. And he's great with kids. Do you have kids?"

I stiffened. "No."

"I mean, he's probably too big and energetic for an apartment. That's the kelpie in him."

I nodded and used the chance to turn towards the ute, taking the keys out of my handbag. "See ya, Pepper." I stole one final glance at him. He was watching me walk away with his deep brown eyes.

"It's just that ... " the girl paused, looking down at her hands, "I mean, I'm not supposed to say this, but – well, he's being put down tomorrow. I mean, if we, if we don't adopt him before then."

I froze mid-step. "What?"

"Yeah, we can't—it's the worst part of the job."

"You can't keep him, with all that money I've just donated?"

"Uh, no, well – it's a spacing issue. And he's been here forever. Probably has no idea what living in his own home, with his own humans, even feels like."

I closed my eyes. When I turned back to Pepper, he went wild at the eye contact, jumping against the gate with his paws poking out in the gaps and his tail wagging with such energy that his whole body was swinging back and forth.

I closed my eyes again and sighed.

*

Pepper sat on his bottom on the passenger seat of my ute, straight-backed like a human. The girl was right about him looking like royalty. I'd even put the seatbelt on him to keep him from flying through the windscreen if I had to brake hard.

He kept staring at me, then back out the front, then back at me, grinning.

The two of us would've been an absolutely ridiculous sight driving along in the ute like that.

He'd finally settled down after trying to jump into my lap repeatedly. He wouldn't stay on the floor of the ute's cab, and I didn't have the heart to put him in the tray.

Not after Mal.

He kept glancing over at me as I drove, a sizable string of saliva connecting his mouth and tongue to my seat. I shook my head. "You win this round, pal." I indicated and turned onto the main road. "You better not cost me anything in vet bills. And you're eating the cheapest kibble I can find. Okay?"

He turned to me and blinked. And I knew right then that he would most likely be eating eye fillet steaks for dinner every night.

"Jesus," I muttered. "What the hell am I gonna do with a *dog*?"

A red leash and two round metal bowls sat on the floor of the ute, a large dog bed in the tray. I'd been upsold when I bought a frickin' *dog*. "Georgie?" the young girl at the pound had called out after me as I started to drive off, Pepper still trying to get in my lap. "Um, a tiny warning. Pepper chews stuff."

I pulled into my parking spot and looked up at my apartment. "Well, this is it." Pepper looked at me curiously as we sat silently in the ute, side by side. "Welcome home, buddy."

47

GEORGIE

The doorbell rang as I was rinsing off one of my chewed-up shoes in the laundry sink of my apartment, seeing if it could be salvaged. "Bloody dog." Pepper sat at my feet, tail wagging. "Yes. That's right. *You!*" I said, holding the wrecked shoe up to him. He just wagged his tail harder. "Hold on," I yelled towards the door. "I'm coming!"

Must be one of the neighbours. I took off the chain and turned the deadlock. My only concern with returning to Sydney was seeing Kevin again. I wasn't scared of him so much as utterly disgusted – but I still never wanted to have to see him again. I'd investigated getting a restraining order, and it seemed possible, but then he'd just be alerted to the fact I was back in Australia. I didn't necessarily want that, either. So I still hadn't made up my mind about what to do – but it was reassuring that the option was available. One thing was certain: with Byron gone, I would never have to worry about being in a room alone with Kevin ever again.

When I opened the door, chewed shoe in hand, I froze. "Hanako?"

She grinned, then tried to suffocate me with a massive hug. "Oh my *god*. You're back!"

"I'm back." I held her out at arm's length and looked at her. "Wow. You are so tall!"

Pepper was running around us, thrilled to bits, jumping up and yelping.

"What on earth … Who is this?" Han said, sounding unimpressed at first, but falling victim to Pepper's deep brown eyes. She crouched down, put his head in her hands, and scratched it roughly all over.

"This is Pepito Rodriguez III. He also goes by Pepper," I said. "I know. Don't give me that look."

"I thought you hated dogs?"

"So did I." It took a good five minutes to settle Pepper down after Hanako's arrival. He eventually lay down on my new couch next to his expensive dog bed, which was untouched, of course. Well, almost untouched. It had some bite marks on its side, thread sticking out everywhere despite the brand's claim of "99% of dogs will NOT be able to chew through this!" *This bloody dog.*

"Wow, Han. I can't get over how tall you've got."

"Yeah. And get this," she said, fishing a plastic card out of her phone case and holding it up to me.

"You got your licence?"

She beamed. "Yep. Finally. I thought Dad was gonna lose his shit. He really hated teaching me to drive. Sat there holding the handbrake in one hand, the handle above his head with the other. He would have preferred a harness to a seatbelt, for sure."

I laughed. It was so good to see her – the first friend I'd seen apart from Roisin and the girls at work.

"Well, congratulations. Come in, have a seat." I gave up and put the shoe in the bin, then walked behind the kitchen island. "You want a tea?"

"Georgie. I may have my driver's licence, but I'm no grandma."

I laughed. "Well, then I only have water to offer you, I'm

afraid …"

"Geez, sound English much? *I'm afraid*," she mimicked.

"Apparently. So how're Kate and Tony? And what happened with school? Did they let you come back after the suspension?"

"*Let* me come back? Pfft. They practically begged."

"Especially the principal, I bet."

"Yeah, especially him. As you Poms like to say, he's a right bell-end."

I pressed my lips together at her put-on accent. "So you decided to finish Year Twelve then."

"Yeah, I decided to keep Dad happy for a while."

I nodded. "Good."

"Besides, I figured I have plenty more chances in life to disappoint him, anyway."

"Oh my god, Hanako." I sat down on the couch next to her and handed her a glass of water. "Maybe Tony deserves a short break from your antics?"

"I'm here, aren't I? He gets an hour off." She grinned. "I'm really glad you called Kate. She gave me your address. Drove here in my new car! Well – not *new* new. I wish. But still. It's so cool!"

"You got a car?"

"Yeah."

"Well, come on, then – show me!"

"I will. But I need to talk to you about something first." Her expression turned serious as we sat down on the couch next to Pepper, who, of course, was hogging the entire chaise.

"O … kaay?"

She paused. "Georgie, are you all right?"

I shrugged. "Yeah. More or less."

"I mean emotionally."

"I got that."

She crossed her legs on the couch and bounced a knee up and down.

"What happened with you and Drew?"

My heart skipped a beat. "Uh, what do you mean?"

I had successfully managed *not* to think about Drew. Well, just about. Although, since moving back to Sydney, it was getting harder and harder not to. I'd visited and swum at all the beaches. Coogee. Tamarama. Bondi. Maroubra.

But I never, ever went back to Gordons Bay.

"Georgie. I know something was going on with you two. You don't have to tell me, but I've been real worried about you. I didn't even have your UK number."

I looked at her concerned face. She'd never been someone I could lie to. She was as brutally honest as me, and I trusted her. There were so many people I had left behind when I left Australia that I didn't even think about. Hanako may have been a lot younger than me, but she just got me. And she was an important part of my life. So I proceeded to tell her everything – right from the day I cut my finger and climbed Drew's fence, to the day he came to work with me, to the phone incident, to the night I got drunk and blacked out in his bed, and finally, to *that* beach day.

The day I'd struggled so much not to think about.

My shoulders sagged when I finished speaking, and I let out a huge sigh.

Han's eyes went wide. "And the next day …"

"The next day I found out Byron had died."

Her hand shot to her mouth. "Fuuuuck."

"Yep."

"Have you told anyone else? About Drew?"

"Not a soul."

She swallowed, taking in all the information.

"How did you know something happened?" I asked her.

"I knew after Kate's Christmas party. It was so obvious he was into you. And after that, I kept hoping you would get together."

"But I was married."

"Yeah. But Byron was a dick."

"You can't say that."

"I can, and I did."

I sat in silence for a moment before putting my head in my hands. "He poisoned Mal."

"Huh?"

"Byron. He poisoned Mal. I've never told anyone about that." A huge weight lifted from my chest, right before the tears pricked my eyes.

"What?"

I nodded. "That's why he had to be put down. Byron gave him something that put him into kidney failure." My voice trailed off halfway through the last word, a lump forming in my throat. I bit down hard on my tongue and looked up at the ceiling. What Byron had done … I couldn't even comprehend it. Poisoning a dog.

That wasn't being a bad husband.

That wasn't even being a bad human.

That was being a straight-up psychopath.

I didn't even know who he really was. And it made me sick to my core.

"Oh my god, Georgie. You can never, ever tell Drew," Han said, eyes still wide.

"Well, I'm not going to *see* Drew, so that won't be a problem."

Even if I did see Drew, I couldn't possibly tell him the truth. The scenario had crossed my mind. Of course it had – I thought about seeing Drew all the time. And it broke my heart to know that I never would.

Didn't he deserve to know what happened to Mal? Mal was his, after all. That was the continuous cycle of thought that went round and round in my head – tell him; don't tell him. But the thing was: Byron did what he did to hurt Drew. And he did it to hurt me. He knew I loved that dog so much. And he knew Mal was Drew's world. Nothing mattered more to Drew than Mal, his beautiful black-and-white rescue dog. His best friend.

Telling him the truth wouldn't bring Mal back. Nothing good would come of it.

I still felt responsible for what Byron had done. And it felt like if I told Drew, then Byron would win – he would hurt Drew as much as he'd hurt me. The final stab in the back.

And I could just see the smug expression on Byron's face. I felt nauseous.

"Why not?" Han asked as I shuddered.

I stood up, put my hands on my hips and faced Pepper as I spoke. "That ship has sailed. Drew wouldn't want to see me, after what I did anyway. I messed that up royally. And he deserves better."

She gave me a stern look. "Georgie. You're a smart woman. But that's just stupid."

"It's not."

"It is. You're talking out of your ass."

Sighing, I picked up the empty mug and glass, and took them to the kitchen, grabbing a sponge to wash the dishes. As soon as I stood, Pepper was at my feet, eagerly awaiting a treat.

"This is his favourite room in the house," I told Han. "This is where he does his best work. He's like a busker playing terrible music – even though you know it's awful, you feel sorry for him and give him money just because he gives you a certain look." I laughed. "That's Pepper. Except it's with food."

"Georgie. I'm serious. You need to contact him."

"I … can't."

"All right. Can I ask you a question then? And you promise to be honest?"

"I'm always honest with you."

"And are you honest with yourself?"

I sighed, putting down the sponge. "What's the question?"

"If Byron had never had the accident, if he'd survived and come home, what would have happened?"

I swallowed. "I was … I was going to leave him."

"And?"

"And no one else knows that, not even my family."

"Okay. Well, that must've been tough to keep to yourself all this time."

I nodded, giving her a tight-lipped smile. A knife was twisting in my stomach, but at the same time, talking about this finally was also releasing something inside me.

"Right. So you would've left him. And then?"

I hesitated. "And then I would've gone to Drew's and told him how I felt."

"And that is …?"

I sighed, staring at my feet. "That I'm in love with him."

Han clapped. "Present tense! Good. We're getting somewhere." She leaned down, picked up her handbag, and pulled out a thick wad of papers. "Did I ever tell you the story of my mum and Kate?"

I frowned, making my way back to the couch. "They *knew* each other?"

"Of course they didn't know each other."

I gave her an odd look, confused. "Okay?"

"Dad met her, like, two years after Mum passed away. Anyway. You know what Mum said to me before she died?"

I shook my head.

"She told me Dad would need to move on, find someone else, be happy. I was eleven. I cried for three days straight. But she was right. And you know what? If she hadn't told me that, I'd have made Dad's life a living hell. I never would have let him get together with Kate. But now, he's happy. He'd probably be miserable without her."

I nodded. "I'm glad you and Kate get along."

"You can't live for the dead, Georgie. Byron is gone. And he's not coming back. But Drew? He's here. He *did* come back. So what are you going to do about that?"

"I … I'm not sure."

"Georgie."

"Han … look. That might have been the case with your Dad, and I'm glad he was able to move on. But the big difference is that *he* didn't do anything wrong. I did. The guilt I feel, the guilt I've felt for over a year, it really weighs you down. I can't just move on and pretend it didn't happen. I can't say *'Yeah, okay, I'll go and be happy with Drew now'* after what I did."

"But you said you would have left Byron."

"And?"

"Okay, listen. Fact number one." She raised her index finger. "You feel guilty about cheating on Byron. Right?"

I nodded. Just hearing that word made me feel ill.

"Fact two." She raised another finger. "You're in love with Drew."

I nodded carefully. And I knew exactly where she was going with her point.

"Which one are you going to let rule your life? Are you going to keep letting Byron dictate your happiness? Follow your heart, or keep letting guilt win? The past is the past. But tomorrow is the future."

I chuckled. "Bloody hell, did you practise this speech?" And more to the point – how was she so wise at her age? Still a teenager … and yet insightful beyond her years. But teenagers often were. I wondered if losing her mother at a young age had made her more aware, and more sensitive, of people missing out on having loved ones in their lives. I swallowed, pushing away the thought of what she'd gone through.

"Drew's a good guy, Georgie."

"Trust me. You don't need to tell me that." I sighed. "But you know what? It's been a year. What's to say he hasn't moved on? He won't want anything to do with me. And I can't blame him. I ruined things big time."

"You are writing him off, Georgie. And you're writing yourself off, too."

I shook my head. "What're those?" I said, eyeing the paper in her hands. It was a pile of crinkled letters held together by a thick red elastic band.

"Do you know where Drew was deployed?"

"Um … Somewhere in the Middle East. Why?"

"He sent you all these. While he was away." She put them in my hands and waited.

My heart skipped a beat, an involuntary sob leaving my mouth as I looked at the handwriting. I hadn't even realised I'd been close to tears again. "But … these are all addressed to you?" I said, flicking through the letters. There were about ten or twelve of them, all identical.

"I got a letter from him a few weeks after he left. It said he was going to write you a letter. But he didn't want it to get into the wrong hands. So he said he was going to send it to me to give to you in private."

I stared at her.

"Obviously, he didn't know what'd happened. And you left, and I had no way of finding where you were. You don't even have Facebook anymore."

"I … deleted it."

"No shit. And the letters kept coming."

I studied them again. "What do they say?"

"How the hell should I know?"

"You didn't open them?"

"Why would I open them?"

My heart was beating in my temples as I sat clutching Drew's letters.

"He came looking for you, you know. When he got home. He didn't even go into his house before he came over to ask where you were."

I was frozen to the spot. "Do your parents know?"

"About you and Drew?"

I nodded.

"Not unless you told them."

My legs were jelly. I couldn't move. Pepper lay on the chaise, unfazed.

"Are you okay?" Han asked cautiously.

I nodded again, fighting back the tears that were still burning my eyes.

"Okay. Then here's what's going to happen. I'm gonna get some ice cream from that hipster place down the road. Then I'm gonna come back in half an hour. And if you decide you want to see him, I'll drive you. You remember where his sister lives, yeah?"

"Vaguely … I think? But, why?"

"Because Drew doesn't live across the street any more. And I have no idea where he moved."

She got up and slung her handbag over her shoulder. "Let's hope his sister is still there. 'Cos you and Drew are sure as hell making this process difficult."

I couldn't help smiling at her.

"So, what flavour ice cream should I get? What's good?"

"I have no idea," I said, clutching the letters like they might run away.

"Of course you don't. You're a rake, Georgie. I'm bringing you back a tub of ice cream." She scratched Pepper on the head, winding him up again before walking out the door, an excited, brown-eyed stare following her.

I looked down and shakily pulled the elastic off the thick pile of letters.

4 8

GEORGIE

There was a letter on the top of the pile without an envelope which I set aside to read first. Heart pounding, I put the other letters in order – thankfully Hanako had numbered them. I stuck my index finger under the corners of the letters and ripped them open, careful not to mess up the order they'd arrived in. I slowly unfolded them, swallowed, and started reading Drew's words. Drew's warm, sincere words. Choking back tears, I suddenly found his absence in my life more painful than ever. And, right away, I could hear his voice in my head, so clearly, like a year hadn't passed.

Dear Hanako,

It's Drew here, from across the road. How are you? I'm away overseas for some time, and I was hoping you could pass this letter on to Georgie for me. For various reasons, I can't send it to her house. Please, could you give it to her for me when you see her next? Thanks so much. I really appreciate it.

Drew

P.S. My Hilux is sitting unused in the front yard. If you need it for driving lessons, it's all yours. My sister lives down the road – you could get her to let you in to mine to grab the keys. Georgie knows where she lives.

Dear Georgie,

Well, first of all, I hope you're ok. I'm really hoping that you are. What happened on Sunday night? I'm so sorry if I did something to upset you. I've tried so hard to think back, to remember, but I've got nothing. Was it seeing me nude? It was seeing me nude, wasn't it?! And I just made a mental note to address this to Hanako to give to you instead of sending it to your house.

So the other night I dreamt about that time we bought all those things from that random shopping list. You made that amazing linguine from it. And also, you got busted by your own butcher for buying bones for Mal!!! And then I remembered that that same night we were chatting about my brother's kids and you said you loved receiving letters. So I decided to write you one. I'm not much of a writer, so if it sucks, I'm sorry. Apart from my replies to Evie and Gracie, I don't think I have ever written a letter. Actually, that's a lie. Once I wrote a secret Valentine's card to my Year 3 teacher. I have a feeling she knew who it was, but she never did respond :)

I've had the first few days here to get used to the weather and settle in, and we've had some weaponry training. From tomorrow, we'll be straight into it.

It's quite cold here, as it's the end of winter, but the mountains are so beautiful – they're all snow-capped and we can see them from the base. I think you'd like them.

Ok, well, I'm off to have some dinner now. The mess hall is massive here. The food's a lot better than I expected. You can literally get heaps of different cuisines – Turkish, Italian, Thai. I had the Italian on my first night. It was good, but it had nothing on your cooking.

Well, I miss you.

My work email is below. I would love it so much if you wrote to me. Even just to say you're ok.

Love,

Drew.

Dear Georgie,

I have no idea how long it takes for these to arrive in Australia, but I'm going to keep writing because hopefully they do eventually arrive. I'm kind of enjoying writing the letters. I feel like I'm talking to you, which I know sounds weird, but it makes me feel better. I've written a couple of letters to the girls, too, and they sent me an email the other day with some photos from Singapore. It was very cute. It's so weird seeing their photos – they're all in shirts and shorts, and going swimming at night, but here it's so bloody cold. Have you ever been to Singapore? And what's it been like in Sydney?

I've been going running every day, usually in the morning, but it really depends on the shifts I'm doing. Running is a lot more boring without Mal. I miss him a lot, but I have so many good memories of him. And a lot of them include you.

My shifts have changed from days to nights, and it took a bit of time to get used to it, but it's all ok now. Being here, it really doesn't make that much of a difference – it's not exactly life as usual. We have two or three watchkeepers rotating each day, so we either do 8 or 12 hour shifts.

Enough about me, though. How are you? I really wish I knew what you were up to, and just that you're ok.

Love,

Drew

Dear Georgie,

I'm hoping you're getting and reading these letters even if you're not responding. Although I guess then that means you don't want to talk to me for whatever reason as I haven't had an email from you yet. So maybe I'm actually hoping you aren't getting these. Who knows.

A couple of the guys and I got together and watched the cricket this morning after night shift. I've never followed it, but it was cool to watch – even though it made me miss Australia heaps!

I really miss you.

Drew

P.S. If you do decide to send me an email, just a warning that everything is heavily monitored here. Calls, emails, letters. So, as much as it pains me to say this, DON'T SEND NUDES!

Love,

Drew

Dear Georgie,

It's almost been a month since I arrived here. A whole month! One down ... five to go. Honestly, it has been so slow. But I've been thinking (I can imagine you asking me, "Did it hurt?" – yes, it did, because my brain is so large). After four months, I get a two-week holiday somewhere. I was going to come back to Sydney, but it's a long way to travel when all I have is that time – the two weeks include the time to get there and back. So I've been thinking of where else I can go, because I will definitely need a break. We work seven days a week, so there's really not much time to relax. Not that I'd expect it, given the nature of the job – and I always knew that coming into it. But anyway, I've been thinking. A lot of the Aussies go to Europe instead of flying home. And sometimes their families fly over to meet them there. It's not too far away from here, a pretty quick flight. So

I've been thinking about where to go. I've been chatting to some of the guys around. Would love to hear your thoughts, seeing as you're the Euro-expert. Any ideas?

Drew

Dear Georgie,

I know it's not exactly timely, but if you saw the news last night about the attacks over here, well, I just wanted to tell you I'm ok. They actually weren't near our base at all. Like I said, by the time you receive this, it's not like it'll mean anything, but I thought I'd let you know. Besides, I know you don't know where I am anyway. So, yeah, this is fairly pointless, I guess.

I hope you are doing ok.

How're the Pool Chicks? I hope Roisin was able to get her car sticker fixed. :)

Drew

Dear Georgie,

It's been a hectic night. I am lying in bed listening to some music and writing this. I was on night shift by myself last night and the rocket alarm went off around 2:45am. Everybody ran to take cover – but in the end it was actually a false alarm. It was scary, though. Everyone was pretty freaked out, as you can imagine.

Nothing else to report, really. Another standard week. I'm surrounded by people here, some really lovely Australians who I spend time with, but this week I just feel really lonely. I was about to write that I wish you were here. But I don't – I wish I was there, instead.

Drew

Dear Georgie,

Sorry I haven't written in a while. It's been hectic, and to be honest, sometimes it's hard to know what to say. There's only one more month to go until I get my break! I can't wait. I honestly can't. Ok, so here's a wild thought. Come with me. Ask Roisin for time off and come meet me in Europe. I want to see you so much, Georgie. Just talk to you. There's so much I want to say, and I can't get it across in these letters. I need to get out of here.

We could go to Italy or something. Do you have relatives there still? Friends? Or somewhere totally different. What about Spain? I went there a few years ago, after another deployment, actually. It'll be June/July by then – middle of summer. We could stay on Las Ramblas and eat tapas at the bars and swim in the ocean and drink sangria and take afternoon siestas. You in?

Drew

Dear Georgie,

I should've said this a long time ago.
I love you.
Drew

Dear Georgie,

How are you?

It's only two weeks until my break. I know it's almost here, and I haven't heard from you as yet – I dunno, I'm secretly hoping you'll surprise me there or something. I know that's unlikely, because you don't even know when or where I'm going. But sometimes logic doesn't prevail here.

Please come.

It's been a pretty cool week here, probably because it's so close to my break. I've been hanging out with some Nepalese people. They're a good bunch. Different nationalities take turns

*guarding our base, and at the moment it's them. The Gurkhas
have a reputation for being bloody tough – and that they are.
Super intimidating looking, but they are really kind. Last night
we had a big cook up and they made goat stew. Had the whole
skull in it and everything. They make a bloody mean curry! We
Aussies get on really well with them in general. And a couple
of nights ago we watched the All Blacks game with a couple of
Danish blokes. That was a great night, too.*

See you in Spain? First sangria is on me.

Drew

Dear Georgie,

*We have pretty limited internet here, but I checked my email
earlier. Being honest – I don't know whether to stop writing
altogether. So here's one final effort. I'm going to organise my
flights today. All going to plan, I'll be getting into Barcelona
on the night of June 14. I actually can't give any more details
than that for security reasons.*

*If you get this, please reply – I don't even care if it's just to
say you are ok, but don't want to see me. This waiting is killing
me. I need to know. And I think I deserve at least that.*

Drew

Dear Georgie,

*I'm sorry about my last letter. I was feeling a bit down. Easy
to do here. I had actually listened to an Incubus playlist that
day, which was the first time I'd heard them since that day at
the beach. I'm so confused. I just don't understand what's going
on. And I really, really miss you. But for now, I think I need to
stop writing these. When I do, I keep waiting and waiting for a
reply. And it's pretty clear I'm not getting one. It's like waiting
for the end of a never-ending tunnel. I feel a bit silly that this*

whole time I've kept imagining you meeting me for a European summer when that clearly isn't going to happen.

Whatever you're doing, wherever you are – I hope you are well, and I hope you are happy.

But for now, I'm done.

Drew

49

GEORGIE

My head hit the window of Hanako's car as I tried to insert the old sim card into my phone. "Jesus, Han, slow down!"

"Do you want to get there or not?"

"I'd rather stay in one piece, actually."

"Speed limits are more of a suggestion, right?" She winked, trying to lighten the mood.

After reading Drew's letters three times, I was a total mess.

My heart was pounding as the phone came to life, my old Australian number still working. I was glad – I knew the monthly bill was still coming out of my account, and I had never bothered to stop it. Now I was grateful. I waited as texts and missed call notifications flooded my screen, then opened the camera roll and looked at the screenshot I'd taken of Drew's email address. I quickly typed an email with my new number, telling him to call me as soon as he received it, and sent it to his Defence email. If he saw it before we got to Elena's house, I could go meet him wherever he was. But I didn't like the chances of Drew checking his work email in the next forty minutes. I crossed my fingers that he had his notifications turned on.

I waded through all my old texts, not wanting to open them

– the sim hadn't been used since Byron died, and I couldn't go there right now.

I flicked past all the unopened messages until I got to the day I'd found out Byron died – *that* Sunday, when I was meant to go round to Drew's – the night before he'd flown to the Middle East.

There were three text messages from him.

Hey Georgie, you still coming over? Are you trying to get pretty in front of the mirror again? I'm giving you ten minutes, then I'm starting without you!

Oh. That's awkward. I meant dinner. Starting DINNER without you.

Hey. Everything ok? I just came round but you're not there. I'm sorry if I made things weird. Anyway. I fly out at 8am tomorrow. Prob leave home at 5 at the latest. I'd really love to see you before then. Please come by … any time. I'm sorry again.

What the hell was he sorry for?

I felt sick.

With a shaky hand, I clicked on his number and held the phone to my ear, grabbing onto the handle as Hanako took a corner way too fast.

The number you have dialled has been disconnected.

"Facebook?" Hanako suggested.

I shook my head. "Deleted it, remember? And Drew never had it."

"God. You pair of geriatrics."

I sat in silence as Hanako pulled up on my old street. It felt surreal being back there after all this time. And it took a good ten minutes, but I finally found what I wanted: Elena's orange front door. Thankfully, it stood out from the houses around it, jogging my memory. Lucky Drew had pointed it out on the way home from work that day.

A random memory flashed through my mind. Drew, carrying two drums of chlorine, grinning, his shorts bleached in patches.

It had been a scorcher of a day, but not once had he complained when I'd asked him to help with something.

He would literally do anything for me – back then, at least. I just hoped all of this wasn't too late.

I took a breath, walked to the front door, and rang Elena's doorbell.

5 0

D R E W

"So, you gonna do the Cottesloe to Rotty swim with me at the end of the month, or what?" Mike said.

"Mate, I need a few more beers before I commit to stupid stuff like that," I said.

He leaned back in his chair on my balcony, putting his feet up and raising his beer towards the sky. "To many more beers and bad decisions. So good to have you back."

I clinked his bottle with mine and took a swig of the cold amber liquid. As I watched the sun slowly setting over Cottesloe Beach, I realised I'd be hard-pressed to remember an afternoon that I hadn't spent in this exact position, watching the ball of flaming red dip down over the smooth water.

Being back in Perth was *good*. Summers here were my favourite. But I didn't like the fact that the end of this one was looming.

"How long since you did it?" Mike said, turning up the volume on the speaker sitting between us on the ground.

"What, the swim?"

He nodded.

"At least … two years?"

"Good. Then you've forgotten the pain."

"Hilarious. I'll think about it."

"It's not even twenty ks. No big deal."

"Oh yeah? What is it then, seventeen?"

"Nineteen point seven."

I looked at him and we both laughed, right as an Incubus song started playing. I froze, the beer in my hand stopping halfway to my mouth for a split second, before I reached down and skipped the song.

"Hey. That's a *great* song," Mike said with a frown.

"Agreed."

He raised an eyebrow. I didn't elaborate, but picked up my phone instead and ordered a couple of pizzas. Mike put his beer down on the tiled floor of my balcony and rolled up his shorts so the tops of his thighs were exposed to the sun.

"Mate," I said with a smirk, "working on your tan?"

"Well, some of us are single, you know. Gotta stay sexy for the ladies."

"You creep."

"Says you. You look like you've just come back from stripping at a bachelorette party."

I turned to him. "You're the one sitting there shirtless, tanning your thighs." I laughed. "Besides, I'm not exactly *not* single."

"Not single? Listen to you, wanting your cake and eating it too. And I reckon your relationship status probably depends on who you ask."

I took a swig of beer and looked out the balcony, thoughts drifting to Georgie as they often did, an all-too-familiar sadness crushing my chest when I thought of her smile – and the fact it was now Jess's smile I was waking up to. I redirected my thoughts to Mike – and what he was saying about Jess. "What do you mean?"

"Come on. Jess is all over you like a rash. You said she's been here, like, every night."

"Well, yeah, pretty much. But it's … I mean, we haven't really had that conversation."

"She was calling you her boyfriend at the pub on Sunday. So you might wanna straighten things out before she moves in or something. Or gets you a kitten. Or both."

I nodded. "Point taken."

"So do you not like her?"

"She's really nice."

"Nice? That's it?"

"She's pretty fun to be around as well."

Mike rolled his eyes. "Tell me how you really feel. I don't actually think you like her one bit."

I tapped my fingers on my beer. "I do. It's … It's just a bit full on."

Understatement of the year. When I'd moved back to Perth, and caught up with Jess again, she'd seemed different. More mature? She had definitely calmed down a little. I'd been so lonely at the start – it wasn't my finest moment. And then, it had been so easy hanging out with her without all the bullshit she used to bring to the table. She really was a nice person. But over the weeks, she'd started turning up at mine out of the blue, more and more frequently, and I started to suspect she was checking up on me. She'd even made hints about moving in together. Hints that I'd ignored, pretending not to pick up on what she was saying. But I worried that one day she'd just move her stuff over, or tell me her flatmates had kicked her out again, or turn up with a cat or something like Mike said – and I'd have no choice. A casual catch-up had inadvertently become a relationship. I'd say I was completely caught off guard by her, but that wouldn't be fair to Jess. I had wanted it too.

Except now, I didn't. Mike had a point. But I didn't have the heart to break it off with her – again. She was sweet, and she deserved more. I was the ultimate frog in hot water – I hadn't realised how serious things had got between us. And it was probably high time I faced the music.

"Ali's coming round in a bit," I said to Mike, literally as I heard a knock at the door. "How's that for timing. Incredible!" Chuckling, I yelled from the balcony, "It's open! Grab three beers from the fridge on your way in!"

But when I looked up, it wasn't Ali. It was Jess. And immediately, my heart sank.

That's not how you're supposed to feel when you are with someone, I reminded myself guiltily. *It's like a chore.*

"Hi, baby!" she said to me, a white handbag hanging from the middle of her forearm. "Oh, hey, Mike," she said, giving him an air kiss on the cheek.

"I was just talking to your *boyfriend* about doing the Rottnest Island swim," Mike said, glancing across at me as I shot him a dirty look.

"Here, have a seat, I'll grab another chair," I said to Jess, standing up.

"Oh, no, that's okay, I can't sit down anyway," she said.

"How come?"

She gave me a mischievous smile. Her hair was in a high ponytail, the bottom of her brown extensions lining the back of her neck. I really didn't understand how those hair things stayed in.

"Because I got this!" She twirled around and lifted her skirt so high it revealed her black G-string, a rose tattoo on her left cheek covered in plastic wrap.

"Oh ..." Mike turned away quickly, understandably seeming uncomfortable. I didn't blame him.

"You got a tattoo?"

She nodded. "It's *so* adorable, isn't it, baby? But sitting, like, *really* hurts. So I'm gonna have to sleep on my stomach tonight. Or … on yours." She giggled, dragging her index finger under my chin. I tried not to grimace. Mike was contemplating what to say, still looking like a fish out of water.

End it tonight.

Nice was not enough. I wasn't in love with her. Not even close. Unfortunately, I knew what the real deal felt like – and it wasn't this.

"I ordered some pizzas," I said. "I got two, but maybe I'll order more if you're staying?"

Her expression soured. "Do you *ever* listen to anything I say?"

"Sorry?" I blinked.

"I *told* you. I'm no-carbing this week. And next."

"Um, right. Sorry. Let's order something else." I took out my phone. "Should we get some salads? Or a—"

"Oh," she said to me, but looked at Mike. "So you *do* have your phone with you then."

Mike stood up and walked inside, presumably to get away from this conversation and get more beer. I didn't blame him – I kind of wanted to do the same myself.

"Why wouldn't I have my phone?"

"I sent you, like, six emails before."

I held my hands out, palms to the sky. "I'm sorry, I don't really check them that often."

"What if it was an emergency?"

"Then I would be wondering why you're emailing me instead of calling."

"Oh my *god*. Don't mock me."

Mike stood behind her and mouthed "*I'm out,*" at me, pointing a thumb at the door. He handed me a beer. "See ya, Jess. Hope you guys have a nice night."

I gave him an apologetic look. Jess didn't even acknowledge

him as he left. "You were avoiding me on purpose," she continued. "Why? Were you two gonna hit the bars? Try and pick up?"

I sighed. "Jess. That's not … Come on. That's not fair."

"Is this about *her* again?"

Mike had once let something slip about Georgie being the love of my life. Unfortunately for me, Jess had overheard. That was *not* a fun night. And Jess wasn't one to let things go.

"Okay, you know what, Jess? I can't do this any more. I'm out."

She stared at me wide-eyed, then laughed. "No," she said, folding her arms, then unfolding them again to point an index finger at me. "Are you actually kidding me right now? *You* said you wanted this."

I didn't, actually. But I was in no mood to get into it. "You're right. But you deserve better. And I'm not in it a hundred percent."

She shook her head. "You're unbelievable." She snatched up her handbag and gave me a dirty look as she charged towards the front door. "I'm going out. And I'm gonna pick up tonight. Maybe I'll have sex with Mike. He's way hotter than *you* anyway."

I didn't respond. She waited a second, then walked out and tried to slam my door. It was one of those soft-touch ones that you couldn't physically slam. Watching her battle with it was almost comical.

But I didn't laugh – I felt awful.

I sighed and picked up my phone. There was a text from Ali asking to rain-check beers. Not the worst idea – I wasn't particularly in the mood to socialise. As I sat back down in the chair and closed my eyes, I tried to tune in to the song playing on the speaker. Mindfulness – maybe I should try it. I didn't know exactly what it was, but people banged on about it all the time. If it was just sitting here, listening to soft music and watching the waves rolling in towards the shore at sunset, I was in. Unfortunately, the peace didn't last long. I was torn from my thoughts by my ringing phone. Taking a breath, I turned it around to look at the screen, hoping it wasn't Jess.

"Elena!" I answered, relieved.

"*Oh my god. Drew!*" she screamed down the phone.

"Yeah?" I laughed at her excitement.

"Drew. It happened. It *worked*!"

"What worked?"

"It actually *worked*. I'm pregnant."

I clocked what she was saying. "Wait. What? You're *pregnant*? For real?"

"We're pregnant!"

"*We're pregnant!*" I heard Therese yelling into the phone.

"Oh my god," I breathed. "Oh my *god*! Congratulations! That's huge!" I shook my head, grinning. *Another niece or nephew.* "So how far along are you? Wow. Wow, wow, wow. This is so exciting!"

"Oh, it's super early – you can't tell anyone yet. Not even Mum and Dad. But I just had to tell you!"

"This is so *awesome*, Elena."

"I know." She took a deep breath to calm herself. "So. How are you?"

"Well, I'm on my balcony with a beer, listening to some tunes and watching the sunset, so ..."

"You bloody west coast people and your beach sunsets."

I laughed and pulled a new beer from the esky as the last of the sun dipped under the surface of the water. "You're just jealous you don't live here any more."

"Touché. So, what else is new with you?" she said.

"Well, Mike is trying to get me to do the Rottnest Island swim with him. Apart from that," I said with a sigh, "really nothing else."

"You don't sound ... You sound a little flat, Drew. You know, for someone on extended leave!"

I had a swig of the cold beer. "Nah. I'm okay."

"Is Jess there with you? How is she? Say hi for me!"

I never understood why Elena seemed to like Jess so much. They were chalk and cheese, and had only ever met once. "I ended it."

"What? When?"

"Um, about ten minutes ago."

"Shit. Are you okay?"

I shrugged to myself. "Yeah. I feel bad, but it's almost a relief, to be honest."

I could hear her moving to a different room to talk to me alone. "Well, I mean I wasn't a hundred percent sure she was *the one*, but I didn't think *that* would happen so soon."

I didn't respond, thinking about her statement.

"Bloody hell," she muttered suddenly, almost as though she were talking to herself.

"What?"

Silence.

"What's wrong, Elena?"

"I … It's nothing."

"Come on. Out with it! It's not triplets or something, is it?" I laughed. "Although, come to think of it, that could be fun … for me, anyway!"

"Oh god … Drew."

"*What*, Elena?"

"I think I may have really messed up."

"Messed up what?"

She took a deep breath. I could picture her trying to compose herself. Like every time she'd come clean to Mum and Dad about sneaking out when she was a teenager. Like every time she'd brought up John when we talked, knowing she'd pushed it too far. I could picture the exact expression on Elena's face when she knew she was in the wrong, or felt utterly guilty.

"Um ... Georgie came over."

My heart skipped a beat. "Huh?"

"She came over. To my place."

I inhaled sharply and sat up in the chair. "What?"

"She came round, uh, to ask where you were. I ... She wanted to see you."

Georgie is back in Australia? My heart was pounding in my ears. And all of a sudden, the slight tipsy feeling I'd had from the beers disappeared, and everything was in clear focus around me.

"When?"

There was a pause, then: "Not long ago, Drew."

"*When,* Elena?"

"About ... About a month ago?"

I stood up and started pacing along the balcony. "A *month*? And at no stage between then and now, did you think to *tell* me? How often have we talked? Six, seven times?"

This is not happening.

"I'm really sorry. I didn't ... I didn't think you'd want to hear from her."

I stopped pacing for a moment and rubbed my temples. "What the hell, Elena. What were you thinking? Why the hell wouldn't I want to talk to her? Did you ... Did you get her number?"

Pause. "No."

"Okay, well where does she live?"

"I don't know."

"What the *hell*. What did you say to her? Did you tell her I was in Perth? Did you tell her I came back from my deployment?"

"I ... No. Well, yes. I told her you were back in Australia. But I ..." She paused again.

My heart thumped. "What?"

"I told her you'd moved on. And that you were happy."

The ground was spinning under me. I hung up the phone and

squeezed it so hard that my hand shook and I thought the screen was seriously going to break.

Was she for real? She knew how I felt about Georgie. Elena and Mike were the only people I had ever spoken to truthfully about how I felt.

Elena was ringing me back, but I was too angry to answer. I turned my phone on silent and the calls stopped after a while. It got dark around me and I lost track of time. The pizzas arrived, and I didn't touch them. I couldn't tell if minutes or hours had gone by.

But I did ring Elena back.

"Drew, I am *so*—"

"Do you know where Hanako lives?" I interrupted.

"Hanako – the girl across the road from your old place?"

"Yes."

"Yeah, I think so …"

"Good. You're gonna go over there right now and ask her for Georgie's number."

"Okay."

My shoulders dropped.

"Drew? I'm really sorry. I'm gonna … I'm gonna go over right now."

I swallowed. "Thank you."

I kept pacing after I'd hung up. Elena was literally a five-minute walk to Hanako's, a couple of streets away. I thought back to the night of the Christmas party, and what Hanako had said to me about Byron. What she'd said about me and Georgie.

Georgie.

In about ten minutes, I would know where she was. I would be able to *call* her. The thought of that was almost unbearable.

I paced some more, then threw on some running shorts and a singlet, and made for the front door. I couldn't sit around waiting.

Beers or no beers, I was going for a run. But as I got halfway down the stairs, my phone beeped. It was Elena. No message in the text, just a single mobile number.

I stared at the numbers. Then I clicked on them and held the phone to my ear.

Each ring sent a vibration through my chest.

"Hi! You've reached Georgie from The Pool Chicks. Leave a message and I'll get back to you."

That *voice*.

"Hi, it's me. Uh … Drew. Can you … Can you please call me back on this number?"

I hung up. Well, that was a very average message. I contemplated calling again, then checked to make sure my phone had caller ID switched on. I walked back inside and kept pacing around my living room, holding the phone. I must've checked about six times that it was switched on loud – *and* on vibrate. I saved her number in my phone.

And a minute later, I got a text from her.

Sunday 16:00 – 33°57'00.6"S 151°09'56.5"E

I stared at the text, wondering if it was a mistype, or whether she'd accidentally used one of those weird font things. But on closer inspection, I realised what the numbers meant.

They're coordinates. I blinked. *She wants to meet me tomorrow at those coordinates.*

With my breath caught in my throat, I clicked on the numbers, highlighted them, and pasted them into Google Maps. *Coordinates – because I'm in the Navy.* I grinned. *Still a complete smartass.*

The map showed the location as a beach right beside Sydney airport, somewhere called Kyeemagh. I zoomed out. It was near Brighton-Le-Sands.

I opened her message again and replied straight away.

Fruit Man will be there.

I opened a new browser and booked a red-eye flight to Sydney immediately.

51

DREW

I sat in the backseat of the taxi looking out the window, heading south. According to Google, it was only a seven-minute drive from the domestic airport to the location Georgie had sent me. I glanced at my watch – not even seven yet, but the sky was already a deep hazy pink from the sun. My flight had left Perth at eleven last night, and I hadn't got a single moment's sleep. I'd watched a couple of new movies in the dark while everyone around me slept, but I would be hard-pressed to remember what they were about.

And when the plane's tyres skidded to a halt on the runway in Sydney, I was wide awake.

The driver dropped me at the car park as requested, and I got out and walked around. The day was already warm, the sky slowly transforming from the pink to a deep indigo – although it'd rained a little overnight, there wasn't a single cloud around. There was a grassy area between the carpark and the beach. I walked down the grass and along a brick footpath. It was quiet; there weren't many people around at all. Making my way down towards the sand and the water, I shielded my eyes with my hand as I studied the area. The airport's runways were to my left, planes landing and taking off almost as frequently as the cars on the road behind me. But the beach was far enough from the road that it was still peaceful and relaxing, despite the hum of the traffic. Maybe watching the hurried movement of everyone else was what made it so peaceful here. I sat down on the sand and watched the planes for a while, trying not to think about how eager I'd been to get here, and the fact that I now had nine hours until it was time to meet Georgie.

Talk about showing up early. But there was no way in the world I was going to be late for this. I couldn't risk leaving the flight until the morning. I lay down on the sand, put the duffel bag under my head and closed my eyes, listening to the low rumble of the A380s coming in to land.

When I woke up, I was covered in sweat, and my face burned from the sun's rays. I tried to remember the dream I'd had. I was in a different place, but I was waiting for Georgie in my dream, too – and she didn't turn up.

What if she doesn't turn up today?

What is she's coming to tell me it's over?

Not that there was anything for there to *be* over.

I shook my head to get rid of this train of thought and checked my watch. It was eleven. I'd done a good job of having a "quick" rest – so much for not being tired. I whipped out my phone to see if there was any food nearby. A never-ending maze of cafés and restaurants lined the main road behind me, about a kilometre south. I needed to get out of the sun for a while, so I crossed the road and made my way down. I picked a nice café, where I ordered a big breakfast. I was starving, too – I hadn't eaten since lunch the day before.

Picking up my phone again, I dialled Elena.

"Drew, how are you?"

"Good. Listen, I'm sorry I lost my temper yesterday."

"Don't worry about it. Totally my fault. I should've, well, I should've been upfront."

"It's all good."

She cleared her throat. "So, what are you up to?"

A coffee was put down in front of me on the table. I picked up the teaspoon and scooped some of the chocolate-dusted foam off the top, thanking the waitress. "I'm in Brighton, actually."

"Oh nice, you gonna hit up Scarborough for a swim, too?"

"No. Brighton, Sydney."

Pause. "Oh."

"Yep."

"Well, you certainly didn't waste any time!" she said with a soft laugh.

"Nope."

"Right. Well, good luck, and keep us posted. I mean that."

"I will. Can I stay at yours tonight? If I need."

Let's be honest. Who knows how all this will go? I was so excited to see Georgie. But a small part of me was also pretty hurt. And confused. In fact, *confused* didn't even start to cover how I felt about her year of silence.

"Of course, any time. How long you here?"

"I have no idea."

She laughed. "All right. I'll see you in a few days, then."

"You'll probably see me tonight."

"No, Drew. I don't reckon I will." I could tell she was smiling.

We hung up and I waited for my breakfast, anxiety in the pit of my stomach taking over the hunger.

Why was I so nervous?

Maybe because you haven't seen her in a year.

And maybe because she's the love of your life.

I puffed out my cheeks with exhaustion. I was so tired of thinking.

Brighton-Le-Sands Beach stretched for kilometres, from the

runways near the dog-friendly Kyeemagh Beach, where the taxi had dropped me, all the way down to Dolls Point. Swimming seemed like a good idea, so I did exactly that after my breakfast. I wanted to go for a run, but I had my bag, and I didn't want to leave it at one end of the beach. And besides, I was *way* too full from the breakfast burrito. So, I walked to Dolls Point and back with the bag, swapping it from shoulder to shoulder every ten minutes, which downright annoyed me after a while. Not to mention, I had to keep reapplying the sunscreen on my shoulders where the strap kept rubbing it off. I was definitely going to have some bizarre tan lines after today.

When I got back to Kyeemagh, I changed into my boardies and dived into the cool water. *"Water's nice,"* I remembered saying to Georgie the morning before we went to the beach. *"Mid to late January is when it's at its warmest. And the visibility is really good at the moment."* It was February, but the water was still warm now. Small schools of silver-and-black fish swam around me. The beach was shallow, and it took me quite a while to swim out into the deep. If things didn't work out with Georgie, I'd have a hard time every time I came to the beach in Sydney. All I could think about was our day of snorkelling.

A feed, walk, and swim transformed me into a new person – the power of the ocean never ceased to amaze me. After drying off, I put a new pair of shorts on and double-checked the coordinates Georgie had sent me – as I'd done so many times already, to make sure I wasn't in the wrong spot. I checked my watch again. Two o'clock. My heart did a flip.

I'd be seeing her in just two hours.

I sat down, my boardshorts drying on my bag next to me, and watched some kite surfers getting their equipment out of their cars. They were setting up the kites and boards on the grass, and then taking it all down to the beach. I moved down to the sand as well, and watched them surfing for a while, hoping it'd make the time go faster.

By three o'clock, my stomach was in my throat. Nausea hit me every time I looked at my watch.

And by quarter to four, I couldn't sit still. I put on a fresh white T-shirt on top of my green shorts, and some cologne, wishing I had somewhere to shower. There was probably a public toilet block with showers somewhere along this incredibly long beach, but it was way too late now. No way I was missing her arriving after all this time because I felt like a shower.

Finally, excitement overtook me, pushing the doubt aside.

But I still had so many questions. Where had she been all this time? Why had she never answered my letters, calls, texts? Why hadn't she left me a note, or told me she was moving to another continent?

When I thought about those things too much, it just made me angry. So instead, I simply focused on getting to see her beautiful face again.

I stood up and brushed the grass off my shorts, flinging my duffel bag over my right shoulder. I made for the sand, stopping at the exact location of the coordinates. It was a bit odd that she'd chosen a spot right here. I turned around to look at the footpath, wondering if I should wait there instead so she could see me. I pulled out my phone to check if she'd called as something jumped up on me from behind, knocking the wind from my lungs and scaring the daylights out of me.

"Holy shit," I gasped, spinning around. There was a brown dog in front of me, but it was like he was on a pogo stick. He kept jumping up, smearing dirt and sand onto my white T-shirt. "Hey buddy, you're a bit energetic, aren't ya?" I held onto his white front paws to stop him jumping for a moment, glancing down at my T-shirt. It was covered in dirt. Wonderful. The dog almost came up to my chest, standing on his hind legs like that. He was a fairly tall dog, but not quite as big as Mal, with a brown-and-black coat and white feet. The tip of his tail was white, too, like it'd been dipped in a tub of paint. He looked at me, tail wagging wildly. Then he pulled away, and as soon as I let go of his front paws, he jumped back up again like he was on a trampoline. "My god. You are wild." I laughed and crouched down, accepting the fact I was covered in dirt and sand anyway, and scratched him behind the ears. He rolled onto his back, ready to accept belly scratches. I smiled at his long eyelashes – they reminded me a bit of Mal's. He darted off suddenly, flinging sand onto me, and chased another dog up along the beach. Wondering where his owner was, I sat down on the sand. I watched him as he came zooming back along the edge of the water before sort of half-tackling me onto my back. I lay on the sand, laughing at him, now soaked as well, and covered in his slobber.

Okay, Drew. Well, this was fun. Now get the hell up and change your T-shirt before Georgie arrives. You are filthy.

I scratched the dog's belly as he lay blissfully beside me, unaware someone was standing behind us.

"So," I heard a woman's voice. I whirled around and looked up at her. "I see you've met my dog."

52

DREW

I scrambled to stand, feeling about as gracious as a newborn giraffe, and brushed as much of the sand off me as I could. Georgie grinned at me, then glanced to her right. "Give me one sec. *Pepper!*" she yelled, turning and jogging towards a group of dogs at the very end of the beach. "Pepper! Come here, *now*!"

I watched as she tried to catch him. It was quite a sight. He did *not* want to be caught. He'd let her get close, then go down on his front legs with his butt in the air, wagging his tail, and as she got close to catching him, he'd dart off in the opposite direction.

Georgie had cut her hair. It was in a bob, just grazing her shoulders. It was slightly darker than I'd seen it before – it looked like it was her natural colour. She was wearing a pair of denim shorts, and a loose-fitting black T-shirt, tucked in at the front.

But what I really noticed was how beautiful she was. As beautiful as the first time I ever saw her. And just like the first time, my heart was warm and full.

She came back eventually, marching Pepper towards me by his collar. She clipped the leash on, smiling at me and trying to catch her breath.

"You got a *dog*?" I said, incredulous.

"No. I got a nightmare."

I paused, then started laughing. She grinned.

"You. Got a dog." I couldn't believe it.

Pepper sat on the sand at her feet, watching me curiously. "He's very cute." I looked up at Georgie as she tucked her short hair behind her ears.

"I like your hair," I said.

"I like that you're here," she replied.

We studied each other for a moment, not speaking. I loved those hazel eyes so much. She watched me carefully, and a moment later, she stepped forward and wrapped her arms around my waist, still holding onto Pepper's leash. I put my arms around her and we stood there hugging for what felt like an hour. I loved her warmth, the fact she held me tight. I loved that she was in my arms again.

"You know," she eventually said into my chest, "I got you a yellow tulip. My plan was to be waiting down here on the sand when you arrived, with the tulip in his mouth." She pointed at Pepper, one arm still around me. I had done the tulip thing for her once, with Mal.

She remembered.

"And?"

"Well," she said, pointing behind her, "he chewed the tulip to shreds and spat it out back there somewhere, and I only got one, didn't I? It didn't exactly go to plan."

"No. Not many things have, lately."

She stared at the sand. "I'm so sorry, Drew." She buried her face in my chest again.

"It's okay," I said, stroking her hair, although I wasn't sure if that was actually true. *Was* it okay? Was *I* okay? As good as it was to see her, there was some kind of barrier there on my part. But I couldn't quite put my finger on why.

She wiped her face, taking a step back and clearing her throat. "Uh, so are you free for the next few hours?"

"Sure."

"Okay, cool. My place is about fifteen minutes away, down there. If, I mean, if you feel like it, you wanna walk down to mine and we can chat there?"

"All right."

Pepper must've sensed we were about to move, and started jumping about eagerly.

"I have … There's some stuff I want to talk to you about. And then, I thought you could stay for dinner. I mean, only if you want."

"Sounds good."

I could hear how short my responses were, yet I couldn't stop them being that way. We walked down the path that ran parallel to the water, down towards Brighton, where she said she lived. She told me how she'd bought a paddleboard, and had been going down to the water after work some afternoons. It was a really pretty beach, very flat – there were no waves at all, the perfect stand-up paddleboarding spot, really. And it would be a cool spot to watch the planes taking off and landing. Apparently you could paddle right up to the runways. She was loving it, she said, although she once thought she saw a shark. And she had gone back to her old job with The Pool Chicks, which I'd gathered from her voicemail recording.

Pepper darted left and right, sniffing, peeing, growling at other dogs as we walked along side by side.

"He isn't great with other dogs," she explained. "He gets really nervous. But he's fantastic with people. Kids, especially. My neighbour's kids basically climb all over him and he just takes it."

When we got to the front of her apartment, which was on a corner of the main road, there was a young woman sitting on the low brick wall near some letterboxes.

"Drew!" It was Hanako, and she was coming over to give me a hug, grinning ear to ear.

"Hi, Hanako. How are you?"

"Good! Good, good. But I won't keep you guys." She was still grinning at me, before turning to Georgie and taking Pepper's leash.

"Do you need the bowls and stuff?" Georgie asked. "Or food?"

"Nope. Still got some from last time. All good. I'll see you guys later."

"See you, Hanako," I said, a bit confused, as Georgie turned to me.

"She's only taking him 'til tomorrow."

I reached down to pat Pepper, and he immediately jumped up and licked my cheek. "Nice!" I chuckled.

"Oh yeah, sorry. He does that."

"You don't say." He was adorable, but incredibly cheeky.

Georgie looked at me for a moment as Hanako walked off with Pepper, not saying anything. "Well, um, let's go up."

I followed her into the building, and into the lift. She pressed a button and smiled at me. "My place is on the top floor. The balcony overlooks the ocean."

"Well, you did always say you wanted to be by the coast."

"Yep. Anyway, it's a pretty old building. Seventies or something. And the apartment is tiny, but it's mine. I bought it."

"Good on you. That's great. Congrats."

"I bought it with my own money," she continued proudly. I was pleased for her, and yet dread continued to fill my chest. The doors opened and she led me down the hall before unlocking the door to her apartment.

There was something too … casual about all this.

I followed her in. The apartment actually reminded me a lot of mine in Perth, the one I'd recently moved into. It was only a one-bedroom, but it had a spacious living area and a balcony overlooking the water.

And really, living by myself, what more did I need?

Obviously, Georgie had had the same idea. I just wasn't sure how she'd thought it'd be big enough for a dog of Pepper's size and energy.

She locked the door behind us and motioned to the couch. A small, round dining table sat in front of the old kitchen bench, set with two plates and some nice cutlery and napkins. I took a seat on her cream-coloured couch. A chewed dog bed sat on the floor next to it. Apart from that, the apartment was neat, clean, and not very full.

"So. I owe you an apology, and a dinner." She smiled as she sat down on the couch next to me.

That's it? She's going to cook me dinner and say sorry?

I cleared my throat. "Um, okay."

"So, I didn't even ask, where did you park?"

"Park?"

"Yeah, your car. I should've told you, there's a visitor spot here. Don't worry. If it's dark later I can drive you back. I mean, if you don't feel like walking."

"I didn't drive here. I flew."

She frowned. "Flew? From where?"

"From my place. In Perth."

"You're living back in *Perth*?"

I nodded.

"And you just … flew here? For me?"

"Yeah …"

Her face crumpled, and tears started streaming down her cheeks.

"Hey, what's wrong?" I said, putting an arm around her.

But she'd started sobbing so much, she couldn't get anything out. Her body was heaving up and down as she gasped for air. I pulled her close to me and wrapped my arms around her, kissing the top of her head, and just held her for a few minutes. She was shaking against me, getting worse before calming down, unable to breathe properly. It was almost like she was having a panic attack.

"Georgie. What's wrong?" Sadness crushed me seeing her like this.

She pulled back and wiped her red-rimmed eyes, then started sobbing into my chest again.

"Hey. It's all right."

She shook her head. "No, it's not. I'm *so*, so sorry. You are always so kind to me – and – do anything for me, and – and – all I do is—" her words disappeared into a jumble of tears and jagged breathing.

She looked so vulnerable, sitting there against me, bawling her eyes out. My chest tightened. Despite being angry with her – *this* I couldn't handle. I stroked her hair softly.

"Drew." She slowly composed herself. "I'm so sorry I didn't come over that night. That's the … That's the night that … I found out …"

Instantly, it clicked. The night she was meant to come over was the night she'd found out about Byron.

No wonder she never came.

No wonder she never wrote.

"Georgie, I'm really sorry about Byron," I said.

She nodded. "Thank you." Taking a deep breath, she leaned her head back against the couch, not speaking. Then she got up to get a tissue and blew her nose. Seeming a little more composed, she smiled at me, sapped of energy.

"Are you okay?" I asked. "What's … Were you in England this whole time?"

She sat down on the couch next to me again, tucking her legs underneath. "It's all right. I'm getting there. But anyway …" She took a deep breath. "I need to explain some stuff, get this out – is that all right?"

I nodded. "I'm listening."

"Okay. So after … *that*, after what happened, I … I felt so guilty, and I was confused. I had reason to believe he was having— He was cheating on me. But anyway. That's neither here nor there. I was going to end it, on that day, before I came around. I couldn't not. But after he died, everything was a blur. I don't remember anything. I don't know how I got through. It was a nightmare – having to get his body home, organising the funeral, dealing with literally hundreds of people. And then – I was just a mess. I moved back to the UK with my dad. And I was there for almost a year. I never even checked my phone. You know how I left it in your car? I never … I didn't even turn it on. Well, actually, I did look once, and it was flooded with calls and texts about Byron. I couldn't deal with it. I didn't see your texts at all, until about a month ago. And also, I never got your letters. But Hanako kept them for me. She brought them over here when she found out I'd moved back. So I read all of them at once, and then I tried to ring, but your phone had been disconnected, or something …"

"Yeah, I got a new phone when I got back," I said when she stopped talking.

She never got my letters.

I'd had no faith in her, and I felt terrible. I wiped my hand down my face, the truth finally sinking in.

She didn't even do anything wrong.

"I *know* I should've told you I left Sydney. But I … It was so confusing. I felt so guilty, Drew … I felt sick for not contacting you before you left. Or trying to once you were there. I just … I kept thinking it was too late. I thought you'd hate me." She started sobbing again.

"Georgie. Hey. It's okay."

"Anyway, I went to see Elena, and she, well, she said you'd moved on." She sniffed.

I'm going to have to tell her.

Clearing my throat, I said, "I was sort of seeing someone for a while in Perth. She was … someone I was with before I moved to Sydney."

She nodded. "Drew, I'm not angry about that."

"Really?"

"Yeah. How could I be? I mean, don't get me wrong, of course I don't want to think about *that*, but I hadn't contacted you in over a year. I disappeared, essentially."

I nodded. It still didn't make me feel better – I still felt like I'd let her down.

"But—" she paused, "you're … Are you still … together?"

I wiped a single tear from her cheek. "God, no. Absolutely not. It wasn't my finest moment, but no."

She took my hands in hers, studying them before weaving her fingers between mine. "That's good." She looked up at me. "Because I am *so* in love with you." She paused, choking up again. "And I thought about you so much when I … while I was gone. I never really stopped. And I … I kept thinking it was way too late to get in touch, and I'd really messed up … and then I read your letters and thought there was a chance, but then Elena said …" She let out a sob … "That you had … that you had moved on, I was so scared that you wouldn't— I mean, even now, you don't have to say—"

"Georgie," I interrupted her and let go of her hands, then picked her up and pulled her onto my lap. I smiled at her, studying her beautiful eyes, before putting my arms around her and kissing her gently.

This was bliss. Her lips were so soft, so warm. Exactly like I'd remembered. Exactly like our first proper kiss, sitting in the dark in my Hilux. Except this time, it felt more intimate, and slow. She was heaven, and my heart felt full. I pulled away and looked at her. "I love you. It's always been you."

She wiped her eyes, before letting out a giggle of relief and leaning down to kiss me again. "Oh my god. I am so relieved," she said, lacing her fingers through mine again. "I've been so scared since I messaged yesterday. That you wouldn't show up."

I squeezed her leg. "Well, I'm here. I told you Fruit Man would show up." I grinned. "It's all over now. All the bad stuff. Okay?"

"Spoken like a true superhero." She smiled, her eyes wet. "Drew, I missed you *so* much."

I squeezed her hand. "Honestly, you have no idea how much I missed you. I was … It was heartbreaking thinking I'd never see you again." I let out a breath. "Life was so … bland without you."

"So, I have to ask. Did you ever make it to Spain?"

"Nah. I worked through the break and came home two weeks early. I didn't take leave."

She looked at me wide-eyed. "So you worked seven days a week for six months straight?"

"Yep."

"Holy shit."

I nodded. "I'm definitely glad to be back."

"I bet."

"So," I motioned at the dog bed, "how come Pepper couldn't be here for this?"

"It wasn't so much that. Hanako likes to take him every now and then for a night. She's trying to prove to Kate and her dad that she's responsible enough for a dog. She's almost eighteen and has never had a pet. She's really using that argument to her advantage." Georgie laughed. I'd missed that sound so much.

"Ah, I see."

"But don't worry. You'll see him again, and I just know he's going to like you more than he likes me."

"Well, that's only fair, seeing how Mal liked *you* way more than *me*," I said, smiling at the memory of him.

But her smile faded at the comment. "Um, actually, I need to tell you something. About Mal."

I swept a strand of her hair off her face and tucked it behind her ear. "Yeah?"

She took a slow, deep breath, like she was contemplating something. "He's going to be in a newsletter next month. Of an animal rescue place. I donated a hundred grand to them, in Mal's honour."

"You donated … a hundred grand?"

She nodded.

The back of my eyes stung. "That is so generous. Thank you."

"You're welcome." She took a breath, visibly relaxing even more. "Mal … changed me. He was an amazing dog."

"He sure was."

We sat in silence for a moment. I noticed a pot of tulips on the balcony. As if reading my mind, Georgie nodded towards them.

"Just like my tulips from Mal," she said, making me want to kiss her even more, and never stop. "So what happened to your place?"

"In Sydney? I rented it out. Really nice family moved in."

"And what about the Hilux? You didn't drive it back to Perth, did you?"

"No. That drive is enough to do once. I sold it to one of the guys in my squadron. Let's just say, never sell a car to a mate, especially if you suck at bargaining!" I laughed. "Unless you're happy to accept way less than what it's actually worth."

Georgie's lips curled up into a cheeky smile.

"What?"

"I gave the Maserati away to a total stranger."

I laughed. "No way. Did you at least drive it first?"

"Yep. On a racetrack."

I laughed again, letting my head fall back onto the couch. "You're joking."

"Nope. It was great. But seriously, having money doesn't buy you happiness," she said, "and it sure as hell doesn't buy you integrity."

I nodded. "Agreed."

"I gave Byron's money away – what I got from the insurance and stuff, I mean. His family got his actual money. What I ended up with, I mostly donated to Surgeons with Heart International. That's what he would've wanted. And the rest to the animal shelter."

I leaned in to kiss her. "You are so sweet."

She gave me a sad smile. "See this?" She pointed to a scar on her ankle. "I was attacked by a dog in Italy when I was four. Right before we migrated. I still remember I couldn't put a shoe on for the plane trip and I was so embarrassed. It was my earliest memory, actually. It was awful – I ended up in hospital with an infection. I hated dogs so much after that; well, more like – I was petrified. I avoided them my entire life. But then Mal …" Her eyes welled up again. "He made me forget all that. If it weren't for Mal, I probably never would have adopted Pepper." She traced the faint pink scar on her leg, the one I knew she got when she took Mal to the vet. "You know Pepper was due to be put down the day after I got him? Mal basically saved his life."

It was my turn to choke up.

"And Pepper practically saved mine. There were some pretty dark days there for a while." She took a deep breath.

I put an arm around her, kissing her forehead and breathing in deeply when I caught a whiff of her perfume. "Well, no more. Okay? I promise I'm going to try to make every day awesome from here on in."

She smiled her beautiful smile at me. The sun was casting a yellow glow across her apartment. It was hot inside, despite the balcony door being open, but I didn't care. I didn't want to let her go. "So ..." I gave her a squeeze. "What's on the agenda for tonight?"

"Well, I was really hoping you'd stay the night, for a start."

"Of course I'll stay."

"And I have a surprise."

"Yeah?"

She stood up and walked to the kitchen, filling two glasses with water from the fridge before coming back and handing me one. "It just depends on a few things. Hold on. First of all. What are you doing living in Perth?"

I had a drink of the cold water. I was so parched from the day, I gulped down the whole thing, not realising how thirsty I'd been. She laughed and refilled it for me.

"By the way. Are you going to get in trouble? Your face is totally burnt. Except for where your sunnies were. It's funny. And also ... really cute."

"I fell asleep in the sun waiting for you," I said. "Um, so, after I got back to Australia, I moved to Perth and took Leave Without Pay. I took six months. So no, luckily there will be no issues about this." I pointed to my face. "But it *is* gonna hurt tomorrow!"

"So then are you back in Perth for good? With work?"

"No. So technically, I'm still posted in Sydney. But after that deployment, I had to bail. I couldn't stand being back here." *Without you.* I didn't say it, but she knew anyway. Her eyes welled up.

"Come here," I said, pulling her to me again. "You gotta stop." I wrapped my arms around her protectively. She was basically on me, and it still didn't feel close enough. But I was so, so happy to be with her again.

I was so in *love* with her. Even more than before, if that was possible.

"I just feel so awful."

"Georgie. It's not your fault. I get it, okay? It was a really awful year. A lot of things happened outside our control." I squeezed her hand. "For *both* of us. Anyway. I've been talking to my boss about taking on a different role in the Navy."

"Yeah?"

"Yeah. One where I would only be deployed every now and then. Or hopefully not at all."

She nodded. "Well, I ... I know I said I love you already, but I also, I mean, you know I want to be with you, right? As in – together?"

"Well, I figured that much, but thanks for clearing it up!"

She hit me on the arm playfully. "Stop it." She wiped her eyes and composed herself. "But honestly, Drew. I never, ever want to lose you again." She smiled sadly at me, then took a long breath. "So, you ready for the surprise then?" She reached to grab her phone after I nodded, opening an email and passing the phone to me.

"Nice phone," I remarked. "Some legend must've bought it for you."

She rolled her eyes. "Come on, hurry up and look at it!"

I scrolled down the email. It was a flight voucher.

I paused, staring. "Whoa – that's ... a lot of cash. What's this for?"

"Spain." Her eyes sparkled.

"Spain?"

"Yeah. Will you come with me?"

I stared at the phone. "You got us tickets to Spain?"

"Well, no, technically not yet, because I didn't know what your work schedule would be like, but—"

I interrupted her with a kiss. "You're so kind. This is so much money, though."

"Drew. I don't care about the money. So will you come to Spain with me, and swim in the ocean and eat tapas and drink sangria 'til we pass out? Please say yes!"

I grinned. "Yes. Yes, I will."

She squealed. "When?"

"Well – I could extend my leave relatively easily. I could go tomorrow, if you really wanted."

"Oh my god. Well, it'll take me a few weeks to organise cover at work, but this is so exciting!" She did a little jig. "Oh my *god*, I'm so happy."

"Me too." Excitement flooded my body. This was the dream I'd had. Night after night, week after week, month after month. And now it was all coming true. "Hey," I said, motioning to Pepper's bed, "what will you do with him while we're away, though?"

She drummed her fingers on her chin. "Hmm. Good question. Let's see. I'll make a list of the people who want to take care of him. Then I'll have to short-list, and conduct interviews, and then choose the highest bidder." She paused, then laughed. "Probably Hanako, to be honest."

"Pepper is one lucky dog."

She squeezed my hand. "So was Mal."

"Yeah. I'm so glad he got to meet you."

She turned so she was facing me, her short brown hair framing her gorgeous face. I couldn't believe this was my *girlfriend*. I could stare at her forever.

"Drew."

"Yeah?"

"We're going to Spain!" She threw her arms up in the air in

excitement.

I laughed. "Yes we are."

"But ... I'm gonna need to take this slow. As in ... us."

"You're worth the wait, Georgie. You always have been."

"But I can move to Perth, if you want. I mean, Pepper will need a backyard if I'm realistic. He's part kelpie. No way he should be in this apartment. He needs a big backyard, really."

"Hold on. So you gave me crap for having a winter dog in a summer country, then went and bought a large, energetic dog for your apartment?"

This made her laugh.

"It's okay," I continued. "I will have to come back to Sydney anyway for work eventually – and besides, Elena is pregnant. Not to mention, you *love* The Pool Chicks. I would never take that away from you."

She gaped at me. "Oh my god! You're gonna be an uncle! I mean – again!"

"Yep. So anyway, I think I'd prefer to live by the beach when I come back to Sydney this time. I mean, I've still got my place, but I don't want to go back to it yet. Maybe one day – but not right now. And the tenants are lovely, and have young kids who adore the pool – I don't want to kick them out."

"Okay, well, we can look at something on the coast. It's nice around here, and a little more affordable than the Eastern Suburbs."

"*We?*"

She nodded.

"You want to move in with me?" I laughed. "That's not really taking it slow!"

"Drew – I've spent enough time away from you. I don't want to do that again. When your lease is up in Perth, let's just do it. Why waste another year? I'm so over it. I'm so over the shit times. If I've learned anything, it's that you don't know when your time's up. I think I meant … like with marriage and stuff. I'm not sure I can go down that path again any time soon."

I nodded.

"But I love you, and I never ever want to be apart again. Okay?"

"Me neither. But I get it, about the marriage stuff. So let's do it then. Let's move in together."

We sat staring and grinning at each other like two teenagers in love. And then we spent the better part of ten minutes kissing each other like two teenagers in love. I had honestly never felt so happy in my whole life.

"I love you so much, Georgie."

"Me too." She puffed out her cheeks suddenly. "Don't get me wrong," she said, "I do worry that I'll annoy you. I mean, we never really, you know, dated."

"Well, we're adults, and I also think we know each other well enough."

"So do I. But what if I *do* annoy you? What if everything I say and do annoys you?"

"I don't think that's going to be an issue." I paused, shrugging. "But you know what? If it is, when we go to bed I'll just lie on my good ear, so I can't hear you talking."

She laughed so hard I thought she was going to fall off the couch.

"Anyway," I said. "You still haven't told me what's on for tonight."

"Ah. Yes. Okay, so I'm cooking you dinner." She motioned to the dining table. "Gnocchi with basil pesto and pecorino, and vanilla pannacotta with mulberries and a pistachio crumb for dessert."

"That's … That's what you were going to cook me …"

"Yeah – on that night. And after that, I believe we still have last year's *Bachelor* finale to watch."

"So we do."

"And *then* we can start planning our Spain trip. Also, we could go for an ice cream and maybe a night beach swim. *Yes!* Can we go for a night swim?" She looked at me wide-eyed, like this was the best idea ever.

I laughed. "Of course."

This is her. This is the Georgie I know and love. She was here all along.

"And then we can come home and stay up talking all night," she said.

"Talking?"

"Okay, well, that's negotiable." She winked at me as we sat grinning at each other. "I am so happy this all worked out," she continued. "But you know – speaking of that, today has been everything I hoped it would be. And I am *so* happy you are here with me. There's just one tiny thing that didn't work out quite as I'd hoped."

"Oh yeah? What's that?"

"You turned up with a shirt on." She shook her head. "You've changed, Drew."

I chuckled. "Well, I guess it's someone else's job to take it off me from now on."

FOR MY READERS

Thank you for supporting me by buying this book, which was entirely independently produced.

Having no agent or big publishing house behind me, your purchase is extremely meaningful to me. If you enjoyed the story of Drew and Georgie, recommending it to your friends and family is the biggest compliment you can pay me, and I thank you in advance. If you have the time, you can also write a review on Goodreads as well as the platform on which you purchased *Tulips from Mal.*

You can now check out the *Tulips from Mal* audiobook narrated by Kate Worsley and Gareth Rickards, available on all audio platforms!

Thank you once again.

gm
Gabriella Margo

Instagram: gabriellamargoauthor
Website: www.gabriellamargobooks.com

FOR FOOD LOVERS

If Georgie's cooking inspired you, you can download some of her recipes for free – hand-picked by the wonderful, real-life Italian chef, Luca Faccin.

Visit **www.gabriellamargobooks.com** and subscribe to get the recipes. You'll also be the first to hear about my upcoming books – and, of course, you can opt out anytime.

FOR DOG LOVERS

You might be delighted to know that Pepper is, in fact, a real dog! (Unlike Mal, who is completely fictional). Pepper's story is similar to that of the Pepper in the book – he was rescued a couple of days before he was due to be euthanised because nobody wanted to adopt him. That's why 10% of my book profits will go to AWL NSW – an organisation that receives no government funding and relies solely on donations.

To leave you with the warm and fuzzies, here is a picture of The Real Pepper – who now lives with his favourite humans – Julie, Cam, Gisele and Louis – in Sydney.

ACKNOWLEDGEMENTS

First of all, thank you to my editor, Claire Strombeck, for your warm but honest guidance. You are a wonderful editor – thorough, encouraging and highly detail-oriented.

Thank you to my proofreader, Katalin Veres, for the (gazillion) final edits of the book; and thanks for being the first beta reader in whatever I write, no matter how terrible it is.

My beautiful cover design and interior typesetting was done by the talented Vanessa Mendozzi – massive thanks to her for putting up with all my changes, questions and indecisiveness.

RC, you dedicated so much of your time to making sure I used correct terminology and described day-to-day Navy operations properly. The hours you spent talking to me, texting me and emailing me, as well as reading the final product, are more appreciated than I can express. Thanks dude, I owe you a pale ale and a breakfast burrito.

To Paul and Nick at Sydney's Best Pool Service – thank you for letting me be a temporary 'Pool Chick' – it was great. But Nick, I will not apologise for the terrible puns throughout the day (thanks for throwing me in the deep end, it all went swimmingly, etc). They were good, and you know it.

Thank you to star chef Luca Faccin for insights into your delicious Italian cooking and for sharing those mouth-watering recipes with me (and telling me why too much chilli is not good!). As officially The Worst Cook in the World, I appreciate all your guidance and passion.

Rob Tener, thank you for the information about your overseas volunteering trips to Tanzania and explaining how it all works. Good on you for being a part of such a good cause, on multiple occasions.

Brooke Robinson – thanks for walking this road with me, offering encouragement, support and understanding. It's a long path to publication, but I'm so glad I met you at Varuna, and I can't wait to see your book in print. To the authors and staff I met at Varuna, thanks for your feedback on Georgie, Drew and Mal.

To Jen White, your encouragement and words of support have never been taken for granted. You are a wonderful writer and friend, not to mention actor, and you have the best stage voice out of anyone I know. Love your work.

Liz and Ben, thank you for your ongoing support and encouragement of all my creative ventures (of which there have been a few …). You guys have a great eye for detail, wonderful ideas, and are generally awesome people.

To my wonderful Beta readers – my original support group, my cheerleaders and most importantly, the best friends ever – thank you for always reading the words I put on a page and encouraging me (even when I know it's utter rubbish).

Julie and Cam: good on you for adopting Pepper, and letting us 'borrow' him whenever we like. Here's to everyone who has, at some point, given an animal in need a forever home.

Thanks to the Australian Society of Authors for advice, courses and support – a wonderful organisation